# REBEL REVENGE

---

## SAINT VIEW REBELS
### BOOK 1

## ELLE THORPE

WWW.ELLETHORPE.COM

Editing by Studio ENP.

Proofreading by Barren Acres Editing.

Original cover by Elle Thorpe. Photo by Wander Aguiar.

Discreet cover by Emily Wittig Designs.

V2.

*For the staff at Goulburn Soldiers Club.*
*Thanks for letting me write there every day.*
*Your chicken schnittys are A+.*
*Elle x*

# 1

## REBEL

The nightmares always came.

Fingers on my skin, biting and tearing, taking what hadn't been offered. Taunts in my ears, reminding me I deserved this because I was trailer-park trash.

Darkness wrapped itself around me, pulling me down, stealing everything good, until there was nothing left except the shell of a woman who woke in twisted, sweaty, fear-soaked sheets.

I had no tears left. For days after, I'd lain in this bed, crying for everything they'd stolen from me. Sniffling while texting my boss to tell her I was sick and couldn't come into the club. Sobbing in pain while I sat in the shower, water running over the filth I couldn't scrub clean.

They hadn't killed me, but they may as well have.

I was dead inside. Used. My spirit broken.

How many days would it be until my body just gave up too?

It was taking too long.

I dragged myself from bed, wobbling on unsteady legs in the dark. For the first time since I'd been dumped back in Saint View and forced to stumble my way home or lie in the gutter and die, I left my apartment. The filthy carpeted stairs in the hallway reeked of piss and left a sticky residue on the bottoms of my bare feet. It was two in the morning, but music still played from behind the door of my downstairs neighbor, and I slumped against the frame to bang my fist against the wall. "Robbie!"

The music paused, and a second later, the door swung open, my neighbor blinking at me through squinty, bloodshot eyes.

"I need a gun."

Robbie leaned on the doorway, crossing his arms over his chest in suspicion, but not particularly surprised by my demand. "Do you know what time it is? Also, what the fuck happened to you?"

I could guess at what he saw. Short hair wild. Bare legs and arms scratched and torn with half-healed injuries. Eyes black with bruises. "Doesn't matter. Do you have a gun or not?"

"Depends on if you're gonna pay?"

I had no money. Nothing more than the few dollars left in my bank account at the end of the pay week. I had no property of any value, nothing to sell or trade for, and there was an eviction notice pinned to my door because my rent was overdue. I shook my head desperately. "Please, Robbie. Just give me one."

"You can pay in other ways." He leered at me, running his disgusting, thick tongue over chapped lips.

I backed off so quick my hip hit the railing of the staircase behind me.

For half a second, I imagined toppling over it. Free-falling through the air. Snapping my neck on impact with the ground-level floor.

Seemed like bliss compared to the pain and fear that had plagued me since that night.

Robbie held his hands up. "Whoa, shit. Settle down. I didn't mean it. What do you want a gun for?"

I didn't answer his question and deflected with a comment of my own. "I could tell the cops all about what you're growing in there. I saw you bringing in another set of lights last weekend."

His eyes widened. "I need those lights for tanning!"

I snorted. "Yeah, and I need a gun so I can use it as a flower vase. Just give me one." I held my hand out, palm up, waiting.

Robbie scowled but disappeared into his home. I peeked around the corner of the doorframe and raised an eyebrow at the hydroponic setup he had going on in his living room. There was a small farm of mid-size marijuana plants growing happily in the middle of it. "Seriously, Rob? Not even in a bedroom?"

He reappeared and flipped me the bird with one hand, the other clutching a small black handgun. "It's a loan, Rebel. I want it back."

I snatched it from his fingers before he could change his mind and hightailed it back up the stairs, hugging it to my chest and hoping none of our other neighbors would decide to take a late-night stroll and catch me with it.

"Hey," Robbie called after me. "If you kill someone, can you at least wipe my fingerprints off it?"

I shut the door behind me, double-checking it was locked, and then leaned back against it, breathing harder than necessary after the short sprint up the stairs.

One bullet in the chamber.

Not enough for all three men who needed to die.

But enough for me.

I stared down at the gun, a tear rolling down my face. With a hiccuping sob, I put it in my mouth.

One tiny pull on the trigger and this could all be over. The dreams at night. The terror during the day. The constant self-loathing and misery, all gone in an instant.

I just wanted it all to stop.

Two framed photos sat on a wall shelf directly opposite where I stood, familiar faces smiling out from behind the glass. In one, my boss and best friend, Bethany-Melissa, or Bliss as we all called her, slung her arm around my neck. On my other side, one of her guys, Nash, rested his arm on the top of my head. The three of us beamed at the camera. It had been taken one day at work when we'd been bored, but I'd loved it so much I'd had copies printed for all of us. Nash had hung his on a wall in his office at Psychos. Bliss had taken hers home to the house she shared with Nash and her two other guys. I'd put mine there on the shelf beside the photo of me and my mom, the only other person I truly cared about.

Now I wondered if I'd put them there specifically for this moment. So I would see them while I held a gun and contemplated ending it all.

Slowly, I lowered the weapon, sobs turning to gut-wrenching cries ripped straight from my soul. I stumbled back to my bed, tucking the gun beneath my pillow. With the safety back on, touching it was the only way I could stop myself from shaking.

The nightmares resumed, but this time, they were almost welcome. They were better than the one I lived while I was awake.

At least I couldn't put a bullet through my brain while I slept.

*T*he disengaging of the lock on my front door woke me. My will to die instantly forgotten as instinct and self-preservation kicked in.

I was out of bed, gun in my hand, fingers trembling over the trigger before the handle even turned.

"I've got a gun," I announced as the door swung open. "I'll—"

The woman in the doorway propped one hand on her hip and stared me down with a look that somehow bordered on amusement, even though there was a deadly weapon pointed at her. "You'll what, Bel? Shoot your dear old mom?"

I dropped my arm in relief, letting the gun clatter to the floor.

That had Mom flinching, but nothing happened. The gun lay silent.

Mom stepped inside, her stiletto heels sinking into the carpet. She squatted gracefully, keeping her knees together despite wearing formfitting cream slacks, and scooped the gun up from the floor. "What on earth are you doing with a Glock, Bel?"

I cringed at the nickname I'd always despised. "Please don't call me that. You know I hate it."

Mom acted like I hadn't spoken. Just dangled the gun from one of her perfectly manicured, talon-length fingernails.

I snatched it from her and spun on my heel, stomping back to my bed. I tucked the gun beneath my pillow once more then curled up on the lumpy mattress and pulled a blanket over me.

She followed more slowly, perching on the edge of the bed, the springs squeaking beneath her weight. She brushed back a strand of my crazy hair, her fingers returning to hover over my messed-up face. "Who did that to you?"

I burrowed farther into the blankets. "Does it matter?"

She sighed heavily in defeat. "I suppose not. This is where I should probably tell you to go to the police—"

I snorted beneath the covers. "I went to a clinic and made sure I wasn't pregnant. But the men who did it? They're from Providence."

"Oh."

The understanding was there in that one-syllable word. It was all that needed to be said. I was a woman from Saint View, the wrong side of the tracks. They were rich white men from the nearby upper-class neighborhood. The cops would sooner dress in drag and do a hula than take my word over theirs. Everyone from Saint View knew how it was. We handled our own business here, because the cops always came down on the side of the rich pricks who called Providence home.

There would be no justice for what they'd done. Not unless I kept myself alive long enough to carry it out.

I wasn't making any promises on that one.

Mother dearest had other ideas. The covers were yanked off me, and bright sunlight flooded in once more. "Nope. You ain't moping. That's not what we do."

I glared at her. "It's not? How many times did I pick you up off the bathroom floor after you wrote yourself off because some jackass dumped you?"

My anger bounced right off her, and she booped me on the nose. "Rich jackass, Bel. They were always rich. And I wasn't crying over them. I was crying because I missed their Porsches."

It wasn't true. She thought I'd been too young to truly remember the assholes she'd dated when I was a teen. The men who'd used her for her pretty face and tiny, perfect body. The men who'd promised her a better life, then reneged on the deal when they found out she had a daughter. The ones who'd left her as beaten and broken and violated as I was now.

My face and the things those men had done to me were nothing new to Miranda. She'd seen it all before, in her own reflection. She knew it was just the way of the world for women like us.

"Anyway." She bounced on the edge of the bed. "You haven't been answering your phone, so I decided to just come tell you my big news in person."

I sat up and pulled a pillow over my lap. "Big news, huh? Did your doctor run out of Botox?"

"No, but clearly yours did. Seriously, Belly, you're getting crow's feet."

She poked at the corners of my eyes, which hadn't

had any wrinkles last time I'd checked, but I was about to turn thirty, and after the last few days, it wouldn't have surprised me if I'd developed a few.

I batted her hand away. "Just tell me."

As much as my mother and I picked at each other, it was our love language. At only thirteen years apart, we'd always been more like sisters than mother and daughter. Miranda wasn't truly capable of being anyone's parent. She'd kept me alive, but once I'd turned six, I'd had to fend for myself. It hadn't dulled my love for her any though. She was a hot mess, but she was my hot mess.

Her face smiling out at me from that photo this morning was the only reason I was still here.

She clutched my fingers in her hand, stabbing me with her nails in her excitement. "I'm getting married! Eeeep!"

I squinted at her, wondering if she was still drunk from the night before, though she didn't look it. "Married?"

"Married! Me! An honorable woman!"

I laughed at the thought of my mother, who had a penchant for drunk dancing on tables and flashing the room her panties, as an honorable woman.

She didn't laugh with me.

I sobered quickly. "Oh, shit. You're serious?"

She shoved me in the arm. "Of course I am."

"You don't even have a boyfriend!"

She tutted at me in disapproval. "Well, not anymore. He's my fiancé now." She held up her hand to flash a rock the size of Texas at me.

I grabbed her arm. "Get the fuck out. What is that? It's fake, right?"

She gasped in outrage. "Hush your mouth!" Then she grinned at me. "It's totally legit. I had it checked!"

I let go of her hand and sat back against the headboard. "Who is he?"

Her excitement disappeared and was replaced with a calm matureness I didn't often see on my mother's face. "His name is Bart Weston. We've been dating for months. He's tall and handsome and the literal sweetest man on earth."

"And rich?" Because they always were with her.

Which always made me wary of them and maybe why my mother hadn't mentioned him to me. She knew my feelings on men with money. I'd seen too much of their ugly. As a result, I'd always kept my own interests to this side of the Saint View-Providence border.

She laughed. "So freaking rich, Belly. You should see his house! It has wings!"

"So do bats, but that doesn't make me want to get into bed with them."

She shushed me, her expression sobering as she picked up my phone, unlocked it, and aimlessly scrolled through. "He's a good one, Bel. I promise. You'll like him."

I dredged up a smile for her because I knew she desperately wanted my approval. "As long as you don't make me call him Daddy."

"Oh, no. That's what I call him, so that would be weird."

I crinkled my nose at her in disgust. "Too much information."

Her laughter was a joyful tinkle in a room that had seen too much misery the last few days. A little of my darkness slipped away with her light surrounding me.

It was nice. The warmth of her. The reminder that outside these walls, people were actually happy, even if I'd forgotten what that felt like.

I clutched my pillow a little tighter. "So. When is this wedding? Summer? You always wanted a beach wedding."

She tossed me back my phone. "I already put it in your calendar for you."

I glanced down at the screen, searching for the entry, and then back up at her, wide-eyed. "This weekend? Are you insane? I haven't even met him yet!"

"Nope! We don't want to wait. He's been married before. I'm old enough to know what I want, so we're just going to the courthouse and getting ourselves hitched."

I blinked at her. She'd always been a whirlwind, but this seemed impulsive, even for her. I eyed her stomach. "Are you pregnant?"

She shoved her hands on her hips and frowned at me. "No, young lady, I am not."

"Then what's the rush?"

She shrugged. "I love him."

I stopped in my list of objections. Of all the men my mother had dated, I couldn't remember her ever saying she loved one.

She squeezed my fingers. "Please, Bel. I really need you to be on board with this. I don't want to marry him without you there by my side."

Her words got right into my chest and strangled my heart. "You want me to be your bridesmaid?"

"Maid of honor. And witness, actually. We're planning a big party for after, but the ceremony itself is strictly immediate family. So say yes, because you're my only family, and it would be too sad to have no one on my side."

I swallowed thickly, choking up on the emotion. "Of course I will. I'd be honored."

Miranda let out a cheer of excitement and flung herself at me, both of us flopping sideways on the bed in a tangle of legs and arms. "Thank God for that. I wasn't sure if I'd be able to convince you to wear a pretty dress when your style is normally ripped jeans and acid-washed T-shirts. But I really need you there. His best man is actually a best woman. And his ex, no less. So I need backup."

"Repeat that, please?" I asked with big eyes. "His ex-wife is going to be his person at his wedding to his new wife?"

"I know!" Miranda shouted dramatically. "That's exactly what I said! It's weird!"

"So weird."

"He says they stayed close after their divorce."

Alarm bells rang in my head. "Is she in love with him still? Or vice versa?"

But Mom shook her head quickly. "Oh, no. I don't think it's anything like that. She's happily remarried to this very handsome man. Has been for something like twenty years. And Bart has never given me any reason to be jealous. I really think they're just good friends. They sent us the sweetest gift."

I shrugged. "I guess that's nice then?"

She nodded. "She's who he wants, and I want him to have the best day ever."

"Very mature of you. Where's the Miranda who stormed into the law office of an ex-boyfriend and accused every woman there of having the hots for him?"

She cringed. "I was on pain medication, Bel! I didn't know what I was doing."

I chuckled at her. "Sure you were."

She laughed back. "Anyway. It's not like that this time. He's...changed me. He doesn't give me a reason to storm his office when I'm half high on Vicodin. He doesn't get off on my jealousy."

I smiled at her. "He sounds great, Mom. I can't wait to meet him."

"Good. You'll love him."

"If he treats you well, and has you feeling this secure and happy, then I already do." The man got top marks just for not making my mother crazier than she already was.

She beamed. "That's perfect, because I have a favor to ask you. You're still friends with that motorbike man who comes into your scary clown club, right?"

I froze. "There's a lot of men from the Saint View Slayers MC who come into Psychos, yes."

She frowned at me. "I meant the tall one you introduced me to once. What was his name? Frog? Fluff?"

I cleared my throat of the lump building in it. "Fang."

She clapped her hands together. "That's it!

If she noticed how his name got to me, then she didn't comment on it.

But all I could think of was the last time I'd seen him.

He'd been at Psychos the night of my attack.

It had been him I'd wanted to go home with that night. Fang with his towering presence and ice-blue eyes. Fang who had taken me to bed on many occasions and shown me everything I'd been missing with any other man.

But not that night. That night he'd seen me chatting with a stranger, gotten jealous, and walked out without a word to me.

That stranger had taken me to his home, where he'd had friends waiting for me. The three of them trapped me inside, blocking the exits, and held me down while I screamed. Until I'd let the painful reality take over.

Fang hadn't come to rescue me, and neither had anyone else.

I swallowed painfully. "What do you want with Fang?"

"Well, Bart has this obsession with motorcycles. He loves them. But he has no idea how to ride one. It's so cute, Belly. He's such a computer dork."

I forced a smile, but the mention of Fang had me unsettled all over again. I'd replayed that look he'd given me as he'd walked out of the club over and over. I rewound that night in my head and changed the outcome until he came over, told Caleb to fuck off, and took me home on the back of his bike.

He'd have worshipped every inch of my body and then tucked me into his bed to sleep.

I wanted that to have been my truth.

And yet it could never be.

Everything good between us had been ruined in that moment.

Mom still babbled on, not noticing I'd stopped properly paying attention. "So, I want to surprise him. Can you ask Fang and some of his friends to pick us up from the courthouse after the ceremony and drive us to the reception venue?"

I cleared my throat. "Mom, they're bikers. Not the clean-cut nice guys with shiny bikes you hire for a wedding."

"No, that's exactly what I need! I don't want Bart to know about it. I really want it to be a surprise, but if I pay someone, he'll know instantly. He'll see it on my credit card."

She never asked for much. She wasn't the type to hit me up for money, though that was probably because I had none. The most she ever needed from me was emotional support when her men dumped her ass.

This one sounded like he wanted to stick around.

"Okay, fine, I'll ask him."

But I was not going to be getting on the back of Fang's bike. I'd go with Hawk or Ice or War or any of the guys.

But not Fang. I couldn't be near him right now. His rejection had caused me way too much pain.

Mom cheered and threw herself at me in another tackle hug, holding on for longer than necessary, squeezing me tight. She pressed her face into my shoulder and mumbled, "You're going to be okay, baby. I promise."

She couldn't promise that. No one could.

She pulled back and pushed to her feet. "Well, now that all of that is settled, I need to get a move on. I've got a dress fitting, cake testing, a meeting with the judge who'll be marrying us since we need them to open the court on a Saturday. All the things!" She trotted toward the door in her high heels, before she paused to look back at me. "Oh! And we're having a dinner on Friday night at the hotel restaurant. So you can meet Bart. He wants to meet his new daughter before the day of the wedding. You'll be there, right?"

I'd never been any man's daughter and I wasn't about to start being Bart's, not at twenty-nine. But I didn't need to poop on my mother's parade either. "Fine. I'll come."

She kissed my cheek. "Thank you. Truly, baby. You're gonna like this one."

It was the kiss of death, those five little words. Because every other time in my life she'd said them, it ended in her back on that bathroom floor, crying her eyes out, while I picked up the pieces.

But today she'd said it with such hope in her voice that I couldn't let her down.

So all I did was smile and nod and promise to meet my new daddy. Whoop-de-fucking-do.

## 2

# FANG

*B*y night, Psychos was an underground sex club filled with erotic displays of kinks that would blow the average person's mind.

But by day, Psychos was a dive. A bar with sticky floors, ripped pool tables, and that damn clown with sharp teeth painted on the wall in terrifying detail.

I fucking hated that clown. A cold sweat broke out across the back of my neck every time I passed it. If I'd had it my way, I never would have stepped foot inside the premises with that thing staring at me the entire time.

There was only one thing that got me here day and night, and it sure as fuck wasn't the cheap beer. I was sure people thought I had a drinking problem. Or hell, maybe a sex addiction.

Rebel was the only addiction I couldn't fucking quit. I had no idea what it was about that little fairylike woman. She'd just shown up here one day, already acting like she owned the place. She'd rocked around in her short, pleated skirt and cropped midriff top, serving drinks to me and the boys from my MC. Her hair all wild, her eyes dark-rimmed with liner. She'd walked right up to me, leaned forward so her barely-there tits were in my face, and asked me if I was going home with anyone that night.

I'd been shocked speechless, while the guys around me had hooted and hollered, banging their heavy beer mugs on the wooden tabletop.

Rebel had smiled quietly and winked at me. "Even if you are going home with someone, I'd be interested in joining in."

Heat flushed my face even now, just thinking about that night. She'd never been scared of me the way other women were. I knew I was nothing special to look at. I could fuck a club slut if I wanted to just get my dick wet, they wouldn't say no. But I never had. I saw the way they feared me. The terror in their eyes as they took in my size, my scars, my tattoos.

I didn't want a woman too scared to enjoy herself when she was in my bed.

But Rebel had never been like that. She'd never had any qualms about letting me between her thighs so I could make her come. Or climbing my body and riding my cock like she owned it.

I looked around the club for her now, gaze skimming past the naked women, couples having sex, or groups with their hands all over each other. Moans of pleasure filtered through the deeply sexy music pouring from the club's speakers, and performers on stages writhed in various stages of undress or foreplay.

None of it did anything for me. It never did.

It was only ever her.

Nash, one of the club's owners strode by, in a hurry to get somewhere.

"Hey." I reached out and grabbed his arm.

He stopped and offered me his hand. "How's it going, Fang? Where you been all week? We've missed you around here."

I shrugged. "One of our sister chapters out in Florida needed some help with damage from a storm. Seemed like a good reason to take a beach break."

Nash raised an eyebrow. "It's nearly winter."

"Not in Florida. Place is hot all the fucking time."

Nash chuckled. The guy was probably five years older than me, but he had this settled-down vibe about him that I knew I didn't share. I was anxious. Unsettled. Rebel usually calmed that feeling in me, but without her around, I was twitchy.

Nash eyed me, focusing in on my leg bouncing. "Rebel isn't on tonight."

"Didn't ask if she was," I answered too quickly.

He raised an eyebrow. "Didn't need to, bro."

I sighed, figuring there was no point bluffing when the guy clearly knew what was up. I wanted his info. "She always works the sex parties." I knew because it was fucking torture, watching her walk around this place in anything from sexy lingerie to nipple tassels and a G-string. If the mood took her, it might be nothing but her birthday suit while she strutted around the club, one-hundred-percent confident in her own skin. It took every-thing in me not to toss her over my shoulder and storm through the club to find somewhere private to sink my dick deep inside her.

But that wasn't how she and I worked.

She wasn't mine.

Even if I wanted her to be.

"She's sick," Nash explained. "She texted Bliss at the start of the week to say she had some sort of stomach bug and that she'd be out for a few days."

"She's been out all week?" I shifted uncomfortably. I'd never known her to take so much as a single sick day. She loved this place.

He slapped me on the shoulder. "She's okay. She'll be back on Monday." He glanced around the room. "Plenty of other women around if you don't want to wait... I know you two aren't exclusive..."

I scowled at him.

He sniggered. "Yeah, like I thought. You don't need to say a word."

"Fuck off, Nash."

He just laughed and carried on his way with an all-knowing expression, as if he knew everything just because he was dating Rebel's best friend and they were all shacked up with my prez and some other dude.

Fuck that. Sharing my woman with two other men?

No thank you.

I shifted uncomfortably on the seat, remembering Rebel flirting with some asshole at the bar last week before I'd gone to Florida. I'd had no choice but to get up and leave. My club had needed me, and I had orders that had to be followed.

It was probably a good thing, though. If I'd stayed, I might have shoved the cocky, all-American asshole's head through a window just for looking at her. Then Rebel would have gotten pissed and told me to fuck off, just like she did every other time I got possessive with her.

She wasn't mine.

She'd reminded me of that a million times.

I needed it fucking tattooed on the back of my hand so I remembered.

My phone buzzed, and I picked it up, hitting a button to light up the screen.

REBEL

Hey. I need a favor.

"Speak of the devil," I muttered beneath my breath. My heart hammered at just the sight of her name.

FANG

Anything. You need soup or something?

REBEL

Soup? Why?

FANG

I'm at the Psychos party. Nash said you were out sick.

There was a long pause, but I knew she'd read the message. Eventually, she messaged back.

REBEL

Yeah. Chest infection.

I frowned at the phone. Nash had said it was a stomach bug. But whatever, I wasn't going to argue.

FANG

I'll bring soup. And some of that chocolate you like. I can be there in ten.

REBEL

> No. Don't. I'm fine. I just need a favor. My mom is getting married on Saturday morning at the courthouse. Finishes at midday. Could a couple of the guys come pick us up and drive us to the reception? Doesn't need to be you.

I made a face at the screen.

FANG

> Why the fuck wouldn't it be me? You think I'm gonna let you get on the back of Hawk's bike?

I waited three whole songs for a reply.

It didn't come. I waited two more, while staring real hard at that read symbol, willing her to type back.

She didn't.

A hand wandered over my thigh, creeping closer to my fly.

I glanced over at the woman who owned it, and she gave me a drunken smile.

"Hey, handsome. Wanna have some fun?"

I said nothing.

She clearly took it as a yes. She shifted to kneel in front of my widespread legs and ran her tongue over her pink lips. With her gaze on me, she slipped her thumbs into the thin straps of her bra and tugged them down her shoulders.

Her tits spilled over the cups, large and full, nipples pink and erect, begging to be touched.

I was about as turned on as I'd been at my grandfather's funeral.

"No thanks." I stood and stepped away, brushing past the woman who called me a prick beneath her breath.

The insult bounced right off me.

I couldn't have cared less.

I left the party behind. There was nothing of interest there for me. Not if Rebel wasn't there.

Outside in the parking lot, people were still arriving, hiding their party outfits—or lack of—beneath coats. Someone yelled out to me, but I ignored them, only one thing on my mind.

On my bike, I gunned the engine and peeled out onto Saint View Strip, the main road that ran through the town. I knew it well. It had been home for the best part of a decade, and I knew which places to eat at and which would result in a weeklong case of food poisoning. I passed the strip club with its flickering neon sign and stopped my bike up two shops down, in front of the Chinese take-out store.

A little bell rang when I ducked my head to enter through the door, and the only person in the store glanced up from her phone. She darted a look over her shoulder toward the kitchen, then back at me, her bored gaze instantly switching to one of fear.

"We don't keep money here."

"Do you keep soup here?" I took a ten-dollar bill from my pocket and put it on the countertop.

She edged toward me slowly with clear distrust.

I couldn't even blame her. She was barely as tall as Rebel, which made me practically twice her size. If I'd intended any ill harm, there would have been nothing she could do to stop me, unless she had a gun stashed back there between packets of rice and sweet and sour sauce.

She snatched the bill, crumpling it in her fingers, then pointed at the big silver vats on the stove. "What flavor?"

"Chicken, please, ma'am."

She nodded and pulled down a clear plastic container and matching lid. With one eye on me the entire time, she ladled in the soup, fitted the lid, and then pushed it across to me.

"Thanks. Keep the change."

She sighed with audible relief as I left the store, the door swinging shut behind me.

Her reaction wasn't unusual, but it didn't mean I liked it. It just made me appreciate Rebel all the more. I hated the idea of her lying in bed unwell for an entire week while I was away. I should have checked in on her.

*Not your girl to do that.*

"Fuck that," I muttered, slipping into the convenience store and picking up her favorite chocolate bar, the same one I always had in the little bar fridge in my room at the clubhouse. I hated nuts in chocolate, but I liked watching her eat them because she made all sorts of pleasurable noises at the taste, and it reminded me of the sounds she made when she let me put my tongue on her clit.

I stowed my purchases in the saddlebag on my bike and drove through the unusually quiet Saint View streets to her apartment.

I'd only been here once before, but I'd memorized her building and her apartment number. The place was a shit heap, in desperate need of repairs, but I took the stairs two at a time, not bothered by my boots thumping even though it was late. There were plenty of other noises from behind closed doors. Arguments. TVs. A dog barking. It kind of reminded me of the clubhouse. You learned to sleep through noise when you lived in a place like this.

I stopped outside her door and stared at the eviction notice pinned to it. I didn't like the look of that. I didn't have much in the way of cash to give her, but I could have a 'friendly chat' with her landlord. Though I already knew she'd be pissed if I did. Miss Fucking Independent would probably rather sleep on the streets than ask me for help.

But that was an argument for another time, when she was well. I sucked in a breath, suddenly nervous. I'd never just turned up at her place out of the blue. Before I could lose my nerve, I rapped my knuckles across the door. "Rebel. It's me." Then I realized she might not even recognize my voice. "Fang...I mean."

I squeezed my eyes shut and slumped against her doorframe. Fucking hell. I couldn't even get a proper sentence out around this woman. And I wasn't even facing her.

The mattress squeaked from inside the room, so I knew she was home. Maybe she was sleeping.

I sighed, putting the soup and chocolate down at my feet and pulling out my phone.

FANG

Soup at your door. Feel better. x

I walked away, down a flight of stairs, then paused when the lock on her door disengaged. It opened a crack, just wide enough for her hand to poke out and grope

around the floor until she snagged on the plastic bag with
her hot soup and probably melting chocolate bar.

She dragged it inside and closed the door without
showing her face, the locks clicking again.

I waited for a text to come in, but nothing did.

Eventually, I wrote one of my own. If I was doing her
a favor, the least she could do was give me one in return.
It was a simple request, but an important one. Because I
really didn't want to have to kill one of my brothers for
having her arms wrapped around them when it could
have been me.

FANG

> We'll be there for the wedding. But,
> Rebel? You will be on the back of my
> bike. Only mine.

## 3

## REBEL

*A*t the heavy footsteps outside and the knock on my door, the panic attack stole over me so quickly I didn't even see it coming. One minute I was fine, the next there was no air in my lungs, leaving them raw and aching while I simultaneously gasped and tried to shove my fist in my mouth so I wouldn't make a noise. I buried under the blankets, trembling but frozen in place, silently begging them to go away.

They'd held me down. Taken turns forcing themselves on me. I hadn't had a gun then, and no way of protecting myself. The one clutched in my fingers now didn't seem like enough.

"Rebel. It's me."

In an instant, the panic subsided.

"Fang...I mean."

His familiar voice was a balm on my ragged, nervous edges. One by one, each muscle in my body relaxed into my lumpy mattress, and I unclenched my grip on the gun.

I wanted to run to the door, throw it open, and wrap myself in the massive man who had always curled my toes. With his huge, thick body and constant scowl, he'd never scared me. Quite the opposite. His ice-blue gaze that followed me around rooms heated my blood and sent tingles to places I really enjoyed.

Until he'd walked out of the bar that night, unknowingly leaving me with Caleb and his pack of wolves.

It was unfair for me to blame him. If he'd known what would happen, there was no doubt in my mind he would have stayed. Hell, he probably would have killed Caleb on the spot. But no matter how I tried to get up off the bed and let him in, I couldn't. My legs wouldn't move. Not until his footsteps went down the stairs.

The scent of chicken soup forced my stomach into a growl of hunger. I hadn't eaten in days. The carved-out hollow of my belly twisted in pain, and my weak limbs begged for the chance of just a tiny sip.

It smelled so freaking good.

I dragged myself from the bed and tiptoed to the door, pressing up to look out through the peephole.

His ice-blue gaze stared back at me. A flight of stairs down, but waiting on the landing, watching to see if I took his gift.

This close, it was all I could smell. My legs wobbled, and I dropped to my knees, knowing I desperately needed that food before I fainted.

I reached up and unlocked the door, then opened it with agonizing slowness, cringing, just waiting for him to slam his way inside and steal what he wanted, just the way Caleb and his friends had.

It didn't come.

Of course it didn't. Because Fang wasn't Caleb. He didn't hurt me. He left sex club parties at midnight and brought me soup. That urge to run to him hit me again, so hard and fast I almost did it.

But my face... I was still black and blue. If I showed Fang, he'd want to know who did it.

Then he'd kill them. I had no doubts the man was capable of it. You didn't get scars like his from living a life on the straight and narrow.

Nobody was killing Caleb and his friends.

Nobody but me.

I reached a hand around the door, almost weeping with relief when my fingers snagged on the plastic take-out bag. I dragged it inside, leaning back on the door to close it and then quickly turning the locks.

I cracked open the lid, taking only a second to inhale the richly scented steam, before putting the entire thing to my lips and swallowing.

It slid down my throat so perfectly warm and tasty, my stomach relaxing instantly as food hit it for the first time in days. I would make myself sick on this, I was sure of it, but I took a few more long swallows, just basking in how good it tasted.

My phone buzzed with an incoming text.

FANG

We'll be there for the wedding. But, Rebel? You will be on the back of my bike. Only mine.

I put Fang's soup down on the floor beside me and reread the message, dread filling me with every word.

It was exactly why I hadn't wanted to ask him. Why I should have just told my mom no.

Putting a woman on the back of your bike was a sacred act in Fang's MC. My bestie, Bliss, had told me all about it, when she'd fallen for the club prez. It would be different for my mom and new stepdaddy. It was clear they weren't anyone's girl.

But me and Fang...that was a different kettle of fish altogether.

One that might have made me all warm and cozy just a few days earlier, if it hadn't sent me running for the hills in terror over making a commitment.

But the point was moot now. I hadn't even been able to open the door for him. Some traumatized part of me rejected the idea of ever letting a man touch me again.

*You asked for this.*

*You've been flirting with me for weeks.*

*You like it rough like this? Yeah, you do, whore.*

It wasn't fair of me to taint Fang with the same brush. He had no idea what he'd done. No idea that just him walking out had sent me careening down a path that would change who I was at my very core. None of it was his fault. All of it mine.

It didn't change anything.

It didn't change he was always going to be linked to that night in my head.

With a belly full of warm soup, I took my chocolate bar back to bed and ate it slowly, savoring every mouthful. Nothing had ever been so sweet.

Except maybe the man who'd given it to me.

*I* finally got dressed on Friday evening, but only because I knew my mom would be devastated if I failed to show up for the fancy dinner she'd planned so I could meet Bart before the ceremony. She'd even called this morning to double-check I was coming.

The conversation had left me smiling. I'd never heard her sound quite so in love. Normally it was all infatuation with her. She liked guys with abs and chiseled jaws and bank accounts with numbers bigger than I even knew were possible.

But with Bart, she didn't mention any of those things. She gushed about how smart he was. How he'd picked her flowers every day for the last week. How she'd had the best night of her life just watching a movie with him. She'd been shocked it hadn't led to sex and had marveled over how good just cuddling had felt.

I'd heard my mother declare herself in love many a time. But when she said it about Bart, something deep inside me recognized she finally knew what that meant.

For that reason, I wanted to meet the man.

And hell, I couldn't feel any worse than I already did, so maybe getting out of the house would help.

I put on a cute black dress, one of the tamest ones I owned. Bart had booked a fancy hotel room for the night, so I didn't have to travel from Saint View in the morning for the ceremony, and we were eating in their posh restaurant. So booty shorts and a barely there T-shirt weren't going to cut it.

I didn't want anyone staring at me. Especially not men. The more understated my dress, the better. I covered up the healing scratches and scrapes on my arms with a cardigan, grateful for the colder weather. Black, opaque stockings disguised the marks on my legs. I studied my reflection in my full-length mirror and decided if anyone asked why I looked like I was about to go to a funeral, I would just say I was channeling my inner Wednesday Addams.

My face was more problematic. But at least the swelling had gone down. So all that was left to do was gingerly dab a thick foundation on top of the bruising around my cheeks and eyes.

"Motherfucking donkey balls," I muttered, blinking fast to keep tears at bay. "Big, fat, hairy donkey balls." Blending on top of tender, injured skin was worse than first-day period pain.

I got through the rest of my routine by imagining kicking Caleb in the face and following it up with a nice stab from the pointy end of a makeup brush.

When I was done, I studied my handiwork from every angle, checking and double-checking nothing showed through. It was sweet. I'd clearly missed my calling as a makeup artist.

I used a female-only ride-sharing app to get myself and an overnight bag into the city, too nervous to just use an Uber for fear a man would pick me up and I'd freak out. The trip went quickly with the driver mindlessly chatting and me staring out the window barely respond-ing. Then we were parking in front of the Grand Metro Hotel, and she was telling me to have a good night.

I got out gingerly, pulling my cardigan a little tighter around me and lowering my gaze to watch where I walked. It wasn't my usual style, but I couldn't strut in like

I normally would have, wide smile for everyone in the room and gaze searching for anyone up for a good time.

The interior of the restaurant was a quiet buzz of low conversation, dim mood lighting, and soft jazz music. The heavy door closed behind me, blocking out the hustle and bustle of the drop-off zone and the high traffic reception area, turning the restaurant intimate and cozy.

I hesitated, waiting for the hostess to notice me. She didn't. I had to clear my throat quietly for her to look up.

"I'm sorry, I didn't see you there."

It was only then I realized how much I'd really succeeded in turning myself into a dormouse. Normally I drew stares without even trying. I wasn't tall like Fang who commanded attention with the pure size of him. Nor was I particularly pretty, though I was vain enough to admit I wasn't ugly either. I would have once proudly announced I was a ten, despite the fact I didn't have long legs and big tits.

But that was because I'd believed it. I'd been confident in who I was, and people responded to that. I'd walked into rooms like I owned them. I was the girl who would stroll right up to a guy she found attractive and tell him she was his for the night.

I'd oozed confidence.

Now I had none. Not anymore.

They'd stolen more from me than they would ever know.

The woman stared at me, waiting for me to respond to a question I hadn't heard.

She raised an eyebrow. "I asked if you had a reservation?"

I cleared my throat. "Oh, sorry. Um, maybe? I'm

meeting my mom and her fiancé here. Her name is Miranda. His is Bart."

She ran her fingernail down a sheet of paper on her desk. "Nothing by those names. Most people book under their last name, though."

If Mom had mentioned Bart's, I couldn't remember it, so I gave ours instead. "Kemp?"

The woman shook her head. "Sorry."

It had to be under Bart's name then. "They should be here any minute. Could I just wait at the bar?"

The woman shrugged. "Sure."

I thanked her and weaved my way through the tables of people, to a large circular-shaped bar in the middle of the room. People sat around it on stools, waiting on their tables to be ready or for other members of their parties to arrive. Bartenders moved around the inner circle, serving drinks in all directions.

I dropped my bag at my feet, scooted up onto a stool, and asked the bartender for a vodka with cranberry juice. He placed it in front of me a moment later, and I sat sipping my drink, one eye on the door, waiting for my mom to appear.

A family of four came in and were seated immediately with a bored look from the hostess. I glanced over again when the door opened once more, but it wasn't my cute mother on the arm of a rich businessman.

The hostess perked right up though, and it was obvious why. The man walking through the door was as blacked out as I was. Black motorcycle boots. Black jeans and tee. A leather jacket that was as dark as night, apart from the metal accents that glittered like stars on his broad chest. He had a helmet beneath one arm, and he ran his fingers through his hair, straightening it.

The hostess flashed him a flirty grin she most definitely had not used on me or the family sitting at table four. Interestingly, he flirted back, leaning in to twist a curl of the hostess's hair away from her face.

What an ass. I almost hoped his date would turn up right now, just for the excitement it would cause.

But no leggy blonde, or any other woman followed him in, and eventually, the hostess stopped panting all over him and pointed at the bar.

I rolled my eyes as he leaned across her podium, plucked the pen from her fingers, and wrote something down on her pad of paper. Surely his phone number.

He took the same path through the tables that I had, brushing by me to get to the empty seat next to me. I stiffened at being so close to him and instinctively shifted my stool in the opposite direction. I busied myself with my drink to try to keep my panic at bay. This was a public area. Nothing was going to happen here in front of a hundred people. Mom would be here any minute. There was no need to freak out and cause a scene.

"Do I smell?"

I glanced around, not sure if he was talking to me, but nobody else was paying him any attention. "Sorry?" I stuttered.

"Reek? Stink? Odor of road?"

I crinkled my nose at him. "Odor of road? What exactly does that smell like?"

He grinned. "Squashed bugs and motor oil, maybe?"

Actually, he smelled vaguely of cologne. One I really liked and could pick out on men just walking past them

at the mall because it was that distinctive. I kinda wanted
to take a deep inhale. "You smell fine."

"Why are you scuttling down the bar like a scared
cockroach then?"

I blinked, confused as to why he was talking to me, let
alone insulting me. "Did you just call me a cockroach?"

He shrugged. "You're small, quick, startled easily, and
all in black. Seemed fitting. Who died by the way?"

"Your manners, perhaps?" The quip was out before I
really even had time to consider how my mouth had
gotten me in trouble before.

He chuckled and motioned for the bartender to pour
him a drink. Whiskey on the rocks. Of course. How typi-
cal. Too macho for something with fruit, I was sure.

I jerked my stool away again, a whole lot less subtly
than the first time I'd done it.

Suddenly I was sliding back to where I'd started,
moved along by his hand on my seat, dragging it back
toward him.

"Where you going, Roach?"

I gaped at him, flabbergasted by his confidence, then
shook my head. "I'm too old for this shit."

"What?" he asked innocently, like he didn't still have
his hand resting on the back of my chair.

I pointedly stared at it, and when he didn't move, I
helpfully lifted it with two fingers, like it was dirty and I
didn't want to touch it. "Keep those on your own chair.
And call me roach again. I dare you."

He chuckled under his breath. "Would you prefer
cock...cock-roach..."

I raised an eyebrow. "Actually, I think cock is already
taken by you, cock...cock-face. If you don't mind, I liked

my chair better over here." I jerked it back to where it had been.

Fuck me. I hated men. Especially the attractive ones who thought schoolyard taunts were conversation.

I looked at my phone. Ten past eight. I'd been late for our seven-thirty meal, but Mom was now forty minutes late. That warranted a text message. I pulled my phone out of my purse.

REBEL

> Hey. Where are you guys? I'm waiting at the bar. Getting hit on by some moron. SOS.

My phone rang a moment later, Mom's name flashing up on the screen. I snatched it up quickly when the cock on the seat beside me darted a peek at it. "Do you mind?" I snapped at him, hitting the green button. "Where are you guys?"

There was a muffled laugh from the other end before Mom's voice came through again. "Oh, honey, I'm so sorry. We completely lost track of time."

I looked at the ceiling in exasperation. Of course she did. Because she was flaky and immature as ever and had probably expected me to call to remind her about a dinner she'd invited me to. I took a deep breath and tried to calm myself. "Okay, well, are you coming now?"

She giggled down the line. "Uh, about that. Bart took a Viagra because I wanted to try this whole tantric sex thing, and now we kinda just gotta ride it out." She laughed hysterically. "Ride it out! I sure am!"

I screwed up my face in revulsion. "Ugh, Mom. Too much information. You just crossed a hard line."

"I'm sorry! I'm sorry! I know. I swear, Belly, we didn't mean for this to happen. I thought it would have gone down hours ago. I can't just leave him like this. I've been trying everything I can think of to get it to...you know."

I pinched the space between my eyebrows, trying hard not to imagine what they were doing in that very moment to get Bart's little problem under control. "Okay, okay. Never mind! You do what you gotta do. I'll see you tomorrow, I guess."

"You will! Because I'm getting married!"

I smiled, never able to stay mad at her for long because she was like an impulsive child. Of course she managed to give her fiancé a never-ending stiffy just hours before their wedding. I didn't even know why I was surprised. "Go enjoy yourselves. See you tomorrow."

"Wait! Wait! Belly, I forgot to tell you something. There's a surprise for you at the restaurant."

Unless it was a credit card to pay my drink bill, I wasn't sure I really needed a surprise right now. Especially because I was pretty sure Cockface next to me was listening to every word. I turned around, and sure enough, he was watching me.

I glared at him.

He smirked back.

Ugh. Exactly why I hated attractive men. The ability to smirk should be removed from their repertoire. "What is it?" I asked Mom. "Is it with the hostess?"

She laughed. "No, no. It's not gift wrapped. Bart's son is there, and he's so cute, Bel! You two would be the most adorable couple."

I blinked at the cock next to me in horror. "No."

"Yes! Bart said he'd be wearing a suit, and he has glasses. A little dorky, but in a cute kind of way…"

I breathed a sigh of relief. Definitely not this guy then, because nothing about Cockface was dorky in any sort of way. But there was a guy drinking alone across the other side of the bar who could have stepped right out of an accounting magazine. If I squinted real hard, he might have been cute. But it was a long shot. To be fair, Mom and I had never had similar taste in men. Which was probably a good thing, considering how close we were in age. It would have been very easy to steal each other's guys if we'd had even remotely similar attractions.

"Do you see him?"

"Yeah, I see him. And now I'm leaving. We can meet tomorrow at the wedding. PS—Thanks for telling me I had a new stepbrother. Info that could have been shared well before right now."

"Oh, don't be mad! I just wanted to surprise you because he's so cute. Go say hi, Bel. Please? For me?"

"I'm going to kill you for this," I muttered, getting down off the stool. "Truly, you're the worst."

"You love me! And you'll love him too, I'm sure!"

I groaned because I did love her. I ended the call and put my head in my hands.

"Family drama?" Cockface asked.

I glared at him. "Do you always eavesdrop on other people's conversations?"

"Do you always speak so loudly that the entire bar can hear your every word? Nothing was stopping you from walking outside, you know. I mean, now whose manners are dead?"

I rolled my eyes.

He laughed. "You're cute when you do that."

I froze. "No, I'm not."

I was doing it again. Drawing attention to myself. Specifically, male attention. Exactly what I was supposed to *not* be doing.

I got off the seat woodenly, clutching my purse and bag with one hand, and forced myself to walk around to the other side of the bar where my new stepbrother was nursing a watery cocktail. At least he wasn't too alpha male for fruit. "Hey. I'm Rebel."

He glanced over at me, his eyes widening. "Uh, hi. Mathew."

He stuck his hand out, and I tried not to look at Cock-face smirking at me from across the bar. I twisted so I couldn't see him as easily and tried to focus on my new brother. I'd never had a sibling. Though I imagined this wouldn't be slumber parties or a lifelong bond, it might be nice to at least have a friend to complain about our parents with.

I tried not to shrink away when his fingers touched mine, but it took everything in me to return his handshake.

But then he just stared awkwardly at me, and the silence drew out.

"So, uh, parents, huh?" I forced a laugh.

He cocked his head at me. "Parents?"

"Yeah."

He nodded. "Annoying?"

"To say the least."

I drummed my fingers on the countertop, feeling more and more anxious with every moment I sat next to him. With too much silence between us, all I could think about was how my skin itched at being this close to a man. How I wanted to dig my fingernails in and scratch until my skin bled.

I got down off my stool and picked up my things. "You know what? We don't need to be besties. I'll see you tomorrow."

He opened his mouth to respond, but I was already hurrying away, wishing I'd had more than just the one drink.

Cockface leaned back on his stool, fingers brushing my arm. "On the run again, Roach?"

"Just trying to be anywhere you aren't, Cock."

He saluted me with a grin, and as I rounded the corner, I found a tiny smile on my face too.

As well as the realization that when Cockface had touched me, I hadn't wanted to burn.

# 4

## REBEL

The hotel room Bart had booked for me was the most luxurious I'd ever been in. If theirs was even half as nice, I couldn't blame my mom and Bart for spending the day in bed and ditching me for dinner. I might have done the same if I'd come up here first. I ordered room service since I hadn't eaten downstairs, and ate it sitting in bed, watching a movie, with the city lights twinkling through the window outside.

For the first time in a week, I slept soundly. The sheets were silk, the mattress free of lumps, and I woke up feeling almost like a new person.

All fine and dandy until I looked at my phone and realized the blackout blinds weren't the cheap, shit kind I had in my apartment that let sun in from the crack of dawn. Oh no, they were the freaking expensive kind that kept it as dark as the middle of the night, even when it was eleven and you were due at your mother's wedding in forty-five minutes.

"Fark. She's going to kill me." I staggered out of bed,

regretting the three extra vodkas I'd consumed from the mini bar after my dinner. In the bathroom, I got the shower going and peeled off the clothes I'd slept in. Not wanting to do it, but knowing I needed to, I cranked the water all the way to the right and let it spray over my naked body. "Oh, finger nuggets. That's cold."

But it did the trick in waking me up. I toweled off at record speed and carefully reapplied my makeup, covering every bruise. Next up was the gold satin dress I hadn't worn in a very long time. The spaghetti straps and low-cut back meant no bra, not that I really needed one with my less-than-a-handful of boob. The hemline fell around my ankles but the skirt had a large split up the thigh.

I stared at myself in the mirror and realized there was no way I could wear this. It was too much. Too revealing. For all the reasons I'd loved it when I'd bought it, I now hated it.

But I hadn't brought an alternative. The only other option was the dress I'd worn last night, which I'd also slept in, so it was a hot mess. I shrugged on my coat instead. It wasn't long enough to cover the slit in the skirt, but I could hold that together with my hand. I was out of other options, and out of time. It was ten minutes to twelve, and I didn't have time to hang around here, pondering over how much skin I was showing off.

On the elevator ride down, my female-only ride-sharing app unhelpfully advised there were no drivers in the area in the next fifteen minutes. That was just great. But there'd been a lot of taxis dropping off and picking up guests the night before when I'd arrived, so I strode out to the drop-off bay, praying I'd be lucky.

A taxi pulled in right as I arrived, letting out an elderly couple who had to have come from the airport, judging by the stickers on their suitcases.

The driver slammed down the trunk and then looked at me. "You need a ride?"

I froze. The idea of being in a confined space with him felt too out of my control. It would be all too easy for him to lock the doors and drive me somewhere private, where he could take whatever he wanted from me.

The man waited patiently for my answer.

I couldn't breathe. I only had minutes to get to the courthouse, but I couldn't do it. I shook my head quickly.

Tears pricked the backs of my eyes. I hated this. It was so far removed from who I was, and yet I couldn't stop the fear crawling up my throat. I didn't want to be this girl.

I sucked in a few deep breaths and gave myself a mental pep talk. Not every man was Caleb and his friends. Not every man wanted to hurt me, and I couldn't live my life in fear. If I was going to be like this, I might as well go back to starving myself until my body gave up.

Or take the quicker option, via the gun locked in my apartment.

I was going to get in the next taxi that pulled up. No matter who was driving.

The next vehicle in was exactly what I'd been waiting for. A female-driven, completely empty taxi.

I waved at her, and she pulled up right in front of me. I could have leaned through the open window and kissed her for having a vagina. Instead, I grabbed the handle of the front passenger seat. "Thank you so much—"

The back door jerked open with a squeak, and I stopped mid-sentence as a man slid into the back seat of my ride. "Hey! This is my—" My mouth dropped open. "You!"

The man grinned at me. "Hey, Roach. You getting in or what?"

I glared at him. "I am, but you're getting out."

"Nah. Need a ride."

"This is my taxi."

He cocked his head to one side. "Possession is nine-tenths of the law, my little insect friend. And I'm the one sitting in the car while you stand there checking me out."

"I'm not checking you out." But of course, because he'd brought it up, my gaze skimmed down his body, taking in the dark stubble on his jaw, the white, open-necked shirt, and a navy suit that fit him to perfection.

He chuckled.

The sound drew my gaze back up to his face. God, it would be satisfying to punch him right in his full, pink lips.

The driver glanced between us like she was at a tennis game. "You getting in?" she asked me eventually.

As much as I didn't want to get in a car with him, he didn't give me that sick, uncomfortable feeling either. And I really didn't have time to hang around, waiting for another female driver to appear. I got in. "Courthouse, please."

"You got it." She glanced at Cockface in the back. "Good with you if I take her first?"

"Ladies always come first." He leaned forward, so his head was in between our seats, but it was me he turned toward. "A motto I live by in all areas of my life."

I glanced over at him, trying to ignore how close our faces were. "Got references to prove that?"

He sat back, shaking his head with a laugh. "How about an on-the-job trial instead? Plenty of room in this back seat if you want to climb over and take me for a test ride."

The urge to make immature gagging noises rose swiftly, but we were pulling up outside the courthouse, and I was saved by the need to pay the driver. "Add an extra-big tip on his ride, okay? You deserve extra for having to hear his verbal diarrhea."

I got my credit card out to pay my bill, but Cockface reached over and tapped his card before I could get mine to it.

Ugh, he was one of those guys, who thought they were all charming and generous, flashing around the fact they had money. "Don't expect me to say thank you. You owed me that for breathing all over my neck while you were trying to be sexy."

"Trying or succeeding? I think the latter."

I put my hand on the door and opened it. "Oh, thank God. Room to escape your rapidly expanding head." I tapped the driver on the shoulder. "Have a great day. Thank you."

She nodded at me, and I closed the door, turning away to stride up the courthouse stairs.

"Wait up, Roach."

I spun around. "Seriously? You're following me now?"

"Don't flatter yourself. I've got an appointment."

I grinned. "With a judge? What did you do? Wait, let me guess. Indecent exposure?"

"Nothing about me is indecent, Roachy."

"Whatever. I'm late. One can only hope the judge locks you up so you can't inflict your less-than-stellar personality on any other woman. Lucky you let them come first because I'm sure they don't stick around for pillow talk."

At the top of the stairs, he held the heavy door open for me. "Plenty of spare pillows in my room at the hotel if you want to find out."

"I'd rather suffocate myself with one." I picked up the pace, scanning the entrance board that had a directory of the day's events and the various rooms they were taking place in. Locating the room that had "Wedding of Kemp and Weston" written next to it, I followed the signs down a long hall.

Cockface kept pace with me the entire way. "I'm Vaughn, by the way."

"I think I prefer Cockface."

"Fair enough. I'm pretty partial to Roach for you anyway."

"You aren't even going to ask my name?"

"Why? I already know it. Rebel."

I paused with my hand on the door to the ceremony room, gaze snapping to his. "How?"

He pushed open the door for me again, but neither of us made any move to go inside. I don't know why he didn't, but I was too busy gaping at him.

He winked. "You're my new sister, Roach."

# 5

## REBEL

*V*aughn Weston dropped his invisible mic and strode on into the wedding like he knew they'd be waiting for us to arrive. I stared, dumbstruck, as he strode up the short aisle and embraced an older man who thumped him on the back and hugged him close.

"Belly!" Mom came down the aisle to meet me in a slinky white gown, but wobbled a little, teetering toward the chairs set up for any attending guests.

I caught her arm, straightening her before she could go careening into them. "Whoa." I took in her bloodshot eyes. "Are you drunk?"

She shook her head vigorously. "No! Not at all. Haven't had a drop."

I wasn't sure that was true, her words were slightly slurred. But she was sober enough for me to tell her off. "That's Bart's son?"

Miranda glanced over her shoulder at the two men embracing, and then looked back at me to shrug. "I guess so! I haven't met him. He lives in California."

I clutched her arm. "You told me he was cute in a nerdy way!"

"He was in the photo Bart showed me. Maybe it was old?"

Christ Al-fucking-mighty. "It must have been from a land before time if you thought that man over there was just cute and dorky."

There was no way Vaughn Weston had ever been either of those things. While I'd had a very embarrassing, awkward teenage years stage, I doubted Vaughn had ever had braces and acne. He'd probably been the bad boy smoking pot behind school buildings and fucking the head cheerleader behind her all-American boyfriend's back.

"Come meet Bart before the judge gets here, okay?" Mom tugged me up the aisle, but she could barely walk a straight line, zigzagging until I grabbed her arm and did the guiding myself.

"Okay," I whispered to her. "So we're doing this drunk."

"I swear, I'm not, Bel." She shook her head a few times and then forced a smile for her fiancé. "Hey there, handsome. I want you to meet my daughter."

Bart stumbled forward, only to be caught by Vaughn who'd lost his casual smirk and had replaced it with a frown of deep concern.

"Hi. Reb-b-el," Bart stammered, like his tongue was too thick for his mouth.

"They're smashed,' Vaughn said quietly to me. "That's my mom and her husband over there. She said they've been like this since they got here."

"Fuck," I muttered and nodded to Vaughn's mom and

stepdad when they introduced themselves as Riva and Karmichael.

They perched on seats in the front row, watching on with worried expressions.

"They can't get married like this," Vaughn said softly. "We're going to have to tell the judge."

"No!" Bart bellowed, lurching forward to clutch my mother's hand. "We're fine. I'm marrying her, no matter what anyone says."

"Exactly what he said," Mom agreed. "This is our wedding. We're not leaving until we're married."

I frowned, but then an older woman entered the room, her big voice booming. "Ready to get hitched? Is everyone here?"

Vaughn looked at me, and I shrugged.

"There's no doubt in my mind she wanted to do this. Did your dad say anything to you?"

"We aren't exactly sitting around, drinking tea, and hashing out our feelings with Dr. Phil, but I doubt Dad would have proposed if he didn't want to marry her."

I sighed. "Then I guess we're letting them do this?"

"Guess so."

Mom kissed my cheek. "Love you, Belly. And I love him. This is good. I promise. We're fine. We haven't been drinking."

I left her at the altar, clutching Bart's hands. I sat on her side of the room, the only guest because I was the only family she had. While Vaughn sat next to his mom and stepdad.

The judge cleared her throat. "Dear friends and family of Miranda and Bart. We're gathered here today to share their love..."

I was sure whatever the judge was saying was lovely, but as the minutes ticked by, my worry amped up.

Something was horribly wrong. Mom swayed, fingers clutched into Bart's to keep her steady, but he wasn't faring much better. His eyes were half-mast, his responses to the judge slurred.

"Oh," Mom groaned, doubling over suddenly, clutching her stomach.

Despite it being the middle of her wedding, I lurched to my feet to grab her. "What is it? Are you okay?"

She straightened with effort and weakly pushed me away. "I'm fine. It's nothing. Keep going. Do the vows. I want to say I do."

The judge glanced at me with a question in her eyes, but I just nodded at her. I didn't know what else to do. I practically hovered over my chair, just waiting for the moment I'd need to sprint to my mother's side again.

On Bart's side, Vaughn seemed ready to do the same. "Dad. I think you should stop. It's okay, we can do this another day."

Bart shook his head limply. "No. I'm marrying her today. I've never loved anyone the way I love her. I want her to be my wife."

I cringed, glancing over at Riva, but she didn't seem bothered by her ex's words. She had her fingers clutched tight in Karmichael's hands, both of them watching on with love and concern for their friend.

"Okay," the judge said softly. "Bartholomew James Weston, do you take Miranda Leigh Kemp to be your lawful wedded wife? In sickness and in health, 'til death do you part?"

"Yes," Bart lisped, barely audible, like his earlier demands had drained him of energy.

The judge bit her lip but turned to my mother. "Same question of you, Miranda."

I appreciated her cutting through the red tape and getting to the point. I wanted to take my mother back to the hotel and call a doctor. This was more than drunk. They'd taken something, and neither of them were doing well on it.

"I do."

"By the power vested in me, I now pronounce you husband and wife. You may kiss your bride."

Bart's lips didn't come close to my mother's mouth. Like she'd been holding on just to say her vows, her eyes rolled back, and her knees came out from beneath her.

"Mom!" I dove for her, colliding with Vaughn who'd tried to catch her too.

Neither of us were quick enough to get to her, and she fell to the floor, an awkward tangle of arms, legs, and wedding dress.

Even through her makeup, the gray tinge of her skin shocked me. It had only been minutes since she'd met me at the door, wobbly but pink in the cheeks.

Now, she looked dead.

Very freaking dead.

I shoved my fingers against her neck, desperately searching for a sign she was still with me. "I can't find a pulse!"

"Miranda!" Bart stumbled forward, but Karmichael managed to catch him.

"Oh my," Riva cried, hand over her mouth. "What is going on? I'm calling nine-one-one." She stood to make the call, while her husband steered Bart to a seat, then knelt to help Vaughn and me.

"Help me get her flat on the floor," Vaughn barked at the older man.

I rocked back on my heels, watching in horror as the two men shifted my mother's lifeless body off the stairs and onto the flat tiled floor. "Is she okay? Is she breathing?" I'd never had to check for someone's pulse before. I wanted to believe that it had been there and I just couldn't find it.

Vaughn put his ear to her mouth but shook his head. "Fuck. Nothing. We need to start CPR."

He linked his fingers together, one hand on top of the other, and put the heels to my mother's chest.

He leaned down on her so hard her ribs audibly cracked.

"Oh my God, no," I cried. "Mom, please. Please. Wake up."

Vaughn kept going, rhythmically pumping her chest while foam frothed at her lips.

I clutched her hand, tears streaming down my face. I squeezed her fingers, desperately hoping for even the tiniest of movements. Just something that would assure me she was still there.

"The ambulance is here!" Vaughn's mom shouted. "Make way!"

But I couldn't move.

I clutched her hand, willing her to live, even when the paramedic gently moved Vaughn aside and took over.

Vaughn sat back on his knees, eyes wide with shock, staring at the officer while he tried to find a pulse.

The man frowned. "No pulse. How long has she been down for?"

"Fifteen minutes," the judge supplied.

Fifteen minutes? How had it been only fifteen minutes when it felt like a lifetime?

The man shook his head and then checked his watch. "Time of death, twelve forty-seven."

"What? No!" I lurched forward, pressing my own hands to my mother's chest.

But instantly, I knew the paramedic was right. It was her eyes. Where they'd once held pride, and love, mischief, and affection for me, now they stared aimlessly.

She was gone. A deathly silence fell over the room as we all stared in shock at the body on the floor.

"Bart!" Karmichael's shout caught all of us by surprise.

Bart's body fell to the floor beside my mother's, as poetic as *Romeo and Juliet*.

None of us had noticed him quietly slip away, sitting on the chair. But I didn't need to check his pulse to know he was gone too. The paramedic launched into a frantic round of CPR, but Vaughn knew it as well as I did. He let out a roar of anguish that I felt right down to my toes.

"What is happening?" Vaughn's mom clutched her husband's arm. "They were a bit off...but...not this."

Police swarmed in, and any response was lost in a sea of stomping boots and police radios.

It didn't matter anyway.

They were gone, and there was nothing bringing them back.

## 6

## REBEL

*I* wouldn't let her go.

I knelt at her side, begging and crying for her to come back until my knees went numb and my throat ached. From outside somewhere came shouting, and sirens, but my whole world had shrunk down to me and the only person in my life who'd ever loved me.

She couldn't be gone.

"Rebel," Vaughn said in a voice as hoarse as mine would have been, had I been able to get out words.

I didn't answer him. I couldn't.

"Rebel, stop. Come on. The police are going to forcibly remove you if you don't come with me."

I didn't care. Let them. I wasn't leaving her.

"Goddammit, Roach. I'm not letting them do that to you." His hands came around my middle, and he hoisted me up off the floor.

"No!" The scream ripped from somewhere deep inside me, some place where the pain was so acute I was

sure I was bleeding. I thrashed out, kicking and screaming, elbows flying, fighting him with everything I had.

His grip only tightened when he hauled me backward
down the aisle, ignoring the way I scratched and kicked
at him. "Let me go! Let me go!"

People lined the hallway, all of them staring at
Vaughn dragging me out. "Help me!" I screamed desperately at them, but none of them moved. Not one person
stepped in to stop him.

Someone held the doors open, and we burst out onto
the street, sunlight momentarily blinding my eyes but
doing nothing to stop the agony coursing through my
body. "Stop, please!"

My cries for help triggered the memories of my
attack. The darkness rushed in, taking out my vision
again, stiffening my muscles until they ached. "I can't
breathe," I whispered. "I can't breathe!"

I was right back there. Trapped by men intent on
hurting me. No escape. Their weight pinning me down.

"What the fuck are you doing? Let her go!"

I knew that voice. It broke through the darkness. He
hadn't been there for me last time, but when I opened my
eyes, he was all I could see. Tall. Strong. His gaze a
mixture of fury and need. All of it directed at me and the
man holding me captive.

"Fang," I gasped out. "Help. Please."

"Who the hell are you?"

The binds around me loosened, the man standing me
up on two feet.

I stumbled at having to hold my own weight on legs
that tingled with lack of circulation.

Fang didn't answer. He caught me with one arm,

pulling me tight to his side, while the other arm swung back and connected with Vaughn's face.

I blinked.

Vaughn.

Not Caleb. Not Caleb's friends.

I shook my head, trying to clear my foggy brain and decipher what was real and what was in my head.

"Jesus, fuck, man!" Vaughn howled. "What was that for? The cops were going to sedate her if I didn't get her out."

"Don't fucking care," Fang growled. "You put your hands on her when she told you not to."

"I was helping her!"

"Not anymore. I've got her."

Vaughn looked at me. "You know this asshole?"

His lip was already swelling. Guilt rushed in that I'd been the cause of that, when all he'd been trying to do was help me. "I'm sorry."

He shook his head and spit out a mouthful of blood. "Tell your guard dog to take a Valium next time. I'm her brother, asshole. I wasn't going to fucking hurt her."

Fang glanced down at me, but I had no idea why Vaughn would have said that. Our parents hadn't even gotten a chance to sign their wedding certificate before they'd collapsed. He was not my brother.

But it stopped Fang from following up his first punch with a second.

Something flashed in Vaughn's eyes, and it startled me to realize Vaughn had just lost his father too. I reached a hand out but stopped short of actually touching him. "Vaughn..."

He shook his head. "Don't ask me if I'm okay. I'm as okay as you are, with the addition of a busted lip."

I cringed. "I didn't mean for that to happen."

He wiped blood from his chin and stared down at it smeared across the back of his hand. "Yeah, well, it did. See you around, Sis."

He walked away, back toward the cops who were barely paying attention to the scuffle, clearly bigger things to deal with when there were two dead bodies inside.

Fang gazed down at me. "What the hell happened in there, Pix?"

I shook my head, letting the familiar nickname wash over me. It was one he normally only used in private, but clearly, he was rattled, too. "I don't even know. My mom... I think she overdosed. She's dead."

Fang swore softly. "I'm taking you home."

"The cops..."

"Fuck the cops. They want to talk to you; they can do it on your time."

I nodded, clutching his T-shirt. He wrapped his arm around me, and I inhaled the familiar scent of him. It was the same cologne Vaughn wore, the one I'd fallen in love with because it reminded me of Fang.

He guided me toward his bike, and it was only then I noticed the other guys from the club. They sat on their Harleys in the parking lot, watching the commotion with interest.

War, the club prez and my bestie's man, had a phone pressed to his ear, but when he spotted me, he moved it slightly away from his mouth, his gaze sharp with concern. "What the fuck happened in there? They wouldn't let any of us in; we've been going crazy out here. They said people were dead. You're okay?"

I wasn't, but I wasn't physically hurt either, which was what he meant, so I nodded.

"Bliss is on the phone. Do you want to talk to her?"

I shook my head. "Not now. I'm tired."

I only realized how true that was after I'd said it. Exhaustion swamped me, even though the sun was still high so it couldn't have been any later than early afternoon.

All I wanted to do was close my eyes and sleep until none of this was true.

"I'm taking her home, Prez."

War ran a hand through his hair. "Yeah, do that. I'll hang around here for a bit longer. Try to find out what the hell happened."

I didn't have it in me to argue. I stood numbly, letting the two men talk over the top of my head, a ringing in my ears starting up that didn't quit until Fang swung his long leg over the seat of his bike and settled with his hands on the handlebars.

"Get on, Pix."

"I'm wearing a dress."

"Like I care." His fingers circled around my wrist and dragged me in. With one yank of my skirt, he lifted it high enough for me to climb on behind him.

I probably flashed more of my panties than I wanted to in the moment, but I doubted anyone was watching me when there were far more interesting things going on.

I gripped the bar behind me, and Fang let out a grumble that resembled a pissed-off bear. He reached behind, hand sliding up my leg in the space left by the split in my dress. He kept his touch to the outside of my thigh, then up to my hip, fingertips pressing in, anchoring me in place.

"I'm riding like this with one arm unless I can feel your arms around me, Pix. I need to know you're okay back there. Can't know that if I can't feel you. Put your arms around me."

If it had been anyone else, I wouldn't have been able to do it. But I knew this man. He would sooner die than hurt me.

So I sank down against him, pressed the side of my face into the back of his jacket, and wrapped my arms around his solid waist.

I inhaled the combined scent of leather, cologne, and gasoline, all of it swirling me in comforting waves. Then I closed my eyes and let the man drive me home.

---

*F*ang slowed the bike on a gravel road, and I finally opened my eyes. I'd kept myself awake long enough to lean into corners with him, but barely. I blinked at my surroundings. We were most definitely not outside my shitty apartment complex in the middle of Saint View.

Woods surrounded us, thick on all sides and easy to get lost in if you were stupid enough to go wandering. Every tree looked the same as the ones before, and there was only one clear road through them, the gravel drive we'd taken.

The big rectangular building we'd parked in front of was familiar though. I'd been to more than a couple of parties here. We'd played pool in the back room, done shots at the bar. Had my ass spanked by Fang in the middle of a common area while the entire club watched after I'd broken one of their rules. That had been fun.

We'd had mind-blowing sex afterward, with me tied to Fang's bed in the clubhouse while he licked every inch of my body.

Good times.

Ones that seemed like a lifetime ago, before Caleb and his friends. Before my mom...

A hiccuping sob rose in my chest, and I put my hands to my face, pressing my fingertips tight against closed eyes, trying to stem the flow of tears.

"Hey, don't do that." His voice was soft as he pulled my hands away. He brought one to his lips and kissed my fingertips.

It only made it harder to fight back the tears. "Please don't," I whispered. "I can't handle you being nice to me right now."

He pulled my arm and helped me from the bike. "Too bad. I'm taking care of you. Can you walk?"

My legs wobbled, but I fiercely nodded that I could.

His disapproval was written all over his scowl. "No, you fucking can't. Come 'ere."

Even if I'd wanted to protest, I couldn't. He had me up in his strong arms before I could get a word out. On instinct, I wrapped my arms around his neck and buried my face there, breathing in his familiar scent because it was the only thing that made sense right now.

"What on earth you got there, Fang?" Queenie's thick Southern accent rang through the clubhouse.

She was the wife of one of the other guys and a good

friend of mine, even though she had ten years on me. She was always sweet, but right now, I couldn't even look at her.

"Rebel. Taking her to my room. Tell the others I'm not available until tomorrow."

Queenie laughed. "Off for some more wild monkey sex, huh? Get it, girl."

That was my reputation. The good-time girl. Lover of men and sex. Life of the party. Confident in my skin.

"It ain't like that, Queenie. Not today." Fang's voice was deep and gruff, even more clipped than normal.

I lifted my head, my watery eyes meeting Queenie's deep-brown ones, and the smile fell straight off her brown face. "Oh, honey. What happened?"

A lump rose in my throat, and I shook my head. I couldn't do this with her right now. It was too much. It was bad enough Fang was here to watch me fall apart. This wasn't who I was. Some weak girl who needed people to look after her. I'd always had my own back. I'd prided myself on how strong and independent I was.

Yet when it came to the crunch, I'd been pathetic. Too weak to fight Caleb and his friends off. Too small to protect myself. He'd broken something inside me, and now I couldn't even get it together emotionally, let alone physically.

I couldn't even save my mom when she was right there in front of me.

I hated the woman I was right now. Hated her with every ounce of my being, and yet I couldn't stop.

Despite Queenie trotting after us, peppering us with questions all the way down the hall, Fang just kept going, straight into his room, kicking the door shut behind us.

There was a pause, then Queenie's worried voice called through. "I'll hang around. If there's anything you need...food, drinks... I'll be here."

"Thank you," I mumbled, but I wasn't sure it was loud enough for her to hear.

Fang sat on the bed, the springs squeaking beneath his heavy weight.

I struggled to get out of his arms, but they tightened around me, keeping me on his lap.

Panic roared in. "Let me go, Fang!"

He did instantly, his grip loosening, and I shot across the room, back to the wall, chest heaving with panicked breaths.

Confusion flickered in his blue eyes. "What's going on?"

I shook my head, trying to get myself under control. "Nothing. I just...I can't do affection right now."

"Okay. What do you need?"

My mom. I needed my mom to not be lying on the floor of a courthouse, while police officers and paramedics and the press swarmed around her limp body. I needed her to be at her wedding reception, eating cake with a man who saw past her flaws and loved her the way I did. I needed her to be pulling me up from my seat while I complained that I couldn't dance, and for her to say, "Who cares, do it anyway!" the way she always had when it was just me and her, dancing around the kitchen in shitty Saint View low-income housing.

I was never going to have that again.

"I need to be sick." I ran for the little bathroom off to the side of his room, crashing through the doorway and dropping to the floor in front of the toilet.

But there was nothing in my stomach. I dry heaved, stomach cramping painfully in on itself every time I thought about my mom, the red-tinged bubbles around her mouth, her staring, unseeing eyes.

Fang knelt on the tiled floor beside me and rubbed a hand down my back. "You're okay, Pix. I got you."

I shook my head. "Just leave me."

"No."

I turned to glare at him. "Why? Why did you bring me soup and chocolate? Why did you even say yes to driving us to the reception? Why did you bring me here? This isn't what we do."

His thick eyebrows furrowed in. "What do you mean?"

"We fuck, Fang. That's it."

"It doesn't have to be it. You know I want more than that."

But it did. Because he was too much. Of everything. And he was all mixed up in that night, and I didn't quite know how to fully separate him. "You aren't my boyfriend."

His mouth pressed into a line. "I'm well aware. But what did you want me to do? Leave you standing on the side of the road while the police brought your mother's body out in a body bag?"

The tiny ounce of backbone I'd found crumbled into a heap. A sob shook my entire body.

"Ah, fuck. I'm sorry, Pix. I shouldn't have said that. Come 'ere."

I couldn't let him touch me again. I'd disintegrate into dust.

When I didn't move, he got the hint. Instead, he

reached over and turned on the shower, slowly adjusting the temperature until steam billowed around the room. He stuck his hand beneath it then quickly withdrew it, swearing below his breath. "It's scalding. Just the way you like it."

"I'm sorry," I whispered. I knew I was hurting him, but I had nothing else to give.

He stepped in, and when I didn't flinch away, he put his fingers beneath my chin and tilted my head up. "You don't need to be. I'll be whatever you need me to be."

And this was exactly why I'd never let myself get too close. Because I'd burn the man. On the outside, he was formidable. Six foot five, thick as a tree, scarred and tatted up so bad that small children ran from him.

But on the inside, he was soft. Gentle. A man who'd give a woman he loved anything she desired.

That woman couldn't be me.

I was selfish with him. Used him. Took what I needed with no thought to how it affected him.

And yet I couldn't stop. Especially not now.

His fingers found the zipper on the back of my dress and pulled it down. He pushed the spaghetti straps down my arms, and the rest of the dress fell away easily, leaving me in just my panties. He knelt at my feet and lowered my underwear as well, his gaze on mine the entire time.

There was nothing sexual about it. As soon as my panties were off, he stood and stepped toward the door. "Get in. I'll get you a towel and something clean to wear."

He closed the door quietly behind him, and I stared at it for the longest time. We'd been naked together probably a dozen times, and it had never been like that. Normally it was all tongues, and hands, and lips. We were throw you up against a wall and slam home hard and fast. We were moans, orgasms, and dirty words.

We weren't whatever we were doing right now.

My head pounded, pain piercing sharply behind my eyes. I got in the shower, because doing as I was told was easier than thinking for myself.

The hot water poured over my head, drowning the lengths of my short hair instantly. It was the perfect temperature, hot enough to turn my skin pink, and soothed over tense, aching muscles. I dropped my head forward, letting the spray pound on the back of my neck and rivulets run over my body.

With water running in my eyes, I blindly groped at the shower caddy on the wall, grabbing a bottle of what I hoped was bodywash, but shampoo would do the same thing. I squirted a dollop of it onto my palm, the scent rising with the steam of the water.

I opened my eyes in surprise and took in the label on the bottle.

It was my favorite. The same one I used at home, because it smelled like peaches and vanilla.

He'd bought it for me. I was sure of it. His bodywash sat in a black bottle next to it, the scent deeply masculine and at complete odds with the one I used.

I could have tried to convince myself that it was a coincidence. Or that he wanted a bottle of something feminine for when he had other women here.

But I knew neither of those were true.

I stood in that shower until the water ran cold, and then I stood there some more, deserving the punishment for the way I treated him.

Fang was not the sort of man you used for a good time. And yet I hadn't ever been able to stop.

I turned the water off and pulled aside the shower curtain.

A neatly folded gray towel sat on the closed toilet lid, along with a faded T-shirt I'd seen him wear. I wrapped the towel around myself and then picked up the T-shirt, holding it to my face and inhaling the scent. It smelled clean but still faintly of him.

I was sure nothing had ever smelled so good or so comforting. Knowing I was playing with fire, I dried myself off and slipped into his clothes.

The hem hung around my knees, and the sleeves halfway down my arms. But it was as soft as I'd thought, and there was no way I was putting on that dress again. I picked it up off the floor and shoved it into the bin by the sink.

"Rebel. Are you okay?"

I wasn't, but I opened the door and stepped out.

He was sitting on the edge of the bed again, with his elbows resting on his knees. He looked up when I entered, his long blond hair falling in his eyes.

In an instant, his expression changed from neutral, to something cold and dark. He pushed to his feet violently fast, and startled, I skittered back into the bathroom until my ass hit the sink. But he didn't stop. He strode right after me, caging me in with his big body, his fingers gripping my chin again so he could see my face.

"What. The. Fuck?"

"What?" I yelped.

"Your face. It's covered in bruises."

Oh shit. I hadn't even thought of that when I'd been

in the shower. I'd so painstakingly covered each and every one of them with heavy foundation that morning, but the shower must have washed it off. I turned away, hoping I could still hide the damage. "They aren't bruises. It's just my mascara running."

"Bullshit. Who did this to you?"

I shook my head. "I'm fine."

"Say you're fine again, Rebel, and I swear, my head will implode. I'm trying real hard not to walk out this door and kill every man who has ever looked at you. So please. Do me a favor, and tell me which one it was, so innocent people don't have to die today."

I twisted out of his grasp and stared at myself in the mirror.

It was like punching myself in the gut.

My face was a mess, even after a week. If anything, it seemed worse with the bruises in various states of healing and all sorts of different colors. I sighed. "No."

Confusion flickered on his face. "No? What the hell does that mean?"

"It means I'm not telling you who did it, because I have it handled."

"Do you see the way my brain is leaking out my ears right now?" His voice was barely above a growl. "A name."

"Why? So you can go over there and kick his ass?"

"Exactly!"

"What do I get out of that?"

He paused. "The satisfaction of seeing him dead?"

"The only satisfaction I want is the one that will come when I kill them myself."

"Them?" The word was a feral snarl on his lips.

Ah, fuck. His fingers clenched into fists, and he paced

the length of the small room like a caged animal. One with big teeth and claws and the capability of busting out at any minute and going on a death rampage.

I couldn't let him do that.

I needed to be the one who did it. I would never sleep well until I proved to myself once more that I was the woman I thought I was. That I could protect myself.

If Fang knew, he wouldn't be able to stop himself. So I had to defuse the situation, because when a man like him said he would kill every man who'd ever spoken to you, he meant it. He'd been a member of this MC the entire time I'd known him. I knew they did things that weren't always on the right side of the law. He had the means and motive to rip Caleb and his friends apart.

I lifted the covers on his neatly made bed and got beneath them. His sheets were soft, his mattress the perfect firmness. I tugged the quilt up to my chin and then silently raised the corner, offering him a space beside me.

He stopped pacing to stare at me. "That won't work."

I said nothing.

He sighed. Then he put his hand to the back of his shirt and pulled it over his head.

I counted the ridges on his abs while he undid his fly and took off his jeans, leaving him only in black boxer briefs.

Like I knew he would, he got beneath the blankets with me.

I flipped over, giving him my back and wriggling onto the other side of the bed. His thick arm banded around my middle, dragging me to him again, his chest against my spine.

"You played me," he murmured into the back of my head.

I'd given him a thing I never had before. Normally after we had sex, I was straight out of bed and blowing him a kiss as I walked out the door.

I never snuggled with him.

I couldn't, because I knew how much he liked it. Every time I got out of his bed, his face would fall, and I'd pretend not to notice.

"I know," I whispered back, letting him hold me in a way he never had before.

In a way I'd never wanted, because being this close to another person was terrifying and stifling.

Except his warmth felt nice. His arms around me made me feel small and protected. I fell asleep, knowing while I was in Fang's bed, nothing bad was going to happen.

## 7

# VAUGHN

*I* stood outside the courthouse with my busted, bleeding lip. Police tape had been put up to create a barrier between the swarm of police officers, medical personnel, and the rapidly growing crowd. Rumors spread and rippled around me, and minute by minute, more onlookers and press arrived.

"I heard it was a murder-suicide," a woman beside me said in hushed whispers. "Imagine that? He kills her then takes his own life because he can't bear to be without her. Like some sort of *Romeo and Juliet.*"

Rage filled me, hot and fast at the gall these women had, to stand right there in the middle of the street and make assumptions like they had any idea who my father was. "Who told you that?" I snapped. "My father wouldn't hurt a fly, so shut your gossiping mouths."

The two women spun around, their eyes going wide at the blood dripping down onto my shirt. One clutched her friend's arm, and they hurried away.

It was just another reason I hated this fucking town

and would never have come back here if I'd had a say in it. It had been a decade since I'd last set foot in Providence, and nothing had changed. It was still full of judgmental old gossips and police officers on a power trip. I'd already had the displeasure of giving them a statement and been warned not to leave town.

That had really pissed me off. I'd planned on getting out of here the minute the wedding reception had been over. Not that I had anywhere to go, but hanging around in Providence wasn't an option either.

Though apparently, for now at least, I had no choice.

The doors to the courthouse opened, and two gurneys were slowly wheeled out.

On top of them, two black body bags.

Around me, the click of camera shutters and flashes exploded, and gasps rang in my ears.

My father was in one of those bags.

Dead.

I hadn't even gotten to say goodbye.

Hurt stabbed through me, hot and sharp as I remembered his last words to me the night before. He'd called to tell me he couldn't make it to dinner, but could I still go and have a meal with my new stepsister. He'd wanted her to have a good night and told me to charge our meals and drinks to his room.

I'd tried to weasel my way out of it, not interested in babysitting some teenage brat, but then he'd gone into a big, long speech about how much he loved Miranda and how he desperately wanted her daughter and I to get along so that maybe I'd consider coming home more. He rambled about Thanksgiving and Christmas coming up and how he really wanted me home for them. How he desperately missed having a family.

I hadn't had the heart to say no. When he'd sent me a photo of my new stepsister, and she'd been a hot-as-fuck woman around my age and not a thirteen-year-old with braces, it had seemed like a fun way to kill an evening.

Now I wished I spent the night with my dad. That I could have just had one nice night with him and left on that memory. Instead of all the ones that had come before, where he'd tried and tried, and I'd held him at arm's length.

I ducked beneath the police tape and ran toward the waiting ambulance. "Stop! Wait!" I didn't know what I was going to do or say, but I couldn't just let them wheel my father's body away and take him to some morgue. It wasn't right. He was one of the good guys. He was supposed to live 'til he was ninety and be surrounded by family and grandkids. Though how he was going to get those grandkids when I was his only child was beyond me. Maybe that's part of why he'd wanted to marry Miranda. Rebel could have given him the grandbabies he'd always hinted about.

Two police officers stopped me before I could get to the ambulances.

"My father is in one of those bags," I begged them.

"I know, but you can't be over there right now. You need to let them do their job."

The fight went out of me. "Can I at least go inside and see my mother? She hasn't come out yet."

The officers looked at each other, and one shrugged.

"We'll have to take you, though."

I stepped back with a nod, and they let me go. I trailed

behind them back inside the courthouse. It was still a hive of activity, and the officers pointed to my mother and stepfather who were deep in conversation with a plain-clothes detective.

"You'll have to wait until they're done being interviewed."

"Of course. I'll just wait here if that's okay."

One of their radios spit out a babble of static-laced instructions that were indecipherable to me but clearly made sense to them.

He reluctantly eyed me. "We have to go, but I'll leave you here if you promise not to get in the way, and to leave once your mother and stepfather are finished."

I put my hand over my heart. "Scout's honor."

With a curt nod, the officer stepped away. He was only a few steps down the hall though, when he glanced back. "I'm really sorry for your loss. He seemed like a kind-hearted man."

I swallowed thickly and turned away before the officer could see the tears welling in my eyes. Fucking hell. Even a complete stranger could see just how kind and generous my father had been.

I'd taken it for granted. Assumed I'd always have more time with him. Made him come to me, because I was always too busy to come to him.

And he had. He'd run a multi-million-dollar business that he would leave for weeks at a time to visit me across the other side of the country. I'd never bothered to do the same for him, despite the fact my job was not nearly as demanding nor important.

I glanced around the room, focusing on anything but the officer's words. I couldn't fall apart. Not here. Nothing appeared terribly out of place, until my gaze snagged on a gold purse, tucked beneath one of the seats on the bride's side of the room.

I prodded my bottom lip with my tongue, playing with the cut while I debated whether I really wanted to retrieve Rebel's bag for her after her asshole of a boyfriend had socked me one just for trying to help her.

My father wouldn't have thought twice.

My mother had cheated on him and left him for another man, and my father had still been the bigger person. He'd let her go and made sure things were good between them, for my sake. As a result, I'd grown up with parents who were best friends, even though they weren't together.

I waited until the cops were all distracted, photographing blood speckles on the floor, and then strode forward, scooped the purse up, and tucked it beneath my jacket. No doubt her wallet and phone were inside, and she'd want them back. I'd be pissed if my phone was held hostage in police evidence, so I would spare her the hassle and drop it off to her.

"Oh, Vaughn. You're here." Mom's voice was laced with tears, and her eyes were red-rimmed. "I'm so glad you came back. We were so worried, but the police wouldn't let us go until we gave them statements." Her high heels clicked across the tiled floor, and she stopped in front of me, grasping both sides of my face and tilting my head down so she could see my expression. "Oh, baby."

I pressed my lips together, not wanting her sympathy because it would only make me cry. I flicked my head toward the cops. "Do they think you did it?

Being the ex and all, you're probably the prime suspect, right?"

She chuckled. "No. Well, I hope not. They didn't say anything like that." The smile fell off her face. "I heard the paramedics say it was an overdose…"

I shook my head. "Do you believe that? Dad didn't do drugs…"

My mom went quiet.

I looked at her sharply. "What? He didn't!"

"No, not in the time that you knew him. He's been clean for a very long time."

I frowned. "Are you joking?"

"We all used to party in our early twenties, Vaughn." My stepdad, Karmichael put an arm around my shoulders. "It's easy to fall back into that lifestyle if the person you're with never gave it up."

I couldn't in my wildest imagination picture my parents or Karmichael partying it up, high on drugs. Not now. Not even in their twenties. But maybe it explained why my rebellious teenage stage hadn't ended until I was twenty-five and married.

My mom's teeth dug into her bottom lip, and she grimaced. "I'm sorry. We shouldn't have said that. You didn't need to know. Now that's going to be the last memory you have of your father…"

I clutched Rebel's purse tighter. "No, it's fine. It's good I know. At least I'm not going to be worried about them accusing you of anything now. Though the press outside is spreading the rumor that it was a murder-suicide, so I guess you're in the clear anyway."

Mom's jaw dropped open in shock, but it was temporary. In the next instant, her features turned fierce. "I loved your father with every ounce of my heart. We've been friends for decades, and I won't have anyone questioning that or his integrity. Murder-suicide is the most ridiculous thing I've ever heard. You let them try saying that to me."

Karmichael put his arm around my mom's shoulder's and kissed a tear from her cheek. "You know your mom. She won't have anyone saying a bad word about Bart."

"Damn straight I won't. He doesn't deserve that."

In spite of the situation, I smiled. Because this was the thing I loved most about her. She had spent her entire life defending the people she loved. Me, my dad, and Karmichael being the main three. But I'd seen her go to bat for her friends, work colleagues, and even random strangers. If there was an injustice, she addressed it. Her soapbox didn't stop at her Facebook profile. She'd been front-row center at Black Lives Matter protests. She'd fought for gay marriage to be legalized. And she'd spent two hours one night, barking down the phone to me about the unjust way a trans woman was being treated on the internet and how she wasn't going to stand for it.

I kissed her cheek. "If anyone says anything to me, I'll be sure to send them to my mommy."

She chuckled and hugged me back. "You do that. What are you going to do now? Are you going home to Brooke?"

I stiffened at the mention of my wife's name but tried to hide it by stretching. "I can't. The police want me to hang around for a while, in case they have any more questions."

Karmichael hummed his agreement. "Mmm. They said the same thing to us. You can come and stay with us until they conclude their investigations. No need to stay in that hotel."

Mom looked at me hopefully, and so I felt like even more of an asshole when I told her no. "I think I just want to be alone."

"We can pay for your hotel."

My face burned with embarrassment. "No. Mom, please."

She hadn't come right out and said, "Hey, I know your company went bankrupt and you're flat broke," but she might as well have. The mortification was all the same.

"I think I'm going to go stay at Dad's place. I'm sure there's probably things there that need taking care of."

My mom slid her hand into mine and squeezed it. "You're right. That's a great idea. That big old house has plenty of room just waiting to be utilized."

I walked them to their car and accepted their offer of a lift to the hotel so I could pick up my bag and my bike. I'd left it in the hotel parking lot because I'd wanted to have a few drinks with my old man to celebrate his wedding.

Now I'd never get to do that again.

It was a shit feeling. One that had me considering stopping in the hotel bar and writing myself off. But that was better done at my father's house where I wouldn't have to drive anywhere afterward. His place had a bed waiting that I wouldn't have to pay for with an already overdrawn credit card. And the bonus of a bar full of expensive whiskeys and vodkas I could drown my sorrows in for free.

I retrieved my bag from my room and checked out, grateful when the woman said my father had prepaid. On the way out to the parking lot, I shoved Rebel's glittery gold purse into my duffel bag and stowed the entire thing in the bike's large saddlebag.

Nothing much had changed in Providence in the decade I'd been gone. The streets were the same, houses familiar because I'd been to parties at dozens of them in high school. They grew bigger and bigger the deeper in I got, with my father's house being right in the center. "Guess who's back," I mumbled as I steered my bike into the driveway.

I tapped the code into the pad by the door, not surprised when it opened. My father had always been a creature of habit. The code hadn't changed since I was a kid. I stuck my head through the doorway. "Hello?"

Not a sound echoed back.

I didn't know why I was still hoping my father would appear at the top of the stairs, take them two at a time to get to the bottom, and engulf me in a hug. I'd seen them take away his body.

I dumped my helmet and my bag in the entrance and closed the door quietly behind me. A wave of exhaustion swamped me, my emotions raw and sharp. I headed straight for the den, which was the last place I'd seen my father's alcohol stash before I'd moved out at twenty-one.

A scraping noise stopped me in my tracks, and I swiveled on my heel, trying to source it. When nothing happened, I shook my head, assuming I was hearing things.

The second squeak was definitely not in my imagination. It screeched down my spine like nails on a chalkboard. "Who's there?" I called. "O'Malley? That you?"

O'Malley was my father's right-hand man, his driver,

gardener, butler, and maintenance guy all rolled into one. But I'd assumed he'd be at the wedding reception. Which I guess now was more of a pre-funeral party. That was if anyone had even told the people who had congregated there, waiting for a happy, newly married couple to arrive. How fucking depressing.

The elderly man didn't call out, but the scraping, scratching noise didn't quit. It could be an animal, trapped somewhere in the house, but what the hell kind of animal made that noise?

Footsteps echoed back, and I froze. Fuck. There seriously was someone in the house. My father didn't believe in gun ownership. Neither did I, but now I was cursing us both. On instinct, I opened the nearest closet and grabbed the closest thing that could resemble a weapon.

A stick vacuum cleaner.

I had no idea what I was going to do with the awkwardly shaped thing, but it made me feel better than having nothing in my hands at all. I was reasonably strong, and hopefully adrenaline would help me out there too. I could swing the thing like a giant baseball bat if I had to.

"Who's there?" I called again.

Still no answer.

A chill raced down my spine. "Please don't be armed with anything more deadly than my Hoover." I crept along the hall toward the sounds, wishing my phone was in my pocket instead of back at the doorway. Fuck. I should stop and go back for it. Just call the cops.

The utility room door flung open, and a man stepped out.

I swung the vacuum.

"Jesus, fuck!" the man bellowed, ducking to avoid the flying floor cleaner.

The cleaner hit the wall and kept going. Right through the plaster.

Vibrations shot painfully through my arms at the impact, and I let go on instinct, jumping back from the gaping hole I'd just put in my father's wall.

"Vaughn?" the other man questioned.

I snapped my head around at his familiar voice and did a double take at the face of the man beneath a Saint View Scorers baseball cap. There was only one person I knew who'd ever played baseball for Saint View, and sure enough, his familiar green eyes stared back at me. "Kian?"

Instantly, his expression hardened. "Fuck. It is you. What the hell are you doing here?"

I raised an eyebrow at his hostile tone. "Excuse me? This is my father's house. What the hell are you doing here?"

Kian folded his arms over his broad chest.

My gaze dropped to the thickly muscled biceps, which I did not remember from back when he'd been the son of our housekeeper, and my best friend.

Kian narrowed green eyes at me. "It may be your father's house, but forgive me for being surprised. It's not like you've seen the inside of it in the last...what? Eight years? Nine?"

"Ten," I corrected stiffly, guilt washing over me again.

Kian shook his head. "Ten. Of course. Only you would walk out of someone's life a decade ago and then think you can just waltz back like nothing happened." He jerked his head toward the damaged wall and vacuum cleaner. "What the hell were you doing with that?"

"I thought you were an intruder."

Kian choked on his laughter. "So what? You thought you'd suck me with it?"

My jaw clenched, and I shoved past him, hating that it suddenly felt like I was eighteen again. "Fuck off, Kian. I'm not in the mood for your shit."

Apparently, nothing changed with him either, except for the fact he'd bulked up and a had a few extra freckles across the bridge of his nose. His hair was shorter than he'd worn it before I'd gone to college. But he clearly still lived to give me a hard time. I stormed farther down the hall, leaving the mess I'd made with the vacuum cleaner. I'd worry about that later.

"Where are you going in such a hurry?"

"To get drunk." I rounded the corner of the den and went straight to a cabinet in the corner. "Does Dad still keep the alcohol in here?" I yanked the cupboard door open, and angels sang in my head. A full bottle of bourbon sat right in the middle, just begging for me to take a swig. I didn't even bother standing or reaching for a glass. I pulled out the cork and took a swig straight from the bottle.

It scalded all the way down my throat, but it was the good kind of burn. Much better than the one in my chest that ached every time I thought of my dad.

Kian leaned on the wall to my left and made a show of checking the cheap watch strapped to his wrist. "Not even three in the afternoon. Bit early, isn't it?" His brow furrowed. "Shouldn't you be at your old man's wedding right now?"

I took another slug from the bottle and rocked back on my heels. "Can't. He's dead."

Kian's shocked silence was so loud it was almost deafening. "Are you joking?"

"Would I be here getting drunk with you, of all people, if I were?"

He stiffly pushed off the wall and walked over to me. He held a hand out.

I stared at it blankly. "What?"

"Give me the bottle."

I passed it over, and he took several long gulps before slumping down beside me on the floor. "Fuck."

He passed the bottle back, and I took it, drinking down as much as he had then abandoning it to the space between us.

"I don't understand." Kian's head thunked back against the cabinet. "Are you sure?"

I squinted at him. "Am I sure? Well, he's in a body bag at the morgue as we speak, so I really hope they weren't just messing around when they called time of death. Wouldn't be a particularly funny prank."

"What the hell happened?"

I shrugged. "Word on the street? Drug overdose."

"No, that didn't happen."

I really wanted the alcohol to kick in faster. "It did."

"Your dad doesn't do drugs."

"Yeah. well, that's what I thought. But apparently, the old man, as straight and narrow as he is...was...these days, once had a wild side."

"Didn't we all?" His voice was laden with unsaid meaning.

I wasn't going there with him. Rehashing the past.

"What are you doing here anyway? I thought you were off playing baseball in California?"

He peered over at me. "I haven't been there in years, Vaughn. You didn't know? Came back when my dad died."

I gaped at him. "O'Malley died?"

"Surely your dad told you? I've been working here ever since."

I pressed the heels of my hands into my eyes. "No. He would have told me."

"Yeah, he probably did."

The meaning behind his words was accusatory. I bristled. "What does that mean? He told me and I just didn't care?"

Kian shrugged. "Self-centered is your middle name."

"Fuck you."

"Tried that once. It sent you running across the other side of the country."

Heat crept up the back of my neck at the reminder of that night. "I left to start my own company, away from the shadow of my father." My cheeks blazed with awkward embarrassment. "And I'm married."

Kian shook his head with a laugh. "Why are you telling me that? In case I get an idea and try to sneak into your bedroom?" He leaned in slowly, inch by inch, until his mouth was barely hovering above mine.

Something in his eyes changed.

Or maybe I just wanted it to.

His gaze flickered to my mouth. "We could pick up right where we left off..."

It was all too fucking familiar. A lifetime ago, but still so fresh in my head because it was something I'd played over and over again for a lifetime. I put two hands on his chest and shoved him out of my way. "I'm not doing this with you. Go home."

And just like that, whatever had been in his eyes disappeared. He leaned back against the wall and took another swallow from the bottle, like he hadn't just brought up the elephant in the room. "I am home, dick-head. Room and board came with the job. Got the same room I had as a kid."

Oh, hell no. I couldn't stay here with him. But I couldn't go home either. There was nothing left for me there, even if I had been allowed to leave the state. "You have a week to look for a new job."

He sat up sharply, the liquid in the bottle sloshing around inside the glass. "What? You're joking."

"Wasn't joking before, not joking now." I grabbed the bottle from him and staggered to my feet. The room spun around me in dizzying circles. I'd had no idea how drunk I was until I stood up. I staggered toward the stairs that led up to my old room.

The one next door to Kian's.

Fuck.

I changed direction. I'd sleep on the kitchen table if I had to. As long as I was nowhere near Kian O'Malley.

## 8

## REBEL

"Where is she? No, War, I don't care! Where is she? Fang's room, right? Fang! You better open that door right now!"

I cracked open an eye at my bestie's hollering in the hallway and wasn't at all surprised when the door rattled a moment later.

Fang groaned beside me but got out of bed, padding across the room to yank the door open. "What?" he snapped.

Bliss was taller than me but still no match for Fang. Not that you'd know it, judging by the way she pushed past his massive frame. She stopped short of throwing herself onto the bed with me and clapped a hand over her mouth. "Your face…"

Fuck. Still no makeup.

In the doorway, War growled in Fang's direction. "That better not have been at your hands, brother."

Fang gave his prez a look that should have withered him on the spot.

It didn't, but War put his hands up and backed right off. "Sorry, sorry. I had to ask. She's my girl's bestie. So there's an unwritten rule that I watch out for her in the same way. They're a package deal."

Every muscle across Fang's back was clenched tight beneath his pale, tattooed skin. "I'd never fucking hurt her. You ever say that to me again, and prez or not, you'll wish you hadn't."

I gawked at Bliss. War was no slouch in the scary bad-boy department. I knew Fang respected War as a man, as well as his position. I'd never seen him be anything but one-hundred-percent loyal and respectful to War.

Yet now he was facing off with him.

Over me.

I didn't know whether to be completely turned on or terrified.

"Should we get some Jell-O out for wrestling?" I joked, trying to lighten the mood. "Sorry, War, I got my money on Fang."

No one laughed.

Bliss reached out and traced a featherlight stroke over the worst of the bruising on my cheek. "Oh, Rebel." A tear rolled down her cheek, eventually dripping onto her shirt.

I shook my head violently. "Don't do that. Please."

"Okay. War told me about your mom…"

I pressed my fingernails into the palm of my hand, concentrating on that sting instead of the emotion welling inside me. "Shit happens, right?"

What else was there to say? If I said how I truly felt, I'd break down crying again and maybe never stop. I turned away, swinging my legs out of the bed only to realize I was still wearing Fang's shirt and nothing else. I could practically feel Fang's gaze on me, completely unrelenting.

"Can you take me home?" I whispered to Bliss.

"I can take you," Fang said quickly.

I stared at Bliss, imploring her to understand without me having to spell it out.

That was the beauty of having a best friend. She got me without me even having to say anything.

"Of course I can."

I stood, and she put her arm around my shoulders, guiding me out of the room.

"Pix..."

It was short for Pixie. Bliss had once described me as a coked-out fairy, and I'd kind of always enjoyed that description. It was accurate. I was a tiny woman who had ADHD, a loud voice, a big personality, and did everything impulsively at a million miles an hour. She was wrong about the coke, though. I never touched the stuff, because I didn't need to. I lived in a permanently buzzed state naturally.

Nothing about me felt buzzed right now. He would have to change my nickname to swamp troll or something of the like. "Let me go, Fang."

I saw the way my words affected him. He didn't want to step aside, but he did, clearly hating every minute.

At the last second, I threw him a bone and linked my pinkie finger with his as I passed. "Thank you. For being there for me last night. When I needed you."

He squeezed my finger but let me go.

At least for now.

Bliss guided me through the clubhouse, and I tried to

ignore the shocked gasp that came from Queenie's mouth when she saw my face.

She mouthed, *"Are you okay?"*

All I could do was nod, grateful for her concern but hating that they were all seeing me like this.

Bliss put me in the front seat of her car and closed the door, but War stopped her before she got in the driver's side. He said something I didn't hear, then put his hands on her little baby bump, rubbing it affectionately, before kissing her mouth.

When they broke apart and moved aside, Fang was all I could see through the windshield. His eyes locked on mine.

I dropped my gaze to my lap, twisting my fingers in the fabric of my T-shirt until Bliss got in and started the car.

"War is staying here to talk to the other men. He wants you to tell them who did this to you so they can take care of it." She turned the car around on the gravel lot and headed for the gates.

Ice, one of the club prospects, unlocked them and waved us through, but even his eyes glinted with the promise of something dangerous when he noticed my injuries.

I slumped in my seat. "Like I told Fang, I have it handled."

Bliss looked over at me with the saddest expression I'd ever seen. "I know you're used to handling your own business. But you don't have to…"

"I want to."

She slowly nodded. "Do I know him?"

*Them*, I corrected silently in my head. But I couldn't

tell her the truth. Caleb was her ex. I'd listened to her talk about how evil and abusive he was.

But I hadn't recognized any of that in the man who'd sat at the end of my bar that night and called himself by a different name. By the time I'd realized who and what he was, it had been too late.

I could never tell Bliss it was her ex who'd done this to me. She'd blame herself for bringing him into my life, or she'd assume he'd done it to get back at her.

That wasn't true. At least not entirely. The things Caleb did were for his own sick pleasure, as much as getting back at a woman who had moved on from his abusive games. Bliss had at least one of her three men around her at all times. Especially now she was pregnant. Caleb couldn't get to her.

I'd been a weak, easy target.

"Have you heard anything about your mom?" Bliss asked gently.

I shook my head, but then realized I didn't even know where my phone or my purse was. "Shit. I think I left my purse at the courthouse. My clothes are all still at the hotel as well. Fuck, they've probably thrown them all out since I was only booked in for one night. Could I borrow your phone? I need to call the police. They might have been trying to get a hold of me."

She nodded at her phone sitting near the gearshift. "Of course. As soon as you're done, I'll call Nash or Vincent and get one of them to go get your stuff from the hotel. They can go to the courthouse too, and see if your purse was handed in."

I looked up the phone number for the Providence Police Department and bounced my leg nervously while I waited for someone to pick up. It rang four times before a woman introduced herself as Officer Lehey.

"Yeah, hi. My mother died..." I ran my hand through my hair as my throat threatened to close up. "She was at the courthouse, getting married yesterday when she collapsed..."

"Hold on a moment, please. I'll patch you through to the detective working that case."

Bliss glanced at me and gave me a questioning thumbs-up. I tried to return it, but it was half-assed at best. She went back to driving, and I rested my head back on the seat and closed my eyes, trying to keep it together long enough to speak to the detective.

His voice was bristly when he barked his name and job title down the line. Detective Simon Richardson, Senior Detective with the Providence Police Department. "I understand your mother was one of the deceased at the courthouse yesterday. Your name?"

"Rebel Kemp."

There was a shuffling of papers. "You were there at the time of their deaths? Your name isn't on any of this paperwork."

"Well, no, it's probably not because I didn't speak to any of the officers there."

"Was there a reason for that?"

I didn't like his tone, but there were things I needed to know. "I want a copy of my mother's autopsy report. I want to know what she overdosed on."

"We'll need you to come down to the station immediately, Miss Kemp."

I scrunched my face. "Can't you just email it to me?"

"There's more that needs to be discussed than just your mother's autopsy report."

"Like what?"

"Like why you left the scene of a crime without talking to police, perhaps?"

I ground my molars. Fuck the Providence police. This was what they were always like. Fucking assholes. I was not in the mood for it.

Apparently, he didn't like my silence, because I hadn't even gotten a chance to reply when he barked down the line again. "This is a very serious matter, young lady. So wherever you are right now, it would be best if you changed course and drove immediately to the station."

I blinked at Bliss.

"What?" she whispered.

"He's demanding I go down to the station. He just young ladyed me."

"Oh, hell no." Bliss knew exactly how I felt about men who liked to throw their weight around. "Condescending prick."

"Miss Kemp? I'll expect you here in the next fifteen minutes then, shall I?"

I snorted. "No, Detective Richardson. You shall not."

He huffed out an annoyed breath. "You've been given a direct instruction by a police officer. So I would inquire as to why you think you can ignore it?"

Oh, this guy was really starting to piss me off. Which, frankly, felt nice because it didn't come with the desire to cry.

I felt a lot more like my old, sassy self when I replied, "Because I'm currently not wearing any panties, and I don't think I'm in the mood for a Sharon Stone,

*Basic Instinct* replay, even if I do have the cutest little snatch around. Pity for you, you'd cream yourself over it."

Bliss turned to me with huge eyes. "You did not just say that."

I shrugged and made no attempt to cover the phone. "He was pissing me off." But then I went back to Detective Dickhead, who was spluttering down the line.

I rolled my eyes. "Relax. I'll come down to the station, Richards. No need to get your knickers...or lack of, in my case, in a knot. Learn some manners though, would you?"

I ended the call and tossed the phone down where I'd found it.

Bliss took a corner, shaking her head with quiet laughter. "You amaze me."

I yawned and looked at the car clock. "Is that time right? Is it seriously nine?"

Bliss nodded. "War wanted me to wait 'til ten to go over to the clubhouse to find you, but at eight I couldn't wait anymore. I wish you'd come back to our place last night."

But I couldn't have. I couldn't deflect any of my friends off with cuddling the way I had with Fang. And Bliss's men were just as dangerous, if not more so. If you caught Vincent on a bad day, he was nothing less than a completely psychotic killer. He loved Bliss—and me, by law of the best friend code—so normally I just found him amusing. But he wouldn't hesitate to take the one thing I truly needed.

Caleb's head on a stick.

It needed to be mine.

"Can we get coffee?" I asked. "My head is fuzzy..."

*With murderous thoughts.* I wasn't sure coffee would truly help, but it couldn't hurt.

She pulled over at the Starbucks on the Saint View-Providence border, and I graciously waited in the car to spare the rest of the customers my panty-free, oversized T-shirt getup. The time ticked on, my headache growing with every second that passed, until Bliss finally emerged, holding two huge cups.

When she was back in the car, I took one from her gratefully, and then we were back on the road to my apartment. It was odd to see kids playing in the communal area, like their entire worlds hadn't been ripped to shreds in the space of seven days. I hoped they never had to feel the way I did, with shit piling on top of shit.

But these were kids from the wrong side of the tracks, just like I was.

So their lives were hardly charmed. Violence and poverty and death would be what they grew up with.

All the more reason to never have kids ,if you asked me.

I went to grab my purse and keys, but of course, I didn't have those. "Do you have that spare key to my apartment?"

Bliss flicked the keys dangling from her ignition. "Right here." She switched the car off. "I'll come up with you."

We walked slowly, side by side, both of us sipping our coffee.

"Do you truly have no panties on?"

I smiled around my steaming cup. "It's pretty breezy down there."

"So you and Fang hooked up again?"

I shook my head. "No. Not last night."

"No one would judge you if you had, you know. You went through something really big yesterday, and if you went seeking comfort, no one would blame you."

I blew over my coffee, trying to cool it enough to drink, debating over how much to tell her. But she was my best friend, and the words just came out. "I don't think I'll be doing that anymore. Not with him. Or anyone."

Bliss stopped and put her hand on my arm. "He...the person who hurt you, I mean...he..." Her eyes filled with tears.

"Raped me, Bliss. You can say it."

A sob burst from her mouth, and she dug her fingers into my skin. "Tell me who, Rebel. I swear, I won't even tell Vincent and the others, I'll kill him myself."

I decided to be honest. "I'm not playing around when I say I can't let you do that, Bliss. Because I'm going to."

She dug her white teeth into her bottom lip. "You aren't just saying that, are you?"

"No."

"I'll help you hide the body." She was dead serious.

I glanced at her and burst out laughing. "Bliss!"

"What? I will! I'd do anything for you."

Just like I'd do anything for her.

We took the last flight of stairs up to my apartment, but I flinched when three men stepped out from against my apartment door.

Bliss picked up my hand and squeezed it, steadying me. "Officers. What can we do for you? That's my friend's apartment you're loitering in front of."

All three of them looked to me, but it was the oldest one who spoke, a man with graying hair at his temples. "Rebel Kemp?"

"Yes," I murmured.

"We're here to escort you down to the police station." His gaze slow-rolled over my bare legs. "Detective Richardson said you should put panties on first."

A trickle of worry spread down my spine. "Do I have a say in the matter?"

His eyes narrowed. "Not unless you want me to arrest you and take you in wearing handcuffs."

What the hell?

"Handcuffs!" Bliss yelped. "You can't do that. She hasn't done anything wrong. I'm calling a lawyer."

"Great. Tell him to meet us at the station, because we aren't waiting around for him to get here. Miss Kemp? Do you plan to put your panties on so we can leave or am I taking you in as is?"

I ground my molars. Fucking assholes. "Wouldn't you just love a peek at my coochie?" I walked past and patted him on the chest. "She bites, though." I snapped my teeth at him and was deeply satisfied when he flinched away.

I used the spare key I'd given Bliss to open the door, and slipped inside, quickly pulling on underwear and clean clothes. Despite my bravado, I really wasn't in the mood to be arrested, so I made it snappy, shoving my feet into white sneakers without bothering with socks.

Back in the hallway, Bliss had the phone clutched to her ear. When I emerged, she looked over, a fierce expression on her heart-shaped face. "I've got Liam on the phone." She stared at the officers; her words sharp as she practically spit them out. "Liam Banks? He's a friend of ours, and a lawyer. A really fucking good one."

It had been a while since I'd seen Bliss so worked up she swore at a police officer. She needed to settle down though, because I did not want her pregnant ass thrown in jail for obstructing justice or something. Her guys would kill me.

"We're well aware of Mr. Banks and his reputation," the office replied dryly. "Trust us."

I'd only met Liam once, when one of Bliss's guys, Vincent, had been kidnapped and tortured. We'd joined forces with him and some others to rescue him, because we all knew the police wouldn't do shit. But judging by the officer's irritation, Liam was a thorn in their side.

Which only made me like the man more. "Tell Liam I'm looking forward to catching up with him over stale police station coffee and donuts." I poked the officer in his round belly. "Assuming you haven't already eaten them all, that is?"

"You're pushing your luck, Miss Kemp. Let's go."

Bliss widened her eyes at me, but I was enjoying sassing the officers. Was it smart? No. But it felt normal, and right now, normal was welcome.

Plus, I had the advantage of being tiny. Barely over five foot. Everyone underestimated me and assumed I was no threat, but it worked in situations like this. They probably already would have slapped cuffs on a man.

But I followed them downstairs and into the back of a squad car. It took mere minutes to get across town to Providence, and even less time to find myself marched straight through the station to an interview room. I grinned at officer tubby tummy. "VIP treatment, huh? No waiting in line. I feel so important."

He pointed at the table with two seats on either side. "Sit."

"Say please."

His gaze narrowed. "Are you enjoying yourself?"

"Immensely," I said, voice dripping with sarcasm.

He clearly hadn't received the memo on sarcasm because he took it literally. "Good. Enjoy yourself now, while you still can. Because in a minute, you're going to be accused of murder, and boy am I going to enjoy wiping that fucking grin off your face."

The smile faded.

He chuckled as he walked out. "Yeah, exactly like that."

## 9

## REBEL

*I* left the police station a trembling, shaking mess. The moment I was out of sight of the horrid, squat building, I doubled over, sucking deep breaths in so I didn't vomit.

Liam patted my shoulder awkwardly. "I'm going to call Bliss for you, okay?"

I covered my mouth with the back of my hand. "Please don't. I'll be fine. I just…"

Liam gave me a sympathetic smile. "Didn't expect them to loosely accuse you of murdering your mother and her fiancé?"

Yeah. That.

"I swear, Liam. I didn't do it."

"I know. Don't worry, we'll sort it all out. You're just an easy target. The poor bartender who wanted her stepdaddy's money. The woman jealous of her mother's rich partner. The mother-daughter duo who worked together to scam a rich businessman out of his life savings, only to have the entire thing go horribly wrong at the last moment when the mother eats the poisoned apple. There's a million different, very creative ways they can spin this, and the Providence police do this all the time. Half the force is corrupt. The other half is lazy as hell, so they go after the easiest target to pin it on. But they don't have anything concrete on you or you'd be in a holding cell right now, waiting for a bail hearing."

I wiped my sweaty palms on my jeans and stood up straight. "Okay. But everything they said in there…"

"Was designed to scare you into confessing. You don't talk to them without me. Ever. Okay?"

I nodded. "Thanks, Liam."

"I'll drive you home."

I followed him to his car and sat quietly in the passenger seat while he chatted about his partners and their boys and his job at the law firm. Clearly, he didn't like awkward silences, and I was grateful for his ongoing commentary because neither did I. I just didn't have the energy to fill it myself.

I directed him to my apartment, a bit embarrassed by how shabby it was compared to his expensive car. But Liam didn't comment or even seem to notice.

He put the car in park and took his seat belt off. "I'll walk you in."

"Oh, no, you don't have to do that."

"Mae would have my head, and then she'd tell Bliss, and Bliss would set Vincent on me, and as much as I love that little psychopath…"

"You don't want to be on his bad side?"

"Not even for a second."

I could understand that. Vincent's alter ego, Scythe,

was a scary motherfucker. Funny as hell, but scary, none-theless.

I let Liam walk me across the apartment complex and inside the building. He frowned at the lack of security on the door but kept moving, sticking close behind me. So close, he ran smack into my back when I stopped abruptly on the last flight of stairs to my floor.

"Hey, Roach."

Vaughn slumped on the floor of my hallway, clutching my gold purse in one hand and a mostly drank bottle of bourbon in the other.

I shoved my hands on my hips "What the hell are you doing here? Are you drunk?"

Liam cleared his throat. "You know this guy?"

I glanced over my shoulder at him. "Yeah. He's my…" I trailed off, not knowing exactly what he was. "He's Vaughn."

"I'm her brother," Vaughn slurred. "Big brother."

I frowned at his handsome, barely lined face. "Don't know about that. You look about twenty-five."

"I'm thirty-one, thank you very much. But I'll let my Botox doc know you said he does good work."

I rolled my eyes. "You're so vain."

"There's a song about that."

Liam's confused gaze bounced between us. "You don't know how old your brother is?"

"We've only been siblings for a hot minute."

Understanding dawned in Liam's blue eyes. "Ah. The dead fiancé's son, then?"

"That's the one."

"Husband," Vaughn chipped in. "The judge had pronounced them husband and wife when they…" He made a tree tipping noise then an exploding action with his fingers. "Boom! Dead on the floor." He laughed, then shook his head, thick eyebrows furrowing together. "It was really not funny though."

Liam nudged me. "Do you want me to get him out of here? I can drive him home."

"Ain't got no home. Kian's there, taking up all the room with his stupid, attractive face."

"Who's Kian?" Liam whispered.

I shrugged. "No idea. But leave him. I'll take care of it."

Liam didn't seem happy about that idea. "You sure? You don't seem to know this guy very well..."

He was right. I didn't. But Vaughn was barely conscious, and I didn't want him puking in Liam's car on the drive home. Plus, my gun was inside. If he so much as looked in my direction wrong, I'd use it.

A little trickle of empowerment straightened my spine. A small reminder of the woman I'd been before the attack. I liked it.

"Truly," I told Liam. "I'll take him inside, get him some coffee, then call him an Uber. We'll be fine."

"Thanks, Sis." Vaughn blew me a sloppy kiss.

I crinkled my nose but crouched to retrieve my purse from his clutches and fished out my keys from inside. At least now I could give Bliss back the spare.

I opened the door, hastily pushing aside a pile of clothes I'd tried on and discarded before I'd decided on the gold dress for the wedding. "Sorry it's messy. I wasn't expecting company." That, and I'd been nursing some pretty violent injuries for the last few days, and cleaning had been the last thing on my mind.

Vaughn didn't make a move to come inside. Just took another slug from his bottle and laid himself out on the floor, like it was a good spot to sleep it off.

I sighed and reached both hands out for him. "Come on. Give me your hands. I'll help you up."

He set the bottle down and put his hands in mine.

Warm. Strong. He gazed up at me with warm brown eyes that suddenly didn't seem quite so intoxicated.

Panicked, I tried to jerk away, but his fingers were already wrapped around mine.

"Pull," he instructed.

I pulled.

I should have known my tiny self had zero chance of moving a big guy like Vaughn. My upward momentum didn't budge him at all.

His downward pressure sent me careening right down onto the floor with him, smack against his too-solid chest.

For a moment, I stayed there in complete shock, trying to work out what had just happened.

The second moment was because I'd noticed how cut his abs were. I could feel them through his shirt.

Deep-brown eyes. Muscles. Tanned skin and a cocky attitude, even when he was plastered...

Oh no. Hell, no. I was not attracted to him. I put my hands on his pecs, trying really hard not to notice how perfect they were, and used them to propel myself away from him.

Vaughn chuckled. "Falling for me already, Roach?"

Liam cleared his throat. "Do you want a hand?"

I spun, big-eyed because Vaughn had made me forget Liam was even still there. As much as I wanted to be a strong, independent woman once more, I also really did not want to touch Vaughn and feel whatever the hell it was I'd just felt. "Yes, please, actually. If you can just get him inside, I'll put coffee on."

Liam came up the last couple of stairs and crouched low, slinging one of Vaughn's arms over his shoulders. "Come on, big guy. Let's get you up so you don't pass out here in the hall."

He got Vaughn on his feet, and he staggered inside.

I pointed to the kitchen counter and the stools behind it. "Just put him on one of those…"

Vaughn crashed down onto my bed, the mattress squeaking and complaining beneath him.

"…or just there will do."

Vaughn fumbled around my bed and picked up one of my lacy bralettes. It was one I used to enjoy wearing at Psychos, whenever we held one of the sex parties and lingerie was my outfit of the day.

"What is this, little sis?" Vaughn groaned. "Fuck me."

I snatched it from his fingers, balling it up and shoving it into a drawer. "Nothing for you to see, big brother. Also, for the record, you're barely older than me, and we are not related, so stop calling me that."

"Do you prefer Roach?"

I glared at him.

Liam chuckled. "Okay, so I see you already have the brother-sister vibe down. Rebel, if you're sure you don't want me to take him, I'll get going."

I eyed Vaughn warily, not at all sure that Liam was reading the vibe between us right, but Vaughn had his eyes closed and clearly wasn't moving anytime soon. Even still, I wanted him to know I could protect myself if I had to. "Go.

You have a family to get home to. I'm sorry for keeping you out late. I'll be fine. I have a gun if my brother here decides to do anything remotely unbrotherly. Hear that, Vaughn?"

He didn't open his eyes, but he did flip me the bird, so I assumed he had the message. Liam left, and I closed the door softly behind him, leaning back on it while I studied the big man in my bed.

He went to take another swallow from the bottle of bourbon, but I caught it before he could get his lips to it. "Nope. That's about enough for you. Next thing you put in your mouth is going to be coffee."

He cracked an eye open. "I'm on your bed, Roach. Next thing I put in my mouth could be your pussy if you play your cards right."

I widened my eyes at him. "Did you seriously just say that to your *sister*."

He waved his hand around dismissively. "Stepsister."

"Oh, so when you want to lick my pussy, I'm your stepsister?"

"When I want to lick your pussy, you're my woman."

I squinted at him. "You're plastered. I'm making coffee. And for the record, I'm no one's woman."

"Coffee is good, then."

I hid a laugh at his drunkenness, but at least he was a respectful drunk. I doubted he even knew where a clit was though, with half a bottle of bourbon in his system.

I waited for the coffee to be ready, even though it was verging on dinnertime and really getting too late for me to drink the stuff if I wanted to sleep tonight. But Vaughn needed it. I brought a steaming mug to the bedside, and he managed to shift into a sitting position, his back and shoulders against the headboard. He sipped his coffee slowly.

"Sorry," he muttered. "I don't normally get this drunk."

I stood away from him, leaning on a wall with my own mug in my hands. "It's fine. Thank you for bringing my purse back. I had my friend's guys searching for it."

"Thought you might need it. I didn't steal anything from it, but I did open your purse to find some ID with your address on it."

"Good of you not to take the three dollars and seventy-five cents I keep in there."

"Did think about taking the condoms though. Glow-in-the-dark ones are cool. Kinda makes your junk look like a lightsaber."

I sniggered. "If you were gay, you could both wear them and have lightsaber fights in the dark."

Vaughn winked. "If I were gay, I wouldn't get to lick pussy though."

I cocked my head to one side. "You're really into that, huh?"

"Aren't you?"

"Giving or receiving?"

He groaned. "Please tell me you do both."

"Wouldn't you like to know?"

He sipped his coffee again. "This is really good."

"I work at a bar. I'm well used to making coffee to sober people up. Don't like just kicking them out at closing time."

"That's nice of you."

I lifted one shoulder. "I just prefer not to have to clean vomit in the parking lot."

He screwed his face up. "Your job sounds horrible."

I shook my head. "It's not. I love it. The owners are my best friends. The guys who hang out there respect me. Those people have my back."

It was when I'd left the bar that things had gone wrong. Psychos was my home. My family. I wouldn't let Caleb ruin that for me. "There's also a sex club behind a secret door."

Vaughn suddenly seemed a whole lot more sober. "No fucking way."

"Way. You should come sometime. Many a pussy just begging to be licked at that place."

"Don't tempt me with a good time, Roach. I might just take you up on it."

Heat flushed through me at the thought of watching Vaughn on his knees, face pressed between some woman's thighs.

I went hotter again imagining it was my thighs.

"Why are your cheeks pink?"

"That's just the light from outside." I turned my back and went into the kitchenette and busied myself by rifling through my purse. I pulled out my phone and connected it to the charger, then scrolled through the list of notifications.

"Pink looks good on you, Roach. Much better than those bruises." His voice dropped an octave. "Who did that to you? That asshole with the motorcycle?"

I blinked. "Fang? Fuck, no. He would never lay a finger on me."

"He your boyfriend?"

"No."

"He wants to be though."

"Maybe."

"He kill the guy who hit you?"

"He would if I told him who it was."

"Why aren't you?"

I put my coffee mug down hard on the countertop. "Because it's not his fight. It's mine."

"You're flea-sized."

I glared at him, pissed off. "So? You think that's going to stop me walking up to him and putting a bullet through his brain?"

Vaughn eyed me over his mug. "Good for you. Not letting you do that, of course. But I like the spunk."

"Like you have a say in who I do or do not shoot."

The words came out of my mouth and hung in the air between us before I really heard them. I stifled a laugh. "Not a sentence I ever thought I'd say, to be honest."

Vaughn wasn't laughing, but I ignored him. He sounded too much like Fang.

Being told I couldn't do something was the best damn way to get me to prove I could.

I went back to my phone and hovered over an email preview from an attorney in Providence. The email was titled, *Last Will and Testament of Bartholomew Weston*. I glanced at Vaughn. "There's an email here. It's a copy of your dad's will."

He cocked his head to one side. "Why would you be getting that?"

"I've no idea." I tapped on the attached document, skimming the paragraphs of tiny writing. I paused mid page, when my name appeared.

"What is it?" Vaughn asked.

I read the words out slowly. "In the event of both my

and my future wife, Miranda Kemp's, deaths, the entirety of our estate will be split equally between Mr. Vaughn Eugene Weston and Miss Rebel Rose Kemp. This includes my business, any cash in my bank accounts, and the property I own at three hundred and five, Smeeton Range Road..."

"What?" Vaughn growled. "Our parents weren't even properly married, and you get half his estate?"

Shock punched through me. "I...I didn't know. It's dated months ago. They must have had it drawn up when they got engaged..."

Vaughn got off the bed, wobbling once, but the coffee and maybe his anger had helped sober him. "Do you have any idea how much my father's estate is worth?"

I frowned at him. "No?"

He laughed bitterly. "Yes, you do. Was this your plan all along?"

I frowned, not sure if he was still talking gibberish because he was drunk or if he was honestly serious. "Plan? What are you talking about?"

He stalked across the room to me, fury in his eyes. "Where did you go after I saw you at the hotel bar the night before their wedding?"

Anger flamed through me at his tone and the unspoken implication behind it. "What exactly are you accusing me of?"

He kept coming, his big steps eating up the distance between us. "Did you do it?"

Fear flickered through me. I put the bed between us, my fingers hovering over the drawer with my gun in it. "Do what? Kill my own mother?"

"You clearly have it in you. You just told me you were

planning a second murder. Third, I guess, since you already took out two people."

I gaped at him. "You're drunk. And insane. I never hurt my mother!"

"Then where were you that night?"

I yanked the drawer open and pulled out the gun, pointing it at him. "Get out."

He ignored the gun and stared me in the eye. "Did you kill my father?"

"I already told you, no! Now get out!"

He shook his head and backed toward the door. "You aren't getting half my father's assets, Roach. Over my dead body."

I waved the gun in his direction. "That can be arranged!"

His jaw hardened. "This isn't done."

"No shit, Sherlock. I'll be seeing you when I move into my fancy new house." It was a dig purely to get at him, because this was what I always did. Ran my damn mouth until it got me in trouble.

But this time, it succeeded. Vaughn backed out of the apartment, and I rushed to lock the door behind him.

Trembling with adrenaline, I perched on the edge of my bed, shakily putting the gun down next to me.

I'd had no idea about Mom's and Bart's will. No idea I'd been named one of the two beneficiaries of a multi-million-dollar estate.

I laughed, a giddy smile breaking on my face.

Only for it to fall just as quick.

Because that would have just given the cops all the probable motive they needed to pin a double homicide squarely on my shoulders.

mom obviously wanted you to have that money, or they wouldn't have put your name in the will. They want you to be looked after." Bliss shoved her hands on her ample hips and pinned me with a matter-of-fact glare, just daring me to argue back.

I'd give anything for curves like hers, but I was stuck with my runty tomboy look. "Okay, fine. Hypothetically, though, what do I do? This email says he's putting the house on the market as of the end of the week. He's not even giving me a chance."

"He can't do that," Nash argued.

"I think we all know that a bartender from Saint View without a cent to her name hasn't got much power against a wealthy businessman with his daddy's money and lawyers to back him up. He'll probably have the place sold before I can even hire a lawyer. And look," I wailed, scrolling through the photo app on my phone, selecting the one I wanted and then flashing it at them. It showed off the sprawling two-story mansion's gabled roof and painted shutters. A wide verandah on the ground level made me want to buy a porch swing where I could sit curled up and watch the world go by. Or something equally romantic. "I scoped out the place on Street View, and it's my dream house."

Vincent crinkled his nose. "It looks haunted."

I slapped his solid arm. "Stop. It's beautiful and charming. Old, yes. But I love it. It has personality. Not to mention the fact my apartment could probably fit in just one bedroom of that place. Think of the parties we could have there."

Bliss raised an eyebrow. "Because we throw keggers and invite the entire football team on a regular basis? The only parties we ever throw are here and of the sexy variety."

I side-eyed her. "We could try having more of a life."

"Tell that to my all-day sickness."

"Halloween is coming up. You'll be well into the second trimester then, right? You should be feeling better. We could throw an amazing party at this house."

Bliss stared at the beautiful house in the photo. "It is a lot nicer than your apartment. You need to fight for it."

I ran my finger over the image on the screen. "Imagine being such an entitled twat that you would even consider selling a house like that. He has more money than sense."

"Agreed," Bliss announced. "We hate him."

I nodded, ignoring the memory of the chemistry sparking between me and Vaughn, before there'd been a will to get his knickers in a twist. I went back to the email and sighed. Vaughn's phone number was listed as a contact in the details section of the front page.

Without thinking about it too much, I typed out a message.

Rebel

WTF with the lawyer? You couldn't have even let it sit for a day? Maybe had a conversation about it? And while we're on the topic of conversations that should have happened, do you not remember how just yesterday you were begging to go down on me? Maybe we should talk about that?

VAUGHN

That was before I knew you murdered my
father to steal his fortune.

REBEL

Where's my eye roll emoji when I need it?
I already told you: I did not murder your
father. I didn't even know I was in the will!
If anyone has motive for murder, it's you!
You knew you'd get squillions.

VAUGHN

I'm selling the house. The lawyer has
paperwork for you to sign. If you agree,
I'll pay you twenty-five thousand dollars.

I gaped at Bliss. "This jackass is trying to pay me off."

"How much?" Nash asked curiously.

"Twenty-five thousand."

"Oh, fuck that guy," Bliss spit out. "Tell him you'll see
him in court."

I wavered. "He'll probably win in court. We all know
that."

"You can't take twenty-five K, Rebel! That's insulting."

It was. "What if I tell him I want the house? He can
keep the business and the cash. I don't care about those.
But that house…" I could imagine myself waking up in a
huge bed every morning, stretching as sun streamed in
the bay windows. I would eat my breakfast overlooking
the pool. Dance around in a gown and slippers. Maybe
plonk a tiara on my head…

But mostly I would just be safe in the knowledge no
landlord was going to kick me out. I'd sleep better at
night knowing I wasn't going to be living out of my car or
crashing on Bliss's couch because my rent was overdue.

That was all I truly wanted. To work at Psychos. To have my friends around me. To have a safe, stable home nobody could take away from me.

Oh, and to kill Caleb and his friends, but that could wait until the housing problem was fixed.

REBEL

> No deal. I want the house. You take the business and the cash and anything else you want. I'll sign those over right now. All I want is the house.

VAUGHN

> No.

I ground my teeth. I was being more than reasonable, I was sure. Yes, the house was worth a lot of money, but it was definitely the smaller portion of Bart's overall estate. I'd really hoped Vaughn would be reasonable.

I tossed my phone down on the counter and groaned. "It's hopeless. He's an ass who wants it all, even though he probably swims in his pool of money on a nightly basis."

"Sounds like something Caleb would have done," Bliss ground out.

I blanched at the comparison. Even though he was being an ass, Vaughn hadn't hurt me the way Caleb had. He hadn't laid a finger on me. When I'd told him to leave, he had.

"They aren't the same," I said quietly, but Bliss didn't hear me. She'd already walked away to retrieve some empty glasses from a table.

Nash had gone back to work too, and I needed to do the same. I put the phone away and headed for the main floor to join Bliss in cleaning up.

Vincent put an arm out to stop me as I passed. "Rebel."

"Yeah?"

"Possession is nine-tenths of the law."

I squinted at him. "Meaning..."

"It's really hard to sell a house that has a tenant in it who won't budge. Doesn't even need to be a legal tenant. Squatters can't be forcibly removed without notice either."

He had a point. I was supposed to have coughed up my late rent or moved out two weeks ago. I was still there and would be until the landlord took me to court and I was forcibly removed. I pressed up onto my toes and kissed my bestie's psychopath on the cheek. "You're a genius."

He blushed pink. "It might buy you some time."

I was being evicted anyway, so what did I have to lose? All I had to do was find a time that Vaughn wasn't home, find a way inside, and make myself comfy.

I smiled to myself just imagining his outrage.

REBEL

You'll regret that.

VAUGHN

That another murder threat, Roach?

REBEL

No threat. Just a promise. See you soon, big brother.

## 11

## REBEL

*I* packed everything I could fit into my little car. Clothes. A TV. My five-year-old laptop that desperately needed replacing. Sheets and blankets. The two barely living houseplants I neglected on a regular basis. My gun that I was definitely not giving back to the guy downstairs. It all got shoved into the trunk or the back seat, until the car was laden down with everything I cared about.

I wouldn't bother with my bulky furniture. Most of it had been picked up off the side of the road anyway and was in dire need of being sent to the dump.

In my half-empty apartment, my fingers hovered over the three square Polaroid photos I'd taken of my injuries. They'd been shot the morning after it had happened and showed the worst of what Caleb and his friends had done to me. I hadn't done it for the police. I knew there was no going to them.

I'd taken them for myself.

So I'd have a constant reminder of what happened when you let your guard down.

Part of me wanted to rip them up and throw them out, but a bigger part knew it was a lesson I needed to remember. So they got shoved into the final box too.

On my last trip down the stairs, I gave the middle finger to my landlord's closed door. He could get rid of the rest of my stuff. I wasn't coming back for it.

I drove into Providence, excitement licking through me with every turn I made. Bliss had gone bug-eyed when I'd told her the plan. She'd tried to convince me to let her help, but she was not the right person for the job. I was essentially breaking and entering, and she would have been a bundle of nerves on the seat beside me, worrying that we were breaking the law.

This sort of thing made me feel alive though. I lived for the thrill of it, and the prospect of wiping the smug look off Vaughn's face was enough to have me bouncing on my seat with excitement.

Maybe I'd still end up on Bliss's couch when he kicked me out and barred the doors. But at least I'd have a new story to tell my grandkids one day. Or Bliss's grandkids. I wasn't sure kids would ever be in the cards for me. I refused to have a baby the way my mom had. If any baby was in my future, I first needed a stable relationship. My chances of that happening, after not one decent boyfriend in the past fifteen years, seemed slim.

I'd be fine though. I had great friends. A job I loved. Hopefully a big-ass house to lounge around in. I wanted to clap my hands in glee.

I parked my car a few houses down from Bart's aging mansion and settled in to watch. There was a truck sitting to the left of the house with O'Malley's Handyman Services printed on the side, but it was too late for a tradesman to still be there.

The only other vehicle was a sleek black motorcycle parked on the circular drive, right up close to the door.

Judging from the helmet Vaughn had carried when we'd met at the hotel restaurant, the bike was his. So, if I just waited for it to leave...

I'd just about drifted off to sleep when the front door opened, startling me awake. I sat forward eagerly, grin spreading wide across my face. I pulled my phone up, opened up my camera app, and then zoomed all the way in on Vaughn.

The image went grainy, but it was enough to see the general direction his fingers moved over the lock pad. "Seven, three, seven..." I chuckled, pretty sure the last number had been a three too. "Thank you, Bart, for not having a fingerprint or eye scanner. That would have been a real pain. Now if your son could just skedaddle..."

Like he could hear me, Vaughn tucked his wallet in a saddlebag and lifted his arms to tug on his jacket.

I refused to notice the flash of abs I got when his T-shirt rose.

The jacket settled around his shoulders, and he pulled the helmet on too, masking his face.

"Good," I muttered, before I'd even thought about why. I was so damn distracted by the chiseled jaw and the dark stubble and the deep-brown eyes I was forgetting Vaughn was now the enemy.

A stupidly sexy enemy.

Finally, he got on the bike and zoomed out of the driveway. I slunk right down in the driver's seat, barely peeking over the dashboard, and thankful my short legs allowed it.

"Go time." I turned on the car and drove straight into the driveway like I owned it. Since I sort of did, according to Bart's will. I hummed the *Mission Impossible* theme song as I darted to the door in the darkness and punched in the number combination I thought I'd seen Vaughn use.

The door popped open on the first go. I felt like calling Vincent and telling him. He'd be proud.

I walked tentatively inside, eyeing everything in the grand entranceway with awe. The ceiling had to be twenty feet high with ornately carved cornices and a huge chandelier dangling from the center. The black-and-white checkered tiles seemed like they went on for miles. My apartment could indeed fit in this space. Maybe twice over.

Family photos hung on the walls, in amongst expensive art. I wandered it like I was at a gallery, too taken in by it all to hurry, even though for all I knew, Vaughn had just ducked out to the store to get a bottle of milk and would be back at any minute.

I paused on a photo of Vaughn in a classic black suit and bow tie, a blond woman in a pure-white wedding dress wrapped around him. My mouth dropped open. "All that talk of pussy licking, and you're married? Shame on you, Vaughn Weston. Shame. Does she know you're a cheating, lying, house-stealing, scumbag?"

I turned the photo down, not wanting to see his wife's smiling, open face after I'd pictured her man with his head between my thighs. Irritation prickled at me. Fuck Vaughn for putting those ideas out there when he had a ball and chain and was doomed to lick only this woman's vag for the rest of eternity.

Lucky bitch.

I stomped up the grand staircase that seemed to be a staple in houses around here. Bliss's place had one too, and so had her dad's. I supposed you had to get up the stairs somehow when you had a house this size. Might as well make a statement out of it.

At the top, I clutched my dying potted plant in one arm and looked both ways. "Houses that are big enough to have north and south wings should be illegal. Who needs so many rooms?"

But then I thought about the fact this house could be mine and decided that maybe I did. It was better than my shoebox of an apartment anyway.

I opened the door closest to the stairs and found what had to be the main suite. The bed was neatly made with soft cream sheets and bedspread, and above it on the wall was a ginormous framed photo of my mom and Bart. She smiled into the camera in a way I'd never seen her smile before.

She was absolutely beaming. The perfect picture of happiness, showing off her engagement ring for the camera.

A lump rose in my throat, and I shut the door quickly, all of it too fresh and raw to deal with. There was so much sadness to come. The official will reading. Funerals. A whole damn life without her. I didn't want to think about any of it.

It was a lot easier to focus on this little feud with Vaughn and stealing his house.

My house.

Same, same.

I hurried down the hall to the next bedroom. "Oh, boy."

It had to be Vaughn's room. It was done up in deep navy blue, from the walls with their white trims to the silky bedspread. It was neat and tidy, apart from a duffel bag stashed in the corner, overflowing with clothes, and a glass on the bedside table with an inch of bourbon still in the bottom.

I bit my lip, looking at it. Had the man been drunk since it had happened? He was out riding right now. I'd slap him upside the head if he was driving drunk. I had no patience for that shit.

Not that he was my man to do that with, but it didn't matter. It didn't fly with anyone.

If I'd been a bigger person, I would have walked out of the room and left Vaughn to his privacy.

I wasn't. I was tiny in stature, and I guess that carried over to my morals too. At least when it came to snooping through Vaughn's bedroom.

The walls were lined with white shelves, each one laden down with rows and rows of trophies. I pressed up on my toes to read the plaques. "Senior Boys State Champion. Fifty-meter Freestyle record holder." I moved on to the copious number of ribbons pinned to a huge corkboard. They were predominantly blue for first place, but there were plenty of second and third too. In every event from butterfly to backstroke to relays. "So, the man swims. Explains the bod."

Like the true snoop I was, I rummaged through his closet, which was stacked with expensive suits and shirts and shoes, though most of them had a fine layer of dust on the shoulders so I suspected they didn't get worn much. The crumpled shirts and jeans in his duffel bag seemed to be his everyday attire. His en suite was just as opulent as the room attached, with marble sinks and shower. Of course, I opened all the drawers, rolling my eyes when there was little inside other than deodorant and a handful of condoms that had expired years ago. "Probably haven't needed them for a while since you're banging that gorgeous, tall, blond wife of yours, huh?" I muttered. "Which, for the record, I am not at all jealous about."

I frowned at myself in the mirror, no idea why I'd felt the need to add that.

I shifted my plant onto my hip. "Time to go find myself a room, Planty McPlantface. One with lots of sun for you. Or do you need shade? Shit, I can never remember. Plant Protective Services really needs to take you away from me."

I wondered at what point you checked yourself in for therapy. Was it the point where you talked to your plants as you wandered around a house you'd broken into? A shrink might actually be overdue.

Nevertheless, I closed Vaughn's bedroom door then deliberately walked the very far end of the hall, wanting my room to be well away from his. It was the sunny end of the house, with light streaming in from a big open window, and I put my plant buddy down on a hall table in a nice, warm patch of sunlight. "Stand guard while I check this out. Shout...or...I don't know, germinate, if anyone comes."

I really needed to get a life, but nerves and excitement were making me giddy.

I opened the door to the last bedroom and gasped at how beautiful it was inside. Clearly a guest bedroom, with a big king-size bed and decorated in all neutral tones. But it was full of natural light and absolutely massive. I gazed around and couldn't help myself. I did a little spin with my arms open wide, like I was freaking Julie Andrews in *The Sound of Music*.

It was my perfect bedroom. A calm, collected, tidy space where my chaotic ADHD brain felt at ease. I could so easily see myself coming here after a night of noise and craziness at Psychos, and just being at peace with being alone.

I'd never had anything like it. Every other house I'd ever lived in had been a hodgepodge of secondhand furniture that didn't match, noisy neighbors, and room-mates with their own brands of crazy. I flopped onto the bed and had a sudden feeling of 'home' for the first time ever. Maybe it was just the fact that this house was mine. Something that could be stable.

If Vaughn would let it be.

I'd come here to try my luck, but half thinking I'd be slinking back to Bliss's house to sleep on her couch by the end of the night. But in that moment, I knew I'd fight to keep it. Tooth and nail if I had to. This house might mean nothing to him, but a true home was all I'd ever wanted. Here, it was so close I could almost taste it.

I needed to go get all my things and drag them in here so I could hole up and prepare to fight when Vaughn got home. But the extra-large Coke I'd drunk in the car while eating a greasy burger and fries was making demands on my bladder. I hadn't even checked out the bathroom yet.

There were doors on the left of the room, but they

were ajar, and an empty walk-in closet with a small dressing area lay beyond them. A dressing area in a guest bedroom. This house was seriously something else.

But that made the door on the right of the room up for grabs, and I had my fingers crossed for another en suite.

I opened the door.

A scream ripped from my mouth, my reflexes taking in the scene before my brain did.

A huge, very naked man exploded up out of the bathtub with a blood-curdling scream of his own.

And for a very long moment, we both stood there, both of us screaming, neither of us moving.

Except, without any permission from me, my gaze swept over his big body.

Holy, freaking, fuck.

The man was stacked. Muscles for days. Tattoos all over. And his dick...

I'd never seen one more beautiful. Even soft, it was something to be proud of. I couldn't even imagine what it would look like hard. Christ on a cracker.

He yanked a pair of headphones off and used them to cover the junk I was so rudely staring at.

"Who the hell are you?" we both yelled at the same time.

He got out of the bathtub and came at me.

I screamed and stumbled back again, fear coursing through me at the huge naked man approaching me. To my horror, I found myself frozen in terror, cringing away from him. "Please don't hurt me."

He froze, arm stretched out. "I'm just going to get that towel, okay? I'm not going to hurt you. I'm not in the habit of hurting bite-size women, even if they are breaking into my house."

I goggled at him. "Your house? Isn't this Bart Weston's place?"

He took a towel from the rack and wrapped it around his narrow waist, tucking it in at the end. "He lives...shit, lived... here too. I worked for him. Maintenance. Driving. Cleaning. Whatever needs doing. But I've no idea why I'm explaining that to you, when I know for a fact *you* do not live here, and so I should probably call the police. If you're here to steal shit—"

I shook my head rapidly, straightening now the man was at least partially covered and seemingly not about to attack me with his giant man salami. "I swear, I'm not. I'm Rebel. Miranda's daughter?"

Some of the tension seeped out of his shoulders. "Oh, damn. You are too. I should have realized. You look like her. You could be sisters. If she was..." He cringed.

"Still alive?"

"Yeah. Tactless. Sorry. I really liked your mom. She was good for Bart. Made him really happy."

My heart squeezed. "I wish I'd gotten to meet him properly. I don't know why she didn't tell me about him sooner."

"They were a bit of a whirlwind, and very wrapped up in their own little love nest. Don't take it personally. Vaughn didn't know about it either until they decided to get married. Not many people did." He ran his hand through the short lengths of his reddish-brown hair. "I'm really sorry about what happened to them. Bart was so good to me. I don't even know what I'm going to do without this job and this house. I've lived here off and on my entire life. It's always been home. I love everything about it."

I could understand that. I'd fallen in love with the house the moment I'd laid eyes on it, too. "Why are you leaving then?"

He sighed. "Vaughn's getting rid of it."

My heart lit up. There was a chance there, and I was going to take it. "I own half the property. Bart left half of everything to me. I don't want to sell it."

The man leaned on the bathroom wall and crossed his arms over his broad chest. It popped his pecs, and I had a vague desire to lean in and lick the water droplets from them.

"No shit?" His eyes narrowed. "So you want to...what, exactly?"

"Live in it. Buy Vaughn out, if that's what needs to happen."

"Good luck with that. I'm sure he's already contesting the will."

"He is. And maybe he'll win, maybe he won't. I don't know. But I don't want him trying to sell this place until I've had a chance to fight for it. That's where you come in."

The man's eyebrows shot up. "Me? What do I have to do with it?"

"I'm moving in...unbeknownst to Vaughn."

A smile lifted the corner of his mouth. "Seriously? Like one of those environmentalists who tie themselves to trees so they can't be cut down?"

"My dying houseplant is already out in the hall, and my car is filled with everything I own."

He chuckled. "So you just waited 'til he left and started bringing your shit in? Freaking ballsy."

I grinned. "He's gonna be pissed when he gets home, right? Any chance he'll find me cute or adorable?"

The guy chuckled. "Oh, so pissed. You're cute as fuck, and totally his type, but his anger is going to obliterate all of that."

I wanted to question him on me being Vaughn's type when he was clearly married to a leggy blonde. Pretty much the exact opposite of me. But that wasn't the most pressing issue. This man could pick me up and throw me out the door like I weighed nothing more than a matchstick. I needed him on my side. "Help me with Vaughn," I begged. "Don't let him throw me out. If we work together, maybe we can keep the house, and your job."

He eyed me, that small smirk never leaving his mouth. Eventually, he stuck his hand out in my direction again. "I'm Kian."

Slowly, I took his hand, letting his big fingers engulf mine. Fuck, he was big. Everywhere. "Nice to meet you, Kian. Do we have a deal?"

He laughed, the sound deep and sexy. "Oh, we have a deal, little demon. We most definitely have a deal."

## 12

# VAUGHN

*T*he only good thing about coming home was the beach. The golden sands ran the length of both Providence and Saint View, connecting the two towns in one beautiful spot. I opened the visor on my helmet and breathed deep, sucking in familiar lungfuls of salty sea air.

With the sun starting its descent, I weaved my way through other cars and took the road that led up to the bluff and the lookout. It was a popular spot with teenagers who wanted to make out, and I'd spent a few nights up here myself, back before I'd left for college, getting naked on the back seat with whoever I was dating at the time.

It was too early for that though, and the cliffs were quiet when I got there, nothing but the waves crashing hundreds of feet below to pierce the silence. I slowed the bike right down to a crawl, inching closer to the edge with every rotation of the tires.

I could just keep going.

Gun the engine.

Ride the entire thing right over the edge.

Rocks crumbled off the cliff face, and I sank down on my bike, letting it roll backward a few inches, away from the plunging cliff face.

But my heart hurt. Everything fucking hurt really, especially after all the binge drinking. I was sober now, but as soon as I got home, I'd be fixing that. I was steadily plowing my way through my father's liquor cabinet, but it wasn't like he was around to stop me, the way he would have back when I'd actually lived here.

What I wouldn't fucking give to rewind the clock and have him scolding me when I stumbled in the door two hours past curfew, reeking of booze.

I'd do it all differently. Him. Kian. Brooke.

I squeezed my eyes shut at the thought of my wife. With a sigh, I pulled my phone from the saddlebag on my bike and punched the relevant buttons to call her cell. I hadn't wanted to do this at home where Kian might hear. I didn't need anyone knowing my business.

"About fucking time, Vaughn," Brooke snarled down the phone.

"Hello to you too, my darling wife," I replied sarcastically. "So lovely to hear the sweet, soothing sound of your voice."

"Fuck you. You were supposed to call days ago. Did you get the money?"

I ground my molars together. "No. I'm working on it."

"Working on it!" she screeched. "Not good enough! I need the money now."

"Then ask your daddy for it."

"You know I can't do that!"

Yeah, because he got sick of bailing her out of her financial irresponsibility and cut her off too. I lost my patience. "Getting money out of a deceased's estate isn't as easy as just snapping my fingers, Brooke. Everything is frozen. And there's...unforeseen problems."

"Problems? What problems? That is not what I want to hear, Vaughn."

"Apparently I have a sister who I have to share everything with."

"You don't even have a sister! You're such a liar. Is this some ploy to screw me over? Keep all the money for yourself?"

I shook my head at the audacity. "Oh, that's rich. I'm the one screwing you over? You're the one who got yourself into this mess."

I huffed into the phone, pissed with myself for letting her get to me, even though I'd sworn after our last argument I would be calm and matter of fact. Nothing good came from us both getting emotional. That only ended in her screaming and me shutting down, leaving, and riding my bike too fast to burn off my emotions.

Maybe she realized it too, because she changed tactics, and her voice turned syrupy sweet. "Baby, I'm sorry. I'm just scared. If I don't produce that money, they're going to come for me."

I wanted to tell her to let them. That she'd dug herself into this mess and now she could get herself out of it.

But I couldn't. I might only be half the gentleman my father was, but I couldn't just let them hurt Brooke. I'd loved her once. At least, I thought I had. It had all unraveled pretty fast after we'd been married and I'd found out about her unsavory little 'habits.'

Habits that had her blowing through my entire trust fund without me even realizing. Habits that had left us with crippling debts we didn't have the money to pay. Habits that had people after her, ready to take their pound of flesh when she couldn't produce the money she owed.

There was no point in leaving her to the wolves. If they killed her, it wouldn't erase the debt.

It would just fall to me.

Like it or not, I was as much in this mess as she was.

"You don't want them to kill me, do you?" She was using that whiny little girl voice she thought was all doe-eyed and innocent. But really was like a banshee scream in my head.

"Of course not."

"Thank you, baby. I'll make it up to you when you get home. In exactly the way you like."

I rolled my eyes. "I'll get you the money, Brooke. But I'm not coming home. I already told you; we're done."

"You don't mean that. Once the debts are paid, we'll go back to the way things used to be."

"No. We won't. I don't want anything to do with you. My lawyers are already working on the divorce papers."

"I won't sign them."

Of course, she'd try to make my life miserable right to the very bitter end. "Then I'll see you in court. I'll call you when I've worked out something with the money. Just... sit tight. Don't answer the fucking door."

I hung up before she could say anything else. I sat there on the bluffs for another hour, watching the sunset and wishing my life was as carefree as it had been the last time I'd been up here.

I'd made so many mistakes.

Eventually, darkness fell and the mosquitos swarmed in, so I pulled my helmet back on and rode slowly back along the beach, then took the turnoff for Providence.

I passed my mom's house and noted hers and Karmichael's cars in the driveway, but I didn't stop. My dad's place was only a few houses down the street from Mom's. It had been great when I was a kid. If one parent pissed me off, I just walked down the road to the other. But half the time my parents had been hanging out together anyway. When my mom and Karmichael had gotten together, my dad had taken it like the true gentleman he was and told her that all he wanted was her happiness.

I still remembered walking in and catching my mother on the floor, begging his forgiveness, only for my father to gently tell her there was nothing to forgive if she was following her heart.

That's the sort of man he'd always been.

My mother had been his best friend and fiercest supporter ever since, steadfastly standing up for him whenever the media decided to try to play him as some evil millionaire developer who didn't have a heart.

A junky brown car sat in my driveway, right in front of the house where I always parked. I stopped behind it and hung my helmet on the handlebars, shaking my head in annoyance. The sooner Kian moved out, the better. He could take his friends and their shitty cars with him.

Inside, I half expected to find Kian and with a bunch of half-drunk buddies, lounging in the living room, watching sports on the big-screen TV. But when I stopped in the entryway, it was quiet. I moved to the back of the house, the outdoor area with the pool and barbecue was another likely hangout spot, but it was quiet too.

That really only left his bedroom.

I paused with one foot on the bottom stair.

Maybe it wasn't a friend's car after all.

Maybe it was a woman's.

Or a man's.

Kian hadn't had a preference back when we'd known each other.

Heat flushed my body, then settled at the back of my neck at the thought of him naked with someone. I plodded up the stairs, my feet suddenly as heavy as lead. My room was right at the top. It would have been easy to just keep walking and go inside, shut the door, put on some headphones until Kian's guest left.

But I was clearly a sucker for punishment. I turned left and tiptoed my way down to his end of the corridor.

The bedframe squeaking was audible even before I pressed my ear up against his door.

Squeak. Squeak. Squeak.

"You're wild," Kian laughed.

"They don't call me Rebel for nothing."

Rebel? No fucking way. Jealousy speared through me, hot and fast, quickly turning into anger. Before I knew it, the doorknob was twisting beneath my hands. "What the fuck, Kian!" I bellowed.

Rebel froze, mid bounce on Kian's bed.

Kian glanced over at me from the couch where he was flipping through an MMA magazine. His mouth lifted in the corner, amused, like he'd been planning this all along. "Oh, look. Vaughn's home. Good to see you, *buddy*."

The word was laced with a clear undercurrent of something else.

Rebel bounced lightly on her bare feet, the mattress dipping beneath her weight. She watched the two of us with interest, then laughed. "Oh my. What is going on here? Do I detect the sweet, sweet smell of two men who've seen each other naked?" She gave an overexaggerated inhale. "Truly my favorite scent. I have no idea why two men together does it for me, but damn, it really, truly does."

Kian leaned over and offered her a high five. "Me too."

She slapped his palm gleefully while I stared at them, dumbfounded. "Again. What the fuck? But same question for you too, Roach. Were you just jumping on his bed? How do you even know each other?"

"Roach?" Kian questioned. He wrinkled his nose. "That's the worst nickname ever. I'm running with Little Demon."

What the fuck was he even talking about?

Rebel flipped her feet out from beneath her and landed on her ass before scooting to the edge. "Settle down, psycho. First, yes, I was jumping on the bed. You should try it sometime. It's fun."

I was sure I was staring at the woman like she'd just grown another eyeball. "My head would go right through the ceiling."

Rebel gazed up at it and shrugged. "Never have to worry about that when you're my height. Yay me for being fun-sized. But anyway. Back to your questions. How do we know each other?"

"We're besties," Kian said, another dig, I was sure, aimed at hurting me.

Because once upon a time, it was me and him who'd been inseparable. Though that couldn't be further from the truth anymore.

"Since when?" I demanded.

Rebel turned to Kian, and he made a show of checking the time on his phone. "About thirty minutes ago, when I found her moving into the bedroom on the other side of my bathroom."

My brain was struggling to keep up. "At the risk of sounding like a record on repeat, what?"

"I moved in," Rebel said with a grin. "I hope you don't mind. I took the room at the end of the hall. You know, since I own half the property now."

I narrowed my eyes at her, spitting out my words. "You do not own half this property. Or anything in my father's name."

A low growl came from Kian's chest. "Watch the way you speak to my bestie, Weston."

Was he for real? He'd known me for decades, her for thirty minutes, and he was taking her side? Hurt stabbed through me at how far our friendship had disintegrated.

Rebel cleared her throat. "I don't want to fight. But I do own half this property, and I'm not letting you sell it."

"If the will remains as it is, and that's a big if, you'd get half the profits anyway. What do you care if I sell it?"

She glared at me. "I get that you're Richie Rich and have no idea what it's like to have no home of your own, but not everyone in this room was born with a silver spoon in their mouth. Some of us think this house is amazing and can't think of a single other place in the world they'd want to call home."

"This is ridiculous." I glanced at Kian for backup. "You cannot possibly want a stranger living here in your home?"

He cleared his throat, looked me dead in the eye, and said, "Why not? That's exactly what you are. At least she's not threatening to kick me out."

I flinched. "I shouldn't have said that."

"Yeah, but you did. So fuck you, Vaughn. I'm on the little demon's side. She stays."

Rebel softened a tiny bit. "I was evicted from my apartment. I have nowhere else to go."

The fight went out of me entirely at the thought of her living on the streets. "You could have led with that."

She raised an eyebrow. "So you aren't calling the cops?"

I turned and walked away. "Don't tempt me, Roach."

I meant it in more ways than one.

## 13

## REBEL

*I* didn't feel as triumphant as I thought I would when Vaughn walked out of the room and back to his own. The door slammed a moment later, and I winced at Kian. "Why do I just feel like we kicked a puppy?"

He sighed. "'Cause Vaughn is real good at putting on the puppy-dog eyes when it suits him. Don't feel bad. He's a professional liar."

I cocked my head. "There's a story there. That was said with the hurt of a man betrayed."

"It's nothing. Ancient history. We're both over it." He tossed his magazine aside and stood, offering me a hand up. "Come on. Let's get the rest of your stuff out of your car now that his lordship has graciously approved your stay."

I followed him, both of us eyeing Vaughn's bedroom door as we passed to go down the stairs. But I was soon huffing and puffing, carrying boxes to and from the car and into my new room, and too excited about the prospect of living in this massive house to worry about Vaughn being a jackass. He wasn't my problem. Especially since the man had a wife who could worry about him.

Plus, Kian was entirely distracting. He lugged the heaviest of my stuff up the stairs, placed it all neatly in my room, until only one box was left.

"I can grab it." I reached for the last, overflowing box.

"It weighs more than you do. Not a chance. Give it."

He swiped it before I could stop him, and I slammed down the hatchback's door, before locking it.

Not that anyone was going to try stealing it around here, when there were BMWs, Porches, and Mercedes everywhere you looked. We walked up the staircase side by side, Kian chattering about the history of the house and how his dad had worked here when Kian was a kid.

"He landscaped the yard, renovated the ground floor bathroom, built the pool house…" He put the last box down on the writing desk in my room and paused mid-sentence.

I glanced over at him. "Your dad was the one who built the pool house, and then…" I prompted, truly curious about the property I'd inherited. I suddenly wanted to know everything about it, from its history to the people who'd owned it and lived here over the decades. It had to be one of the original properties in the area, perhaps once surrounded by land that had been sold off to make way for the new houses.

But Kian had lost interest in the story. He plucked three square photos from the top of my box and stared down at them. Horror stole the color from his face.

Oh fuck. I should have buried those deeper. I stormed

across the room and snatched them from his grasp. "Those are private."

He spun and glared at me.

I flinched at the intensity, and he backed right off, hands up. "Shit. Sorry. But what the fuck, Rebel? What are those?"

I swallowed thickly, exhaustion swamping me after a long, emotionally charged day. I didn't have it in me to lie. "Photos to remind me of the injuries I sustained after I was attacked."

He ground his jaw. "Who did it? A boyfriend?"

I shook my head quickly. "No. I made a bad decision in going home with a man who had friends waiting..." Tears pricked the backs of my eyes, emotion welling up in my chest from just looking at those photos again. I didn't even want to talk about it for fear I'd cry. But then it was too late. The tears spilled over and coursed down my cheeks.

"Fuck," Kian ground out. He wrapped his arms around me, dragging me to his chest in a bear hug.

I stiffened in his arms.

He must have felt it. He pulled back quickly. "Shit, sorry. That's probably not what you need right now after what they did. Not everyone is a hugger."

I was stunned to find that though his embrace had taken me by surprise, it hadn't scared me. Kian gave off an overgrown teddy bear with golden retriever energy sort of vibe. It was hard to feel scared around a man who encouraged you to jump on his bed.

But at this point, I didn't trust my own judgment. So I let him back off, even though the hug had felt kind of nice.

Kian tapped his fingers against the box. "I can promise you, though Prince Stick Up His Ass can be a royal dickhead, he won't hurt you. I've known him long enough to say that with one-hundred-percent certainty. And full disclosure? I'm good at hurting people, but I've never laid a hand on a woman, and I never will."

He sighed when I didn't say anything.

"Talk is cheap, though, huh? I bet you went home with that guy, thinking he was nice too. Am I right?"

"I wish you weren't."

He mulled that over for a moment, his gaze dropping to the photos in my hand. I tucked them into my back pocket quickly, but he'd already seen them. Seen every bruise and cut Caleb and his friends had put on my body, none of them pretty.

Kian shoved off the wall abruptly. "Come with me."

Without waiting for me, he strode purposefully out of the room and down the hall.

Curious, I followed, jogging to catch up to his long, determined strides. "Where are we going?"

"To the shed."

I frowned, not exactly sure what was so exciting about a shed, presumably filled with tools and lawn-mowing equipment.

Kian led me out of the house and around the side, where a large metal shed was hidden from view of the pool and entertaining area. It wasn't locked, and he let himself in, going straight for a drawer on the right of the neatly organized space. "I know they're in here some-where. Aha!"

I tried to peer over his shoulder, but he was so much

bigger than me and there was a lot of stuff in the way. Bags of fertilizer. Something called Oxyanedride, that was probably a pool cleaner, judging from the other equipment around it. A lawn mower and a rake. "I can't see. What is it?"

He ignored the question. "Grab my drill, would you, please? It's just on that tool bench."

I grabbed the power tool in question and followed him back upstairs to my room. He waited for me to enter, then kicked the door closed, his big body blocking the exit.

A flicker of fear almost instantly exploded into a firestorm of terror.

It was just like that night all over again. I was trapped. Men blocking the exits. Not letting me leave until they got what they came for.

My chest tightened in panic, and I darted for the bathroom door, the only unblocked exit.

"Rebel," Kian barked. "Wait. Stop. Look."

Despite the adrenaline rushing my body, I did.

Two small silver slide locks sat on Kian's palm. "One for this door, one for the bathroom door. I swear to you, Vaughn and I won't ever lay a finger on you. But I thought you might feel safer anyway if you could lock yourself in here when you feel like you need to."

The pounding of my heart slowed, the fight or flight response dying off as Kian turned back to the closed door and measured where the lock would be installed.

I moved to sit on the bed, tucking my knees up and wrapping my arms around them while I watched him work. "Thank you." It was barely more than a whisper, easily lost in the noise of the drill.

But Kian nodded. "You're welcome. If this is going to be your home, you should feel safe here."

I wanted that. So desperately. I wanted to feel like I didn't have to sleep with a gun under my pillow. I wanted to feel safe walking the streets again or having a drink with a man I found attractive. I wanted to be the woman I'd been before Caleb had stolen that sense of peace.

I couldn't let him win. Right now, Caleb was walking around town, powerful in the knowledge he could do what he liked and face no repercussions.

While I'd become some scared mouse I barely recognized.

"I'm going to kill them."

Kian paused in his drilling and looked over at me.

I waited for his shock. His judgment. Some sort of reaction. But he just put the drill down and picked up a chisel. "Okay. How?"

I blinked. "How? That's what you're asking me when I say I'm going to kill three men?"

He put the tool down and turned to give me his full attention. "I saw those photos, Rebel. I saw what they did to you. They don't deserve to breathe." He shrugged. "And better to have a plan than to just do it in the heat of the moment. That's sloppy and a surefire way to get caught. So yeah, I'm asking you how?"

"Something painful. Brutally painful."

He chuckled. "Okay, okay. I like your style."

The corner of my mouth flickered but then died. "You probably think I'm some weak little girl who can't stand up for herself, huh? I swear, I'm not. If you'd met me before, you'd have a very different opinion. I'm not the girl in those photos. I work at Psychos. You probably don't know it. It's a bar in Saint View. Rough as guts."

He raised an eyebrow. "Psychos? Yeah, I know it."

Something about the way he said it made me pause. "You've heard it's a sex club, haven't you?"

He grinned. "Is it?"

"You're not an undercover cop, are you?"

He scoffed. "Hardly."

"Then, yes. At times, it is. But most of the time it's just a dive bar. I'm not beating my own chest when I say I ruled that place. I took no shit from any of the guys there, and they learned fast not to piss me off or they'd get a taste of my brass knuckles. I'm small. But I'm scrappy."

"I don't think you're weak, Rebel. Weak women don't decide they're moving into the house they inherited, despite the fact other people already live in it. You've been ballsy as fuck in the single afternoon I've known you." He sat on the bed next to me. "So let me help you."

"Help me what? Kill a few men?"

He shook his head. "As much as I might enjoy teaching those pricks a lesson, I think that's your wrong to right. Yeah?"

It was a relief to hear him say that. I couldn't tell Fang or Bliss their names. Bliss's guys and Fang would completely ignore what I wanted, because they could get the job done quickly. They weren't like that to be assholes, but they were too close to me. They would think they were protecting me.

But I needed to do it myself. I wouldn't feel whole until I'd proved to myself I was the woman I'd always thought I was. Strong. Powerful. An independent, take-no-shit sorta girl.

It was my whole damn identity, and without it, I was lost.

Kian cocked his head in my direction. "What are you doing tonight?"

I shrugged. "Nothing other than unpacking."

Something devilish glinted in his eye. "I got to know you some this afternoon. I think it's only fair I show you something of me. You in?"

I nodded. "Sure."

Kian pointed toward my closet. "Get your shoes on, little demon. We're going to a fight."

# 14

## FANG

*I* paced my room at the clubhouse like a caged lion. Up and down. Back and forth, wearing a hole in the already thin carpet. The moment I heard War's voice drift back from the common room, I was out there, storming right up to him, not caring I was interrupting his conversation.

"Prez," I bit out, voice hoarse. "I need to talk to you."

War slid his gaze from Hawk, our VP, to me. Slowly, he raised an eyebrow.

I understood why. It wasn't like me to make demands on him. I never spoke out of turn, if I ever spoke at all. That wasn't my place. I'd pledged complete and undying allegiance to this club, and to me, that meant not questioning its leadership.

If War said jump, my only question was how high.

"It important?" War asked.

It was to me. "Yes."

He gave me a nod, then turned to Hawk. "Give us a minute?"

Hawk frowned, not used to being dismissed in favor of a lower ranking member, but he eventually shuffled toward the bar. "Need a drink anyway."

Didn't we all. Except I couldn't afford to not be one-hundred-percent mentally focused right now. So drinking was off the table until I'd done what needed to be done.

War folded his arms across his broad chest. "Okay. You have my attention. What is it?"

"Has Bliss told you who hurt Rebel?"

He shook his head. "No. You'd be the first person I'd tell if I knew, brother. Vincent, Nash, and I are all itching to know too. The minute we do, we're on our way to the asshole's house to take care of business."

I cracked my knuckles. It wasn't enough to calm the restless ache inside me that stemmed from knowing someone had hurt my woman and gotten away with it. "I need to know," I said hoarsely. "It's fucking killing me."

War slapped a beefy hand on my shoulder. "I know, brother. I know. But until she tells us their names, there's nothing we can do."

"I need a job," I practically begged. "I can't hang around here, just sitting on my damn hands. I want to start a fight with every person who even looks my way. I can't take it. I'm scared I'm gonna hurt someone I care about. Or that my head is going to fucking explode."

War's sympathy was palpable. "I know how you feel. I was the same when it was Bliss in that situation. But we have nothing on right now. Just gotta sit tight 'til something comes up."

I couldn't do that. "What about your old man's murder?"

Someone had hired a hitman to take out War's parents. His mom had made it, but his father hadn't been so lucky. We'd found out who the hitman was, but that wasn't who we cared about. The person who'd ordered the hit was who needed to go down.

War patted my arm. "That time is coming. Trust me, when it does, you'll be the first man by my side. But until then, fuck, bro. You need to find somewhere else to channel that aggression. Don't go starting shit here, you know I ain't got no patience for brothers fighting brothers. Take it somewhere else."

He was right. I nodded obediently.

War gave me a half-smile. "Go get laid or something. Rebel ain't the only one around here willing to ride your horse-sized cock. Any of the girls would be happy for a round."

But that wasn't true. The girls who hung around the clubhouse generally were up for it, and were often seen draped over the laps of the other guys, or bouncing on their cocks for the rest of us to watch.

But I saw the way they stared at me when I entered a room. Like everywhere else, they feared me too. Some flinched away. Others averted their eyes, hoping I wouldn't notice them. I got it. I was huge, with a face only a mother could love, and mine hadn't even done that.

I didn't want a woman who was scared of me.

I just wanted the pixie who had never looked at me in any way other than with pure desire.

Being the center of Rebel's attention was addictive. Once you'd had a taste, there was no going back. No other woman's gaze felt the same.

There was no going to get laid unless it was Rebel's sweet body writhing beneath me.

Since that wasn't in the cards, the only other thing was violence.

I stalked outside to my bike, shoved on my helmet, and gunned the engine. It roared to life beneath me, vibrating through my bones in a way that normally settled my nerves but today only made them worse.

The tires kicked up rocks as I slammed my hand on the accelerator and shot out of the compound. Woods surrounded me on both sides, until I came out on the road that led up to the bluff. I steered away from it, though, taking the turnoff into Saint View.

I didn't need pretty views tonight. I needed the rough, underbelly of the ghetto and the people who called it home. I passed Psychos, searching the parking lot for Rebel's junk bucket of a car. But it wasn't there. Which lined up with War saying she wouldn't be back at work until next week.

The last time I'd seen her there, I'd left, jealous over her talking with another man. The memory played over in my head while I drove, getting clearer and clearer with every mile that passed beneath my tires.

The realization jolted, and I took my hand off the accelerator, letting the bike slow. Had it been him? The pretty boy sitting at the end of the bar while she worked, looking completely out of place in a Saint View dive?

Bile rolled around in my stomach.

No.

It couldn't be. Because if it was, her attack was my fault.

I should have stayed. Should have watched over her.

Instead, I'd left in a jealous funk, like I had any right.

That urge to use my fists flooded me once more. If there'd been a wall to punch, I probably would have, just so the feeling had somewhere to go. "Fuck!" I bellowed into the night; the word whipped away by the rushing wind. I pushed the bike as hard as I dared, only one destination in mind now.

On the edge of town, the Dark Demon Boxing Gym sat surrounded by industrial buildings. By day, the place bustled with a mixture of businesses, but come closing time, the entire place emptied out.

Except for fight nights. They weren't officially hosted by the Dark Demon, but seeing as the fights took place in their parking lot, and apart from a service station around the corner, they were always the only building with lights on, some liked to call it Demon night.

Like always, the cars parked in a large circle, leaving their headlights on so they all shined into the center of a makeshift ring. I parked my bike on the outskirts and pulled my helmet off but sat there for a minute, checking out who else was here.

People milled around everywhere, loud music pumping from someone's car stereo. At one end of the lot, a guy took bets on the first matchup—two guys, both stripped of their shirts, and warming up in the circle of car headlights.

There was a carnival vibe to the gathering, with a lot of laughter and shouts of greeting when people recognized their friends.

Through the crowd, a tiny woman appeared, and I did a double take, squinting through the groups of people. She disappeared, but I was on my feet anyway, storming through the crowd, not knowing if I'd seen her because she was there or just because she was on my mind twenty-four seven.

"Rebel," I barked out, spotting the dark-haired woman again. I scrubbed my eyes, really not sure if I was seeing things. There was no reason she should be here. I'd never seen her at a fight before. She'd never mentioned going.

But then again, I'd never told her I went to them either.

I reached for the woman's arm, only to have a man step in front of me and growl, "I wouldn't."

I backed off. "Sorry. I didn't know she was your girl. I thought she was someone else."

The woman turned around. Her eyes went big. "Fang? What are you doing here?"

There was no mistaking her now. Or the way my heartbeat went into overdrive just from being in her presence. I glanced at the guy she was with, the one who'd defended her.

Not the guy from the bar that night. He was vaguely familiar. I was pretty sure I'd seen him here on other occasions, but never with Rebel before.

Jealousy surged again, but unlike that night at the bar, where I'd walked out, this time, I wasn't letting it get the better of me. I wasn't moving. I wasn't going anywhere. Not without her.

"You know him?" the guy and I both asked Pix at the same time.

I ground my molars at the familiar way he talked to her. I didn't like it.

She rolled her eyes at our standoff. "Okay, cool your

testosterone-filled tits, you two. I know you both. Kian, this is Fang. A friend of mine from the Slayers MC."

Friend.

I fucking hated that word. She'd never been just a friend from my point of view. It wasn't what I wanted from her. It barely even scratched the surface of the things I craved from that woman.

"Fang, this is Kian. My new roommate."

My gaze whirled from Kian to my tiny pixie. "Your what?"

"Roommate. I moved into his house today."

"The fuck?" I'd heard her, I just didn't fucking want to have. "You just moved in with some guy? Do you even know him? Or is he just some perverted creep who advertises his room for rent and only accepts women he wants to fuck?"

Kian's mouth pulled into a tight line.

The guy was big, but so was I.

She folded her arms beneath her tits and glared at me. "Honestly, sometimes I really wish I was into women. It would be so much easier. Kian didn't advertise for a roommate. It's a long story. But while you're pissed, you may as well know, there's also another guy living there. Vaughn. You met him outside the courthouse the other day."

I stared at her blankly. All I remembered about the courthouse was getting to her, taking her home, making sure she was safe.

"He introduced himself as my brother?"

A lightbulb clicked in my head. "That jackass?"

Kian grumbled. "Watch yourself. I'm the only one allowed to call him names. Even if they are true."

It didn't matter anyway. I wasn't interested in this guy or any other. "What are you doing here?" I asked Rebel. "It's not safe."

She glanced between me and Kian, both of us towering over her. "Oh, I think I'm about as safe as it gets right here. Kian brought me to watch him fight."

Kian stretched his arms over his head and twisted to crack his neck. "Actually, I brought you to see if *you* wanted to fight."

Her eyes went big. "What?"

The growl from my chest was completely feral. "Over my dead body."

Rebel took a step toward me. "I'm kinda with Fang on this one. I can't fight at something like this. Have you seen me? I'll die."

I practically crowed with victory

Kian folded his arms across his chest. "I didn't mean fight tonight. But you just told me you're scrappy. And that you've got some wrongs to right. Maybe this is where you get your confidence back."

"No," I spit out.

Rebel squinted up at me. "Did you just speak for me?"

I bit my lip, knowing I had and that she was rightfully putting me in my place. But fuck. I could not stand here and watch her fight. I'd seen the women who came to these things. They weren't just scrappy. They were brutal and not above cheating. Not that there were really any rules to these matches, other than respecting when the other person conceded.

I never wanted to cut her wings.

But I didn't know how to support her getting hurt either.

Pix was tiny, and everything in my body screamed *protect her.*

It had since the very moment I'd laid eyes on her.

She turned to Kian. "I'm not fighting. I'm not trained."

"Then let me train you."

"I'll train you," I said quickly. I knew exactly how physical fighters got with their trainers, and the thought of this guy all over Rebel had my fingers unconsciously clenching into fists.

She shook her head. "It's a yes to the training, but you can't both do it."

Kian glanced at me and then jerked his head toward the ring. "Up for it? The better fighter trains her."

Rebel's eyes went wide, and she put her hands up in a stop motion. "Whoa. No. That's not what I meant."

Kian's eye held a challenging gleam.

Like spoke to like. He was as keen for a fight as I was. I needed the pain. Needed to hurt for what I'd done. Even if it meant Kian winning and being the one to train her. I stuck my hand out. "Deal."

He grinned at me. "I like you more already. May the best man win."

"Wait, wait!" Rebel jumped in between us. "You can't fight each other. Fight someone else, whatever, but I don't know who to cheer for if you're both in the ring. What if you get hurt?"

"I won't," we both said in unison.

Even I almost smiled at that one. Because he would.

I would too, but I would welcome it. The sting of a punch in the face was a whole lot better than the stabbing reminder that she'd been hurt because of me.

Kian waved to the guy who organized the fights. "Joe. Me and Leather Jacket here. Yeah?"

Joe's gaze slid to me. "You up for it, Fang?"

I nodded.

Joe pointed over at the ring. "Get ready then. You're up next."

I cracked my knuckles in anticipation.

Kian put his hand on the small of Rebel's back, and it took everything in me not to rip it right off. But she didn't seem to mind.

"Let's find you someone to stand with," Kian said. "I'm not leaving you here on the sidelines alone."

Sometimes other guys from my club were here, but I hadn't noticed any of their bikes. They were probably all hanging out at the clubhouse, choosing beers and sex over getting their asses kicked.

I didn't plan on getting my ass kicked. But I was in agreement with Rebel not standing alone. Once I was in that ring, my concentration needed to be fully on my opponent. I couldn't be watching out for her as well.

Kian jerked his head at another guy. "There. Colt!"

He guided Rebel through the crowd, and I followed close behind, not willing to let her out of my sight.

A younger guy spun around and nodded at Kian in return. The two shook hands when they got close enough.

Colt indicated to the people he was standing with. "Have you met my family? That's Banjo, and Rafe. And this"—he pulled a dark-haired woman tight beneath his arm—"is Lacey."

"Nice to meet you," Lacey said with a warm smile.

Kian held a hand out to her. "Kian. This is Rebel."

"And that's Fang, hovering behind me," Rebel chipped in.

Colt glanced at me. "Good to see you, man. I remember you from back when I used to fight. Haven't seen you fight for a while. I don't get out here much anymore now we have a little one at home."

I didn't remember him, but I shook his hand and grunted a reply at him.

Lacey stared at Rebel. "Have we met before?" Her eyes widened. "Oh, wait, I know. You work at Psychos, right? My friend, Bliss, owns the place."

Rebel smiled. "It's my home away from home. And if you're a friend of Bliss's then you're a friend of mine. Mind if I stand with you guys? Tweedle Dumb and Tweedle Dumber here want to kill each other in the ring, and I'd prefer not to get covered with their caveman blood."

Lacey laughed. "Ah, yes. I know all about that with these three."

All three guys frowned at her, but she waved them off and linked her arm through Rebel's. "Come on, I'll show you where the spatter-free zone is."

She dragged Rebel off, and Lacey's guys followed after.

Colt tossed us a glance. "Don't worry. I'll keep an eye on them. I might not have been fighting lately, but working at the prison keeps me on my toes. I got it."

Kian and I both nodded.

He eyed me. "Ready? These guys seem just about done."

We both looked into the ring right as Joe lifted the arm of a man with a bleeding nose, declaring him the winner. He let it drop then called out, "Kian. Fang. You're up."

Kian pulled off his T-shirt, dropping it onto the hood of the nearest car.

I shrugged out of my jacket and then my shirt, leaving us both bare chested, in jeans and boots. Not ideal fighting attire, but these fights were really all about boxing, so it didn't matter too much our legs were restricted by unforgiving denim.

Kian and I both entered the ring, and a cheer went up from the crowd.

"May the best man win," Kian said with a grin.

The words hit me right in the chest. I wasn't the best man. The best man wouldn't have let his girl get hurt on his watch.

Right then and there, I gave up any intention of winning.

## 15

## REBEL

*I* didn't know whether to be horrified or turned on. I clutched Lacey's hand as the two men entered the ring and circled each other.

"You okay?" she whispered to me.

I realized I was mangling her hand. I loosened it. "Sorry. This is making me nervous. Do you watch Colt fight?"

She glanced over at her men, the three of them deep in conversation, but eyes on Kian and Fang in the ring. "I used to, back when we were in high school. But then we had a baby, and Colt calmed down a bit." She eyed the fighters. "Are you with both of them?"

I widened my eyes. "Am I...oh God, no. I'm not with either of them."

She nodded. "I wasn't judging. I'm well used to polyamorous relationships. If you couldn't tell from those three."

I glanced at the men again. They were younger than me, in their early twenties maybe, but I wasn't blind.

They were good-looking guys. I winked at Lacey. "Lucky you. Is that how you know Bliss? Are you guys starting a gang bangs of Saint View Instagram page or something?" I cringed as soon as I said it. I barely knew this woman. "Sorry. I normally try to let people get to know me so they realize I'm not an ass when I unleash the sarcasm."

Lacey chuckled. "It's fine. There's no Instagram page, but our common lifestyle is how I met Bliss. So it was a fair call. We should have an Insta. I'll put that on the agenda for the next gang bang. A little social media discussion between orgasms never goes astray."

I sniggered, enjoying that she didn't take herself too seriously. "I don't know how you guys do it. I can't even hold down one man, let alone multiple."

Lacey gave me a sly wink. "Have you ever tried though? There's nothing like having three men, solely focused on you..."

I nodded at the two guys squaring off in the ring. "Right now, I think they only have eyes for each other."

She laughed. "Hey, that's hot too."

Hell yeah, it was. But I already knew there was no chance of that with these two. Fang was as straight as an arrow. Kian, though...Something had happened between him and Vaughn. I was sure of it. I was dying to know what.

Our laughter, or at least mine, died when Kian's first punch connected squarely with Fang's jaw.

That was all it took. One punch for all out chaos to reign.

Fang retaliated with a quick follow-up, slamming one fist across Kian's face, the next to his midsection.

I gasped at the force of the heavy blows, each one

thumping loud enough for me to hear over the shouts and cheers of the crowd.

They were all living for it.

While I was sick to my stomach, nausea clutching at me, wringing my stomach.

They were doing this for me. This was so stupid. I was not worth the pain they were inflicting.

Fists flew. Blood sprayed. Heavy breaths were forced through split lips as the two went at each other.

Kian was all form and grace, his movement beautiful in a deadly sort of way. Someone had trained him and trained him well.

Fang was the opposite. A street fighter through and through, but no less dangerous.

Kian's next punch sent Fang to the ground, his back sliding through the gravel.

"Fuck, that's gonna hurt tomorrow." Colt winced.

But it was hurting me now. Kian followed up with a punishing round of blows, while tears welled in the backs of my eyes for the man on the ground. I'd seen many a fight, working at Psychos. But nothing like this. Nothing like seeing Fang down on the ground, being savagely attacked and doing nothing to stop it. I wouldn't have thought it possible if I wasn't seeing it with my own eyes.

He was better than this. Maybe not as good as Kian, but something was very wrong here.

"He needs to concede," Colt murmured. "Kian has him."

Everyone could see it. A hush fell over the crowd as Kian kept going, pummeling Fang's face and torso, each blow landing like a sledgehammer against cement.

Fang had stopped fighting back.

He'd stopped even trying to defend himself.

His gaze slid to mine and caught, and in his eyes, I saw every ounce of remorse.

He knew. I could see it in his eyes, in the depth of agony there that had nothing to do with the pain Kian was inflicting on him right now. He knew the attack had happened that night after he'd walked out of the bar and left me alone. He knew, and he was blaming himself, letting Kian punish him for my poor choices.

"Stop," I croaked out. "Make them stop. He's going to kill him."

Lacey glanced over at me; worried expression etched into her pretty features. "He has to tap out. Kian will just keep going if he doesn't."

Fang would never tap out. Never. I knew it instinctively. He'd rather die.

Especially if he was punishing himself.

I let go of Lacey's hand and rushed into the ring.

"Rebel!" she yelped. "You can't, you'll get hurt!"

I ignored her, lunging for the two men grappling on the ground. "Stop!"

I think everyone, including me, was shocked when Kian froze, fist midair, ready to connect.

"Enough," I choked out. "You've got the job. Stop."

The crowd booed, clearly there for the bloodshed.

I dropped to my knees and traced light fingertips all over Fang's face. "Are you okay?"

"I'm fine," Fang said through gritted teeth. "He was going easy on me."

If that was Kian going easy on someone then I could barely think about what it would look like if he went all out. But since he was being such a tough guy, I let my anger roar and overtake the worry. I drew my arm back, fingers clenched into fists, and let it fly at Fang's face.

I might have been little, but I still knew how to throw a punch. It connected solidly, the impact jolting through my arm painfully, but I ignored that, no stranger to pain. "Then that's for trying to get yourself killed!"

I used his solid chest to push myself up and stormed away, ignoring Kian and Lacey calling my name and the crowd hooting and hollering at me, laughing and jeering. I shoved my way through the crowd, shrugging off all the pats on the back, and "Good one, girl!"

I didn't want those. I wasn't proud of punching Fang.

But fuck, he made me mad.

The shouts of the crowd grew dimmer as I stormed into the night, weaving through the parked cars, the lights of the fight dropping away the farther I ran.

Fang's bike was parked on the outer edge, as far away from the action as you could get and shrouded in near complete darkness.

"Rebel."

I froze at his voice behind me. I'd known he'd follow, but I'd hoped that by getting a head start I'd be able to lose him in the crowd. I should have known that wouldn't be possible. He always came after me. Protected me. Once, when I'd broken a club rule, he'd refused to let anyone else punish me. My punishment had come from his hands, and in the form of a public spanking that I'd thoroughly enjoyed and followed with a delayed orgasm.

The only lesson I'd learned was to break more rules.

But this was different. He was punishing himself over something I'd done, and that made me feel like shit. The feeling had nowhere to go, except out. I lashed out, kicking at his bike, sending it toppling to the ground.

I blinked at the bike on its side, shocked at what I'd done.

I turned big eyes on him, suddenly terrified I'd pushed him too far. Bikes were everything to the guys in his club. A sacred item. They took care of them like they were babies.

I'd just sent Fang's, with its pretty, shiny paintwork, into the gravel.

"I'm sorry," I yelped, backing up. "I didn't mean to take that out on you. It's not even about you. It's about…"

He loomed over me, strong strides swallowing up the distance between us in an instant. With his face mostly in shadow, he was terrifying. A giant beast of a man, power in every muscle, a predator stalking its tiny, mouthy prey.

My back hit a brick wall.

Nowhere else to run.

"I'm sorry," I tried again.

The distance between us disappeared, eaten up by his enormous presence. He crowded me in, face bloodied and battered. Chest heaving either from the fight or from chasing me, I had no idea. His ice-blue eyes pinned me to the wall as much as his body did.

No escape.

Nothing to do but pay for my crime.

Fang dropped to his knees and circled his arms around the backs of my thighs. His face pressed into my belly as he hugged me tight. "I'm sorry," he murmured. "I'm so fucking sorry, Pix."

I froze, staring down at the massive man on his knees for me, begging my forgiveness.

"It was that guy at the bar that night, wasn't it? The night I left you there..."

A lump rose in my throat swiftly. "Caleb. I went home with him. He had friends waiting."

An unearthly sound ripped from his body. Something between a howl of pain and a roar of outrage.

It made one thing clear.

He was in agony. Not from the injuries Kian had inflicted on him. But from the blame he'd placed squarely on his own shoulders.

"It's my fault. Everything that happened that night could have been prevented if I'd just stayed." His guilt shuddered through his body as he held on to me like I was his life raft, the only thing keeping him from crumpling.

A tear slipped down my cheek, and I clutched the back of his head, holding him to me. "It's not your fault." The tie keeping his long hair back had come loose during the fight, and now I stroked my fingers through the sweat-soaked lengths, trying to comfort him.

"Please forgive me," he whispered, pressing his lips to my belly. "I'm so fucking sorry. I let you down."

I shook my head into the darkness, even though he wouldn't see it. "I let myself down."

His lips found the tiny slip of skin showing between my cropped shirt and jeans. I gasped at the contact, his lips hot against my belly. He trailed kisses across every inch of the gap, his hands sliding up from the backs of my thighs, over my ass, to my lower back, holding me in place.

I dropped my head back against the wall, reveling in

the familiar feel of him, as desperate to take the guilt from him as he was to take it from me.

His kisses turned open-mouthed, tonguing at the flat planes of my stomach and belly button.

He found the button on my fly and raised his head, blue eyes seeking my permission. "Let me make it up to you."

The slaps and kicks and cheers from the continuing fights filtered back, but there was no one nearby. The darkness would shroud us from any eyes that happened to look back this way.

I wasn't sure I would ever have sex again, but that wasn't what Fang was offering.

Caleb and his friends had certainly not touched me like this. So gently and sweetly. They hadn't asked permission the way he was, down on his knees, begging to let him make it up to me in the only way he knew how.

Giving me all the power, even though he was twice my size.

I nodded, a trickle of fear, replaced by a breath of desire.

He was beautiful like this, with the darkness softening his scars and harsh lines. But then he'd always been beautiful to me.

He silently undid the button, and the zipper below, pressing kisses there as he went.

One sharp tug on the legs of my pants had them down around my knees, exposing the plain black panties I'd put on that morning.

He breathed deeply, his lips on the fabric covering my mound, then nuzzled in between my thighs, licking the insides.

"I've missed this," he murmured. "The taste of your skin. The scent of your arousal." He twisted my panties to one side and groaned. "The sight of your slit."

He drove his tongue between the lips of my pussy, rasping over my clit, making me jump at the sudden rush of sensation.

I dropped my head back against the brick wall. It was hard and rough behind me, at complete odds with how soft and gentle the man between my legs was. He explored every inch of my most intimate areas, prodding his tongue against every sensitive place, checking my reaction to each.

"I need you to tell me if you're hurt, Pix. If you're hurt here. I don't want to make it worse. Only better."

I shook my head. "I was. But not anymore. All that's left behind now are the injuries in my head."

He licked my pussy slowly, luxuriously, like he had all the time in the world and every intention of using every second. "I'm going to kill him, Pix."

I grabbed a handful of his hair and yanked it back sharply. "No. You aren't. Promise me you won't."

His tongue darted out to touch my clit. Though it felt amazing, and would have been easy to let him get back to the task at hand, I dug my fingers into his hair harder, keeping him back. "Promise me. I have to do it, Fang. It has to be me."

He looked like he wanted to argue, but something in my expression must have stopped him. A little of his fight disappeared. "I need to be there, then. When it happens. I can't have you going up against him alone. I'll lose it."

I could give him that. I wasn't too proud to admit

Caleb scared me. I wanted revenge, but I could let people have my back. That was just smart.

I might not have finished high school, but no one had ever accused me of being stupid.

"Okay."

My acceptance chased away a couple of the demons lurking in his eyes. He put his head back down to finish the job he'd started.

"Oh," I whispered, accepting his open mouth, fitted around my clit while he sucked gently. "I'd forgotten how amazing you are at this."

He huffed out a displeased noise. "Then let me do it more. I'll do it every day if you let me. I think you know that."

I did. When he reminded me so perfectly of exactly how good he was with his tongue, it made me question my reasons for keeping him at bay.

"I want you on the back of my bike, Pix," he murmured between licks. "I want it so fucking bad it hurts."

I squeezed my eyes shut.

It was as good as a marriage proposal from a guy like him. Putting a woman on the back of your bike was a sacred act to him and his club, and we both knew it.

This was why I'd kept him at arm's length.

'Cause Fang was the man you fell in love with, when you were whole and healed and ready to settle down.

If I tried to keep him before I was there, I'd ruin him.

I'd destroy everything good between us and make him miserable.

He was ready, his inner demons all laid to rest.

But I was so bitterly broken.

We didn't fit.

"Stop talking," I whispered, knowing I couldn't say what he wanted me to say. "Stop talking and make me come. I don't want to think anymore."

I knew it wasn't what he wanted, but it was a consolation prize at the very least. He stared up at me and put two fingers inside his mouth, coating them before putting them to my entrance.

"Go slow," I begged him. "Please."

It was fear talking, but I needn't have worried. Fang was the most considerate man I'd ever had in my bed. He was safe and familiar. He watched and waited on my every cue, studying my body like he was preparing to be quizzed later. If I so much as thought about flinching in discomfort, he was all over it, switching up his tactics, changing his routine until I was moaning with desire and begging him to keep going.

He knew me. He knew what I liked.

He rimmed my entrance, playing with the arousal there while he flattened his tongue on my clit, taking long licks. He waited until I was fully relaxed, then nudged his fingers inside, stretching me perfectly. They instantly curved to stroke my G-spot in just the way I liked.

My mind numbed out. Pleasure took over.

Unconsciously, I rocked my hips toward him, and he matched my pace, fucking me with his fingers and his tongue. He pulled from my slick heat to drive his tongue up into me, before switching back to his fingers and repeating. His warm breath tickled across my skin, and his beard rasped on my inner thighs.

All the while, those eyes watched my face, making sure I enjoyed every moment, my pleasure his too.

An orgasm built deep within me, encouraged by every move he made. He reached up, hand beneath my T-shirt to cup my breast, thumb and forefinger clamping onto my nipple.

"Oh!" I moaned.

It was exactly what I needed. I grabbed at my other boob as my rocking became thrusts against his face, taking him deeper inside me. The orgasm took hold and demanded my attention.

"I'm going to come," I moaned.

"I know, Pix. I always fucking know."

I clutched the back of his head, keeping his mouth to me while his fingers pounded up inside me. He added a third, the stretch so sweetly perfect I fell right over the edge. "Oh!"

I came on his tongue with a rush of pleasure that blinded me. Nothing else existed except for him and me and the whirl of pleasure he'd created. I slumped against the wall, legs trembling with the force of the orgasm and unwilling to hold my weight.

I knew he'd have me.

He did.

He stood, wrapping his arms around me to bury his face in my neck. A hug while the aftereffects of the orgasm rattled through me, my body limp as a wet noodle.

"I want more, Pix. Please. Let me show you I deserve it."

I was too scared to ask him what he meant by that. More orgasms? Good. More of anything else, I wasn't sure I had that to give.

Someone cleared their throat from the a few feet

away. "Sorry to interrupt, but I'm leaving. Just wanted to see if you needed a ride home, Rebel?"

Kian stood with his eyes averted to one side, giving us the privacy we clearly did not deserve since we hadn't even noticed that the fights had ended and people were making their way back to their cars. Fang stood between us, blocking me from view long enough that I could get my pants up.

He looked down at me questioningly, and I knew I hadn't answered his question.

But I wasn't going to. Not when I didn't know the answer. Not when Kian was standing right there waiting to drive me home.

For now, orgasms would have to be enough.

## 16

### REBEL

*F*ang refused to let me ride home with Kian, insisting he hadn't just licked my pussy 'til I'd come just to let me drive home with some random guy I'd only known a day. I let him put me on the back of his bike, just for tonight, because right now, I did have a case of the warm and fuzzies when it came to him.

He'd taken a full-on beating for me. It had been completely unnecessary, but the Saint View thug in me found it kinda romantic. I didn't care for flowers and chocolates. Clearly, all you needed to turn my head was blood and violence.

I was sure that said something about my mental state, but I couldn't afford a therapist anyway.

By the time we got back to my flashy new house in Providence though, Fang had me worried. He'd taken the last two corners unusually slowly, and by the time we stopped in front of the house, and I got off to say goodbye to him, his eyes were unfocused.

I peered at him in the darkness, his face barely lit by the automatic porch light. "Get off."

He blinked, albeit slower than usual. "What?"

"Get off. I can't believe I just let you drive me home. Do you have a concussion?"

He shook his head. "No." But there was a wince in his voice.

"Can you shake your head like that again?"

"I'd really rather not."

"Yeah, that's what I thought. Off. You're not going back to the clubhouse. I'm not gonna be the one responsible for you riding your bike off the bluff road because you got too dizzy to see."

"I'll be fine."

"I've got a big-ass bed in there, just waiting to snuggle in." I knew it was the one thing that would get him to stay.

He looked up. "You want to snuggle? You, Rebel Pixie Kemp?"

I shoved my hands on my hips. "That's not my middle name, you know. And I snuggle!"

He chuckled on a laugh. "About as much as snakes do. But hold your tits, I'm coming. Just give me a minute for the world to stop spinning."

Kian pulled up in the driveway a moment later and wandered over. "What's going on?"

"Nothing," Fang snapped.

I rolled my eyes. "Quit being a dog pissing on your territory. Kian isn't trying to hump my leg; he's allowed to ask what's going on when we're blocking the doorway to his house." I turned to Kian. "I think he's got a concussion."

Kian peered at him and held up one finger. "Can you follow this?" He moved his finger to the left an inch.

Fang glared at him, making no effort to perform the simple task. "Can you follow this?" He flipped him the bird and waved it around in his face.

Kian laughed, but I huffed out a sigh of impatience.

"Just do it, Fang."

Fang nodded at Kian. "Fine. Do it again."

Kian held his finger up, moving it side to side.

"What's the prognosis, Doc?" Fang scrubbed a hand wearily over his face. "Is my brain any more fucked up than its usual messy state?"

Kian shrugged. "Fuck if I'd know. I don't even know what I'm doing, but it's what my coaches used to do to me. You can follow my finger, so I'm assuming if your brain is fucked up, it's probably just your usual state of being."

"I want him to stay here tonight. So I can keep an eye on him."

Kian nodded. "Probably a good idea. No sex though."

I frowned. "Did your coaches tell you that too?"

"No, but I'm right next door and I don't want to hear, 'Oh Fang! You're so big! Fuck me, Daddy!' all night."

Fang's mouth flickered in amusement, and I widened my eyes at him more than Kian's overly girly and way-off-base impersonation of me. It was unusual for Fang to be anything other than a monosyllabic grump.

But I couldn't let the comment pass without addressing it. I leaned on the wall, crossing my arms beneath my tits, and grinned at Kian. "Why? Jealous?"

Kian leaned in, breath misting across my cheek when he dropped his voice low enough only for me to hear.

"Nah, little demon. 'Cause when I fuck you, I'll have you panting so hard you can't even utter a sound."

My eyes widened. He might as well have fucked me right then and there, 'cause despite my normal quick wit, I was at a complete loss for words. Until that moment, I hadn't even been sure he wasn't gay.

But that doubt had been laid to bed and tucked in with a kiss of promise I wouldn't be able to stop thinking about for a while.

Kian moved on though, like he'd just asked me to pick up toilet paper at the store. He held an arm out to Fang. "Come on, big guy. Let's get you upstairs. Can't have you sleeping out here, and if you go down with her trying to help you, you're gonna crush her."

I was sure it was only the implication he might hurt me that had Fang agreeing to Kian's help. I trailed after them, more worried with every step because Fang really was wobbly on his feet. Kian got him into my bed, and he was asleep almost instantly.

Kian and I stood side by side, watching him.

"Seriously, should I be worried? What if he has a brain bleed? I don't think you're supposed to go to sleep when you have a concussion."

But Kian shook his head. "Nah. I didn't smack him in the head too much. If anything, I'd be more worried about broken ribs. Your boy doesn't protect himself real well. I swear, I wouldn't have gone up against him if I'd known he wasn't a fighter."

I sighed. "He is. He let you win."

Kian frowned. "Why?"

"Because he's too damn sweet for his own good."

"You say that like it's a bad thing."

"It is. It's how you get your heart broken."

Kian patted me on the back, like maybe he understood a little about what that felt like. "I'm going to bed. If he's too out to take care of any needs you might have... that promise I made you downstairs is always available. Night or day. On tap...twenty-four seven."

I shoved him, and he laughed.

"Night, little demon. I'm real glad you're here. It's been too fucking quiet around this place."

I watched him walk away, through the bathroom that connected our bedrooms. "Me too," I whispered to the quiet room. "Me too."

## 17

# VAUGHN

*T*he morgue had left a message on my phone, politely requesting I come down and collect my father's belongings that had been on his person when he'd died.

I hadn't felt up to it for a few days, preferring to drink until I forgot about it, but each day when I woke up hungover, it weighed heavily on my mind. I couldn't keep drinking, or it would become a serious problem. So the next morning, I left before I could get drunk and drove to a cold-looking building in the industrial part of Saint View. Glancing around warily at the graffiti on the walls of the run-down buildings, I locked my father's car, hoping it would still be there when I returned.

The entire place gave me the heebie-jeebies, just knowing inside lay dozens and dozens of dead bodies, all chilling in a freezer.

What a fucking job.

The woman who greeted me when I opened the door though was anything but gloomy. Her dress was bright yellow, her arms covered by a pink cardigan, and she had her hair braided into two strands that hung over her shoulders pigtail-style, held in place with rainbow hair ties. "Good morning!" she announced so brightly I jumped at the sudden, unexpected tone. "What can we do for you today?"

"I need to pick up my father's belongings. Someone called me."

"Last name?"

"Weston. Vaughn...I mean, I'm Vaughn. He's Bart. The dead person in question is Bart. I'm not dead. Clearly. Shit."

She smiled tolerantly, like she put up with rambling idiots like myself on the regular and tapped her lime-green-painted fingernails across the keyboard. "Right! Here you are. ID 7876." She repeated the numbers beneath her breath as she turned to a row of large cabinets behind her and rummaged through one of them. "Here you go, honey. There's a note that the clothes he was brought in wearing were destroyed due to the possibility of contamination with a poisonous substance. But the items in his pockets and his jewelry were checked over by the police then deemed unrequired for their investigations. So, they're all yours, if you want them." She pushed across a small plastic bag with only a couple of things inside. His wallet and phone. A gold wedding band and a folded piece of paper.

My hand shook as I took them from her, and she gave me a sympathetic smile.

"I really am very sorry for your loss."

"Thank you."

She paused for a moment. "Would you like to see the body?"

I glanced up at her, sure my face was white. I could practically feel the blood draining from it. "What?"

"Some people find it comforting. Especially if the death was quick. It's maybe a chance to say anything you didn't get to say while they were living."

I hesitated. There were things I wanted to say. Things I'd always thought I'd have more time for. "Is he...like, blue or something?"

She put a hand on my arm reassuringly. "It's not as scary as you might think. Most people tell me they're glad they did it, even if they didn't want to at first. But it's totally up to you."

I wasn't sure I could live with any more regrets. I already had so many. I nodded.

She came out from behind the desk and led the way to a door at the far end of the room. She punched in a code, and I held the door open for her, then followed behind. "It's just down here." She muttered the ID number again, then found a matching number on the wall of silver drawers.

I tried really hard not to think about how many bodies were behind them.

She put her hand on the handle, pausing to look over at me. "Are you ready?"

No.

"Yes."

She flicked off a lock and pulled the drawer out.

My father's dead body lay on top of it. His skin was pale and did have a blueish tinge, but if I ignored that, I could perhaps pretend he was just sleeping. It was either that or run out of the place screaming.

"Not so bad, huh?" the woman asked.

I couldn't speak, but she seemed to understand.

"I'll give you some time. Just come on out when you're finished. You don't need to do anything. I'll tidy up when you're done. There's a chair here if you'd like to use it."

It was maybe more a matter of need than want. I wasn't sure my legs would support me for very long. I sank down into it gratefully. It was better from this vantage point to. From sitting height, I only saw his profile.

I didn't know what to do. Was I supposed to talk? The room was so deathly silent, I couldn't stand not filling it. "Well. That was a wedding day no one will forget in a hurry, huh?"

I rubbed my face with my hands. This sucked. This sucked so bad. I didn't know what to do. I held up the bag of his belongings. "Picked up your things. Wallet, keys, phone, ring. Don't know what this bit of paper is…"

It was easier to reach inside the bag and take the paper out than it was to keep staring at my father's too-pale skin. I unfolded it slowly and skimmed over the first few lines of text.

*Dear Miranda.*

*I stand here before you on our wedding day, the happiest I've ever been in my fifty-two years. I can wholeheartedly say my life changed the day you came into it. With your big voice, big ideas, and even bigger heart. I'm sure I fell in love with you at first sight...*

I squinted at my father's body. "This isn't what you read at the ceremony." He and Miranda had both recited standard vows, repeating after the judge.

I looked down at the beautiful words and wondered why. Had he chickened out? He shouldn't have. It was a shame Miranda never heard these.

I glanced around the room, wondering if her body was in here. I didn't know what I believed about souls or the afterlife, but my father's words deserved to be read aloud, so I continued.

*"I promise today, as I stand before you with complete and wholehearted devotion and admiration, that all our worst days are behind us. Because even though there will be hard times to come, we'll fight them side by side, my hand in yours, the two of us together.*

*I have never known love like the kind you have shown me. I promise to return it every day. I vow today to love and honor you. To take care of not only you, but your daughter, Rebel. I vow to be the man who protects you both, after so many others have failed. That will never be me, Miranda. You and your daughter are safe with me.*

I put the paper down. "You really loved her, huh, old man? Maybe it's for the best you went together."

I could only imagine losing a love like the one my father had found would be crippling. At least he'd been spared that pain.

"I really hope there's some sort of afterlife, Dad. I hope you get to spend forever with her." I bowed my head, staring down at my lap.

An uncomfortable feeling settled over me. My dad had vowed to protect both Miranda and Rebel. I didn't know what he was protecting them from, but it made a lot more sense now as to why his estate had been split between the two of us.

I'd failed my father in so many ways over the course of my life. Acting out at school. Taking for granted the wealth and privilege his hard work had given me. Never coming back to visit once I'd finished college. I'd been so wrapped up in me. In the things that had pushed me out of this town and made me never want to return. I'd forgotten the one man who'd always supported me.

I swallowed thickly. "I'm so sorry. I wish I could change it."

But there was no going back now. Only going forward.

I'd accused Rebel of some awful things. I'd let my grief get the better of me, and it had come out in anger. I hated I'd done that. She was grieving too. She didn't deserve the things I'd said when alcohol and hurt had gotten the better of me.

I choked down the lump in my throat and stared at the vows again. Rebel's name was the only word that stayed clear, the rest of them blurring as I blinked back the moisture welling in my eyes.

"I'll take over where you left off," I promised him. "I'll protect her. Make sure she's taken care of. If it was important to you, then it's important to me too."

Some of the heaviness lifted off my heart. Maybe it was just the relief at admitting I'd done something wrong and was going to try to fix it. I had to sort out Brooke's mess, and I needed money to do that. Fast. But Rebel wouldn't go without.

"I don't know how you became the man you are. I don't think I can even be half as good." I stood, gathering up my father's things and took one last look down at him. "But I'll try."

## 18

## REBEL

*I* woke in the morning, wrapped in blankets like a warm and toasty burrito, but the other side of the bed was cold to the touch. Instantly, panic filled me, fearing Fang had snuck out and driven himself home, or worse, gone woozily stumbling through the house with all its staircases, and was currently lying at the bottom of one with a broken neck.

But when I made it out onto the second-floor landing and peered over the railing, there was no dead body. Sounds did float up the stairs though, frypans banging and clashing together, and oddly, laughter.

I jogged down the stairs in nothing but the T-shirt I liked to sleep in, the hem brushing my upper thighs. In the doorway to the kitchen, I leaned on the doorframe, smiling at the sight before me. "Wouldn't have picked you for an apron sorta guy, Kian."

Both he and Fang, who was sitting at the kitchen bench chopping vegetables, lifted their heads.

Kian groaned, his gaze sweeping my body. "Don't

wear that in front of me! I don't need big boy over there starting round two because I looked at his girl."

I glanced at Fang.

He was holding the knife a little too tightly.

I put my hand on his back as I slid onto the stool beside him. "Settle."

His hand instantly went to my thigh, clamping down on it, holding me in place. But he spoke to Kian. "I'm not starting anything with anyone she wants looking at her. Only those she doesn't. She can tell me if I need to kill you."

Kian chuckled. "Righto. Remember who won that fight last night."

"You know I let you."

I clapped my hands together. "Okay, okay. We're not getting into that again. You both have very big muscles and you're both headed for the MMA. Good for you. Moving on, I'm starving, and that smells great. What are we having?"

"Omelets."

"I'm drooling already."

Fang's thumb rubbed absently over my skin.

I liked it more than I should have and was a bit miffed when he moved his hand away to continue cutting up onions.

"So, Fang and I were talking before you came downstairs, and he tells me we're going after this Caleb guy and his friends who attacked you." Kian tapped an egg swiftly to the edge of a mixing bowl. The eggshell split down the middle, and he pried it apart, letting the insides drip down.

"We're?" I asked. "No, not we're. I am. Fang is backing me up."

Kian pouted. "Come on. Let me play too. I've watched a ton of *Law and Order* and I reckon I'd be an amazing detective. I guarantee I can find the name of Caleb's buddies in no time. Then it's showtime. Let the ass-kicking begin." He cracked his knuckles. "It'll be fun to watch you hurt them."

I shook my head. "An ass-kicking is too kind. It needs to be more than that. I want to..."

Kian leaned his elbows on the kitchen counter, completely enraptured with the topic. "Want to what? Finish that thought."

I'd let it trail off because I didn't know how it would be received. But if they were going to help with this, then they needed to know what they were in for. "I want to make it hurt. Torture them. String it out so they're scared, never knowing when it's coming."

"Jesus fuck, Roach. That's dark." Vaughn wandered into the room, already dressed, his dark hair slicked back. He grabbed an apple from the fruit bowl on the table and took a bite out of it. He glanced at Fang. "Who are you? Don't tell me you moved in here as well? Seriously, Roach, you can't just move in whoever you feel like. It's bad enough you've made yourself at home."

I glared at him. "He hasn't moved in. And don't be an asshole. The two of you already met outside the courthouse."

Vaughn narrowed his eyes. "You're the prick who punched me!"

Kian pressed down on the countertop to hoist himself up onto it. "Oh, really? That's interesting. Now everyone here has taken a swing at everyone else. What a fun little circle of violence that is."

I cocked my head to one side. "When did you and Vaughn have a fight? Not that I blame you, 'cause he's an ass. I hope you won."

Kian scoffed, "Of course. It was like taking candy from a baby."

Vaughn said nothing, just glared at Kian. If looks could kill...

I really wanted to know what had gone down between the two of them. But now wasn't the time. "Anyway, can we get back to my plan for torturing Caleb Black and his asshole friends?"

Vaughn glanced at me sharply. "Caleb Black? Who runs Black Industries? What do you want with him?"

There was going to be no secrets kept from men I shared a house with. But I still didn't want to tell Vaughn. Not after the way he'd done me dirty, trying to hustle me out of what had been left to me. Especially when I needed it a whole lot more than the trust fund baby did.

Kian tapped his spatula on the edge of the pan. "You should tell him. He knows people the three of us hood rats don't. He can probably get you the names, addresses, and Social Security numbers of the other two guys in a heartbeat."

I ground my teeth, knowing Kian was right. I didn't have those connections to the business world. Vaughn did.

But I was stubborn. "I can do it myself."

Vaughn rolled his eyes. "Fine. Whatever. Have your little powwow down here. I'll leave the three of you to it."

"He hurt her," Kian called out.

Vaughn stopped in the doorway. "What?"

"Kian! Shut up!" I hissed.

"Be mad if you want, Little Demon. I want you to get your revenge more than I care about you getting shitty with me."

He had a point, but it only pissed me off further. I grabbed an apple from the basket and hurled it at his head.

He caught it easily, giving me a wink. "Gotta be quicker than that. Fighter's reflexes."

Irritating man.

But my gaze drew back to Vaughn.

He was a thundercloud in the doorway. "Hurt you how?"

I just stared back at him.

"Tell me, Roach, because I'm imagining all sorts of really bad shit. Tell me I'm exaggerating."

I couldn't. I was sure his imagination probably didn't even scratch the surface of what Caleb had done to me.

"He...raped you?"

The nod I gave was tiny, but it was all he needed.

Vaughn's fist slammed back against the drywall, making the entire wall shake. "I'm in."

I blinked. "In for what?"

"Whatever this is. Whatever we're doing, I'm in."

I raised an eyebrow. "You just said I was dark."

"When it comes to Caleb Black, you could never be dark enough."

A chill raced down my spine. "What do you know about him?"

He shook his head. "Nothing I like. You said he had

two friends with him? Can you give me a description? Anything identifying about them?"

Kian chuckled. "We watched *Law and Order* together."

Vaughn glared at him. "Shut up, Kian. This is serious."

It was, but it was also overwhelming. I'd tried really hard not to think about that night ever since it had happened, and now, I was having to dredge up all those memories and relive them like they were happening right then and there. "One was shorter than him, one was taller. The shorter one had a business suit on when he arrived. Closely cropped hair on the sides, a little longer on top. He was chubby, and he had a lion—"

"Tattoo on his arm?"

I blinked. "Yes."

"The other one had acne scars? Like not just a couple. A lot?"

I nodded.

"How do you know that?" Fang asked quietly.

Vaughn had pity in his eyes. "I went to college with them. But I haven't spoken to any of them since I moved away."

Heat flushed through me. "You were friends with them though?"

Vaughn went quiet.

I shook my head, anger spiking. "How could you? Did you know what they like to do in their spare time?"

"What? No! Of course not." He reached out to me.

I flinched away.

In an instant, Kian and Fang were both between us, putting distance between me and my stepbrother, who'd just happily spent his formative years hanging out with a couple of gang rapists.

I suddenly wasn't hungry anymore.

"Rebel..."

"First time you haven't called me Roach." I got off the stool stiffly. "Thanks for making breakfast, Kian. I'm not hungry anymore though."

He tossed the spatula into the sink. "Me neither."

Fang put his arm around my shoulders. "Let's go for a drive."

Anywhere was better than here. I knew it wasn't Vaughn's fault and I actually believed him when he said he didn't know what they were doing. Hell, for all I knew, they weren't even doing it back then. I really hoped that was the truth, but my gut told me Caleb Black was as dark as his name. He'd hurt Bliss and Vincent. He'd hurt me. It wasn't much of a leap to assume we weren't the only ones.

It only confirmed for me yet again that it had to end here. With me. No matter what it took. "A drive sounds nice."

Fang escorted me around Vaughn, and I avoided looking him in the eye. I ran upstairs to change, then grabbed my purse from the entranceway. Outside in the crisp morning air, I rubbed my chilled arms briskly. "It's cold out here."

Fang pulled his jacket on. "Yeah, I got up early this morning and made a fire to keep the house warm. Wasn't expecting to be out here with you, but your jacket is beneath the seat."

I blinked at him. "I have a jacket?"

He shrugged. "After I drove you home the other day, I

realized you didn't have one suitable for being on my bike. So I bought you one..."

He handed over the leather jacket, still with the tags on it.

I caught sight of the price tag and did a double take. "You can't afford this."

He pushed it toward me again. "You need it. Queenie helped me pick it out. She swore you'd like it, but if you don't, I'll take it back. Get you something else..."

I slipped my arms into the sleeves and smiled up at him. "It's perfect. I've never owned a single article of clothing that cost this much."

He reached behind me, to the tag at the back of my neck, and snapped it off. "Now you do."

He moved back, his face mere inches from mine. His gaze darted to my lips.

I sucked in a breath.

The thing about Fang and I was, we hooked up. We kissed in the heat of the moment, tongues tangling as foreplay, winding us both up for the main event.

We'd never kissed without it leading somewhere else.

Nerves suddenly flooded me, and it was like I was thirteen all over again, never been kissed, and standing in front of a boy, wondering if it was going to happen.

He seemed just as indecisive.

The moment passed.

He cleared his throat and straightened. "Come on, let's take your new jacket for a test drive."

I nodded, getting on the bike behind him and wrapping my arms around his waist. He tried to start the engine but jerked his hand away from the accelerator like it had burned him. He swore low beneath his breath to cover the sound of pain he'd let slip.

I peered around his broad back. "What happened?"

"Nothing. I'm fine."

I slid farther around, and for the first time that morning, properly looked at his hands.

Two fingers on his right hand were swollen to twice their normal size. Which was alarming because his hands were huge to begin with.

I slapped his arm. "That's broken."

He shrugged. "Probably."

"You need an X-ray."

"Nothing getting drunk won't fix."

"You aren't getting drunk at ten in the morning." I slid off the bike and took my keys from my purse. "Come on. I'm taking you to the hospital. They can check your head while we're at it."

"We were going for a drive."

"Yeah, well, we still are. Just now it's to the ER." I folded my arms across my chest when he didn't budge off his bike. "Move it, Fang!"

He raised an eyebrow. "Anyone ever tell you you're bossy for someone so short?"

"Only every other day. Can we go now?"

He grudgingly got off his bike and walked to the driver's side of my car. "Don't know what it is about you that makes me want to do whatever you tell me to."

"It's my charming personality," I sassed him. "Now scoot to the passenger side. Nobody drives my car but me."

He squeezed the handle. "Wasn't planning on driving. Was just opening the door for you."

I bit my lip. "Oh. That's...nice. Nobody ever does that anymore."

"Yeah, well, I do."

I slid behind the steering wheel, and he closed the door before walking over to the passenger side. He crouched to adjust the seat, pushing it all the way back to accommodate his long legs.

It was still comical to watch him try to fit his six-five body into a hatchback made for short asses like me. He had to twist awkwardly but he did manage to get himself inside.

"I've had Matchbox cars bigger than this thing," he muttered.

I sniggered the whole way to the hospital, laughing every time I looked over at him because he truly was like a pretzel and clearly uncomfortable.

After I parked the car, he undid his seat belt. "Wait there. I'll get the door."

But he groaned in pain as he tried to get out. It was more than him just being shoved in like a sardine. He'd taken a beating last night, and it was clearly bothering him more than he was letting on.

I got out and jogged around to his side of the car, opening the door for him.

He scowled at me. "That's my job."

"Yeah, well, I don't think we'll ever be going anywhere in this car again, so at least now we're even."

"I'll buy you a bigger one."

"With the millions in your piggy bank?"

"I play lotto."

I sniggered. "My mom always used to say that, too..."

Fang looked down at me. "You miss her?"

I shrugged. "It's stupid. It's not like we lived in each other's pockets. I could go weeks or even months without seeing her in person. And yet now, because I can't..."

"You want to."

I nodded. "I know that's dumb. I just wish I'd loved her harder when she was here. When I was younger, I'd prepared myself to bury her young. She was reckless, you know? And she had big feelings. She fell hard and fast for every guy she met, and so many of them were scumbags. For the entire six months she dated Linden the Loser, I thought I was going to come home from school and find her head crushed in on the kitchen floor. The man had a vicious temper, and he took it out on her all the time. It got so bad that I was almost surprised when it didn't happen."

The hospital doors opened for us, and Fang led the way to the nurses' check-in point.

"I hate men like that," he said softly as we joined the line. "Men who make a woman feel small to make themselves feel big."

I had my own Linden the Loser, I realized with a start. His name was Caleb the Cunt. I clenched my fingers.

Fang took my hand, slowly massaging it, pressing warmth into my cold fingers, until I relaxed.

"He can't hurt you anymore. That's never going to happen again."

I nodded. I knew. Not because Fang was going to protect me. As much as he might try, he couldn't protect me every minute of the day.

But I would protect myself. I would talk to Kian about it tonight. Get a training schedule set up. I was a decent fighter to begin with, but I was like Fang. No style. All scrappy fury. It hadn't been enough against Caleb.

The nurse behind the plexiglass raised her head when we reached the top of the line and did a double take at Fang. "Oh my. I mean, can I help you?"

I almost laughed. It was the way so many women in the bar and at the clubhouse reacted to Fang. I wasn't sure why I never had. Maybe because I'd seen plenty of truly scary men over the course of my life. I knew a legitimately bad man couldn't be figured out because of what he looked like on the outside. Caleb was a truly bad man, and he looked anything but when he was dressed neatly in a suit and driving around his hundred-thousand-dollar car.

Fang seemed scary, but there was a gentleness about him that most men didn't have. I'd seen it from the minute he'd walked into the bar on my very first shift there.

Fang held up his mangled fingers. "My girl says I need an X-ray."

The nurse glanced at me with huge eyes. "You're his girl?"

I could tell what she was thinking. How did we even fit together?

Wouldn't she like to know.

Maybe it was that, her staring at me with such incredulity, that had me saying, "Yeah. I'm his girl. I think he has a few broken fingers. Possibly a concussion too, though he seems a bit better this morning."

"Take a seat, and we'll be with you when we can."

Fang put his good arm around my neck and guided me over to a seat. He didn't move away once we were sitting, and I found myself cuddling into his side, warm and fuzzy feelings tingling their way through all the places we touched. I was surprised at how much I liked hearing him declare me his. He dropped a kiss on my head absently, and it lit up a part of me I hadn't known would react like that.

*Shit*. I had the sudden realization this man could turn me into a snuggler if he kept up this behavior.

The thought was a little scary. I'd never known much affection. I'd never really had a proper relationship, and I'd never known my father. My mom had loved me, but she hadn't been much of a hugger. It was a dangerous loss of control to let someone touch me freely.

But one that maybe I was willing to take with Fang, because of every man I'd ever met, he was the one I trusted most.

We'd see. We weren't there yet. But sitting with him like this, just enjoying the feel of him beside me, made me want to try.

"Lucy Tinsdale?"

I jerked my head at the voice of a doctor calling his next patient. He searched the waiting room with a roaming gaze, one that finished on me.

Horror froze me to the spot.

Recognition dawned in his eyes, but he quickly moved on, ushering Lucy through security doors for her assessment.

I couldn't move. It took every ounce of my being not to scream in terror when his gaze returned, before the door slammed shut behind him, the locks automatically engaging.

Like some spell had broken, I slumped forward,

elbows to my knees, sucking in deep breaths. For the minute he'd been there in the waiting room, just feet away from me, I hadn't been able to breathe.

Fang's warm hand came to the center of my back. "Pix, you okay? What just happened?"

I couldn't talk. Fear had wrapped itself around my throat and was squeezing the life out of me.

Fang became frantic, twisting in his seat, trying to get a look at my face. "Tell me what to do. Do I call a nurse?"

I shook my head frantically and forced myself to sit up straight. The room spun, but I managed it.

He dropped his hand to my thigh, squeezing reassuringly, and I focused on that. On him. On the fact that with him beside me, that fucking asshole would never get to lay a finger on me.

Not again.

"Please talk to me," he whispered. "I don't know what's happening, but you're fucking scaring me, Pix."

"I'm sorry," I whispered. "I didn't mean to."

"Don't apologize. You have nothing to be sorry for. One minute you were fine. Better than fine, actually. The next you're frozen and hyperventilating."

"That doctor…"

His eyebrows furrowed, and then he glanced at the closed door. "What about him?"

"Lion tattoo…" It was all I could get out before panic took over my system again.

But it was all I needed to say.

Understanding lit up Fang's blue eyes.

In a second, he was on his feet, storming to the door the doctor had disappeared through. His fist slammed against it. "Open this!"

My mouth dropped open.

The entire waiting room full of people swiveled to stare at him, me included.

He clearly didn't care. He rammed his fist against the door again. "Open this fucking door, or I swear I'm going to kick it down."

"Sir," the nurse behind the safety glass, which was clearly there for this exact reason, tried to calm him. "Please. We know the waits are long at the moment, but we'll be with you as soon as possible. Your hand is not considered an emergency, and there's other cases that take priority over yours."

It was the complete wrong thing to say to him, though I couldn't blame the nurse for trying.

"I don't fucking care about my hand! Do you know one of your doctors is a rapist?"

The woman shook her head in disbelief. "Sir, if you don't sit back down, I'll have to call security."

"Fuck security! Call the fucking cops to arrest him!"

The woman behind me tutted a little too loudly to her husband. "Drugs. They make you paranoid. Hopefully the police get here quickly."

Dread pooled in the bottom of my stomach. I didn't know exactly what Fang was involved in with his club. But I doubted much of it was legal. There was a high likelihood he had outstanding warrants. Even if he didn't, if the police arrested him here, I wouldn't put it past them to try to pin something else on him. They'd already proved themselves completely incompetent by suspecting me of murdering my mother. They'd take one look at the Slayers emblem on the back of his jacket and he'd be locked up.

I needed to get him out of here. I ran to his side, pulling down the arm he was using to bash on the door. "Stop. We need to go before they call the cops."

He gazed down at me, eyes wild. "Let them. I'm going to fucking kill him." Without waiting for me, he gave up on the emergency room security door, which had proved its worth by keeping him out, and stormed to a hallway that led who knew where in the hospital.

I had to run to keep up with him. "Fang. Stop."

He shook his head, slamming his way through the halls while nurses and orderlies jumped out of his way. "There's gotta be a back way into emergency through here."

I trailed after him, helpless to stop him, noticing every nurse who picked up a phone to call security.

His gaze flickered over every sign, searching for a way to get to my attacker.

An alarm sounded overhead, blaring and sharp. "Code eleven. Code eleven."

I didn't need to work there to know that a code eleven had to be the signal for giant biker on a rampage.

"Fang!" I jumped in front of him, arms out, so he'd have nowhere to go but stop or mow me right down. He was so lost to his bloodlust; I wasn't even sure he'd stop.

He did.

Right as a storm of boots sounded from down the hall.

"Oh, thank goodness you're here, Officer Johnson. He's down that way. Big guy. Long, dirty-blond hair in a ponytail and a leather jacket. He's got a young woman with him."

I widened my eyes at Fang, and finally, some sense

seemed to reach his hopped-up-on-adrenaline brain. "Fuck," he muttered.

"Yeah, you don't say," I hissed at him. I glanced around, searching for somewhere to go. The hall split in three directions, one pointing to X-ray, the second to oncology, the third to maternity.

We could take one and hope the cops chose one of the other two.

But judging by the number of boots I'd heard running down the corridor, they had enough to split up.

I took door number four. The one that was open and led to a storeroom on our left. I shoved Fang in ahead of me and closed it with a quiet snick. A lock engaged. We could get out, there was a handle inside, but I suspected they'd need a key to get in from the hallway. Hopefully that would deter them enough to go on down the halls and away from us.

Fang's eyes flashed, his chest heaving. "I need to find him."

I pinned him with a glare. "This is exactly why I didn't want to tell you. Get your shit under control. I don't have time to get arrested today."

He leaned against a bare brick wall and dropped his head back against it, staring at the ceiling. "Just the thought of knowing what he did..."

The footsteps outside got closer. I held my breath, not making a sound.

A protective growl started deep in his chest, a terrifying noise in a space as enclosed as this.

And loud. At any moment, it was going to turn into a shout of outrage.

He was going to give us away.

I lifted up on my toes and put my hands to the back of his head, tilting it down so I could press my lips against his.

He pulled back, eyes flickering between mine in the dim light of the supply cupboard. "Pix?" His eyebrows furrowed together in confusion.

This wasn't what we did. Outside his bed, we didn't kiss.

Just the briefest touch of his lips had me wanting more.

But his confusion had me regretting the choice, and as the footsteps moved away, I dared to explain myself. "I'm sorry," I whispered. "The cops were out there, and you were growling like a hungry bear who'd just spotted a chubby hiker. I was just trying to shut you up."

He let out a quiet groan of need. "Shut me up some more, then."

But it was him who took control. With one hand on my hip, he pushed me back against the wall on my side of the narrow closet, his other hand cradling the back of my head. He surrounded me with his big body and slammed his mouth down on mine.

My eyes closed all on their own. A gasp slipped from my mouth as he took my lips, kissing me with the knowledge of a man who'd done it plenty of times before, even if the dynamic was totally different.

His mouth was warm and soft, his beard scratching lightly across my skin, only making me want more of him. He stroked my lips with his tongue, and I opened for him, the kiss deepening.

"Oh," I moaned softly, taking his kiss and giving him

back exactly what he'd been wanting from me for the longest time.

He gripped me so protectively that if that door opened, and the entire Providence Police Department stormed in, I doubted they would have been able to get to me.

I speared my fingers into his hair, kissing him back with everything I had, holding him as tight as he held me.

It was him who broke the kiss. Moving his lips away from mine to rest our foreheads together. We both breathed hard in the tiny space between us, breaths mingling, all the drama outside forgotten.

He had an uncanny ability to do that.

To make me forget about anything else.

It was why I always ran to him when I needed to forget my problems. Why I always let him fuck me into oblivion when something upset me.

The attack had stopped me from doing that with him. When Caleb had stripped every inch of dignity from my body with his rough hands and unforgiving cock, he'd also taken away the one coping mechanism I'd allowed myself.

Not having sex with Fang left me wide open and vulnerable to other things.

Like feelings.

Sex was so much easier.

I pushed him back, creating a little room in the space between us. "Why did you stop?"

He breathed heavily and stared down at his crotch. "'Cause kissing you like that, creates that. I need to be able to walk out of here once the coast is clear."

I stepped forward, putting my fingers to the button on his fly. "There's other ways of taking care of that."

"Pix," he warned. "Don't. That isn't what I meant. You don't have to."

"But what if I want to?"

He put his fingers beneath my chin and tilted my head up. "Don't do it just because you think it's what I want."

The problem was he wanted so much more. So much more I couldn't give. I saw it in the way he watched me. In the way he protected and touched me so gently. No man had ever looked at me the way he did.

His appearance had never scared me. But the things he wanted from me did.

I'd seen that sort of love too many times before. It was how my mother had found herself broken on the floor, with only a ten-year-old to comfort her.

I couldn't give him all the things he wanted. The thought of handing that sort of power over to any man was too much. I wouldn't be her. Lying on the floor, too heartbroken to move.

I couldn't give him the sort of love he wanted or deserved.

But I could give him this.

I slid to my knees, taking his jeans with me. I stared up at him while I forced his boxer briefs to follow, his thick dick springing free.

All the women who thought Fang's appearance was terrifying would die a thousand deaths if they saw how beautiful his cock was. I stroked my hand over it. "Prettiest dick I ever did see."

Fang chuckled, brushing my hair back off my face

and tucking the short lengths behind my ear. "It's so weird when you say that."

"Why? It is pretty. Pretty and perfect."

"It's a dick, Rebel. Nothing pretty about a one-eyed monster."

I grinned up at him. "You think highly of yourself to call it a monster."

He quirked one eyebrow. "You've seen bigger?"

I had not. He had porn star peen, there was no doubt about that. Monster was a fitting name. I didn't doubt him when he'd once told me he'd had women just nope right out as soon as they saw it. Hell, the first time we'd had sex, his exact words to me had been, "If it's too much, I understand."

It was not too much. The way he loved was the only thing that was too much about this man. That was the only thing that scared me. His monster peen was not a problem.

"Actually, I saw Kian's the other day, and he gives you a run for your money."

His fingers fisted in my hair. "I'm gonna pretend you didn't just say that, but only because your lips are going to look so fucking good around my cock."

This was where we were good. When it was all hot sex and desire. Too many other things had crept in over the past week or two, and getting back to our usual was comforting and safe.

I opened my mouth to take him in. At first, just the head. I ran my tongue all over it, paying particular attention to the thick vein, starting on the underside. Then I slid him deeper, coating every inch of him so he slid easily in and out of my opening.

It was impossible to take every inch of him, even if I deep-throated. I didn't really feel like asphyxiating today, even if I was in the right place for a medical emergency. But I used my hand at his base and pulled off to lick every inch of him when my jaw needed a break.

"You're so beautiful," he murmured, not taking his eyes off me for a second.

"Bet you say that to all the women who get on their knees for you."

He shook his head. "Only you, Pix."

Despite myself, my heart swelled. He was telling the truth. I could see it in his gaze.

I sucked him harder and faster, using one hand on his shaft to help my mouth along while the other gripped his balls. His hips jerked, and he thrust shallowly into my mouth, unable to hold back.

I waited for the terror. For the reminder Caleb and his doctor buddy had forced me to my knees too.

But I kept my gaze firmly on Fang's face, which chased away the demons. He was as beautiful as his cock when he was lost to pleasure.

Pleasure only I gave him.

I selfishly liked that he never went elsewhere. Maybe it was because he thought no other woman would find him attractive enough to want to do this.

If he ever showed this side of himself, how gentle and sweet he was, they would. He'd have them lining up around the block.

It was probably only a matter of time until he realized that and stopped waiting for me.

"Gonna come, Pix. You're too good at that."

It was his way of warning me. Of giving me a chance to end it there or jerk him off 'til he came.

I'd taken it every other time I'd done this for him. I'd switched it up and planted myself on his cock and ridden him 'til he couldn't hold on anymore. But this time I just kept going.

"Pix," he warned again, like he was sure I didn't want this, and I was playing with fire.

"Come in my mouth," I begged him breathlessly. "Let me do that for you."

God knew he deserved it after everything he did for me.

"Fuck." His balls tightened, and he let go, releasing into the back of my throat.

I swallowed him down, everything he had, until he slumped back against the wall.

His blissed-out expression had me tingling from head to toe. So freaking proud that I'd put that expression on his face.

Slowly, I stood, wishing I could do it all over again, just to see him stare down at me like that.

He put his hand to the side of my face and rubbed his thumb over my bottom lip. "I didn't deserve that. You told me not to go after those guys. I get one opportunity, and look what I go and do. Get us locked in a supply room while a hospital full of cops searches for us."

"Can't really blame you. The carrot was dangled right in your face. I might have done the same if I wasn't so stupidly paralyzed with fear."

I hated how I'd reacted. I might as well have been right back there in Caleb's house, while they taunted and teased me, blocking the exits, telling me exactly what they were going to do to little sluts like me who led men on.

Fang's expression turned protective again, and he slid his hand to the back of my neck and pulled me to his chest. "Come 'ere."

I let his arms wrap around me. Accepted the comfort I always found so hard to tolerate. I didn't know why he was different.

When he tilted my chin and took my mouth again, probably tasting himself on my lips, I didn't stop him. The kiss felt too nice. It wormed its way down into my heart, where I knew it would destroy me.

I couldn't bring myself to stop it.

## 19

## VAUGHN

*I* had things to do. An appointment with my lawyer. An entire company that was still running thanks to my father's diligent staff who all adored him, but I needed to get in there and talk to his business partner. There were decisions that needed to be made and plans to be put in place.

Then there was my darling wife and her disasters that had somehow become mine.

But instead of doing any of that, I was sitting outside of Black Industries, staring at the dark tinted windows, with hate coursing through my veins.

I might not have known Rebel very well, but hearing Caleb had hurt her rolled my stomach.

The reaction had gone further than just hearing the news that a random woman had been attacked. I heard things like that on the news all the time and felt sympathy and anger, but then I went on with my day.

The problem was, she was a woman I was responsible for. My dad had clearly wanted her taken care of. If I hadn't needed the money so fucking badly to bail my damn wife out of her mess, I would have just let Rebel have half. If I'd never met Brooke, I would have still had a nice fat trust fund and not a damn care in the world.

My phone rang, and I glanced at it, irritated by the interruption. "Ah, shit." My lawyer, Nathan. I was five minutes late for my appointment, and he was already on my case. Freaking Type A people. "What?" I snapped into the phone, not caring I sounded like a spoiled brat. "I'm busy."

"Yeah, well, aren't we all? We had a meeting."

"I'm coming."

There was a pause where I went back to staring at the people coming and going from Black Industries. Was it my imagination, or did they all look depressed?

"So that complete silence I hear is your engine running? Or you jogging up the stairs of my office as we speak?"

I cracked my neck to ease the tension mounting there. "Fine. I'm not coming. Can we just do this over the phone? Something came up."

He huffed out an irritated sigh. "I've set in motion the relevant paperwork to contest the will and I called in a few favors. You can put the house on the market. We'll deal with the fallout later."

I tapped my fingers against the steering wheel impatiently. "Yeah, about that. I think I've changed my mind."

"What? Since when?"

Since I'd found her in my guest bedroom, curled up asleep, innocent as anything when she wasn't sassing the crap out of me.

Since I'd realized she had nowhere to go.

Since I'd pulled my head out of my California-tanned ass and remembered my old man wasn't some elderly, infirm, losing-his-marbles millionaire. He'd been young and smart and kind. Generous. And he'd wanted Miranda's daughter taken care of. Who the hell was I to say no to that? I hadn't stepped foot in Providence in ten years. I barely took my father's calls, and generally only when I wanted something. What made me any more deserving of that money than Rebel?

Half of the estate would have to be enough for Brooke's goons. It was all I had.

"Have you forgotten that you stormed in here a few days ago and demanded I get you ten million dollars in cash?" Nathan demanded down the phone line.

"No. I still need that."

"Then sell the house and everything in it. Because going up against some new stepdaughter who works as a bartender in Saint View is going to be a lot easier than going up against your father's business partner. I can't get at the money in the business. Harold Coker isn't stupid."

I ground my teeth together at the insinuation Rebel was. "Don't talk about her like that. She's not dumb."

"I looked into her. She has a ninth-grade education from Saint View High, of all places, and has only ever held down minimum-wage jobs. I'll put my money on her not being the sharpest tool in the shed. We can probably buy her off with fifty K."

I ended the call without saying goodbye. "Fucking elitist prick," I said to the empty car.

Not that I could talk. I was no better. Brought up with every advantage and an asshole because of it. I couldn't even blame it on my parents. My dad was good and generous, right down to his toes. My mother was all for supporting the underdog.

What did I do? Beside marry a pretty blonde because I needed a woman on my arm. That was about the only thing I'd achieved in my thirty-one years.

Look where that had gotten me. Back in my childhood home, questioning everything I'd ever thought about myself.

But at least I wasn't Caleb Black, who strode out of his building with his phone attached to his ear. He had his long-sleeved collared shirt rolled to his elbows, but his suit pants, tie, and shiny shoes all screamed businessman with expensive taste. He barked something into the phone, face stony before entering the coffee shop next door.

"Shit." I couldn't see inside the building from where I sat, the sun's glare on the glass windows reflecting back at me. Before I could consider exactly what I was doing, I was out of the car, collar flicked up against the cool wind that warned winter was coming, and strode into the coffee shop after him.

Caleb was impossible to miss. He sat in the middle of the room at a round table, talking on the phone loudly, zero care given the rest of the patrons were just trying to enjoy a quiet cup of coffee.

Troy Hugh, who'd gone by his last name when we'd been in college, sat beside him, staring off to my left with his old acne scars still visible on his cheek. I followed his line of sight and landed on the young woman making drinks behind the counter. She couldn't have been any older than eighteen, but he watched her with a degree of intensity that made me uncomfortable.

I ordered a drink, and when the older woman taking orders asked me which table I was sitting at, I found myself pointing to the one behind Caleb and Hugh.

"Okay then, honey. Go on. We'll bring it over."

I tipped her generously and made my way through the café, avoiding making eye contact with the two men. I took a seat facing their backs and busied myself with the little sugar packets on the table, hoping they wouldn't turn my way.

I needn't have worried. As soon as Caleb finished his call, Hugh nudged him and pointed to the young woman behind the counter.

"Her."

Caleb glanced over with a bored expression then back at his friend. "Her face looks like she fell out of the ugly tree and hit every branch on the way down."

Hugh sniggered. "Yeah, but those tits. Fucking huge. Can always put a pillow over her face when I bang her."

I gripped the sugar packet so hard it ripped and spilled all over the table. Someone needed to put a pillow over his head. And push down on it. I'd never liked these guys. Something had always been off about them.

The door opened while I was simultaneously fuming and sweeping sugar crystals into my palm. By the time I lifted my head, Leonn Edrington was dumping his man bag on Caleb and Hugh's table and slumping down into a chair facing his friends. Which also meant if he looked slightly past them, he'd see me sitting there, eaves-dropping.

It had been a decade since we'd last seen each other, but I didn't think I'd changed so much they wouldn't recognize me. I'd recognized the three of them easily enough, even though Leonn had put on at least twenty pounds, and Hugh was prematurely balding. Caleb looked exactly the same, the poster boy for wealth and privilege. He hadn't changed at all. He'd had that air about him since we'd started kindergarten together.

Hugh flicked his head towards the barista. "Whatya think? Hot or not? I vote yes. Caleb votes too ugly to be fuckable."

Leonn glanced over, but he was clearly distracted by something else because the blonde didn't hold his attention for more than a second, and he didn't answer his friend's question.

Caleb cocked his head. "What's wrong with you?"

Leonn glared at him. "What's wrong with me? Maybe if you ever answered your fucking phone, you'd know. I've been calling you!"

Caleb glanced down at his cell and shrugged. "Been on calls most of the day."

"Yeah, well, lucky you, that your morning was so sweet and calm. Want to know how my morning went?" He didn't wait for either of the men to answer. "I just spent the morning in lockdown at the hospital after that little bitch you brought us accused me of raping her."

I couldn't help it. I glanced up. I had to know if they were talking about Rebel.

The man's face was mottled pink and purple in his outrage.

It probably matched mine. If the waitress hadn't come over and placed my coffee down on the table in front of me, I might have flipped it.

Hugh laughed, and when Caleb turned side-on to look at him, I could see the amusement on his face too.

Leonn glared at them both. "It's not fucking funny! The boyfriend is massive, and he was wearing a Slayers jacket. He went on a rampage through the entire hospital searching for me."

Definitely Rebel and Fang then.

Caleb took a sip of his drink before he answered. "Well, you're still alive. So what do you want me to do about it?"

"I don't know. Something! If she's going around accusing me, then what makes you think she's not going to say the same about the two of you? We were all there. What if she goes to the cops?"

Caleb sat back, folding his arms across his chest. "Then we'll sue her for slander. Watch how quick she changes her tune then. They always do. She knows she's just a Saint View slut. Nobody is going to believe her against us. Now can we talk about something more interesting? Like my Halloween party?"

I couldn't hear any more of it. I pushed my chair back, cringing when it made a grating, scraping noise across the tiled floor.

All three men turned to me.

Caleb was the first to recognize me. "Vaughn?"

I shoved my fingers in the pockets of my jeans and tried to act surprised, like I hadn't just heard every word of their conversation. "Caleb? Shit, hey. It's been a long time." I let my gaze slide to the other two men. "Leonn. Hugh. The three of you still hang out?"

Caleb nodded. "Yeah, from time to time. College friends are the best kind, right? Not that we've heard from you in forever."

I rubbed the back of my neck like I was embarrassed.

"Yeah, well. I moved to California after graduation. Got married. Haven't been back since. You guys never left?"

The three of them shook their heads, but the other two let Caleb do the talking.

"I started Black Industries. My building is right next door. Own the entire twenty-seventh floor."

I raised my eyebrows like that impressed me, because I knew that was what he was hoping for.

Caleb pointed to his left. "Hugh here is my right-hand man."

"Wow," I drawled. "Nice job, working for your bestie."

Hugh frowned, and I couldn't blame him. I had said it slightly condescendingly. I turned to Leonn. "Just heard a bit of your conversation. You're a doctor?"

Leonn glanced at Caleb for direction.

It was on the tip of my tongue to mutter, "Yeah, asshole. I know exactly what you did."

But that wasn't going to get me anywhere with them. I shook my head, faking sympathy for Leonn and his work problems. "Bitches be crazy, right? My wife is the same. Don't know why I married her." That was actually vaguely true, but I wouldn't have normally been quite douchey enough to say it out loud to anyone.

The worry in Leonn's expression rapidly changed to relieved laughter. "Don't know why we even bother, right?"

Caleb deftly changed the subject, leaning forward on his elbows to study me. "Sorry to hear about your old man. Let us know when the funeral is. I'd like to come and pay my respects."

I nodded. "Sure. Will do."

"How long are you in town for?"

I shrugged. "A few weeks maybe. Got some things to tie up with my dad's business and belongings."

Caleb glanced at Leonn then back up at me. "I'm having a Halloween party next weekend. You should come? Would be a good chance to catch up properly. Some of the other guys from college will be there. Should be a good night."

"Yeah? Sounds great."

It sounded shit and like I'd rather poke my eyes out with a rusted fork than hang with the three of them, knowing what they liked to do for sport. But what was that saying?

Keep your friends close but your enemies closer?

Getting inside their inner circle and finding out whatever Rebel needed to know for her revenge plan could come in handy. Fuck knows I kinda owed her one, after trying to take the house out from under her.

Caleb handed me a business card. "My number is on there. Send me a text, and I'll send you back the address. Your wife in town?"

I shook my head. "Nah. Left the old ball and chain back in Cali."

Caleb chuckled. "I know how that feels. I just got rid of one myself a few months back."

"Good for you."

"We'll have something a little special at the party. In the form of sluts. What your wife doesn't know won't hurt her, right?"

It felt like a test. To see if I shared their values and could be trusted. I laughed and channeled my inner frat boy. "Slut me up, baby."

They all laughed, and we shook hands, promising to catch up at the party.

The instant I walked outside the smile fell from my face.

I felt dirty. If I could have walked right into an acid wash, I very well might have.

For all that I hated the man who I'd become since I'd moved away from this town, for the first time, I realized it could have been worse if I'd stayed.

## 20

## KIAN

With Rebel, Fang, and Vaughn all out of the house, I got on with my usual tasks. The lawn needed mowing. The pool needed autumn leaves scooped out. Garden beds needed tending to, readying the plants to survive the winter. With a property this size, there was always plenty to do.

It hadn't been my dream to follow in my father's foot-steps and spend my life waiting on rich folks. But not everybody got what they wanted in life. Some of us needed to work in order to keep food in our mouths and a roof over our heads.

Basic survival outweighed hopes and dreams every time.

At least this place was familiar to me. I knew every nook and cranny like the back of my hand after living here for as long as I could remember. We'd moved in here when my mom had died, and my father couldn't afford the rent on the little three-bedroom house we'd had in

Saint View. I'd been eight and in awe of the massive house my father worked in.

The day we'd moved in was the day I'd met Vaughn.

We were the same age. Young enough to not see our differences, and we'd become fast friends.

Oh, how that had changed.

I slammed my shovel down into the ground, put my weight on the edge to get it right down deep, then turned it over. The ground was getting hard. I'd really left this a few weeks later than I should have, but if I'd known Bart and Miranda were going to die, I might have done a lot of things differently.

Rebel's car flew in the driveway at pace, bouncing over the curb with a squeaking protest from her suspension.

I jumped away from the erratic vehicle, choosing life over being flattened like a pancake, and stared at her as she got out.

She was grinning like the Joker.

It was entirely disturbing.

I put the shovel down and wiped my hands on the back of my pants. "Why do you look like you were just in a real-life episode of *Grand Theft Auto*? You're supposed to slow down for driveways, you know." I toed at the driveway with the toe of my work boot. "I think that's part of your undercarriage marking the pavers."

Rebel just laughed. "You know when I said we were going for a drive? Yeah, well, that happened. But it was just a drive with cops chasing us!"

I widened my eyes at her. "What the fuck, Rebel?" I glanced down the road, like a swarm of police cars might descend upon our quiet suburban neighborhood at any moment.

Fang slowly got out of the car, his face a little green. He leaned heavily on the doorframe. "She's exaggerating. There were no cops chasing us. Though she certainly drove like there were. If you have an anti-nausea tablet, I could use one."

I didn't even think he was joking, but Rebel scoffed, her eyes bright with delight.

"Okay fine, maybe there weren't actual cops chasing us, but there could have been! You don't know that sedan behind us wasn't an undercover car."

"It was driven by an eighty-year-old lady with blue hair, Pix. I think we could have taken her if it had come down to that."

Rebel punched her fist into the air and gave a victory crow. "Hell, yeah, we could have! Old bluey would have gone down! Pow, pow!"

I shot Fang an alarmed look. "Is she always like this?"

He shrugged. "Pretty much." He walked by me and slapped me on the shoulder. "Get used to it if you're going to live with her. She'll keep you on your toes."

"I can see that." I watched Rebel dance around like a fighter, taking swats at her imaginary opponent. "What really happened?"

"Saw one of the fuckwits who hurt her. Tried to kill him. Ended up hiding in a closet for a bit while the cops searched the hospital, but they didn't have the manpower for anything too thorough. We got out unseen. Not that I could convince Rebel of that. She drives like a chipmunk hopped up on cocaine."

"I heard that!" Rebel complained, shoving her hands on her hips to glare at him.

He just gave her an indulgent smile, then dropped his voice and spoke to me, "You around for a bit? I need to crash. I think I really do have a concussion. I can barely keep my eyes open, and this hand is throbbing like a motherfucker. I don't want to leave her alone though. Seeing him again..."

I understood, and the guy really did seem like he needed to be horizontal. "Go. I've got her. She'll be okay."

He went inside, the door closing behind him.

I slid my attention to the wannabe car racer. "So. You had an adventure, huh, Little Demon?"

She winked at me. "Story of my life. There's always something."

"What are you doing now? You gotta go into work yet?"

"Not 'til five. I'm on night shift. You want some help?"

"Gardening?"

"Yeah, why not. I need to burn off some off this energy before I explode. Give me something heavy to swing or some pavers to lift. Boulders to roll. Whatever. That shovel will do." She grabbed it from my fingers and drove it erratically into the ground, spearing one of my baby plants in half.

She cringed. "Oops. Was that a weed?"

"A weed I very carefully planted during the summer..."

"Ah, shit. Sorry. Got a carried away. Adrenaline makes me jittery."

I took the shovel from her hand. "Maybe, for the sake of all these other little plants that have not yet had the pleasure of even reaching their first birthdays, we do something else."

She cracked her neck. "I'm wired."

"I can see. I get like that too. But you know where I channel it instead of being a psychopathic plant murderer?"

She gave me a questioning look. "Sex?"

I blinked but then realized she wasn't actually far off base. "Well, yes, but that isn't what I was going for here. Fighting. You said I could train you. You still up for that?"

I frigging missed fighting. I was just searching for any excuse to get back into it and to have something in my life other than this job and this house, and bloody Vaughn resurfacing out of the wild blue yonder.

Her shoulders slumped at my offer. "When I saw that guy at the hospital, I froze. He looked right at me, and I just sat there and did nothing, trembling and contemplating pissing my pants. It was Fang who did all the impressive stuff."

There was so much regret in her voice. I hated that for her. "We can fix that, so next time you don't freeze."

She bit her lip. "I forgot how much bigger he is. How much bigger they all were. I'm so fucking short and weak. It never seemed like a problem before. I had my knuckle-dusters, and that was all I needed. But I had so much false confidence. I know I'm not a complete pushover, but every time I went up against some big guy at Psychos, there were other people around to back me up. Nash— that's the guy who owns the bar with my bestie, Bliss. Or Vincent, the security guard. Or Fang and his guys from the MC. The one time none of them were around, look what happened." She dropped her gaze to the floor, the shame in her stance killing me.

I couldn't help it. I stepped in and put my finger underneath her chin, hoping like hell Fang wasn't watching me touch his girl through the bedroom window. "Hey." I lifted her face to stare down at her. "You got overconfident. It's a danger, sure. And this time, you got beat. That doesn't have to be the case during the rematch, okay? You know your weakness now, and it's not that you're small. I've seen women take down men twice their size. It might actually be your biggest advantage, because they're going to underestimate you."

Her expression hardened. "I hate being underestimated."

"Yeah, girl. That's the spirit. So show me what you got."

She gazed around. "Right here on the driveway?"

"Why not? You think the next time they come at you they're going to politely ask you to step onto some cushy mats?"

"Fair point. I suppose the same would apply if I complained I don't have my knuckle-dusters."

"The little demon learns quick."

She grinned. "So, what? I just come at you?"

"Why not? Give it a go. See what happens."

She made a show of stretching her arms over her head and linking her fingers together to stretch her back. She stuck her hips out to one side and leaned to the other, her shirt riding up over her hip and showing off a sliver of her belly.

Like a moth to a flame, my gaze dropped to that tiny

strip of skin, caressing every inch of it, because my fingers couldn't.

Fuck, she was hot. Cute as hell, but with a banging body. Tight thighs. A barely-there handful of tits. All big sass and smart-mouthed. Just like I liked them.

Her shoulder rammed me right in the stomach, winding me before I even realized what she was doing. I spluttered, taken by surprise, only to find her tiny arms wrapped around my neck in a chokehold.

Jesus fuck. She'd said she was scrappy. I'd made the very mistake I'd said her attackers would.

I'd underestimated her.

I broke the hold she had on my neck, and she backed off, letting me breathe.

Good of her.

She grinned at me with that wicked, hyped-up smile from earlier. "Come on, Kian. Don't go easy on me."

I coughed, sure my throat was bruised. "I wasn't," I said honestly.

She may as well have been a rooster preening.

That was all I needed to sweep her feet out from under her with a low kick. She fell onto the grass at the side of the driveway, groaning at the impact.

"Come on," I encouraged her. "If you aren't broken, get up."

She glared at me, eyes suddenly burning with anger. "I'm not fucking broken. Don't say that to me."

"Then get up and prove it."

She pushed to her feet, fire flashing in her eyes.

"What?" I taunted her. "You didn't think I'd fight back because you're a girl? I wouldn't disrespect you like that."

She charged at me with a yell that would have woken Fang if he wasn't half out of it.

But unlike the first time she'd gotten her shoulder to my gut, this time, I was waiting for it. I caught her mid charge, and spun her, so her back was to my chest. I pinned her arms beneath mine and held her tight, not letting her move.

"Your hand is on my boob, Kian."

I've never let someone go so quick. "Fuck! Sorry. I didn't mean it. I swear, I wasn't trying to catch a grope. I'm just not used to fighting women. I don't normally have to worry about where I put my hands—"

Her kick was sharp and strong, and aimed at my knees.

Only I made the painful mistake of crouching at the same time, trying to catch her expression to see how badly affected she was by my ill-placed hands.

And the kick caught me straight in the crotch.

Pain splintered through me, taking out my vision for a second. When it came back, Rebel was staring at me, white-faced.

"Fuck! I'm so sorry!" She jerked forward.

I could only put it down to instinct when she rubbed at the spot she'd kicked.

I was instantly hard, despite the pain. "That's my dick, Rebel," I said in the same dry tone she'd used a moment earlier.

Later, when I replayed the moment while lying in my bed with an icepack on my junk, I would swear she gave it a single extra rub before she called practice finished for the day.

## 21

## REBEL

*I*t took an hour of sitting in my car, giving myself a pep talk before I could force myself inside for my shift at Psychos. Even then, I had to chant under my breath about how Psychos was not to blame for everything that had happened after I'd left that night.

I'd been okay when I'd stopped in to talk to my friends. The place had been filled with bright sunlight and casual chitchat.

But something about the deep shadows outside and being back here to work had me on edge, reliving that night in my head over and over.

My gaze went straight to the end of the bar where Caleb had sat, calling himself by a different name, and completely charming me with his cute stories and all-American smile.

How fucking stupid I'd been.

A man appeared at my side, and I flinched before I realized who it was.

"How you doing, shorty?" Nash had a dishcloth wrapped around his fingers and his worried dad face on.

"Fine."

"Bliss and I understand if you can't come back yet. Now or..."

I glared at him. "Don't you dare say ever."

"No one would blame you."

"I really love you, but if you say that to me again, I will take a pool cue and ram it in your poop hole. Capiche?"

Nash, well used to my mouth after years of being my boss, shrugged. "Right then. Now that that's been settled, there's a shipment of drinks to be put away, and it's busy in here. Game's on, and it's a nail-biter. I'll be in my office, keeping my poop hole intact if you need me."

I fought not to smile at the man who'd become some sort of surrogate dad-big brother combo to me. "See that you do."

Despite the threats of violence, the conversation had actually helped. It confirmed I could either work through the triggering feeling being back here brought on, or I could walk out the door and never come back.

This place was my home.

Caleb had already taken too much from me. I wasn't letting him take this too. I had a family here. Giving up this job meant giving up on them. It wasn't happening.

War watched me from the group of tables where his club always hung out. Fang wasn't with them. He was still passed out in my bed when I'd left, which was a little worrying. War waved a hand in my direction, and I nodded back at him, but it didn't relieve his concerned expression.

Bliss hurried out from behind the bar with a tray of

drinks. She stopped when she saw me though. "Hey! You okay?"

I brushed her off. She didn't need to be worrying about me when we had a bar full of patrons who needed food and drinks. I hurried to help, cranky at myself for sitting in the car so long, psyching myself up, when I could have been in here lending a hand.

From his usual spot, leaning against the wall, arms crossed over his chest, Vincent watched me too.

"What?" I asked him in exasperation. "Why is everyone staring at me? I'm not going to have a complete breakdown in the middle of the bar."

He raised one eyebrow slowly. "I don't know about everyone else, but I'm just looking at the massive booger hanging out of your nose."

I flipped him the bird, realizing with that one comment it wasn't Vincent at all. "I'd say it's nice to have you here tonight, Scythe. But feel free to let me know when Vincent is back. You know he's my favorite."

Vincent had a diagnosed case of dissociative identity disorder, and Scythe was his psychopathic alter ego. Pointing out nonexistent nose fruit was a clear sign Scythe was in the building. Vincent had manners.

Scythe was funny though. I enjoyed his sense of humor when it was him at the controls. Even if I did adore his much sweeter, somewhat less murderous side.

They were Bliss's guys. But they'd always had my back, and I loved them for it.

Except when they were all hovering like mother hens. Bliss might have liked feeling smothered, but I did not. It just made me more determined to put my demons with this place to bed and get back to the way things were before.

I'd put away all the drinks, collapsed all the cardboard boxes they'd come in, and had moved onto washing glasses when, "Hey, Roach," came from the end of the bar.

I glanced up sharply, heart pounding at Vaughn's tousled hair and dark-eyed smolder. Lust roared through me, hot and uncontrollable, based on nothing other than the pure stupid attraction I felt for the man.

It died the second I noticed where he was sitting. "Get out of that seat."

Vaughn frowned and stared down at the stool beneath his ass. "What? Why? Is there something wrong with it?"

I couldn't handle seeing him sit there. I grabbed his arm and yanked it to the left. "Any seat but that one. I can't look at it."

"Is that...?"

I nodded, breathing deep through my nose.

Vaughn got off the seat and switched to one at the opposite end of the bar.

I released the stranglehold I had on the scrubbing brush. "Sorry. I just..." Couldn't deal.

"It's cool. I get it. But while you're triggered, I need to tell you something."

I cringed. "Can it wait until I get home? If you're going to tell me you've moved my shit out while I was working, fine. I'm not going to keep fighting you on it. Just tell me where you left my stuff and I'll sleep in my car."

"I didn't touch your stuff. Not only because there's a giant, kinda scary man in your bed and if I'd tried to rip your sheets out from beneath him, I don't know that I would have survived to tell the tale."

I fought a smile. He was annoyingly cute when he wasn't being a dickhead. "Shoot then."

"You're not going to like this, but I talked to Caleb, Leonn, and Hugh today. That's their names. The guys who attacked you."

I let that sink in for a moment. "They sound like such nice, normal names, don't they? Like, do you think when their mothers were gazing down at them in the hospital, picking out these proper, distinguished names, that they ever thought for a second their darling babies would turn into violent monsters?"

"I would hope, if they'd known, they'd have asked for a refund."

I scrubbed at a lipstick mark on the rim of the glass clutched in my fingers. "Why were you talking to them? Just organizing to have a little bro catch-up?" It was an uncalled-for jab, but I barely knew Vaughn. I couldn't trust him yet, even if my lady parts did get all excited at the sight of him. Something in my gut wanted to give him the benefit of the doubt, but my gut hadn't done too well for me lately, so I was relying fully on my brain.

While ignoring the lust-filled thoughts that flooded it whenever he was around.

"No. I saw them at a coffee shop. Overheard Leonn freaking out about Fang's little rampage through the hospital."

I grinned at that. "No shit? He was rattled?"

"Very. Caleb threatened to sue you."

I rolled my eyes. "Of course he fucking did. Anything to shut me up." I peered at him, still not fully believing his story. "So you just happen to hang out at the same coffee shop as Caleb Black?"

"Guess so." He ran neatly trimmed fingernails along the edge of a paper coaster with the scary Psychos clown logo printed in the middle. "I wasn't planning on talking to them. But they spotted me when I left. Caleb invited me to his Halloween party next weekend."

I glanced up. "He's having a party? At his house?"

Vaughn appeared distinctly uncomfortable. "Yeah. Sorry, I shouldn't have brought that up. You probably didn't want to hear that."

"I want to come."

The words surprised me probably more than they surprised him.

Vaughn's dark eyebrows drew together. "Ah, no."

I leaned over. "Ah, yes. You owe me."

His eyes went all squinty, trying to work me out. "What the hell do I owe you for?"

"Trying to steal my half of the inheritance."

"I'm letting you sleep in my house!"

I waved that off like it was nothing. "You were a douche. You call me Roach, for Christ's sakes. That's not very nice."

"Do you want me to stop?"

I actually didn't. I maybe enjoyed the nickname. It was tough-sounding, and I could identify with a name like that at the moment. It was a hell of a lot better than something girly like sugar or princess.

So I didn't answer his question. "Come on, Vaughn. I need to know everything about them."

He shifted his weight and rested his elbows on the bar top. "I went to school with them. I'm still in contact with people who run in their circles, I'm sure. I can dig around for you, find out whatever you need to know. About their families and where they live. Where they work. There's no need for you to go anywhere near them."

I narrowed my eyes, not liking any of the words coming out of his mouth. He was missing my point. What I really didn't need was someone taking my power. Again. "I need to face where it happened. Coming back to Psychos tonight made me realize that. I need to stand there and know it's never going to happen again."

He shook his head. "Do you even hear yourself? You're playing with fire. Taking stupid risks in the hope of feeling something that isn't grief over your mom. I'm not letting you do that."

Not letting me? He didn't get it. It wasn't about my grief at all. It was that they'd stolen something from me that night. My confidence. I needed it back. I didn't know who I was without it. "I get you've never felt powerless. It's not your fault you grew up male, white, and with money. But that isn't my story. I can't walk down the street without seeing them in every face. I can't fucking sleep at night, Vaughn. I close my eyes, and they're always there. I need to prove to myself that I can be around them and not freeze. I don't want to be taken by surprise, like I was at the hospital."

His teeth dug into his perfect bottom lip, hesitation still in his eyes, but maybe a little bit of understanding too.

I took my chance to drive my point home. "I don't just want to know where they live. If they're married and have families. I want to know the things they don't admit to their wives. I want to know all their deepest, darkest secrets." I put the over-scrubbed glass into the drainer so hard it rattled. "Then I'll use all of it against them to really make them hurt. I can't win against them as a group. I need to work out a way to divide and conquer. Work out how best to hurt each of them individually."

Vaughn watched me intently. "You're really serious about this, huh?"

I stopped what I was doing and stared him dead in the eye. "If you'd experienced the things they'd done to me, you would be too."

He swore softly under his breath. "Pieces of fucking shit."

"To say the least."

He steeled me with a hard look. "If I take you, and I mean *if*, Rebel. If I take you, you have to wear a mask the entire time. They can't know it's you. You rattled Leonn today just being in the same hospital as him, and then he went running to Caleb. I don't know what they'd do if they knew you were there."

I waved off his concerns. "Not a problem. Plenty of costumes require a mask."

"And you stay with me. You don't wander off."

I saluted him. "Yes, sir."

"I'm serious, Rebel. My dad clearly wanted you taken care of. I was a shitty son while he was here so the least I can do is watch out for you. He would have wanted me to treat you like a sister."

I remembered the way Vaughn had looked at me that night at the hotel, before I'd realized who he was. He was stupidly attractive with his dark features and a smirk that did things to my insides.

I wasn't sure I liked him talking about me like I was

his sibling. I'd never had a brother or sister, but if I had been as attracted to a blooded relative as I was to Vaughn, I would be checking myself into therapy before I ended up on some reality show, confessing to the world how nobody understood our special love.

Fucking hell. The sister thing needed to get nixed in the bud. "Then let me have my half of the inheritance."

He sighed. "It's not that easy."

It never was when it came to money.

A roar from War's side of the bar came up, and I glanced in their direction. They were all staring up at the big-screen TV, where a hockey match was playing.

All but one guy. I hadn't even seen him come in, but my heart gave a happy squeeze.

Fang crossed the room to lean on the bar beside Vaughn. "Hey, Pix. Can I get a beer, please?"

"Politest damn biker I've ever seen," Vaughn muttered.

I pulled down on the beer tap, letting the amber liquid run into a clean glass. "You could stand to be a little more like him, you know."

I pushed the beer across the bar to Fang and waved him off when he tried to pay. "On me."

"Can I get one, too?" Vaughn asked.

I poured a second beer and sent it in his direction. "Three dollars."

"You just gave him one for free!"

"Yeah, well, there's no *sibling* discount around here."

Vaughn glared at me but shoved his hand into the pocket of his jeans and produced a few dollar bills. "Fine then. *Sis*."

Fang ignored our bickering and reached over the

countertop to swipe at a stray bubble on my forearm. He flicked it off his fingers into the sink. "Hey. We're all going back to the clubhouse for a party after the game. Do you want to come?"

"Sure. Sounds good. We're closing up after it finishes anyway."

Vaughn looked between me and the fifteen men all sitting around tables, their MC jackets on the backs of their chairs, their bikes all lined up outside the window. "You are not seriously going to a party with all of them?"

He had his Providence-raised, Judgey McJudgeface pants on, clearly. It was so entitled. I knew better than anyone that wearing a business suit didn't make you a good guy. The Slayers might appear rough and ready, but none of them had ever laid a finger on me.

"Why wouldn't I?" I challenged him.

Fang twisted to glare at him. "Are you implying she wouldn't be safe with me and my brothers?"

Vaughn held his hands up. "Hey, I'm just trying to look out for her."

Irritation prickled at me, probably a leftover after him calling me his sister when some very core part of me didn't have even remotely brotherly thoughts about him. "Who says I want that, Vaughn? Those guys are my friends."

"I'm sure you said that about Caleb too."

Shock punched me right in the gut, and before I could stop them, tears pricked the backs of my eyes. "You're a fucking asshole," I seethed at him. "One minute you're being all nice. But just give you a minute and you're back to being a prick..."

To his credit, he did appear apologetic. "I'm sorry. I

didn't mean it like that. Try seeing it from my point of view."

"I did. You still look like an asshole." Fucking men, thinking they knew better than me.

He turned to Fang for support, and to my surprise, Fang didn't immediately bark something harsh out in my defense. In fact, it was quite the opposite. "Come to the party as well then," he relented with a sigh.

"What?" Vaughn and I said in unison.

Fang rubbed a hand over the back of his neck uncomfortably, his blue-eyed gaze steadfastly fixed on me. "Hey. I think he's a jackass too. But you live together. And in some messed-up way, I think he's just trying to protect you."

"I am," Vaughn grumbled.

"I can't blame him for wanting to know you're safe."

I watched Vaughn for a second, and he actually did seem hurt that I was cranky with him. "Fine. You can come. You're so uptight. You look like you need to chill out and get laid anyway."

I regretted my choice of words the moment they came out of my mouth. I didn't want to think about Vaughn getting laid.

He finished the last few mouthfuls of his beer. "I'm ready."

Fang looked at me and chuckled. I laughed with him.

"What?" Vaughn asked, glancing between us. "What's so funny?"

Fang stood and slapped him on the shoulder. "You aren't ready, my friend. Not even a little bit."

"The Slayers' parties rival the sex club we have here at Psychos," I explained. "You good with that?"

Vaughn cleared his throat, suddenly not quite so cocky. "Sure."

I raised an eyebrow. "Maybe the question should have been, is your wife good with you cheating on her at one?"

To my surprise, he huffed out a laugh, though it had a slightly bitter tinge to it. "My wife spent my entire trust fund on her alcohol, drug, and gambling addiction. She's slept with all of my friends back in Cali and didn't even care enough to try to cover it up. I don't think she gives a shit what I do, as long as I cough up the money she needs to pay her debts."

I blinked at maybe the first honest thing to have come out of Vaughn's mouth since I'd met him.

He dropped his gaze to the bar top.

I could practically see the regret written all over him.

"Shit." Fang took his wallet from the inside of his jacket and took out a few bills. "Pix. Pour the man another drink. Top shelf. On me."

I grabbed a bottle of bourbon and poured two shots. One from Fang. One from me. 'Cause that was a lot of pain that had just come tumbling out of his mouth.

Vaughn slumped on his stool and accepted the drinks. "Thanks."

He knocked them back in quick succession. "Just so you know, I didn't tell you that so you'd feel sorry for me."

I did anyway. At least a little bit.

Vaughn finally met my gaze. "I just wanted you to know I'm not a cheater. I saw how badly my mom's infidelity hurt my dad. I wouldn't do that."

I shrugged. "My opinion of you doesn't matter. I wasn't judging you."

My digs about his wife came from somewhere else entirely. A place that felt a lot like jealousy.

Fang pulled him up from the bar. "Let's go get you laid, brother. 'Cause after that story, I think you need it. We'll wait for you in the parking lot, Pix."

The two men walked out side by side, Vaughn glancing back over his shoulder at me.

I looked away. "Great," I muttered to the rapidly emptying bar. "Now they're buddies, and I get to go watch my stepbrother score. Just how I wanted to end the night."

## 22

## REBEL

*W*e drove in a parade from Psychos to the clubhouse. First Fang and his guys on their bikes, then me in my car, and Vaughn in his. I mostly kept my eyes glued to Fang's broad shoulders leaning over the handles of the bike in front of me. He looked damn fucking good like that, his waist narrow, jeans tight around his perfect ass. His hair was wrapped in a tie at the nape of his neck, the long lengths bundled up into a bun, and I itched to take it out and run my fingers through it.

That was where my attention should have stayed.

Except every few miles, I glanced back at Vaughn, driving his father's car.

A tingle of anticipation wormed its way through me. I was suddenly sure bringing Vaughn here was a very bad idea. But he'd promised to take me to a party, so tit for tat, I guess.

Fang circled around to wait for us to pass through the heavy steel gates with the Slayers' logo in the middle, before closing them behind us. In my rearview mirror, Vaughn glanced all around. I wondered if he was slightly panicked about being out here in the middle of the woods, surrounded by fences too tall to jump.

Nobody got in or out unless the Slayers approved it.

I parked my car in the farthest spot from the door, knowing the guys parked their bikes in the prime positions. Vaughn was smart enough to park next to me. He got out, and I met him at the front of our vehicles.

He squinted at the building in the darkness. "You seriously hang out here? It's a prison block."

The clubhouse was ugly. Squat and rectangular. Industrial.

I linked my arm through his. "I do sometimes. I like it. You probably won't, but I do."

"Why wouldn't I like it?"

I shrugged, leading him toward the doors where Fang was waiting. "This isn't a Providence party, Vaughn. Ain't nobody here sitting around discussing their trust funds or holiday homes like you're probably used to."

"Do you really think I'm that boring?"

I shrugged with a grin. "We don't call you guys the Providence Pod People for nothing."

He turned to Fang, untangling himself from my hold. "I can't deal with her. Introduce me to your friends?" His gaze landed on Kiki and Amber, two of the regulars who liked to hang out at the club. "Especially them."

I rolled my eyes. "How predictable."

But the men didn't hear my sulking. Fang led the way over to the bar, putting a pause on Kiki and Amber's chatter while he introduced them to Vaughn.

I normally had a lot of time for Kiki. She was sweet as

freaking sugar for a woman who had to have had a rough life to end up one of the club girls. But today my greeting fell on deaf ears. Her gaze wandered all over Vaughn, lingering on his face. Amber practically pushed her out of the way to take his offered hand.

Instead of shaking it, she drew him in close, pressing her tits against his chest and whispered something in his ear.

Vaughn's cheeks went pink.

I flicked his arm, kinda hoping it hurt. "You're blushing,"

Amber winked at me. "You'd be blushing too, if you'd heard what I said." She grinned. "Love you, Rebs, but not like that."

"He's my brother, you know," I grumbled at her.

"Stepbrother," Vaughn corrected. "We've known each other for all of about a week."

Kiki laughed but pulled me in for a hug that held on longer than it needed to so she could whisper in my ear, "If you don't want us going there, just say the word, girl. Stepbrother or not, if you have dibs, we'll back off."

A very large part of me wanted to say the word.

A big, fat 'don't touch him' word.

I didn't have that right.

I kissed her cheek. "Go at it. He's all yours."

She squeezed my arms. "He's so hot. I don't know how you haven't self-combusted just being near him."

I kind of didn't either.

Fang put an arm around my shoulders and a drink in my hand. "Come on. Let's go sit on the couches. Leave this lot to do their thing."

I sat on one of the old brown leather couches

arranged in a haphazard circle that encouraged conversation.

And exhibition.

To my left, Aloha had Queenie on his lap, a handful of her plump ass in one hand, a beer in the other. She had her legs straddled across him, knees digging into the couch cushions while he kissed her deeply. She ground over his lap, dry humping him without a care that everyone else was there drinking, talking shit, or watching.

That was about as tame as these parties got.

It was something I'd always liked about them. Anything went, and it was always without judgment or shame. On this very couch, Fang had once put me over his lap, lifted my skirt, and torn off my thong so he could spank me.

I went hot at the memory.

Fang leaned in, lips to my ear. "You're blushing. You thinking about that night I made your pretty little behind pink?"

"No," I said, too quickly to sound believable.

Fang chuckled. "Mmm-hmm. It matched the color of your pussy."

Despite my protests, my nipples went hard.

I distracted myself by glancing over at Vaughn and the two women. Kiki had her arms draped around his neck but noticed me watching them.

To my horror, Fang waved them over.

"What are you doing?" I hissed at him.

"Getting to know him. You're living with him, Pix. I can't be there twenty-four seven. Kian gives me good vibes. I don't know about this one yet."

"I can look after myself."

He sighed, a distinct air of hurt in his tone. "Yeah, I know. You never hesitate to remind me. But just humor me, okay? Don't you want to get to know him a bit more?"

"Not really," I grumped.

Fang chuckled softly before putting his beer to his lips. "You're attracted to him."

I elbowed him. "I am not."

"If I put my hand into your panties right now, I wouldn't find them wet?"

I needed to distract the man because he was hitting too close to home. "You would," I sassed him back. "But that's because you're sitting right next to me, reminding me of the time I nearly came on your lap in front of a room full of people, just because you slapped my ass."

He nuzzled his face into the side of my neck. His breath was warm and smelled faintly of beer. "Show me."

"Show you what?"

"How wet you are for me."

My heartrate sped up. Vaughn sat on the middle of the couch in front of us, his arm around Kiki. She tilted her head back, whispered something to him, and he grinned, putting his mouth down on hers.

Jealousy coursed through me.

Fang's big hand landed on my thigh. I had ripped fishnets on beneath a short denim skirt, and his warmth easily radiated through the barely-there material. Inch by inch, his hand slid up until his pinky brushed the hem of my skirt.

Vaughn's gaze was pinned firmly on the same spot, even with Kiki going for gold on his mouth.

I shifted, heat coursing through me from both men.

Fang kissed my neck, and then up to my ear. "He wants you too, you know," he whispered.

"He does not," I murmured back. "He's quite happy over there with Kiki shoving her tongue down his throat."

"We both know he'd rather be over on this couch."

I didn't know that.

But I liked his gaze on me, even as another woman tried to stake her claim.

A rush of power hit me. It was a heady feeling to have both men watching me, waiting to see what I was going to do. What I was going to allow.

All of it on my terms.

Eyes on Vaughn, I uncrossed my legs.

It was a silent signal for Fang to go ahead.

He placed an open-mouthed kiss on the side of my neck, sucking gently, while his hand slid up my skirt and then between my thighs.

He groaned into my skin, rubbing his finger against my clit.

It was so good, I instantly wanted more. More of his touch and his kisses and the way he made me feel.

More of Vaughn's eyes hooded with desire as he watched Fang rub me in intimate places.

"You're drenched, Pix. Those panties need to come off. Here or in my room?"

"Here," I whispered boldly.

It was what the old Rebel would have said.

It was what this current version desperately wanted.

"You want him jealous."

There was no point denying it. I nodded.

"How bad?"

I glanced over at Fang, always so willing to give me

anything I wanted. But his dick was hard behind his jeans. He was clearly getting off on this as well. I swallowed. "Do your worst."

"You might wish you hadn't said that. It just makes me want to cause a scene."

My heart hammered, and for half a second, I thought maybe I'd gone too far. That I should take back the permission I'd just given him. Instead, I let him brush my panties to the side, flashing Vaughn.

His gaze was hot on my pussy that was very probably dripping from a combination of the two of them. In retaliation, he dragged the spaghetti strap on Kiki's dress down, exposing one of her tits. She had a whole lot more going on than I did, her breast spilling over his hand when he cupped her there. He put his head down to take her nipple in his mouth, but his eyes were on me the entire time.

Fang pushed a finger up inside me, and I did nothing to stop the moan that slipped out of my mouth. He alternated between my clit and pressing inside me, quickly adding a second finger when one clearly wasn't enough.

Kiki was an actress through and through, and one who liked the limelight. She moaned loudly at what Vaughn was doing to her, and a few of the other guys looked over, one starting a slow round of applause for her. She winked in their direction, well used to putting on a show for them.

Vaughn didn't even seem to notice.

He only had eyes for me.

Kiki pulled her other dress strap down, letting it settle around her hips, both breasts on display for anyone who wanted to see them. With a show, she got to her knees in front of Vaughn, and Amber leaned over to undo his pants. "Let's see your cock, handsome."

That jealousy surged again, making me breathless even though I had another man's fingers inside me, working me toward orgasm.

Vaughn surely wasn't going to let them blow him right here with everyone watching.

But yes, apparently, he was. The challenge was there in Vaughn's eyes when he raised his hips up off the couch so Amber could drag his jeans and underwear down.

I hadn't picked him to be into this. The public nature of what we were doing.

But his dick was hard, and his expression searing.

I clenched around Fang's fingers, needing more, needing distraction from Amber putting her head into Vaughn's lap and deep-throating him like it was a fucking Olympic sport.

"Stand up," Fang ordered.

I was weak with need and so lost in watching Vaughn, I didn't argue. I just stood.

It was a mistake. From the higher viewpoint I could see every slide of Amber's tongue as she sucked him. As well as the way he threaded his fingers through Kiki's hair when they alternated.

Fang yanked down my fishnets, dragging them right down my thighs, over my calves, and then off my feet.

But it was me who pushed Fang down on the couch so he was lying.

He gripped my leg, massaging it. "Get over here, Pix. You know what I want."

I climbed up his body, legs spread across his broad chest where I paused, waiting because I knew him.

He flipped my skirt up, flashing my bare ass and pussy to the room, then dragged me over to his face. His tongue licked right through my center as I sank down over his lips and tongue.

Pleasure roared its way through me. Spiraling from my nipples that begged for the same treatment Vaughn had shown Kiki. Right through my belly, and lower to where Fang did the thing that Fang did best.

The man ate pussy like he'd been born to do it. Like his life's mission was giving his woman the utmost amount of pleasure one could receive before their lady bits set up a fan page for his talents. His fingers dug into the sides of my hips and guided me over his face, rocking me back and forth and bouncing me on his tongue.

Every time I thought he would suffocate and tried to move myself off him, he dragged me down farther, refusing to let me stop.

The orgasm raced toward me, building and mounting at speed.

I made the mistake of looking over at Vaughn.

His dick was somewhere buried in Kiki's shiny pink mouth. His eyes were at half-mast, hooded with desire. But when Amber tried to kiss him, he gently moved her away, his gaze on me the entire time.

I could tell from the way he shifted that he was close to coming. His hips drove up, while Kiki's mouth slid down. She moaned like a porn star, her free hand pressing between her legs to get herself off while she sucked him.

Vaughn groaned, watching her, then his gaze slid to me.

"Rub your clit," he ground out.

"I am," Kiki panted around his dick. "I'm going to come."

He hadn't been talking to her.

He'd been talking to me.

I put my fingers to my clit and rubbed. Just the way he'd told me to, while Fang tongued my opening.

"Come with me," Vaughn demanded.

"Yes!" Kiki shouted, fingers deep in her pussy. "I'm coming."

He ignored her but fucked her mouth harder and faster to shut her up. Kiki came with a gasp, but it was me Vaughn was waiting on. Me he was holding out for.

Fang tucked three fingers up inside my tight slit, and I came in a blinding rush of color and feeling. The orgasm exploded through my body with a force I didn't know possible, though I was no stranger to getting off.

Vaughn clutched Kiki's hair and finally let me go. His eyes closed and he lost himself in the feel of her mouth, sucking down everything he poured into her. His groans of ecstasy combined with Fang's talents had me panting and whimpering and desperately clutching the back of the couch for support when the orgasm became all-consuming.

When it finally slowed and the world came back to me, I found both men staring at me.

The heat of the moment gone, I tugged my skirt back down and turned to Fang. "Take me to bed. Let me return the favor."

I wasn't fucking him in front of Vaughn.

He was going to have to use his imagination for that one.

## 23

# FANG

*I* followed Rebel down the hall to my bedroom, closed the door, and leaned back on it.

She threw herself down on the bed and buried her face beneath the pillows.

I waited, giving her the time and space she needed.

Eventually, she poked her pretty little head out from beneath the mounds of pillows I'd bought for her. I didn't give a shit about the stupid things. I didn't even use one most of the time, too used to sleeping flat on a mattress that I couldn't break the habit.

But the scratchy sheets I used to own were replaced the first time I'd taken her to bed. From then on, I'd bought nice ones. Ones with big numbers on the package 'cause Queenie had told me they were the good shit.

I didn't want to give Rebel any reason not to come here. Hell, I would have bought sheets made of pure gold if that had gotten her to stay here permanently.

I wish it was that easy to keep her. But I didn't only

call her Pix because of her size. She was the very definition of a pixie, flittering around, impossible to tie down.

No matter how badly I wanted her, I would never clip
her wings.

"What's up, Pix?" I asked her eventually, when she
hadn't resurfaced.

"Oh, I don't know," she wailed. "I just let you make me
come while Kiki and Amber were deep-throating Vaughn
until he choked them with his man spoof."

"I don't know. Kiki looked like she was enjoying
choking on his man spoof, as you put it."

"Would you hate me if I said that was part of the
problem?" She cringed. Then rushed on before I could
even say anything. "I'm a horrible person. You are so
sweet and good, and I am the worst."

I was hardly good nor sweet, and she was far from
horrible. I knew horrible people. I'd not only grown up
with them but surrounded myself with them even now.
Not my brothers, though none of them were angels. But
the people we dealt with on a daily basis were question-
able at best, even if War did try to work with those who
held the same morals and ethics we did. It wasn't always
possible.

Pushing off the wall, I put one knee on the bed. I
wrapped my fingers around her ankle and pulled it,
sliding her down the bed and out from beneath the
pillows.

Fuck, she was gorgeous, with her cute, upturned nose
and wide eyes, her face framed by the wild, messed-up
lengths of her hair. "You, Pix, are the least horrible thing
in my life. You have no fucking idea how not horrible you
are." I crept my fingers up the insides of her calves and

spread her knees. "Especially when you're lying in my bed with no panties on and still wet from riding my face."

She spread her legs wider, letting me crawl up the bed and settle in between them. I hovered over her, my dick still hard behind my jeans, pressed up against her core, my weight all on my forearms.

"You wouldn't say that if you knew what I just did," she whispered.

"You came on my tongue."

"Because Vaughn told me to."

Her face was completely open and vulnerable. It was one of the things I loved about her. I always knew exactly where I stood with her because she was honest to a fault. "I know."

She paused mid self-loathing wail. "You knew?"

"I heard Vaughn tell you to come with him."

"Maybe he was talking to Kiki. She certainly seemed to think he was."

"He wasn't." You didn't say that sort of thing to a woman you didn't care about. I doubted Vaughn had even cared whether Kiki was getting off or not.

But Rebel, he cared about.

I'd seen enough of the way he looked at her before I buried myself beneath her pussy. The attraction between them was so obvious a blind man would have noticed. I dragged her strapless top down with one sharp tug and took her nipple in my mouth, sucking and licking her.

Her fingers found my hair tie, and she pulled it out, snapping it around her wrist. She stroked her fingers through the loose strands of hair, scratching lightly against my scalp while watching me suck her tits.

I loved she didn't even come close to filling my hand. It just made it all the easier to lick every inch of her.

"Pix," I murmured around her nipple.

"Yeah?" Her voice sounded far off, the way it did when she was getting lost in the things I did to her. "If you want Vaughn, I understand."

She stopped stroking my hair and sat up, shoving me away. "What does that mean?"

I sat back on my knees. "I want you to have everything you want."

"I don't want Vaughn."

I raised an eyebrow. "Yeah, and I don't want your pussy for breakfast."

The corner of her mouth turned up. "Was that humor, Fang...fuck, I don't even know your last name."

"It's Garrisen."

"Mine is Kemp."

"I know."

She sighed. "Of course you do. Because you're a good guy."

More like because I'd been stupidly fucking in love with her for at least a year, so I paid attention whenever she was around or when mutual friends spoke about her. I prowled forward, resting my hands on the mattress, either side of her ass, so our faces were closer. "You aren't a bad person, Rebel. I know what this is. Where I stand with you. If that's all I ever get to have with you, then that will be enough."

She covered her face with her hands and shook her head. "Nooooo. That's not fair to you. I wish I could give you more, but I just have nothing to give. I watched my mother fall for men over and over, and it always ended with her on the floor in the fetal position, barely able to function. She had me to pick her up and put her to bed and bring in money to pay the bills. I don't have that luxury. I can't afford for a man to destroy me. Not even one as sweet and good as you."

Her shoulders shook quietly.

I wrapped my fingers around hers and drew them down so I could see her tearstained face. "I'll never hurt you."

"You would never mean to. But, Fang, you would. Or worse, I'd hurt you. I couldn't live with that."

My desperation wasn't pretty, but this felt a whole lot like slipping right back to where we always did. With the two of us being fuck buddies and nothing more. I didn't want that. "I can share you, Pix. It might fucking kill me, but if that's what you want, then I'll do it. It works out pretty well for War and Bliss and the other guys."

She went quiet for a moment, stroking her fingers across the stubble of my beard. Eventually, she answered. "It's not fair of me to ask that from you."

"It's better than where we'll end up if I smother you and make you run." I leaned into her touch and closed my eyes. "You just need to promise me one thing."

"What?"

I opened my eyes to gaze into hers. "I need you to pick guys who are going to watch out for you like I do. Hell, it might be a good thing. I could actually sleep today because I knew Kian was there for you when I couldn't be. I like him."

"You do?" She cocked her head to one side. "You aren't bi, are you?"

I snorted on a laugh. "I don't like him like that."

She giggled. "More's the pity. The two of you would be freaking hot together."

I pressed her back into the bed. "I'd rather get hot with you."

She wrapped her arms around my neck and smiled softly. "Me too."

The pride that rushed through me at making her smile was ridiculous. It was such a small thing, but it lit me up inside every time. I hadn't been lying when I said I'd do anything, including watch her date other men, if that's what brought her happiness.

I wasn't happy if she wasn't. I was man enough to recognize I didn't fill every gap in her life. She wouldn't be my Pix if I tried to keep her in a cage.

I hoped Vaughn and Kian knew that too.

I'd make sure they did. No one was fucking hurting her ever again. Not even me.

I undid the button on her skirt, and she helped me lower it down her hips. Her sweet little pussy was right there, bare and just begging me to suck it again. So I did. I buried my face between her thighs once more and reveled in being back in my favorite place in the world. This room. At this club. Where outside, my brothers had my back, and in here, I had the woman I would compare every other to.

None would ever come close.

I needed her naked. Needed to mark every inch of her body with my kiss, and my hands, and my tongue, before she let anyone else do it. Her top was already around her middle, but I pushed at it, and she dragged it off the rest of the way.

She lay quietly beneath me, her eyes big when I dragged my gaze up her body to her face.

I stopped. "Are you okay?"

She nodded. "Better than okay."

"I need you to tell me how far I can go."

"I'm yours."

They were words I'd always wanted to hear her say, except I knew she didn't mean them the way I wanted her to. I would be okay with that if it killed me. "I want to fuck you, Pix. But I'm scared I'm going to hurt you."

She shook her head reassuringly. "You won't. Of all the people in this world, Fang, you're the only one I trust to be the first after…"

After those fucking assholes had taken what wasn't theirs.

She pressed my head down between her legs again. "You don't get angry when your tongue is down there." She winked at me.

I was sure I fell in love with her all over again. But I shoved that feeling aside and made her come, working her body just the way I knew she liked.

Her moans were loud, echoing around my sparsely furnished room. I hoped every man outside heard them. Vaughn in particular, so he knew what he had to live up to.

With her blissed-out on the bed beneath me, I put one hand to the back of my shirt and yanked it over my head, then stood and took my boots and socks and jeans off.

She blinked open her eyes and curled up on her side, gloriously naked.

"Condom," she murmured.

"I'm always careful with you."

"I know. I just want you to be extra careful now."

I ripped the top off the condom, but she held a hand out for it. "Let me."

I let her take it from my fingers and hissed when she stroked her hand up and down my shaft a few times. Her other hand cupped and massaged my balls. The fact she was there, naked in my bed, her arousal and my saliva still shining on her inner thighs, had me counting sheep in my head to make sure I didn't finish this too soon.

Eventually, she rolled the condom on and lay back on the bed.

A flash of nerves appeared in her eyes when I covered her body. "You can say no, Pix. Any time. Before or during. You know that, right? This is only about you and what you want."

She wrapped her legs around my waist, letting my erection nudge at her entrance. "I want this," she whispered. "It was a big part of my life, and I want to know I can still enjoy it. That they didn't take that from me too." She strained up to kiss my mouth. "Just go slow. Don't stop kissing me."

I nodded, my heart fucking ripping open at her vulnerability, while pride swirled through me as well, knowing it was me she trusted to do this. Me she wanted when she was scared.

I wanted to tell her I loved her.

But I knew it would ruin it. That it would have the exact opposite effect I was hoping for. So I used my tongue to explore her mouth instead of saying a word. I kissed her until she hugged me tight, planting my body on top of hers. I kissed her until she made tiny whimpering noises of need, and she rocked her hips back and forth, trying to get me to her entrance.

I kissed her until she dragged my hips down so my cock filled her. Then I waited until she pulled off my mouth breathlessly and begged, "Please!"

With my lips on hers, I thrust into her. I had her so primed, there was no resistance, but I still moved painfully slowly, driving us both crazy, but it felt too good to hurry.

I rocked in and out of her body until her hips rose and fell in erratic thrusts as she lost control, needing more than the pace I'd offered.

"Fuck me, Fang. Stop holding back. Please!"

It was the permission I'd been waiting for. I gradually picked up the pace, each stroke gaining a little momentum until we were at the perfect tempo.

"Harder," she groaned.

I knew exactly what she meant. I grabbed her hands, pinning her to the bed and driving home, my pubic bone grinding on her clit so her eyes rolled back. But I kept the pace the same. Silent, strong thrusts, deep inside her until her breaths turned to pants and her moans grew loud once more.

I fucking loved how vocal she was. What you saw with Rebel was what you got. There was never any holding back.

"Fang!" she moaned.

"Milo," I whispered in her ear.

Her eyes flew open in surprise.

I didn't stop. But I had wanted her to know something about me.

She smiled softly, but then I slammed back inside her, and her shout of pleasure was all I heard. It filled my ears, my chest, my entire being.

Those three little words sat on my tongue again, but I buried them in her neck instead.

"I'm coming!"

She didn't need to tell me. I felt it in the spasm of her pussy, it suddenly gripping tight around my cock. The words I wanted to say turned into groans of ecstasy as she drove me right over the edge with her.

The room spun so I closed my eyes and thrust my hips against hers, riding us both out until she begged me for mercy.

Coming inside her was always the sweetest form of torture.

I flopped down on the mattress, wanting to be on top of her but terrified my weight would crush her. Instead, I pulled her on top of me, the both of us a sticky, sweaty mess of arms and limbs and well-satisfied urges.

She dropped her head down on my chest, and I kissed the top of it.

"You need to get off me so I can take care of the condom."

She shook her head. "Just one more minute. Then you can go."

I wasn't ever able to say no to her. I stroked my fingers up and down her spine, feeling each ridge and bump, sure they were more prominent than the last time I'd had her like this.

"Are you eating?"

She lifted a sleepy head. "Yeah. Sure."

But her eyes didn't meet mine.

I swept my hands over her rib cage which was all too prominent. I would take care of that. I would convince Kian and Vaughn to keep an eye on it too.

Whatever she needed, I would get it for her.

## 24

# VAUGHN

*I* woke up in an MC clubhouse with a crick in my neck and two women wrapped around me.

Neither was the one I really wanted to be naked with though. She was down the hall somewhere, probably still asleep, since I couldn't hear her moans and cries of pleasure anymore.

Thank fuck.

Amber stirred, blinked her eyes open, and smiled at me. "Hey, handsome. You have fun last night?"

I pulled my arm out from beneath Kiki's head and scrubbed a hand over my face. Fun? Sure. Getting off was always fun. But it had been mixed in with a whole heap of frustration because I couldn't get the image of my stepsister riding some guy's face out of my head.

Or the things I'd said to her.

Ugh.

Amber reached beneath the blankets and circled my morning wood with her fingers.

I jerked out of her grasp and clambered over Kiki. "I should go. It's gotta be getting late."

Amber sat up and pouted at me, round fake tits like melons on her chest.

They were hot. But not what I wanted.

Rebel's sweet, perky tits were.

I found my pants on the floor and yanked them up, buttoning the fly. My dad's car keys jabbed me in the thigh, which reminded me I'd left my phone somewhere too. I located that by removing a lacy pink bra from a lamp table and found my phone sitting silently beneath it.

I poked the screen and cringed at the messages that popped up. Several calls from my lawyer. I put on my shirt, kissed Amber on the cheek, told her I'd see her around, and to tell Kiki thanks for a great night.

She was still pouting when I opened the door, but then my phone rang, and I couldn't worry about her anymore.

Nathan the lawyer again. That couldn't be good.

Something heavy hit the door of the room to my right, and an annoyed bellow came from the other side. "Somebody shut that fucking phone up! Some of us are trying to sleep!"

Pissing off a club full of burly bikers was probably not the smartest idea. I hustled down the hall to the communal area, where the party had taken place last night. I could barely look at the two brown leather couches that had been the scene of a really good time. The rest of the room was a complete disaster, with empty bottles, half-eaten pizza, and various stray articles of clothing strewn about, just waiting for someone to wake up and get their clean on. I took a seat at the sticky bar, trying not to touch the counter, and answered the call. "What's up, Nathan?"

"'Bout fucking time you answered. I have great news."

His voice was entirely too chipper for this time of the morning. Though when I glanced out the window, the sun was pretty high, so it maybe wasn't as early as I'd initially thought. "Get on with it then."

"Your stepsister is going down for the murder of your dad."

"What?" Surprise forced the word out louder than expected. There was another shout from down the hall, but this time I didn't care. "Say more words, Nathan."

"I've got a buddy down at the station. I hit him up for some details on where they were at with the investigation into your father's death, and he said they're pinning it on the girl. Your name was on the suspect list too, but I sorted that out."

My head spun. "How?"

"Money talks in this town, Vaughn. You know that."

I gripped the countertop, nails bending against the unyielding laminate. "Rebel didn't kill our parents. She loved her mom. Have you met her? She's pint-sized. She couldn't murder a fly."

"That's part of their case against her. Don't need to be big to poison someone."

"Poison..." I shook my head. "She was with me the night before the wedding. And the morning of. Rebel didn't poison anyone."

He sighed. "I really thought you'd be more excited about this. This is good news for your case. If she's tied up in jail for the rest of her life, the money and the property and the business are all yours. If she's deemed the murderer, it's an open-and-shut case to get the entire estate awarded to you. That is what you wanted, Vaughn. That's what you told me you needed, to take care of your wife's...indiscretions."

I lowered my voice to a hiss. "I never said I wanted an innocent woman in jail to do it."

"You don't know she's innocent. The autopsy report said that poison could have been ingested anywhere from two to forty-eight hours before they collapsed. Do you know where she was for every minute of that time?"

I didn't. But my gut said they were wrong about this. So freaking wrong.

"Cancel the contest to the will, Nathan. I already told you once, but actually hear me this time. I changed my mind. And for fuck's sake, get me whatever the cops have on my father's and Miranda's deaths. I need to know everything."

"But I—"

"Do you want to keep your job?"

Nathan huffed down the line. "Well, of course, but I would—"

"Then do as I fucking say!"

I slammed my finger down on the end call button so hard my knuckle cracked in protest.

When I looked up, Fang was in the space between the living room and the hallway to the bedrooms. His face was like thunder.

I put my hands up. "Sorry. Sorry. I didn't mean to yell and wake everyone up."

"What's going on with Rebel?" His words were as deadly and cold as black ice. "I heard your side of the conversation, and I didn't like any of it. Don't tell me I brought you into this clubhouse only to find you're some sort of rat, making deals behind her back or throwing her under the bus."

We stared at each other across the room. I had no idea whether telling him was the right thing to do, but then I wasn't leaving without Rebel. She needed to know what she was up against. I needed to do something. "Cops are pinning our parents' deaths on her."

Fang shook his head. "No."

"That's what I said."

"I'm going down to the police station."

"Good." I shook my keys in his direction and pushed to my feet. "I'll drive."

"Neither of you are going down there," Rebel announced from behind Fang's broad back.

I hadn't even noticed her standing there because he took up so much of the room.

Fang put his hand to the back of her neck. "Pix, it's bad. They're—"

"Pinning it on me. Yeah, I know. I already had the pleasure of speaking to them."

I blinked. "You knew?"

Fang glared at her. "Why didn't you tell me?"

She shrugged. "Because I knew you'd lose it like you did when you saw Leonn at the hospital."

Fang dropped his gaze to the floor, probably knowing she was right. Every muscle in his body was stiff with holding himself back. I could tell, because I felt the same way. I wanted to storm out of the door, drive down to the station, and demand to know why they were wasting their time concentrating on Rebel when the real killer was out there somewhere.

My father would roll over in his grave if I let the woman he'd wanted taken care of go to jail for his murder.

I'd already been such a disappointment to him. I couldn't deal with the thought of continuing that.

But Rebel's glare was all business. I had a feeling she'd throw herself in front of my car if Fang and I tried to make a getaway in it.

"Sit. Both of you."

Fang immediately did as he was told, slumping down onto the couch.

I had reservations. "On the sex couch, bro? Really? No one has even cleaned that thing yet."

Fang raised one eyebrow. "Is that what's really bothering you? Or the fact you can't stop thinking about how I licked her pussy 'til she coated my face in—"

"Okay! That's about enough of that," Rebel butted in, her cheeks pink. "Sit somewhere. I don't care. But Vaughn, we need to talk."

I eyed Fang, feeling punchy. "If it's about the way you came because I told you to—"

She cut me off with a glare, and I conceded with a smirk.

"Fine. Fine. I'm sitting."

"Can we just forget last night happened and never talk about it again, please?" she asked.

I didn't want to do that, but I wasn't going to argue. Especially since Fang was nodding. Of course he was. He was the lucky bastard who'd had her in his room all night. I'd be feeling pretty smug if that had been me too.

Rebel brushed her hands off, like that was all taken care of, then turned to Fang. "Can I get a big sheet of paper and a marker, please?"

I lifted my head. "What for?"

But Fang didn't question her. He stood and disappeared into a room with a 'private' name plaque on the door and returned a moment later with a poster-sized sheet of paper and a black Sharpie. "This do?"

She took them from him, kissed his cheek, and knelt on the floor in front of a low coffee table.

"We playing school?" I asked her. "You want to be the teacher or the student?"

She raised an eyebrow at me. "We all know the girl from Saint View could teach you things beyond your wildest imagination, Vaughn."

I frowned at her. "I'm the one who had a threesome last night."

Fang glanced over at me, laughter flickering at his lips. "He said that like it was something out of the ordinary. Was that baby's first group sex experience?"

I didn't respond.

Rebel's mouth dropped open. "Shit! I think you're right." She peered at me. "You were a threesome virgin?"

"I've been with my wife since I was nineteen. I didn't exactly get a whole lot of time for fooling around."

They looked at each other and laughed.

Rebel side-eyed me. "Fuck. Thirty-something and only ever had one partner. You have done other positions, right? Or are you strictly a missionary man?"

Heat crept up the back of my neck. "Just tell us what the paper and marker are for, would you? Nobody cares about how many threesomes I've had."

"I don't know. It's kinda fun watching you squirm." Fang folded his arms behind his head and leaned back on the couch, a shit-eating grin playing all over his face.

Rebel pressed her teeth down on her lip, like she was biting back amusement, and slowly let it pop out. "Okay. Enough teasing Mr. Vanilla. If you two actually want to help me, instead of running down to the cop shop and getting yourselves arrested, here's what you can do. Help me work out other suspects. If the cops are determined to pin it on me, then we need to give them other places and people to investigate."

She uncapped the marker and scrawled "Suspects" across the top of the page.

"What are you, fifteen?" I muttered, watching her draw a bubble-shaped cloud around the word.

She glared at me, then wrote down her first suspect's name.

"Me!" I shouted indignantly. "Are you serious?"

She lifted a shoulder. "Hey, if I'm a suspect because of the inheritance, you should be too."

She was right. But it didn't matter. "My lawyer paid the cops to not look in my direction."

Rebel shook her head then put an asterisk next to my name. "That"—she stabbed her pen into the paper —"means I suspect you even more now."

I rolled my eyes. "It wasn't me."

"That's what Ted Bundy said too."

I groaned. "How about we add some other names to the list? Like Fang."

Fang laughed. "Why me? What's my motive?"

"I don't know. Miranda was pretty hot. Maybe you wanted to trade the family car for the Lamborghini."

Rebel threw the marker lid at me. "Did you just call me a family car, Vaughn Weston? Can you even make it through one full day without being an asshole?"

"Apparently not."

"I'm not putting Fang on the list. That's ridiculous. Who else? How about your mom and stepdad?"

I shook my head. "Not a chance. My dad literally stepped aside so the two of them could get married. If anyone would want to kill anyone out of that threesome, it should be my dad wanting to kill my mom. But that was twenty years ago anyway. Would be a long time to hold a grudge if you were upset enough to wait this long."

Rebel tapped the marker on the tabletop. "That checks with what my mom said about your parents. Shame."

"Shame my mom isn't a murderer? Nice, Roach."

She flipped me the bird. "They're going on the list, but not with an asterisk. Yours still stands."

I rolled my eyes. "What about your dad?"

"Tenneson? Please. Haven't seen him since I was about three. So that's doubtful."

"He should still go on the list. Along with your mom's exes. Jealousy is a big motive for murder."

She started writing. "Give me a minute. There's a few."

I waited while she wrote down a list of names.

Fang peered over her shoulder. "Ugh, Linden Whitchel? I hate that guy."

"Yeah, me too." Rebel put an asterisk next to his name. "She could pick 'em."

"I'll try not to be insulted on my father's behalf," I muttered.

They both ignored me, and eventually Rebel got to the end of her mother's little black book.

"Guess your dad didn't have any other exes?"

I shook my head. "One and done."

"Aw, like father, like son," Fang mocked.

I was really beginning to hate that guy.

Rebel ignored him. "Give me someone else who would have benefited from your dad being dead?"

I mused on that for a moment. "My wife, I guess. If I get money, so does she, since we're still legally married."

Rebel asked me how to spell her name, and I gave her the letters so she could write them down. "His business partner too. Harold Coker."

Rebel scribbled that across the page too. "This is good. The list is getting long."

"I think you need to think outside their immediate circles too. Who else had opportunity? The judge?"

Rebel peered at me. "I don't remember her name."

I didn't either, but I was sure I could find it. "Just put judge for now. She's a bit of a long shot anyway, but we can look it up if need be. Hotel staff would have also had opportunity. Dad and Miranda both stayed in the hotel for two nights before the ceremony."

"Friends of your mom's?"

"She didn't have many." Rebel cleared her throat. "Speaking of friends, though... Kian."

I frowned. "That's as stupid as accusing me."

"Is it? He was close to your dad. People are more likely to be murdered by someone close to them than some random hotel employee."

"I've known Kian since I was a kid. He didn't do it."

It really freaking irked me Rebel wrote his name down on the list anyway.

My leg bounced like it had a mind of its own. I didn't know what had come over me last night. Rebel was the pain in my ass I'd first assumed her to be. "I think that list is pretty comprehensive. I'm sure the cops will be grateful for it."

Rebel and Fang both gave me that, "Oh, he's so sweet and innocent" look.

I was getting really sick of them doing that. "What?" I demanded.

"You're such a Providence boy at heart, aren't you? Must be nice to assume the cops will actually do their job, just because you're a rich white guy. We aren't all as lucky as you, with the ability to just pay them off." Rebel put the lid back on the marker and sat back, reading over the names she'd added to the paper. "We aren't making this list to hand over to them, Vaughn. We're investigating it ourselves. You going to help? Make use of all those *Law and Order* episodes you used to watch?"

My wife's threats rang in the back of my head. If the cops had taken me off their suspect list, then I needed to get back to Cali. As much as I didn't want to be married to Brooke, I didn't want her dead either. We'd been together since we were nineteen. There was no forgiving the way she'd lied and cheated. She'd ruined everything good between us. But every day I stayed here was another day she was alone, just waiting for an ambush. That didn't sit right with me.

I wasn't wanted here. Kian had made that clear. And Rebel...last night hadn't changed anything between us. It was just sex. Not a big deal. I didn't need to be here to take care of her. I'd make sure she had money. She had Kian and Fang for whatever else she needed. "I'll talk to the cops for you, but I'm not some sort of private investigator. We need to leave that to the professionals. I'm sorting out this will and the funeral and then I'm out of here."

Rebel's face fell, her voice turning quiet and cold. "Fine. I'll send you a postcard from prison."

I blinked, shocked at the way one single sentence set my plans to flames. I barely knew Rebel. I should have just been able to walk away. And yet I knew if I did, that expression on her face would haunt me. "Fuck, you do guilt trips better than my mom does. Like seriously, did you take a course on that or something? Is it just a chick thing?"

She didn't say anything.

Her silence screamed in my head, mixing with memories of her bruises and the shitty little apartment she'd lived in. Images from last night replayed over and over, her head thrown back in pleasure, hips rolling, wild, free, and so fucking beautiful. She had friends who loved her. A job she adored.

I craved what she had.

I craved her.

Last night had proved that.

"Fine," I said stiffly. "Let me take another look at that. I guess we have some work to do."

I tried to ignore the way she beamed at me. It did things to my insides that only cemented the idea, even if I did run back to California, she wouldn't be so easy to forget.

## 25

## REBEL

*I* had to go to work, and War called some sort of club meeting that required Fang's attention, so our amateur sleuthing was put on hold after we'd made our suspect list. But I was distracted all night while I pulled beers and bussed food to tables. Every name on the list rolled around in my head, along with a ticking bomb, just waiting to explode.

I had no idea if or when the cops would come for me. But if Vaughn's lawyer was right, it seemed like it could happen at any time.

I couldn't think about that too much or the panic would consume me. I'd seen too many innocent people go to jail to think it couldn't happen to me too.

I fell into my big soft bed in Vaughn's house after my shift and tossed and turned until the tiny hours of the morning, when exhaustion finally took over.

I could have sworn it was only ten minutes later when Kian bounded into my room and cannonballed onto my bed. "Wake up, Little Demon!"

His heavy weight sent my much smaller body nearly right off the bed. In my half-sleep state, I grappled at the sheets, trying to get a grip on something that would stop me sliding right onto the floor.

The covers just came sliding down with me.

I hit the carpet with a bone-jarring thud that ricocheted right through my body.

Kian's handsome face peered over the bed at me. Eyes wide with surprise, he barely held back laughter. "What just happened?"

I reached up and pushed his face away. "You catapulted me off my bed!"

He burst into laughter that made his handsome face way too attractive for this time of the morning. "It was not my intention, but at least you're up. Let's go!"

I glanced out the window, and my mouth dropped open. I pointed at it. "Is that sky orange because the sun is still *rising*? What the hell time is it?"

"Five thirty."

"Five thirty in the morning?"

"Best time of the day, and you're missing it. Come on!"

He grabbed my arm and dragged me up off the floor, though I would have preferred he'd left me there. I wasn't fussy about where I slept. I just wanted to actually get some.

But Kian shoved me toward my walk-in closet. "Go. Get dressed. We're going running."

I stopped, and then it was my time to laugh. "Ha, that's funny. I thought you just said running. You meant, you're going running and buying me a bucket-sized coffee on your way home, right?"

"Coffee is terrible for you. Running is good. Natural endorphins are where it's at, Little Demon."

"How am I the demon when you're the one in here before six and bouncing around like you just took an upper?" I narrowed my eyes at him. "Did you? 'Cause if you want me to run, you might have to share."

He laughed. "I don't even drink coffee. You really think I put drugs in my body?"

I groaned. "Oh shit, I live with a 'my body is a temple' person. Tell Vaughn I changed my mind about living here. Sleeping in my car might be preferable."

He raised an eyebrow. "You want your revenge on Caleb or what?"

There was probably nothing else that would have got me motivated to work out at this time of the morning. Nothing except for that.

He grinned, knowing he had me. "You aren't a bad fighter. But the sort of training we're going to be doing? You're going to need the fitness. And from what I can see, your current lifestyle is not exactly what I call athletic."

I tossed a sock at him from my drawer. "Insulting. I run. If bears are chasing me."

"You don't eat."

I glanced at him sharply. "Haven't had much appetite with everything going on."

"That has to change. I'm not the only one who noticed. Fang sent me a text last night, asking me to watch you."

Anger poured through me. "He better not have. He's not my mother." Not that my mother had ever really paid attention to my calorie consumption.

"Don't get pissed. He's scared. And frankly, so am I.

You need the fitness, which means you need the calories, or you'll have nothing to build muscle with. What's your favorite foods? I'm a good cook. I'll make whatever you want, whenever you want."

"Coffee is my favorite food."

"Not a food, Little Demon."

I sighed. "The omelets you made the other morning smelled really good."

He nodded. "Run first. Then omelets. Promise you won't run off somewhere before you can eat them?"

My stomach was churning at the thought of food, but I knew he was right. I'd lost weight since the attack, and it wasn't healthy. I needed to be stronger to take on Caleb.

"Fine. Let's go ruh...ruhhhh... Kian, I can't even say the word at this time of the morning. It's dirty."

Kian sniggered from the other side of the closet. "Get dressed or I'm coming in there and doing it for you."

I stuck my head out of the doors, being careful to cover up my half-naked state. "Pervert."

"That sounds like more procrastination. I'm not joking. I will come in there and put a sports bra on you myself if I have to. Can't say I have any practice in that. Plenty of practice in taking them off though, if you ever require such a service..."

I grinned at him but decided enough men had seen me naked in the past two days so dressing myself was the preferred option. I rummaged through all my clothes and came up with a cutoff pair of shorts and an old Rolling Stones shirt. I didn't even own a sports bra, but there wasn't much bounce to my barely-there boobs anyway. A regular old crop top would have to do.

I found a pair of beat-up old Converse in a box I

hadn't unpacked yet, put them on, then presented myself to Kian.

His gaze swept over me. "You look like you're going to an emo punk rock concert."

"If that were true, I'd have more eyeliner on."

"Where are your sneakers?"

"These are sneakers. If you don't like my outfit choice, we could go shopping instead? That sounds like way more fun than running."

He shook his head. "I will take you shopping and get you some decent sneakers, but after running, and after food."

I grumbled at him but followed him down the stairs and out the door anyway. The cold morning air hit me in the face, and I turned back around. "Nope. It's freezing. There's a reason bears hibernate in winter. I now identify as a bear. Bye."

He caught me by the shoulders and steered me back along the path to the road.

I dragged my feet with every step.

"Gonna be a slow-ass run if I have to poke you the entire way."

I sighed overdramatically and picked up the pace since I was out here, and Kian was clearly not giving up.

Kian jogged alongside me, grinning at me like I was his star pupil. "That's it! You're doing so well. Breathe in through your nose. Out through your mouth. You were born for this, Rebel! Go girl!"

I stopped and stared at him.

"What?" He ran around me in circles.

"Your pep is inciting violence. I just had a flash of me pushing you off the Saint View bluffs, and it brought me great joy, even though you were shouting motivations at me the entire way down."

He sniggered. "Fine. No more pep. We can run in silence. Even though that's really boring." He broke off and headed down the road again.

I moved my ass to keep up with him.

For a minute, the silence was bliss. I loved every second of it.

Until he started singing.

Kian belting out Britney Spears songs in an off-key warble was disturbing. But clearly, Kian didn't do silent contemplation.

"Tell me about Vaughn's dad."

Kian stopped in the middle of the "Toxic" chorus. "Bart? Nicest guy you'd ever meet. Went out of his way to be good to people."

"You knew him well?"

He shrugged. "We weren't best friends or anything. We didn't stay up late at night sharing secrets. But there's not really many secrets when you live with someone anyway, even if you are just the hired help."

"What sort of secrets did Bart have?"

He shrugged. "There were some late-night phone calls, I guess. I just assumed they were from his business partner. They didn't always get along."

That sparked my interest. "What makes you think that?"

"Nothing terribly exciting. A few arguments floating out from behind Bart's study door. The occasional look between them when they thought no one else was paying attention."

"A look? Like a sexual one?"

He huffed out a laugh between sucking in breaths of air as we jogged along. "No. Bart wasn't the one exchanging sexual looks in that house."

I widened my eyes at him. "Who? Vaughn?"

He wiggled his eyebrows at me. "Maybe."

"With you?"

Kian didn't say anything. He just ran faster.

I pumped my legs to catch up with him. "Kian! You can't just drop a bomb like that and then run off."

He glanced over at me, laughter in his eyes. "Maybe I just said it to get you to run faster."

"Well, it worked. Tell me more and a girl might even sprint."

"Thought you wanted to know about Bart and his business partner?"

"I do."

"If you ask me, Harold is the one the cops should be investigating. Bart held the majority share in the company. Fifty-one percent. With Vaughn in California and clearly no desire to ever work for his father, old Harry could have easily assumed he'd get to be the big boss if Bart was out of the picture. Seems like a pretty good motive to me."

It was, and good information to have.

But I couldn't stop thinking about what Kian had said about Vaughn. "Were the two of you together?"

"Me and Bart?" Kian coughed.

"I meant Vaughn, but should I ask about you and Bart? In theory, you have a good motive for murder too."

He stopped running to stare at me. "Why on earth would I kill him?"

I was grateful for the break and took my sweet-ass

time, doubled over with my hands on my knees while I sucked in giant lungfuls of air. "Because you were jealous of my mom maybe? Maybe you were in love with Bart? Maybe you were in love with both of them? You could have been having threesomes every night for all I know."

"Pfft. Your mom would have told you if we were banging."

"You don't know that."

"I do. Because I know Miranda had no filter, much the way you don't." He grinned down at me. "Trust me. If we'd been screwing, you would know about it. That's how good I am."

I cocked my head to one side. "You know, when guys talk themselves up like that, they're normally compensating for something."

He started up a slow jog again, running backward this time so I could see the devilish smile on his face. "If you ever want to find out, I'm just on the other side of the bathroom. Speaking of which, first one home gets first shower. And there's limited hot water, just so you know."

He took off running, leaving me trailing behind, my calf twinging with pain and my chest aching from exertion. By the time I got back upstairs, the water was already running in our shared bathroom, and Kian was singing a Christina Aguilera song at the top of his lungs.

"Ugh!" I was a hot and sweaty mess, and Kian was infuriating.

Vaughn appeared in the doorway and leaned on it. "He do that thing where he makes you race him home for the shower?"

"Yes!"

"He's annoying when he does that. I could never beat him either. Come with me."

"I'm hot and grumpy and tired, Vaughn. I think I pulled a muscle while I was running as gracefully as a gazelle."

"I saw you through the window. Your legs are too short to be gazelle-like. It was more like watching a chicken with its head cut off."

I glared at him. "I really don't know why I moved in here."

He smirked at me. "Come on. You want to get Kian back? I didn't grow up with him not to know his pet hates. Cold water is one of them. I swear he got fast just because he never wants to be second in the shower."

That I could get behind. I limped after him, my supposed chicken leg knotted with cramps. I followed Vaughn down into the laundry room where he made a show of leaning on the sink. He flicked up the handle, letting hot water pour from the faucet. Then he held one finger up, telling me to wait.

"Vaughn!" Kian yelled from upstairs. "You traitor! You did not tell her the laundry runs off the same hot water heater! Where is your loyalty?"

He shrugged. "Apparently with the chicken-legged, house-stealing, face-riding roach."

On his tongue, it almost sounded like a compliment.

## 26

## REBEL

*I* was rubbing the cramp out of my calf when Kian came crashing back into my bedroom, hair dripping wet, water droplets all over his chest, and a towel wrapped around his waist.

He raised an eyebrow at me. "Since when are you Team Vaughn? I thought it was you and me against the world?"

"You left me for dead in the middle of a run."

"I don't like cold water."

"So Vaughn said. Keep your friends close but your enemies closer."

"Which are we?"

I shrugged nonchalantly. "Remains to be seen."

He clutched his heart dramatically, spun around a couple of times, and then collapsed back on my bed. "Your words wound, Little Demon."

"You're making my blankets all wet!"

He stuck his arms and legs out like he was making a

snow angel and waved them back and forth, wiping his wet body all over my bed.

I was sure the look I shot his way should have sent him to an early grave, but he just flipped onto his belly, leaning on his arms to watch me. "Your leg hurt?"

"No, I just rub it like this because the skill transfers over to seasoning chicken breast."

He sniggered and pushed my hands away. "Let me do it. I give great massages."

"What makes you think I don't?"

"Your hands are too small. Big hands make for better massages. It's just a fact."

I shoved my aching leg in his direction. "Fine. Prove it."

"Lie on your belly. Let me get some oil."

"Don't have any."

"I do."

"For jacking off with?"

"I find strawberry-flavored lube preferable for jacking off actually."

I raised an eyebrow with a laugh. "Why does the flavor matter in that situation? Hmm?"

He scowled at me. "On your belly, Roach."

I wagged a finger at him. "Nuh-uh. Only Vaughn is allowed to call me that."

He grabbed a bottle of body lotion from my bedside table. "Fine. I can make do with this."

I rolled over onto my belly, and he squirted lotion all over the back of my strained calf.

With slow, practiced fingers, he kneaded the tight muscle.

I squirmed in pain, trying to get away, but he pinned

me to the bed. "Hold still. You'll thank me once it stops hurting and starts to feel good."

I gritted my teeth, but soon enough, I found he was right. The strained muscle eased, and his touch became pleasurable.

Maybe a little too pleasurable.

His fingers worked their way up the back of my leg, moving away from my sore spot and up my bare thigh.

A sigh of pleasure escaped my mouth.

"Good?" Kian asked.

"Very good. You are indeed the master of massages."

His fingers brushed the loose leg of my shorts. "There's tension right up the back of your thigh."

"Is there really, or is that just your coy way of feeling me up?"

"A bit of both. Tell me to stop."

I didn't want him to. It felt nice.

His fingers slipped beneath the edge of my shorts and slid right up, until his fingertips touched the crease where my thigh met my ass. "Seriously, Rebel. Tell me to stop."

He was right. This was going well past the realm of a friendly coach-student, after-workout rubdown. And yet, I still said nothing.

His fingers moved beneath the elastic of my panties and higher to grope my ass. To his credit, he kept up the massaging action, smoothing his thumb into my flesh.

"How's my booty?" I asked, turning my head to the side to peek back at him. "I'm pretty proud of her."

"Is she as badly behaved as you are?"

"I think she's the source of all my evil powers to be honest."

Kian groaned. "Don't tempt me to pull these little shorts off and spank her."

Heat bloomed between my thighs. I flipped over onto my back before he could reach between my legs and notice. It forced him to remove his hand, but he was still on my bed. Still in nothing but a towel.

And I had a very real need building between my legs.

When he lifted my aching leg and draped it over his shoulder, I gasped.

If he'd been Fang, his next move would have been to go down on me.

But Kian straightened my leg out and leaned his weight forward, increasing the stretch.

"If you learned this from your coach, I hope he at least bought you dinner first."

Kian's smile was always so bright. He had a dimple in one cheek when he smiled really big. That damn dimple did things to me.

"I slept with my track coach all through college."

"I'm not sure I'm surprised."

"Why. You want to sleep with me right now, Little Demon?"

My fingers itched to pull his towel and see what was straining beneath it. "I've heard it's good cardio. Much better than running."

Kian laughed and pushed back to his knees, dropping my leg to the bed.

It fell like dead weight in disappointment.

"As fun as that sounds, I made you a promise of breakfast, and we are running out of time."

"We are? Where are we going?"

"Vaughn let it slip last night that you're planning on going to Caleb's Halloween party with him."

"Ugh, of course he did. Tattletale. I guess he told Fang too?"

"No, he was weird about it when I suggested Fang might appreciate that info. So I told him. We decided we're coming too."

I sat up, instantly a whole lot less turned on. "How about no?"

"You're gatecrashing, why can't we?"

"'Cause I'm a tiny person who will blend in with the crowd. You and Fang might as well walk in with fireworks exploding out of your hats while shaking your hips in grass skirts. You couldn't be any more 'look at me.'"

"I respectfully disagree. I'm allergic to grass, so I would never wear a skirt made from one."

I folded my arms across my chest and glared at him.

He held his hands up in mock surrender. "We'll all wear costumes and masks. No one will know who we are. And hey, if everyone is staring at us, that gives you even more opportunity to fly under the radar."

He actually had a point.

"I get to choose your costume," I declared.

He raised an eyebrow. "Only if I get to choose yours."

"I'm not agreeing to that."

He huffed out a sigh. "You drive a hard bargain. But I submit. You can choose. I don't care what I wear. But there's no way I'm letting you near those guys without people who are watching your back. Vaughn alone isn't enough, and it isn't fair for it to be all on him. Caleb will have an entire party on his side. You need more than just one man."

It seemed like I somehow suddenly had three.

---

*I*t was that time of year where costumes were available in every department store. But Kian had driven us into the city on a mission, with the assurance he knew the very best place to get amazing ones. Somehow, he'd talked both Fang and Vaughn into coming in the same car as us and had subjected us all to an hour of old Jessica Simpson songs on the drive in.

I was pretty sure Fang's ears were bleeding as we pulled up in front of a parking meter, and Vaughn and Fang practically dove out of the car, desperate for silence.

Kian glanced over at me. "Was it something I said?"

"More like something you sang. Let's go."

To his credit, Kian hadn't been lying about the amazingness of the pop-up costume store. They'd taken over an old warehouse for the weeks leading up to Halloween and filled the place with everything dark and spooky you could think of. There was everything in that one space, from decorations, toys, candies, and row upon row of costumes.

Kian made a beeline in that direction, while the rest of us followed behind at a much less enthusiastic pace.

But my mood picked up when we reached the costumes and there were hundreds to pick from. I shifted through the racks, bypassing Robin Hood, Ariel from *The Little Mermaid*, and a slutty nurse costume. "Can't deal with a man in tights. Ariel had no feet. And a slutty nurse is so cliché."

Kian glanced over at me. "I vote for slutty nurse. Much better than scales and no feet."

"Hard pass."

I took out a pig costume and held it out to him. "Yours."

He took it in. "I'd rather go as a slutty nurse."

I grabbed that from the rack and thrust it in his direction. "Even better."

"Rebel," he warned.

I laughed, pushing them back in. "Fine. What about a farmer for you, Fang? If Kian goes as the pig, the two of you are couple dressing."

He stared at me with wide eyes. "Are you joking?"

"Cowboy for Vaughn."

Vaughn shrugged. "That's not so bad. I could pull off a sexy cowboy."

I spun the costume around in delight. "Sexy indeed. The chaps are assless."

The look of horror on his face gave me great satisfaction.

Until he took out a poofy pink fairy-tale princess-style dress and held it up in my direction. "Oh, this is so yours, Roach."

Kian grinned wickedly. "The tulle! The beads! The...pink!"

"I hate everything about you both."

Kian just slung an arm around my neck. "Just joking. We get you never grew out of your emo stage."

I elbowed him in the ribs. "My look is not emo!"

He laughed, clearly finding himself amusing. "That Paramore T-shirt you're wearing says otherwise."

"From the man who probably has a Celine Dion tour shirt in his closet."

His mouth dropped open in mock outrage. "You went through my room?"

Fang, clearly sick of our shit, held up a Batman costume. "Mine."

Vaughn glanced his way, fingers pausing on the rack of clothes. "Would have picked you as a Thor, personally. All that long blond hair..."

I would have too, but there was a clear reason Fang could not go to that party dressed as Thor. "Thor doesn't wear a mask. Leonn knows Fang's face. Batman is a better choice."

"Dibs on the Joker then, since I don't need to cover my face." Kian pulled it out and held it up against himself.

I chuckled at Vaughn. "I guess that means Robin is all yours."

"No way. You just said you hate a guy in tights."

I raised an eyebrow. "Assless-chaps cowboy is still available."

He rolled his eyes. "Fine. I'm Robin."

I nodded in approval. "Go try them on then. Make sure they fit. We do not need to get to the night of the party and have to drape a sheet over one of you and call you a ghost because you split the ass in your pants. None of you are exactly standard sizes."

Fang and Kian were both a lot bigger than the average man. Not only tall but solid. Vaughn was slimmer but also over six feet.

I probably looked ridiculous standing in the middle of them. All five foot nothing of me, surrounded by big guys.

Can't say I was complaining though. None of them seemed to be either.

"Which one are you choosing?" Fang asked as the others went inside the changing room.

I shoved him after them. "You'll see."

I picked up two costumes I'd been eyeing, knowing one wasn't suitable since there was no face covering, but I had other plans for it.

From behind the changing room doors came the rustle of men shedding clothes for their costumes and Kian and Vaughn bickering about the Halloween they'd worn the same costume. Both thought they'd worn it better.

Fang was quieter, and my excitement grew as I shed my own clothes in the little cubicle and slipped into the combination of leather and lace.

A biker girl costume. A kinda slutty one.

But when I took in my reflection in the mirror, it was one I definitely wanted Fang to see me in. Short pleated black skirt. Knee-high black boots. A lacy bralette worn beneath a leather motorcycle cut. And an old-school, open-faced helmet I perched on my head, leaving the straps dangling.

I peeked out through the curtains that didn't quite fully close on my dressing room.

Fang was already out of his, checking out the fit of his Batman costume in the full-length mirror set up by the costume racks. He didn't have the mask on, but the suit clung to him like a second skin. It hugged every toned muscle of the man's body, shaping over his perfect ass, broad shoulders, and washboard abs.

My mouth went dry.

I stepped out from behind my curtain to stand slightly behind him.

In the mirror's reflection, I had the pleasure of seeing Fang's expression when he caught sight of me. He did a double take of surprise, and his gaze turned hot.

Without turning, he murmured quietly, "You pick that for me?"

I nodded, ignoring Kian and Vaughn who both stepped out of their changing rooms, mid argument, and stopped to stare at me too.

Fang's growl of approval was exactly what I'd been hoping for.

I wasn't expecting the way he spun around and picked me right up off my feet. I squealed in surprise, but it didn't deter him. Neither did Kian and Vaughn standing in the way. He barged through, me with my legs wrapped around his waist, his hands beneath my ass. Vaughn and Kian had to scurry out of the way or be bowled over.

Fang wasn't waiting for anyone.

He carried me into a changing room and jerked the curtain closed behind us.

It didn't quite close the entire way, and I went to tell him, but then he had me pressed up against the solid back wall of the cubicle, his big body against mine, and his tongue in my mouth.

There was no room for thought after that. My entire being became all about him and the way I could feel every inch of his solid dick beneath his flimsy costume. He ground himself against me, rubbing my clit with his erection through our clothes and kissing me until my head spun. God, I wanted him so bad. Every time he stared at me with those eyes, I lost all willpower to say no.

One look. One murmur of "I need you now," and I was ripping off his costume, trying to get him naked.

He tried doing the same to me. He moved my panties to the side and pushed two fingers up into my pussy. Then kissed me harder to muffle the sound of my moan.

"Shh." He moved his mouth to my neck. "Everyone will hear you."

I'd completely forgotten we were in the middle of a store, with Kian and Vaughn on the other side of a barely closed curtain.

I was shocked to realize some part of me wanted them to hear me.

Maybe even wanted them to be watching through the crack of the curtain.

The thought filled me with heat, my entire body flushing hot. I kissed Fang harder, rocking my hips against his and whimpering in frustration that he wasn't already inside me.

I didn't dare open my eyes.

I didn't want to know whether Kian and Vaughn were watching us or not. I wasn't sure I was ready for the answer.

Finally, we got Fang's costume down far enough that his cock slid through the arousal gathering between my legs.

I so badly just wanted to drop down onto him. Sink onto his massive cock while he held my weight. But... "Condom," I breathed, panting because his dick was so torturously close to where I wanted it. It was agony to hold myself still.

"Fuck. There's one in my wallet, but this isn't my changing room."

I looked down in surprise at the clothes on the little bench.

"It's mine," Vaughn said dryly from the other side of the curtain.

I widened my eyes at Fang and clapped a hand over my mouth to stop myself from laughing. "Uh. Sorry about that."

Fang seemed like he was batting back laughter as well. "Got a condom in here by any chance?"

I choked on the fact he had the audacity to ask. But I suspected Fang might have chosen Vaughn's dressing room on purpose, just to needle him.

Couldn't say I was mad. Needling Vaughn was a fun pastime.

"Please," Kian sniggered. "Vaughn has zero need for condoms since he's only screwing his wife. But here you go."

Kian stuck his outstretched arm between the gap of the curtain, a condom in a silver packet clutched in his fingers.

"Oh my God. Kian!" I yelped.

Fang shook his head but then shrugged and plucked it from his fingers.

I just stared at him.

"What?" he shrugged. "It's either that or we're doing it bareback."

I buried my face in the side of his neck, some weird combination of embarrassed and horny as hell.

Kian twisted his hand into a thumbs-up sign before I batted it away and he withdrew it from the cubicle with a good-natured laugh.

"Thank me when you've come then, huh?"

Fang ignored him, already ripping open the condom and rolling it down his length.

He was inside me in the next instant, seating himself fully, plunging in deep.

The "Oh!" of lusty surprise I let out was indecent.

"Fucking hell, Roach," Vaughn complained in a hiss. "There's people working out here!"

I couldn't stop though. Fang pulled out and then slammed back home again. Every time he did it, his dick touched my G-spot and his pubic bone hit my clit. He'd managed to find the perfect angle, and there was no stopping the orgasm barreling down on me.

I'd never been much good at being quiet. It had never been in my nature.

From outside, a song was hummed.

The tune slightly off-key but familiar.

Fang picked up the pace, driving into me in the same rhythm that Kian hummed outside the curtain.

"You are not humming "My Heart Will Go On," right now, are you?" Vaughn asked his childhood friend, all pissed-off frustration.

"Don't knock Celine, brother! You know how I feel about her!"

His humming rose to a crescendo, and I probably would have laughed if Fang hadn't ripped aside my bralette and squeezed my nipple.

With him deep inside me and the added sensation of him working my tits, Kian's performance outside the cubicle drifted away.

The orgasm took hold, blocking out all other sounds and sights in a blinding flash of color.

Fang covered my mouth with his, burying my shout of

surprise with his tongue when my pussy clenched around his solid, thick cock.

"Fuck," he groaned into my mouth. "You're so tight when you come, Pix. So fucking tight."

"Could have done without that information..." Vaughn complained from the other side.

Fang extended one arm above the top of the curtain and flipped him the bird.

But he didn't stop fucking me. He slid in and out, the two of us coming out of our orgasms to grin at each other and kiss like horny teenagers who couldn't keep their hands off each other.

Like we had all the time in the world, he drove in and out of me until he couldn't take it another minute.

He finally let me drop to the floor, but didn't move away, his body still pressed against mine. He kissed the top of my head while we caught our breath then nudged my head back so I was staring up into his eyes.

His expression turned serious. "You can't wear that to the party. I will fuck you on every available surface if you do. That costume is catnip."

"I already chose another one for the party."

He ran his finger down the center of my chest, between my tits and down my stomach to circle my belly button. "Good. Get dressed. But tell the cashier we're taking both."

## 27

# CALEB

*H*arold Coker's office was bigger than mine, had a better view, and was closer to the city center.

All things that irked me.

On arrival I'd offered my sympathies on the recent death of his business partner, Bart Weston. But the pompous prick had droned on ever since, sitting at the head of a long rectangular table in his boardroom, preaching to the rest of us about a new business deal he'd just made worth more money than I'd ever seen on a contract.

Another thing I really didn't like.

I refused to let that show. On the outside I was a focused and determined man, with only one mission on my mind.

Making these men my acquaintances.

I was the youngest in the room by at least fifteen years. Most of these men were my father's age, and they acted like I was the baby of the group. Which meant I had to work twice as hard as anyone else to gain half the respect and trust.

Also fucking irksome.

I wanted to stand up and yell I was more talented than any of them. That my company would one day leave theirs in the dust, and I wouldn't fucking look back.

But that wasn't how one got to the top.

No. You caught more flies with honey than vinegar.

Which was why I'd asked Bethany-Melissa to marry me. People liked her, and having a wife on my arm, one who was the daughter of another respected businessman, would make me seem older. More settled and mature. More like one of the old boys who loved to bitch about their ball and chains.

I clenched my fingers around the armrest of my chair. I could still barely believe everything that ungrateful bitch had done. Fucking slut, running around with three men from the Saint View slums like the common piece of gutter trash she was.

She embarrassed me every minute of every day.

Fucking her little best friend and hearing her scream had barely taken the tip off my hate for the woman who'd betrayed me.

She was just like all the others. All sluts, the lot of them. Only good for sucking my cock.

I didn't need a bitch.

Harold dismissed the meeting right at five, and I stood slowly, letting the room empty out before I strode toward the man who'd hosted the gathering. I pasted on my most charming smile. It worked on both men and women. "Harold. I just wanted to tell you how inspirational you are. That Simpson deal is the stuff of legend. I'm so impressed."

Harold's barrel chest puffed up, and if it were even possible, I was sure I saw his ego inflate.

"You like that? I'm barely getting started. By the end of the year, I'll have much more impressive figures to report."

I wanted to roll my eyes, but though he was a dickhead, he wasn't top of our field for nothing. He probably would have more impressive numbers at the next meeting, and I'd be stupid to insult the man. Sucking up his ass might have grated every nerve I had, but I could swallow that pride if it got me where I needed to be.

I was destined for the top and willing to do whatever got me there.

"I'd really love to hear more about it. Maybe over a game of golf? I have a reservation at The Royal if you'd like to join me this weekend?"

Harold raised an eyebrow. "The Royal, huh? Great course. Hard to get into."

I was aware. The only reason I'd managed to make a booking was because my father was a part shareholder. Harold mustn't have known that though, and I wasn't about to tell him. I mimicked a golf swing while I waited for his answer. "I could definitely use some more hours on the green. You'll probably pummel me into the ground. You're pretty good, right?"

"Was twelve over par last I played that course."

I whistled like I was impressed.

I wasn't. I'd been nine over, beating his score, but I could let the old codger win if it meant strengthening the relationship. "I can get us on at ten?"

He patted my shoulder. "No can do, unfortunately. Ted, James, Simon, and I are away this weekend."

I froze.

Ted, James, and Simon were all business acquaintances who'd been sitting at this very table a few minutes ago. The fucking old boys club I'd spent the last two years trying to get into. Clearly, that hadn't worked well if they were all going away for a weekend together and hadn't even invited me.

I took a breath that did little to calm the anger at being passed over yet again. "Well, that sounds fun too. Another time." I went to leave the room before I could blow a gasket.

Harold caught me by the arm. "Why don't you come too? You can afford a trip to the Bahamas, can't you?"

It was fucking insulting he'd even ask about whether I could afford it, but I brushed that aside and focused on the fact I'd been invited. "Have your secretary forward mine the details. First round of cocktails is on me and Black Industries."

Harold shook my hand. "That's the attitude. Let me walk you out."

I was beaming when we exited the boardroom and stepped into the reception area of Weston and Coker Investments. A leggy blonde sat on the black leather couch in a tiny red miniskirt and heels that matched.

Great fucking tits. No flab on her thighs. Totally bangable.

I got ready to turn on the charm when she looked up from her magazine, bypassed me completely, and ran into the arms of Harold. "There's my man!"

He kissed her with the enthusiasm of a horny teenager, and she sighed happily in his arms.

I had to clear my throat uncomfortably for them to separate.

Harold chuckled. "Caleb Black, meet Luanda Coker. My wife. Caleb and his partner, Bethany-Melissa, will be joining us this weekend."

Luanda clapped her hands. "Oh, lovely! I can't wait to meet your wife. Us girls are planning all sorts of dinners and breakfasts and golf and the beach!"

I put a hand in my pocket, trying to appear casual. "Actually, it'll just be me."

Harold frowned. "Where will Bethany-Melissa be?"

I cleared my throat, debating whether to lie, but too many other people already knew. "We actually aren't together anymore."

Luanda put a hand over her mouth and gasped. "Oh no!"

I fake smiled at her sympathy. "It was for the best. But it's okay, I'm really just ready to move on and be single for a while and concentrate on my career. A weekend away with you all will be just what the doctor ordered."

Luanda looked to her husband and made a face I couldn't understand but he obviously did.

He rubbed a hand across the back of his neck awkwardly. "Listen, about that, we'll have to take a rain check. I didn't realize you and Bethany-Melissa were no longer together. This weekend is about family. We're all bringing our wives and kids…"

"But you'll be talking business too, I'm sure." The words came out sharp. Probably because I could see where this was going and I was preemptively pissed about it.

"We will, but I think it would be awkward to have a bachelor there. You'll come next time, when it's just us boys, okay? Plus, you wouldn't want to miss that reservation you have at The Royal. It really is the most beautiful course." He leaned over and pushed the down button on the elevator, a clear dismissal. "Make sure they validate your parking downstairs, okay?"

He hurriedly guided his wife away, leaving me standing there waiting for the elevator doors to open.

I kept a polite smile on my face until they closed behind me and then let out a scream of anger into the tiny box that hurtled toward the ground floor.

Another fucking woman trying to ruin my life. Harold had been quite happy to have me along until his bitch had told him otherwise.

Now I was missing out again. They'd spend the weekend discussing the details of the deal. Details I could have used to expand my own operations and now wouldn't get to, and why? Because Bethany-Melissa didn't know what was good for her? Because Luanda had a magic fucking cunt that made Harold gaga?

The rage inside me built by the second.

On the ground floor, I stormed across the lobby, certainly not stopping to get my damn parking validated, like some street rat who couldn't afford the parking costs. How fucking insulting. Didn't he know how much money my company had turned over last year?

I got behind the wheel of my new Lamborghini and navigated my way out of the city, my anger mounting with every red light, every car that drove too slow; every dumbass pedestrian who wandered across the road at a snail's pace.

I was so tempted to run them down. If the entire city hadn't been covered in security cameras, then I probably would have. It would be natural selection. Taken out for being too damn stupid to cross the road somewhere fucking else.

By the time I got on the freeway that would take me back to Providence, I was fucking fuming. I put my foot down on the accelerator, pushing the car well over the speed limit and not caring one ounce. The cops could chase me if they wanted to. I'd be faster than them anyway, so let them try. I made it back to the Providence exit in record time, only slowed by a car in front of me who took the turn like he had all the fucking time in the world. I rammed my fist on the horn but then swerved around him into the breakdown lane to pass him before he could even respond.

When the cars were side by side, I glanced over, my middle finger raised, even though I knew they couldn't see me through the dark tint.

There were four people in the car, but only two I'd met before. "Get fucked," I muttered, recognizing Vaughn and the woman on the seat beside him. Bethany-Melissa's best friend. The one Leonn, Hugh, and I had shared not that long ago.

She was a slut too, just like her best friend. The fact she was in a car with three men right now was all the proof I needed.

They were all the same. I hoped Vaughn had as much fun with her tight little holes as I had. He could have her. As long as she kept her stupid mouth shut, she could spread her legs for every man in town for all I cared.

I stomped on the accelerator again, zooming past them and losing them easily in the suburban streets of Providence. Leonn and Hugh would already be at my house with a bit of luck, setting up for the Halloween party tomorrow. We could get some beers and pizza when it was done. Maybe get some women over to do the one damn thing they were useful for.

I cruised the last few streets to my home, getting hard over the idea of having a woman bouncing on my cock later that night.

"What the fuck?" I muttered, pulling the car up in the driveway. The green lawn was half decorated with fake tombstones, skeletons, and jack-o'-lanterns. A string of lights lay in a pile, waiting for someone to untangle it. The mist maker I'd bought was set up by the garden, the box it had come in still lying on the lawn, not yet discarded.

None of it was out of place, except for the three people standing in the middle of it all, their shouts audible even over the roar of my engine.

They all looked over at me, and the woman, heavily pregnant, stormed over.

"Is that you in there, Caleb Black, you son of a bitch?" She slammed her fist against the window.

I've never opened a door so fast. She had to scramble backward to avoid getting hit by it.

"Who the hell are you? Do you have any idea how much this car is worth?" I checked for any damage, but there was nothing. Bitch got lucky.

She shook her head, her chest heaving. "Do you seriously not remember me?"

I let my gaze flicker over her face, but I was no more aware of who she was than when I'd driven up. "Why would I?"

I hated how important women thought they were. Like I should remember all their names. As if I cared. Arrogant bitches. None of them were so special, and social media needed to stop telling them they were. They'd forgotten their place.

"Do you rape so many women you don't even remember their faces?"

Leonn and Hugh glanced around, cringing at the shrill tone of her voice. My property was large but still suburban. I had neighbors within earshot, and this bitch shouting accusations was sure to draw the attention of someone sooner or later. I grabbed her arm, digging my fingers in until she yelped in pain.

I loved the rush of power that came from making a woman submit. Especially after a day like today. I hauled her in close to me and hissed in her face. "Say that again, slut, and see what happens."

She fought me, and the urge to slap her took me fast and hard. But if any of my neighbors had heard her shouts and were peeping out their windows, I wouldn't be able to cover for striking her. There was no explaining that. Our current hold could be construed as two lovers about to kiss if you weren't close enough to hear our conversation.

I let her shake her arm free. She stared at me with all the same fire and hate I had for her. Good. At least the feeling was mutual.

"This baby is yours," she spit in my face.

I looked down at her swollen belly and then laughed. "No, it's not."

"It is," she insisted. "You're the only one..." Her voice broke off. "There's no one else it could be."

"Liar."

"I'm going to the police as soon as he's born. Getting a DNA test will prove it. Prove what you did to me. The hospital has the photos from the night he was conceived, but I had no proof it was you. Now I do. They'll trace his conception date back to that night. My lawyer says my case is strong."

A muscle ticked in my jaw. I would have continued to call her bluff, but I remembered her now. The police had questioned my whereabouts the night of her attack, and Leonn had covered for me. The police had been quickly persuaded to investigate other suspects.

But if what she'd said was true, and my genetic offspring was inside her belly right now, then she might not be bluffing.

"What do you want?" I clenched my jaw. "Money? How much? A hundred bucks?"

She laughed bitterly. "You really think you can buy me off that easily? You destroyed my life, Caleb. Now I have to look at my son or daughter every day, knowing what a monster their father is. I have a lifetime of payments to make for what you created. A hundred bucks! Hell, a hundred thousand doesn't even come close. A million dollars, Caleb. A million dollars a year for the rest of my life."

I snorted at her ridiculousness. "You're insane."

"Am I insane, or do you want to go to jail? If this kid is born without the first million in my account, I go to the cops. Every year on his birthday, I'll expect a payment, or I'll be straight down to the police station. If you're late by even one day, same deal. Do you get the idea?"

I glared at her smug face. The stupid bitch thought she had the entire thing figured out.

Leonn sighed. "Just give it to her, Caleb. You have the money."

It wasn't the point. The point was there was yet another weak-willed woman trying to dictate what I did with my life. How I spent my money. How dare she?

"Get her inside."

"What?" the woman asked sharply. She backed away a step, fear flashing in her eyes for the first time since this whole thing had begun.

I liked that.

I grinned, reveling in her terror. Enjoying watching her realize she'd pushed me too far.

Leonn and Hugh stepped in behind her, grabbing her arms.

She opened her mouth to scream, no doubt, but Hugh was quicker. He slapped his hand over her mouth and dragged her toward the house. I hurried to get the door open and shoved the three of them inside, hoping none of my neighbors had noticed what was going on.

"Put her in the basement. No one ever goes down there, not even the maid." I shut the door behind them.

Sounds of a struggle floated back but got quieter and quieter as Leonn and Hugh hauled the woman to the basement stairs.

If they were smart, they'd throw her down them.

Hopefully, the fall would kill both her and the bastard baby she carried.

## 28

## REBEL

$\mathscr{I}$ got home from my shift at Psychos just after one in the morning to find Kian's truck missing from its usual spot at the side of the house. I instantly wondered if he was with a woman and then berated myself over the twinge of jealousy that panged inside me at the thought.

Vaughn's bike and his dad's car were both there, though the house was dark, so he was likely asleep. I let myself in quietly and trudged up the stairs, looking forward to bed.

Vaughn's room was dark and empty, the door open enough that I could see straight in at his bed. There was no annoyingly attractive stepbrother inside it.

But a soft light came from beneath the door of his father's room.

The one room of the house I thought none of us had entered since it had happened.

I hadn't been ready to go through my mom's things, and I'd thought Vaughn wasn't either. He hadn't brought it up. I'd clearly been stupid to think it was something we should have done together.

I twisted the handle on the door and let myself in.

Vaughn looked up when I entered, and for half a second, I thought I saw guilt flash in his eyes. But then it cleared and changed into something colder. Harder.

"What are you doing in here at one in the morning?" I asked, rubbing my bare arms in the drafty house. I caught sight of something in his hand and gasped, storming over to take it from him. "What are you doing with that? It was my mom's."

I ran my fingers over the familiar necklace. It was one I'd bought her not long after I first started working at Psychos a decade ago. It had been her birthday, and I'd been excited to finally be able to buy her a proper gift. Something nice, though in hindsight, I realized the eighty bucks I'd spent on it probably didn't actually qualify as something precious.

But she'd acted like it had been.

"I think you were right about Kian." Vaughn's voice was hoarse.

I racked my brain, trying to think what he was referring to. "Unless you're talking about the fact he definitely should have gone with the pig costume, you're going to have to explain better."

Vaughn turned around a framed photo on his lap.

It was of Mom and Kian, the two of them dressed to the nines, faces pressed together, both beaming at the camera.

"I found it on a shelf in her side of the wardrobe."

That was surprising. It seemed a bit odd that she would have a framed photo of her and another man in her bedroom. But I shrugged it off. "It's hardly the two of them writhing around in bed naked together, Vaughn. Men and women can be friends, you know?"

He side-eyed me. "Like us?"

I scoffed, while heat threatened behind my cheeks. "We're barely acquaintances. I don't see any photos of us together in my bedroom."

"I watched a man eat your pussy 'til you came all over his face."

I glared at him. "Keep bringing that up, and I'll assume you were jealous."

"I was."

Oh, sweet Jesus. I turned around before he could notice the blush creeping across my cheeks. "That has nothing to do with Kian and my mom."

He pointed to the bed and the array of photos on top of it. "They're all variations of your mom, my dad, and Kian."

"He does work here."

"You love your friends at Psychos, right? You said they were your family."

"They are."

"How many photos of them do you have printed out in your room?"

There was one of me, Bliss, and Nash. But that was all. There definitely wasn't anywhere near the number of photos Vaughn currently had spread out on the bed. I swallowed, the desire to protect my mom still strong. "I haven't finished unpacking yet."

"Bullshit. You see my point. This is weird."

"Or you're jealous."

He raised an eyebrow. "Already told you I was."

I wondered if he'd been drinking or if it was the late hour that had his tongue loosening. "Not about that." I pointed at a photo of Kian and Bart. "Vaughn, there's nothing in these photos that indicates anything weird going on. Why would Mom frame a photo of her and her lover and keep it in her bedroom for her husband to find? Why would there be just as many photos of Kian and your dad? Were they having an affair too?"

"Kian's bi."

"You don't say. Picked up on that the day I met him. My point still stands. Just because he's bi, doesn't mean they were having some sort of polyamorous relationship." I picked up a photo of all three of them. Kian was holding some sort of award, and my mom and Bart stood either side like proud parents. "This looks like a family."

A twinge of pain flashed across Vaughn's face, and his shoulders slumped. "He replaced me with Kian. I was the asshole son who ran off to another state and never came back. So he found someone to take my place."

I put my hand on his arm. "Or, your dad was just a good guy. He loved you even if you were a Douchey McDoucheface, but maybe he saw Kian needed someone to love him too. If he's lived in this house since you two were boys, he probably thought of Kian as a son even before his dad died. And probably before you left."

Vaughn pushed to his feet and stalked across the other side of the room, leaning on the wall. He rubbed at his forehead, eyes all squinty like he was developing a headache. "Fuck. You're right. I'm being a paranoid prick." His gaze met mine. "Sorry for implying your mom wasn't being faithful. That was a dick move." He dropped his gaze to the floor. "I don't know why I'm like this. I can't just fucking trust people. I always assume the worst. I hate that I do that."

I bit my lip. The man looked miserable. I hated that. I knew all too well how bad it felt and I couldn't handle watching anyone else go through it without trying to help. It was why I'd always been there for my mom, when any other sane person would have given up and left her to lie in the bed she'd made for herself. "Vaughn."

"Yeah?"

"At the risk of potentially becoming friends, can I hug you?"

He cocked his head to one side. "What on earth for?"

"Has anyone even hugged you since your dad died? I saw your stepdad consoling your mom. Your wife isn't here. You and Kian have some weird history thing going on where you can barely be in the same room as each other. I just thought maybe you needed a hug."

"You're tiny. Your hugs are probably the equivalent of a mouse trying to hug an elephant."

My mouth dropped open at the audacity. "I'll have you know I give BEAR hugs, Vaughn. Big, grizzly, king-of-the-wilderness type of hugs. I'll show you."

I strode toward him, arms out.

He dodged. "No, thanks."

I kept going. "No, you definitely want a hug. I can see it in your eyes."

He shook his head, but a smile was pulling at the edges of his mouth. "No. I definitely do not."

"Let me hug you, Vaughn."

"Get away from me, Roach. I don't hug." He edged his way around the room like I was a wild animal ready to strike at any moment, keeping the bed between us.

But he'd lied. He'd hugged me in the courthouse after my mom had died. I was sure he needed the favor returned right now. "You will take my cuddles and love them!" I launched onto the bed and ran across it, jumping off on his side and cutting off his path of escape.

I wrapped my arms around his middle and squeezed him tight.

He held his arms out at the sides, stiff and uncomfortable. "What is happening right now?"

"It's called affection, Vaughn. Learn to like it."

Slowly, the stiffness went out of him, and his arms came tentatively around me.

I grinned triumphantly into his chest. "See? Not so bad, is it?"

"You're a pipsqueak."

"Maybe so, but my hugs are good."

He mumbled something.

"What was that?" I teased. "Did I hear you say 'You're so warm and cuddly, Rebel. I do indeed declare you the Saint View Snuggler!'"

"That's not a thing," he grumbled.

I laughed.

But I did notice neither of us let go and this hug was dragging on a long time. His arms were strong around me. His heat radiated into me, warming my chilled limbs.

Slowly, moment by moment, something changed in the air between us. I became all too aware of just how hard his chest and abs were. How despite our height difference, we fit perfectly together. How I'd been fighting an attraction to him since the moment I'd met him.

"What did you actually say?" I whispered.

His thumb stroked across the back of my neck in a

way that was well beyond friendly. "I said I was glad you weren't flinching away from me anymore. You know, after your attack..."

And just like that, the spell was broken. For a minute I'd felt like my old self, but now Vaughn's touch was too much. Too tight. Too restrictive.

I went to step away, but he held me tighter. "You don't have to go. I give in to the power of your arms." He was joking, good humor in his voice, matching the energy I'd been putting out there before he'd brought up my attack.

Only now, everything felt wrong. The room was too small, the walls closing in. Panic lit up inside me, coursing through my veins. I managed to get my hands up in between us and push hard on his chest. "No!"

He let go of me instantly, watching wide-eyed as I stumbled back toward the door. "Rebel, wait. What's wrong?"

Tears pricked the backs of my eyes, mostly because of the look on his face. The regret. The confusion. It was all my fault, but I couldn't say it. Couldn't voice that in my head I was back there, locked in a room with men intent on hurting me.

I ran to my room and slid the latch on the door before getting in beneath the blankets. Outside, Vaughn called to me, and sometime later, he and Kian had a worried conversation about me not being ready to go back into the lion's den that weekend.

But it was the complete opposite. I needed to go to this party. I needed to face my enemies head-on.

Because I wasn't this scared little dormouse, too afraid of my own shadow to even function.

I needed to put an end to the panic. To the fear. I

needed to face it. Stare it in the eye and tell it I was Rebel freaking Kemp.

And I would not be intimidated any longer.

*J* couldn't sleep. I tossed and turned all night, exhausted, but sleep never came.

I was still awake when Kian and Vaughn both got up and showered. Kian knocked quietly on my door and asked if I was okay and did I need anything? I called back in a scratchy voice that I was fine on both counts.

"Call me if that changes, okay? I'm just putting it out there that you do not have to go to this thing tonight. No one will think you're any less of a badass."

I smiled into my pillow at that. Maybe that was true, but I would think less of me.

Vaughn didn't come to my door before they left. I couldn't blame him. After last night, I wouldn't have either. I got up and got dressed, but my hands trembled the entire time.

I went into the bathroom to put some makeup on and stared at myself in the mirror. "Get it together. You aren't a scared little girl. You've been through worse."

I lifted my chin and pulled my shoulders back, but my damn traitorous hands wouldn't stop. I needed a distraction. Pre-attack, I probably would have called Fang. He was the best at keeping my mind off my problems, with his lips and tongue and cock. But that wasn't going to work today. He would be here later to go to the party with us, but until then I needed something to do to fill the hours, so I wasn't constantly thinking about coming face-to-face with the men who'd attacked me.

I could clean, but Kian was a bit of a neat freak and took his duties seriously. Though I had no idea who was even paying him at the moment. I guessed it was Vaughn's dad's business. At least I hoped it was. I really didn't want him picking up after me and Vaughn and scrubbing every surface of the house for free.

I wandered around the big empty kitchen and decided to bake something for when they got back. Maybe a 'sorry for freaking out on you' apology cake for Vaughn. I walked into the pantry and searched for a box of cake mix or something similar but came up empty-handed. Of course, because Kian was a great cook who had probably never baked a cake from a box. I trailed a finger along a shelf with four different types of flour and marveled that there were so many options. I didn't even know there was anything other than all purpose flour.

But that was fine. I was resourceful. How hard could baking a cake be when I had the internet on my side?

With an online radio station blaring punk rock from the early two thousands and a recipe for carrot cake displayed on my phone, I started combining ingredients. Flour. Milk. Butter... They all went into a big mixing bowl, and I stirred them together, feeling like Martha freaking Stewart.

Eggs were next. I yanked open the refrigerator and pulled down the carton of eggs, only to find it suspiciously light. "Ugh," I groaned to the empty kitchen. "Whyyyyy."

That had to have been Vaughn, putting an empty

container back in. Kian was too OCD about his kitchen. I called Kian.

He picked up on the first ring. "Hey! You're on speaker in the car. Vaughn's here. Did you think of something you need?"

"I'm baking a cake."

"Uh, okay? Did you already burn it and want me to just buy one while we're out?"

My mouth dropped open. "No, I did not burn it! You ass. You remember how little faith you had in me when you're orgasming over how freaking good it tastes."

He chuckled at my fiery, riled-up answer. "But there is a problem, right? Or else you wouldn't have called."

He had me there. "There's no eggs."

"I know. I'm getting some at the store."

"How long until you get home?"

"A couple of hours."

I crinkled my nose at the thought of sitting around for a few hours waiting for him to show. My ADHD knew no such thing. "Is there some sort of egg substitute I can use?"

"In a cake? Sure, if you want it to taste like shit."

"Not exactly my aim."

"You could run to the store yourself?"

"Sounds like more effort than I can currently muster. Ooh shit! The oven is smoking!"

"Oh Lord," Vaughn said in the background with a groan. "Will the house even be standing when we get back? Please don't burn the place down. I don't even know if the insurance is still current."

It was almost a relief to hear him putting me down. It

was a lot safer than the way he'd been talking in the early hours of the morning with his arms wrapped around me.

Kian ignored him. "Turn the oven down. Something probably spilled over last time I cooked and is just burning in the bottom. I'll clean it out later. Then go next door to Kathleen and Paul's place. Kathleen is the sweetest. She'll loan you an egg or two. Tell her I'll replenish her stock when I get home."

I brightened at that idea. I liked the idea of not having to wait or go down to the store myself. "Thanks, Kian. You're a good guy. Can't believe Vaughn ever thought you might have killed our parents."

"What?" Kian demanded.

Vaughn groaned.

I grinned, enjoying the payback for him dissing my baking skills. "Discuss that amongst yourselves. I've got eggs to hunt down."

I hung up to the tune of their squabbling. I was a shit stirrer, and I knew it, but someone had to get the two of them talking.

At the front door, I slipped on a pair of slides and strode up to the road. It was only then that I realized I hadn't asked Kian which side sweet old Kathleen with the plentiful supply of eggs lived on. I shrugged and gave it a shot, heading for the house to the left of ours.

The house was quiet as I approached, and I knocked on the door while admiring the shiny black paint and gold door knocker. When our house was officially mine, maybe I could ask Kian to do the same to ours.

From inside, sprightly footsteps thundered downstairs. I frowned at the noise, because Kian had made out that Kathleen and Paul were older. I wasn't sure how many people in their sixties or seventies could run down a staircase without rolling an ankle or breaking a hip. I was only thirty and I'd had a few dicey moments on the extravagant staircases the houses in this town seemed to favor.

I wasn't all that surprised when a young woman in her twenties answered the door.

What was surprising was the bikini she had on. "Hey. You aren't the pizza guy."

Pizza Guy was gonna be real disappointed he hadn't been on time if he liked tall, athletic brunettes.

I shook my head. "No. I'm not. I'm guessing you aren't Kathleen or Paul?"

The woman smiled and pointed back toward my place. "Oh no, you have the wrong house. Kathleen and Paul are two doors down that way."

"Ah. The other side of my place then. Gotcha. Thank you. Sorry for interrupting."

I turned to leave, but she grabbed my arm.

"Wait, you live next door? With Kian?"

"I do. Just moved in a few days ago. My mom lived there before she…"

The woman clapped a hand over her mouth. "Oh! You're Rebel? Miranda's daughter? Of course you are! You look just like her!" Her face fell. "I really liked your mom. She was a lot of fun."

Sounded about right. Mom had always liked to party. It seemed like she'd done a lot of it with people who weren't me. That hurt a bit, but I knew it was me who'd put distance between us. Once I'd been old enough to realize I was the daughter and I shouldn't have to take care of my mother, it had been easier to draw some boundaries. We'd both benefited from them. She'd had to stand on her own two feet more, and I'd gotten some breathing space.

But after the photos last night, I was really beginning to realize my mom had a whole life I knew almost nothing about.

"I was so sorry to hear about what happened to them." The woman leaned on the doorframe. "You must be so sad."

I forced a smile. "Thank you. It's been difficult." That was the truth. I didn't need to see my mother daily to miss her now. I'd loved her. That was why her death hurt so much, not because we'd lived in each other's pockets.

The woman crossed her arms beneath her barely covered boobs. I wondered how she wasn't freezing to death and figured I'd better get on with it before she turned blue.

"I only came over to see if I could borrow an egg. I'm baking. I didn't mean to keep you from...whatever you were doing."

"Oh! Sorry, I should have grabbed a coverup when I heard you knock, but I'm on my way to the hot tub out back. She winked at me. "Got a guy waiting for me. But quick, come in and grab an egg." She smiled over her shoulder at me. "I'm Sasha by the way."

"Nice to meet you, Sasha."

I followed her through the house and into the kitchen where she pulled open the refrigerator.

"Do you live here alone?" I asked curiously. I was assuming the guy in the hot tub didn't because of the way she'd introduced him.

"Yep. My parents died in a car crash a couple years back, and now it's mine."

"Oh gosh. I'm so sorry."

She smiled, taking out an egg carton and handing it over the countertop to me. "Take as many as you need. You can come over here for eggs anytime. Kathleen is a bit of an old biddy. She loves Kian, of course, because every time he waves at her she practically swoons at his feet. Completely different person to me. She isn't one for the ladies."

"Thanks for the heads-up and the eggs."

She leaned her elbows on the countertop. "Before you go... Can I ask you something?"

"Sure. I owe you for the eggs."

She gazed at me with awestruck eyes. "Do they have any suspects in your mom and Bart's murders? I know it's poor form to ask, but I love true crime and I'm so interested. I have so many theories."

I frowned at that. "You do?"

She nodded, and her long dark waves bounced around her face. "Oh, yeah. I mean obviously, Bart's son. Never met the guy, but the heir to the throne who never bothers to visit and the one time he does, his dad kicks the bucket? So suspicious. Then there's Bart's business partner. Also a dick from what I've seen of him at parties. The first wife, of course. Her husband. And don't tell him I said this, but Kian is also on my list."

"Really?" I'd been the one to put Kian on the suspect list in the first place, but I hadn't really been serious. My conversation with Vaughn last night had really only confirmed that Kian was what you saw. He was all sunshine and smiles and golden retriever energy.

He didn't have a dark bone in his body.

But I could humor Sasha.

Her eyes lit up, like she'd just been waiting for someone to discuss all of this with. "Well first, he had means, motive, and opportunity."

I held my hands up. "Slow down. Why does he have means?"

"Oxyanedride was the main substance found in their bodies, right?"

Warning bells rang in the back of my mind. "Where did you hear that?"

"Nowhere reliable, which is why I'm trying to confirm it with you."

I shook my head slowly. "I don't know. I haven't seen the autopsy report."

"You should be able to get that now. My sources say they found a copy online."

"You have sources?" I blinked at the woman, half in awe, half in disbelief. She couldn't have been older than twenty-one.

She ignored my questions and went on. "Anyway, Oxyanedride is found in pool chemicals. In concentrated form, it can be lethal. Kian does clean that big-ass pool over there. My guess is he has access to it."

A sinking feeling started up in the pit of my stomach, but Sasha carried on like she was reporting on some fictional case she'd seen on *CSI*, getting more and more excited with every fact she listed off.

"Next, opportunity. Well, he lives with them. Easy access to all their foods and drinks. Hell, he could have even stabbed them with an injection in their sleep."

"That seems unlikely."

She waved her hands around, too hyped up for my skepticism. "Whatever. It's always someone the victim knows. Kian knew Bart and Miranda better than anyone."

It made me think of the photos again. How many there were, and how Vaughn had thought it strange. I'd talked him out of it, but maybe it was? Sasha certainly seemed to be implying that more was going on than met the eye.

"Surely not better than Vaughn's mom and stepdad? I forget their names...I did meet them at the wedding..."

"Riva and Karmichael. And for the record, I think Kian knew them *much* better than Riva and Karmichael, if you know what I mean. The three of them did live together. All alone. In that big house. You can't tell me that's not a weird situation. Good-looking guy like Kian. Your mom and Bart were the hot older couple, searching for a third..."

I tried to stem the anger flooding in at her implying there was something scandalous happening between the three of them. It was nothing more than pure gossip. But Sasha lived right next door. If anyone was going to know what had happened in that house over the last few months, maybe it would be her. I could at least listen and keep an open mind.

She leaned forward, her voice dropping low like she was telling scary stories. "But here's the kicker. The night before they left for their wedding, I heard screams. And not the, 'Oh, Daddy, fuck me harder,' sort of screams. The bad kind."

"Masculine or feminine?"

"Unless there was another female there that night, it was definitely your mom. I was outside putting my trash out, and I heard it clear as day. They must have had a window open, because I was standing there eavesdropping, as you do, and then they slammed the window closed." She sighed dreamily. "I would have given anything to be a fly on the wall in there that night. If I'd known it was going to end in murder, I would have snuck over with a glass to press up against the wall."

"Did you tell the cops any of this?"

"They didn't question me. And I've watched enough crime shows to know I have no proof. But it's fun to hypothesize, don't you think?"

I gave her a tight smile. "Probably more fun when it's not your roommate accused of murdering your mother, but sure. Fun."

Sasha cringed, suitably ashamed. "Shit. I'm sorry. I got carried away."

The doorbell rang, pinging through the otherwise quiet house.

Sasha glanced over. "That probably is the pizza guy."

"I'll let him in on my way out."

Sasha trailed me to the door and collected her pizza while I trudged home with the eggs. But when I got inside, I just switched the oven off and sat at the kitchen counter, staring into space.

I'd just convinced Vaughn that Kian was harmless, but now maybe I wasn't so sure.

I pulled out my suspect list and put an asterisk next to Kian's name.

## 29

# VAUGHN

"*I* just need to stop in at the hardware store before we go back to the house, okay?"

I groaned. "Have you gotten any quicker at doing that since we were in high school?"

Kian's gaze strayed to a guy in cement-splattered workpants and a shirt with "Hennessy Exterior Painting" printed on the back. The guy's biceps bulged from carrying two enormous cans of paint toward a truck with the same logo painted on the side.

Eventually, he dragged his gaze back to me. "What do you have against the hardware store, Vaughn? Truly, how did it hurt you? Because for as long as I've known you, which is a fucking long time, you've always complained about the place."

I ignored the flicker of something inside me that hated the way Kian had noticed that guy. "It's not the place I hate. It's that when you drag me here it's a minimum one-hour stay. Often more like two. They need a bored friend's section where tortured people like me can congregate."

He snorted on a laugh. "And do what? Play video games? Do arts and crafts, or sing along to an acoustic guitar?"

"So we can formulate a plot to get our loved one to actually leave the damn store in a reasonable amount of time."

Kian glanced at me. "I'm your loved one, huh?"

I didn't answer.

He parked the car and got out, striding off so gleefully I was surprised he wasn't skipping and clicking his heels together in midair. I trudged along behind him.

He glanced back over his shoulder. "You could just learn to love browsing the aisles. Picking out new power tools makes every day better."

I begged to differ, but whatever. Kian shoved a cart in my direction with a warning not to ram the backs of his heels like I'd done when we were in ninth grade.

The memory amused me. "I was hoping if I injured you bad enough, we'd get to leave before you moved into aisle twenty-seven and built yourself a nest."

He shot me a look. "Ha ha. Hilarious." But then his eyes got a faraway expression in them. "If I lived here, I could make so much stuff. I'd be the king of DIY."

I grabbed the list from his hand, knowing if I didn't take over the show we'd be here until closing. "Batteries. Tile adhesive. Oxy-something or other..."

"Oxyanedride. It's a pool cleaner."

"Right, I knew that."

"You've never cleaned the pool once in your thirty-one years. How would you know that?"

He had a point. "Fine. I've never cleaned a pool. I've never had to cook or clean for myself. I'm spoiled white trash. Happy?"

Kian sighed. "No, not happy. I don't live to piss you off, Vaughn. Though apparently, I'm not the only one who makes you all grouchy. What was with you not even saying goodbye to Rebel this morning?"

"Didn't realize that was in our roommate handbook." I strode away with jerky steps, taking the trolley with me. I wasn't even sure why I was being so pissy. Might have had something to do with Rebel. Might have been the uncomfortable feeling I got in the pit of my stomach every time I thought about taking her to that party tonight.

Might have been Kian potentially murdering my father.

Or him checking out a guy right in front of me. None of them were exactly my idea of a good time.

When Kian caught up to me, he had a bucket of tile adhesive in his hand. He put it down in the shopping cart, then jumped in front of it so I couldn't push it any farther. I tried to reverse, but he wouldn't let the cart go.

"You like her," he declared. "You like her, and it's killing you to watch her with another guy."

That was easier than admitting I was still gutted from the way she'd pulled away from me this morning. And that him checking out guys kinda pissed me off.

"Yeah, well, you like her too," I grumbled.

To my surprise, Kian nodded. "She's gorgeous. And funny. I like having her around."

"She hasn't got a dick," I added on bluntly.

He raised an eyebrow. "Could you be any more

jealous?"

"What the hell do I have to be jealous of?"

"That guy out there in the parking lot... Just 'cause I check out a guy doesn't mean shit. And anyway, how do you know she hasn't got a dick? She could be trans."

"And I could be the fucking prime minister of Mars. I've seen her naked, Kian. Trust me, there's no dick."

Kian could barely conceal his grin. "When did that happen?"

I shrugged. "At Fang's clubhouse the other night."

"You get her off?"

"What? No. He did."

Kian nodded, then steeled me with a glare. "You would have gotten her off though, right? I taught you at least that much before you up and married—"

"Shut up."

He raised an eyebrow. "About your wife or how I taught you all about getting off?"

Heat flushed my face. "Don't be a fucking dick, Kian."

"Don't be so in the closet, *Vaughn*. Nobody cares if you used to like me jerking your cock."

I wasn't doing this with him. Because people did fucking care. People had cared and people had gotten hurt. He was opening up old wounds, and I wasn't in the fucking mood after everything that had gone down with Rebel during the night. I stormed off down the next aisle, even though it was clearly marked 'ropes and pulleys,' neither of which was on Kian's list.

Caleb Black stood in the middle of the aisle, a length of thin rope in his hand. He glanced up when I entered, and I felt like I'd stepped right inside a pressure cooker. If he'd heard what Kian had said...

"Caleb!" I overcompensated with a wide smile and pointed to the rope. "Planning to rob a bank and take hostages?"

Caleb frowned and shook his head. "What?"

I chuckled. "Sorry. Bad joke. I'm looking forward to your party tonight. It's okay if I bring a date and a couple of friends, right?"

He squinted at me. "Your date hot?"

She was, but I didn't get why he'd ask. "Yes?"

"Good. She can come. No uglies. Your friends too, if you want, whatever. We've got plenty of beer." He held up his length of rope. "Gotta get back to the house and tie down some of the inflatables. They were flapping around a bit when the breeze kicked up this morning. See you tonight."

"See you then."

Caleb stalked away, and Kian appeared.

"Where were you?" I asked.

"Giving you a minute to cool down, then I heard you say Caleb and I thought I'd better not interrupt. That was Caleb as in..."

"The piece of shit who hurt Rebel? Yeah, that's him."

"He reminds me of a snake. Was it me or were his eyes too close together?"

"It wasn't just you."

Caleb walked away to pay for his rope.

"You believe he's using that to tie down inflatable skeleton decorations?" Kian asked.

We both stood in silence, our earlier argument forgotten against a common enemy.

"I'm not taking my eyes off Rebel tonight," Kian muttered.

Neither was I.

## 30

## REBEL

In the middle of a messy kitchen, half-made cake batter sitting in a bowl waiting for my attention, all I could think about was storming upstairs to Kian's room. I wanted to search through his things and find some sort of proof that backed up the things Sasha had said.

Or better, proved she was wrong.

But Kian had been nothing but a friend to me since I'd moved in here. He'd gone out of his way to make me feel at home when everything had felt unsettled. He'd helped me with my training out of the goodness of his own heart. He'd cooked and cleaned and never asked for anything in return.

I couldn't take Sasha's word over his. I couldn't invade his privacy when he'd installed those locks so I could have mine. It just didn't feel right.

After not listening to my instincts too much lately, I wasn't making that mistake again.

If Kian had something to do with my mother's death, I'd find out one way or another.

A knock at the door had me jumping a mile. I rushed to it and peered through the peephole.

Fang.

Exactly who I needed right now. I swear to God the man seemed to have a radar that must start pinging whenever I was feeling out of control.

Just him standing there on the other side of the door brought a calm feeling of safety that was intoxicating. I threw open the door and launched myself at the man.

He caught me with an *oof* of surprise. But he didn't put me down. He dropped a bag at his feet and hefted me up higher in his arms so our faces were level.

"Hi," I chirped at him, leaning in and brushing my lips over his, but then decided that wasn't a satisfactory greeting and deepened the kiss, pressing my tongue against his lips and smiling to myself when he tightened his arms around me to accept it.

Finally, he pulled away and focused his gorgeous blue eyes on me. "Hi yourself. What did I do to deserve all that?"

I slid down his body to stand on my own two feet and picked up his bag for him, dragging it inside. "I just like you. You're exactly who I wanted to see right now."

"You're always the one I want to see, Pix. Give me back that bag, it's heavy."

I flexed an arm at him. "I'm strong."

"You are. But you're also a pipsqueak, and I'm not letting you carry my shit. That's my job. Give me the bag."

I huffed at his indifference to my guns display. I thought I was starting to see a little more definition, thanks to Kian's morning workouts, but maybe that was wishful thinking. I handed over the bag though, because there was no way he was going to let me carry his shit. I swear, the man would carry me around everywhere if I let him. I never lifted a finger if he was in a hundred-mile radius. It was odd after spending so much of my life taking care of someone else. I'd never had someone do it for me.

He followed me into the kitchen, surveying the mess I'd made. "I hope Kian isn't home to see you destroying his kitchen."

"It's not destroyed. I'm baking."

"There's flour on every surface. And why is it so hot in here?" He unzipped his leather jacket.

I ran a finger through the light dusting of flour on the countertop. "I had the oven on...then I got distracted and went next door, and that became a longer conversation than I had expected, and when I got back the kitchen was nicely heated."

He shrugged out of his jacket and hung it over a kitchen chair. "You could bake a cake in here, even without putting it in the oven."

The temperature likely had something to do with the thermostat I'd cranked up that morning when the house was chilly, but I burst into laughter before I could explain. "What is that?" I pointed at Fang's chest.

The tight black T-shirt simply said, "Peter, Pumpkin Eater," in bold orange text.

He gave me a wicked grin that immediately sent a jolt of lust through me. "There's a matching pumpkin costume for you in my bag."

"There is not."

He raised an eyebrow in challenge. "Open it and see for yourself."

I was totally calling his bluff. I knelt at his feet and unzipped his duffel bag. I could barely contain myself when on top there legitimately was a bright-orange pumpkin outfit with a cute green Peter Pan collar. I took it out and shook it in his direction, laughter spilling over.

"Put it on." His gaze raked over mine. "Let me eat you."

I looked up at him. "You're not serious?"

"Have I ever joked about going down on you before?"

Come to think of it, he hadn't. "The guys will be home soon. We should go upstairs."

"Put it on, Pix."

A shiver of anticipation and the dominant tone in his voice rolled through me. "Right here?"

"Pumpkins belong in the kitchen, not the bedroom."

I pulled off my T-shirt and went to put the costume over my head, but his frown stopped me. "What?"

"Since when do pumpkins have underwear? Take it all off, Pix."

"It's the middle of the day!"

He shrugged. "When you got a craving, you got a craving. Off."

I threw my shirt at his face playfully, but he just peeled it off, his gaze sweeping across my cleavage and bare stomach. He watched every movement while I took off my leggings and panties, and finally, my bra.

"Happy?" I asked him in challenge as I stood stark naked in the kitchen.

"As a pig in shit. You should never wear clothes."

"I'd get cold. Pass me the pumpkin."

He picked it up and tossed it over his shoulder. It hit the floor somewhere near the refrigerator. "Nah. Like you better just like this."

He closed in on me, leaning down to kiss me hard. His tongue stroked against mine, demanding, while heat rushed to my core at being so completely naked while he was still fully dressed.

And maybe a little at the fact all the windows were open, and Kian and Vaughn would be back at any minute.

I squeezed my thighs together.

Fang kissed me searingly deep, a promise of all the things he could do to me. His tongue was a wicked tease, flicking and tasting, promising once he used it on my pussy, I would forget my own name.

"Need to taste you," he murmured. "Every inch of you. Let me."

"Yes," I whispered over his lips, a real need for him to get between my thighs starting up.

But the man lived to torture me. He ran his lips down my neck, taking little sucks of my skin as he went. He pressed kisses across my breasts until he got to my nipples.

On his knees, his head was the perfect height for playing with them, and he took his time, sucking one into his mouth, his fingers toying with the other. He licked and rolled my nipples until I was so horny, I wondered if I could come from nipple stimulation alone.

With him on his knees for me the way he was, it was a serious possibility.

I ran my fingers through his hair, stroking it back from his face and pulling out the tie at the nape of his neck to let it fall free. God, this man was beautiful. I had no idea how other women didn't see it. How they didn't see the way his eyes devoured you. The way his stare lit up every part of me. The way his scars and tattoos and piercings only added to the whole bad-boy appeal.

Bad on the outside. So freaking good on the inside.

It dawned on me, maybe other people didn't see him like that because he didn't show them that side of him.

I was grateful for it every time.

His lips trailed down my belly, and I could barely breathe in anticipation of him getting to the spot I needed him most.

He didn't disappoint. He never did. It was like he lived to go down on me, and he took his sweet-ass time, prodding his tongue between my folds, tasting my arousal, coating his lips and beard in it without a care. The scratch of his bristles against my sensitive flesh only heightened the sensation, the soft lick of his tongue soothing and sweet.

An orgasm started up its warning signals, and he felt them before I did. He pulled away and kissed my mound. "Turn around."

I whimpered at him stopping, but he was insistent.

"Turn around. I'm tasting every inch of you."

My eyes flared at the implication. "Every inch?"

"Every. Single. One." It was said with such certainty, it left nothing to the imagination.

And yet, I couldn't shut up. "You mean...you're going to lick my...pumpkin hole?"

He chuckled. "Turn around and find out."

Oh. My. Fucking. God.

But bless me, pumpkin gods, 'cause I was going to sin. I turned around.

"Lean over the table, Pix. Spread your legs."

I wasn't even sure my damn legs would cooperate. It was probably lucky he wanted me to be half on the table. At least it would support my weight.

He spread my legs wide, exposing every inch of me to him, and if I hadn't been so damn turned on, I might have been mortified.

But Fang had never made me feel anything but completely desirable. So even like this, legs spread, ass in the air, I never thought to tell him no.

He put his mouth to my pussy once more, tonguing my clit while he pumped two fingers in and out of my core. I moaned loudly, the orgasm building again until Kian and Vaughn could have walked in with lunch and I wouldn't have cared. I would have demanded Fang keep going and the boys could just take a seat and wait until we were done.

Too bad if their lunch went cold.

I ground back against his hand. Savored in the lick of his tongue.

Waited for it to move higher.

When it did, I let out a shuddering moan that could have been heard halfway down the street. It was too good, too much, and yet not enough all at once.

His fingers pumping inside me, hitting my G-spot with every thrust never stopped. He added pressure to my clit with his other hand, while his tongue went to places no pumpkin eater could tell their mother about. He tongue fucked me 'til I was weak, and until I begged for more.

His jeans came down in a heartbeat.

A condom wrapper ripping.

My fingers diving between my legs to rub my clit because I couldn't bear to let the orgasm trail off again.

His dick sliding in was the perfect stretch. He withdrew then pumped back so slowly it was almost torture, but I found myself matching his pace, easing up on my clit so I wouldn't get overstimulated.

His finger on my ass was all the stimulation I needed. He rubbed a thumb against my tight rear hole and then leaned over me, growling in my ear, "I want to fuck you here. So fucking bad. You have no idea how fucking tempting this little hole is."

"Do it," I moaned, desperate for more.

I'd lived a pretty adventurous sex life. There wasn't much that was brand-new to me. Anal had not been something I loved with other partners, but none of them had ever treated me the way Fang did. None of them had ever touched me the way he did. Taken their time, built me up, edged me until I'd legitimately begged them to fuck me there the way I just had with him.

"Soon, Pix. Not now. You need more prep. When I fuck you there it'll be as sweet and easy as taking your pussy because you'll be so ready for me. I don't ever want to hurt you."

Tears formed behind my eyes, but I quickly blinked them away. I felt too much for this man. Way too freaking much.

I rubbed frantically at my clit, and he seemed to get the idea that we were edging feelings that were too big for me to utter.

Sex was easier. Sex didn't have to come with the

strings that were currently threatening to wrap their way around my heart and tie me to him.

He fucked me harder, pumping into my pussy while fingering my ass.

I came with his name on my lips and his cock buried deep inside me.

His own shouts of relief mingling a moment later.

His lips on my spine. His breaths on my skin.

My heart beating, just for him.

## 31

## REBEL

*S*ometime after dark, I pulled on a black Lycra bodysuit. The thing clung to every inch of me, showing off every curve and dimple. I slicked my short hair back and fit the mask across the top half of my face.

Downstairs, Batman, Robin, and the Joker waited for me.

I eyed Vaughn in his Robin costume. "You look hot."

He scowled, like I hadn't been one-hundred-percent serious. "I look like a joke."

Fang elbowed him. "Can't all be Batman."

"Says Batman," Vaughn grumbled.

Kian grinned, his teeth extra white beneath face paint. "Hey, I said we could swap and you could be the Joker. You didn't want to put the face paint on!"

"I just got a facial, Kian!"

Me, Kian, and Fang all stared at him. Simultaneously, we all burst into laughter. Laughter that turned into hysterics, until I was glad I wasn't wearing makeup because tears streamed down my face from laughing so hard.

Some of it was nerves, and I was grateful to get them out now. We were all on edge, but teasing Vaughn for his upper-class upbringing and expensive taste was always good for some light relief.

Eventually, even Vaughn laughed. "I was joking by the way."

Kian snorted. "You weren't, but that's fine. I so enjoy when your hoity-toity side comes out to play." He turned to me and Fang. "Do you think there'll be little cucumber sandwiches cuts into triangles for Vaughn's sensitive palate at this party? Or should we pack him a lunch box?"

I covered my mouth to hide my smile, while Fang pressed his lips tight to keep it together.

Vaughn shook his father's car keys in our direction. "If we're finished making fun of me, can we get going? We're already late."

"Party don't start 'til I walk in," I announced, grabbing my purse from the hallway table.

Fang frowned disapprovingly at me. "You're incognito tonight, Pix. Don't draw attention to yourself."

"When do I ever?"

All three of them stared at me, and I waved them off.

"Stop."

"He's right." Kian crossed his arms over his chest. "Don't get carried away."

"I'll be fine."

Even Vaughn looked like a stern principal, telling off a naughty schoolgirl. "You might not be. We should have a code in case you need to bail."

"Or I could just say, let's bail?"

He shrugged. "That, or pull your ear three times."

"I think you're taking your Robin costume too seriously. I get it. We don't need no superheroes tonight. We're just observing. But that goes for all of you too. If I'm worried about anyone drawing a crowd, it's you guys."

Kian's gaze rolled over my catsuit-clad body. "We aren't the ones dressed all in Lycra." He glanced at Fang and Vaughn's Lycra tights. "Well, at least not all of us. Those two might draw some stares too."

Vaughn groaned, clearly grumpy about the entire thing, from being stuck as Robin right through to having to wear tights. "Can we please get this show on the road? The sooner we're all back home safe and sound and out of wedgie pants, the better."

I strode for the door. "Couldn't agree more. Let's go."

We piled into Vaughn's car, and he traversed the streets of Providence, most of the houses all decorated for the holiday. In Saint View, we didn't bother, because people just stole stuff right off your lawn. But Providence was like a scary funhouse tonight, with skulls and witches and ghouls all out on the town, ready to party. It was nearing eleven, and the streets had cleared of trick-or-treaters, but the adults had come out to play.

As we drove into Caleb's neighborhood, a growing sense of unease settled over me. His entire street was lined with expensive cars. There were clearly a lot of people at this party. I wasn't sure if that was good or bad for us, and I wondered if the guys were trying to work it out too. All four of us in the car lapsed into silence when an obnoxious Lamborghini pulled up in the driveway and Caleb got out.

Every muscle in my body was stiff, watching him stroll to the front door and letting himself in.

Kian broke the silence. "Sticking together as a group might not be possible," he said softly. "Not if we want to watch all three of them. But at least one of us is with Rebel at all times."

I opened my mouth to complain and shut it again when he glared at me.

"Don't even think about it. You are not ready to take them on yet."

It drove me nuts that he was right, but he was.

He softened when he saw the expression on my face. "Not yet, but soon, Little Demon. You need time."

I nodded. Seeing Caleb, even from a distance, had reminded me we were playing with fire.

"Good, we've got that all agreed on," Vaughn murmured. "Because I'm parking the car up here. We'll have to walk the rest of the way in."

Fang looked to me, a question in his eyes. "Last chance, Pix. We can still turn around."

But I shook my head. I needed to do this. Needed to see the place where it had happened.

I got out of the car, slamming the door shut behind me, knowing they'd all follow.

They surrounded me. Kian to my left. Vaughn on my right. Fang at my back. Their strides fell in time with mine as we strode toward the house from my nightmares. All of us marching into a war I couldn't escape from. Not until I could end it myself.

A short line of people waited at the side gate where a bouncer stood guard. It was clearly the way in, so we joined the tail end. I fidgeted with my purse, straining to see around the group in front of us. The bouncer let a couple of guys in but then stopped a man and a woman.

The bouncer handed the man a form on a clipboard and a pen. "Sign this."

"What is it?"

"Disclaimer for the event."

The guy skimmed through the three pages of text, flipping the pages up while he squinted at the small writing in the dark. "This so we don't sue?"

The bouncer didn't answer. "You need to hand your phones over too. There's no recording allowed."

The guy signed it without reading anything, put their phones in a big bucket that was already half full with other people's property, and the couple were let in.

"No phones?" Kian muttered. "What the hell?"

There was no way for the guys to hide theirs. They literally had their phones and wallets in their hands because their costumes didn't come with pockets.

"Don't worry about it," I said beneath my breath. "Just go along with whatever he says." I reached inside my purse and slipped my phone into a hole in the lining, obscuring it from view.

The group of guys in front of me passed no problem, but the bouncer put his hand up in front of us.

He looked at me with a sneer. "Who's responsible for the slut?"

My mouth dropped open. "Excuse me?"

There was a titter of laughter from behind me, and I spun around to glare at whoever it was. All I could see was Fang's broad chest though, which practically vibrated with anger.

It was so bad I had to put a hand over his heart to calm him.

He settled into something that was a little closer to a purr.

Vaughn cleared his throat. "What's your problem, bro? Caleb said I could bring my girl."

The bouncer thrust a clipboard at Vaughn. "Sign then, if she's yours."

Vaughn glanced at me.

I wasn't impressed, but I nodded. We hadn't come all this way for nothing. I wasn't turning back now.

Vaughn read the text, explaining it as he went. "It's a lot of legal mumbo jumbo about staying out of areas marked do not disturb, security cameras are in use, as well as 'don't sue if you get injured' sort of statements... Fucking hell, three pages? What is all this?"

I shifted my weight from foot to foot. "Just sign it. People are staring." It was either that or turn around and leave. That would feel like running away, and Caleb would win again.

Vaughn glanced up and found a small crowd gathered behind us.

"Hurry up, bro," someone called. "Halloween doesn't last all month. We only got tonight."

The bodyguard huffed out an impatient sigh. "She ain't coming in unless you sign it. So sign or say goodbye."

For a moment, I thought Vaughn was going to refuse. But eventually, he signed the paper and thrust it back to the guy. "There. Happy?"

"Keep running your mouth and I'll be real happy to toss you out on your ass. Phones."

The guys reluctantly put theirs into the bucket.

"I didn't bring one," I announced. I held out my open purse, careful to keep the hole closed with my finger. "Nothing in here but my wallet, keys, and some tampons."

The guy poked a finger at my things, and I held my breath, praying he wouldn't notice the phone sitting in the bottom of the bag, obscured by the black liner.

A muscle ticked in Vaughn's jaw as his fingers clenched into fists. "Don't touch her shit, bro. Didn't your mother to teach you to look with your eyes, not your fingers?"

The bouncer glanced up from my purse. "What did you say?"

I could see exactly where this was headed. Into a fight before we'd even stepped foot inside. I grabbed Vaughn's hand and squeezed it. "Let's go."

He looked down in surprise at my fingers wrapped around his, but he followed me through the gates, the other two guys close at our heels.

"I don't like this," Fang muttered.

I tried to make light of the fact that my gut was screaming to get out of here too. "It's just a party."

"A really fucking big one. I forgot how you rich people do this." Kian let out a low, impressed whistle.

I was sure my eyes were big too. "Is this what your parties were like in high school, Vaughn?"

He wandered toward the pool, lit up with lights. Around the edges, people sat or stood around in groups, some dancing to the music pouring out over the speakers.

"I don't know this many people."

There were a lot of people there for a backyard party, but then most people didn't have backyards the size of small countries. Everywhere I turned, there were bodies moving around, laughing, talking. Everyone had costumes. Some simple like Dracula capes and fangs, some more elaborate like a guy in a Viking costume, his hair braided into intricate strands.

But one thing stood out most. "Where are all the women?"

Fang gazed around, his eyes narrowing on the handful who were all outnumbered twenty to one. He stepped in closer. "Nowhere alone, Pix."

I normally would have sassed him and told him no man controlled me.

But this was weird. The vibe wasn't right. I tried to catch the gazes of the other women, but none of them looked my way. But none seemed particularly bothered to be in the minority either. A couple seemed to be loving it, flirting and chatting away with the guys who surrounded them.

"Maybe we're overthinking it. Maybe Caleb just has no friends who are women."

"That checks," Vaughn mumbled. "He got laid a lot in college 'cause he's a pretty boy, but none of the girls liked him much once they got to know him. He never had a girlfriend last long."

Until Bliss. I blamed her previous shitty self-esteem for her making such a bad choice in being with Caleb. Thank God she'd found herself and kicked Caleb to the curb.

Shame I'd also fallen for his charms.

I spotted Hugh holding court on a pool lounger and shuddered. His pockmarked face starred in my nightmares, right alongside Caleb's and Leonn's. I'd never forget it. I'd probably have nightmares as long as I lived, while he just got to sit there like royalty, enjoying himself without a care in the world.

"That's him, isn't it?" Fang asked in a voice barely above a whisper. "The third guy."

Vaughn nodded for me, because I was too busy trying to keep myself calm.

How could someone be so cruel and then just go on with their life, like nothing had even happened? Why did he get to do that while I suffered every damn day?

"Vaughn," I croaked out. "You know them. Go sit with them. Get him drunk. Let him talk. Find out anything you can about him. I want to know all his weak spots."

So I could use each and every one to torture him.

Vaughn hesitated, but I begged him with big eyes. "Please. I need to know who they are. Where they work. If they have families. Who they're friends with. Their strengths. Their weaknesses." There was a crack in my voice as I begged. "Knowledge is power, right?" I swallowed thickly. "I have so little power left. I just need something..."

To my surprise, Vaughn put his arm around my neck and drew me in, kissing the top of my head.

When I gazed up at him, questions in my eyes, he jerked his head over at the bodyguard.

"He was watching, and I said you were my girl. Need to make it seem real, right?"

Oh.

I stepped out of his embrace, and he headed over to Hugh and some other guys.

Kian watched him go, tension across his entire frame.

Eventually, he turned away. "I need a fucking drink. This party is too much."

We'd barely been here ten minutes, but I couldn't agree more.

"There's a guy from my gym over by the drink table. I'll go say hi and get us something." He looked to Fang. "You got her?"

"Always."

Maybe it was the party and the vague sense of danger I felt in the air, but I'd never been happier to hear someone say they had my back. I made a circular motion with my finger. "We're going to do a lap. We'll be back by the time you finish talking to your friend."

Kian nodded. "Rebel..."

"Yeah?" I gazed up into his warm eyes.

"Just be careful, okay? The worst thing you can do as a fighter is get cocky and underestimate your opponent."

I didn't think I was underestimating Caleb. I knew exactly what he was capable of. The bruises might have faded, but I'd carry the scars always.

Fang and I left Kian and wandered toward the house, but we were stopped by black-and-yellow warning tape that had the back doors closed off. A printed sign pointed partygoers toward the pool house bathroom, but it was clear they didn't want anyone in the house itself.

Fang gazed down at me. "I'm assuming the tape isn't going to persuade you to leave it be?"

"You know me so well." I glanced around, making sure no one was paying any attention, then ducked beneath it.

Fang grumbled, but he followed. We stuck to the shadows and moved quickly to the back door, but I didn't think anyone was really paying us any attention. The party was very much all in the other direction.

I pulled on sliding glass door and swore softly when it was locked. "Shit."

"Move over. These things are stupidly easy to break into."

I stepped aside and raised an impressed eyebrow when Fang gave the door a sharp upward tug that had it sliding open.

"I didn't know you were so adept at breaking and entering."

"Comes in handy from time to time. Get inside before someone notices."

The house was dark inside, no lights on, which worked in our favor. No one would notice our shadows lurking around inside. The kitchen countertop and dining room table showed the aftermath of party setup. They were strewn with empty boxes and discarded wrappers, scissors, tape, and balloons. Down the hall was a door that probably led down to the basement. It had a slide lock, firmly in place, but no padlock to keep it secured.

Fang pointed at it. "Think Caleb wants to keep his fine china and childhood figure skating trophies safe from the drunks?" he asked beneath his breath. "Hate to break it to him, but that thing ain't keeping anyone out without a padlock. At least not from this side."

I sniggered, moving past the door with a mental note to come back to it later once we'd made sure no one else was in the house. "He seems like the type to be a figure skater, doesn't he? I bet he did it professionally with sequined shirts and the whole shebang."

It lightened the mood just enough that walking into the living room by the front door took me by surprise. I hadn't expected it, disoriented from entering the property from the back.

I froze to the spot, dropping my purse on the floor when my fingers weren't strong enough to hold it, and stared at the room where three men had destroyed me in a matter of hours.

"Pix?"

I couldn't talk. All I could do was stare as that night played over and over in my head. We'd come through the front door. Caleb had been kissing me, and at first it had been fun. He was hot, and we'd had chemistry.

Then his friends had arrived, and I'd realized who he truly was. Not the cute real-estate salesman he'd led me to believe.

But my new best friend's abusive ex. Hell-bent on hurting her by hurting me.

Or maybe he just got off on hurting women in general and I was just convenient since I'd been stupid enough to let him drive me right into his web of lies.

I couldn't forget his voice. It taunted me. Echoing around the empty room like he was right there in it.

Tears rolled down my cheeks. Tears for my best friend. Tears for the woman I'd been before. Tears for every woman who'd ever had a Caleb in her life. I took off my mask to wipe my eyes, and Fang engulfed me in his arms.

He lifted his mask so I could see his face. "I love you, Pix," he whispered. "I hate seeing you like this."

I blinked up at him, mouth dropping open in shock. "You...what?"

His eyes were kind as he stared down at me. "You know I do. I always have."

A sob hurtled up my throat and exploded past my lips. I dug my fingers into his shirt and cried on his chest, too overwhelmed to say anything, though I knew what I wanted to say in my heart. My tongue just couldn't form the words. Not here. Not in this house where too many other memories tainted the words I wanted to say.

All of a sudden, I didn't know why I was doing any of this. I couldn't remember one good reason for wanting to come here, to this place, and relive that night. I'd thought I'd needed it.

But maybe I just needed him.

Fang was enough to exorcise my demons. At least for tonight.

I pulled back. "Can we go somewhere? Just you and me. I...I don't want to be here anymore."

He gave a curt nod. "Of course. I'll get—"

The front door flew open, a man entering with a six-pack of beer in one hand and a shopping bag in the other. "Caleb! I got the stuff. Let's lock these doors and get the party started."

The open door let in enough light from the street that Fang and I were like deer caught in headlights.

Leonn's gaze stopped on mine, and his eyes went wide. "You're..." His gaze flickered to Fang. "Oh, fuck. Caleb!"

Leonn's bellow rattled through the quiet house. Panic speared through me. We'd both taken our masks off.

Shit.

Fang thought faster than I did. In a second, he had Leonn shoved up against the wall, a hand over his fat lips.

"Shut your mouth," he hissed, low and deadly. "So help me fucking God, you utter one more sound, and I'll take great pleasure in snapping your neck right here."

I grabbed his sleeve, knowing he was fully capable of carrying out the threat. "You can't! There's two hundred people out there in the yard! Those papers Vaughn signed said there were security cameras..." I looked around the room wildly and didn't see anything, but that didn't mean they weren't there. "What if there's some in here?"

Fang leaned on Leonn's fat neck, glancing around the same way I was before his blue-eyed gaze finally came to rest on mine. "What do you want, Pix? We gotta decide now. We let him go, and he's running straight out there to tell Caleb we're here. Game over."

Leonn tried shaking his head, like he wouldn't do exactly that if Fang released him.

I laughed in his face. "As if we'd believe you." I tried to think, but my mind was a whirlwind. I had him here. One of my enemies. It was exactly what I'd wanted. But I wasn't ready. I wasn't prepared. This wasn't how this was supposed to go down. I didn't just want to kill him.

I wanted to make it hurt.

I wanted him scared and begging, just the way I had.

The walls suddenly felt like they were closing in. I needed to get out. I stuck my head out the front door and glanced over at the gates where we'd come in. There was no one there. The gates had been locked with a shiny silver padlock, the bouncer gone.

Why the fuck were the gates locked?

So no one could get in?

Or so no one could get out?

A sinking feeling in my stomach threatened to take over and cloud my brain with confusion, but I pushed it all away. "Get him out here." On the ground in front of me lay a coil of rope, holding down an inflatable skeleton. I knelt and frantically untied it, not caring if the skeleton floated away in the breeze.

I held it up triumphantly to Fang, and he yanked Leonn off the wall.

"What's your plan here, Pix?" Fang asked in a hushed whisper as I wrapped the rope around Leonn's wrists as tight as I could.

"I don't know," I admitted, adrenaline pumping through me, but not having the desired effect of sharpening my mind. "I really have no idea. Tie him up, put him up the side of the house for someone to find later after we're long gone."

Fang ground his molars. "That's not much of a plan."

"I know!" I glanced around frantically. This wasn't the way it was supposed to happen. We were just supposed to observe tonight. "You got anything better?"

"Shove him in the car and kill him?"

Leonn barely even reacted. It was like he'd already accepted his defeat. He just stood there silently, not even struggling.

It sent an anger raging through me I'd only ever felt one other night. I shoved him in the chest. "Why aren't you scared?"

He mumbled something behind Fang's hand that I couldn't make out. Fang pulled his hand away to let him talk with a glare that clearly said, 'you scream, and I'll end you.'

Leonn's eyes looked dead. Any spark in them completely extinguished. "I deserve to die."

I ground my molars, trying to decide what to do. Eventually, I shook my head hard. "You do. But not like this. This is too easy."

Fang held him while I got real close, right up in the face of one of the men who'd hurt me.

"I'm coming for you. Just know that. You won't know when. You won't know how. But one day soon, you'll know true fear."

"Just kill me," he begged.

"Not a fucking chance," I growled in his face, the words practically demonic.

Rage coursed through me. I hated this man. Hated him with everything I had inside me, and that hate had nowhere to go. I ripped off Fang's cape and shoved it in Leonn's mouth, muffling his pitiful cries. "Tie him up. Leave him around the side of the house. Kneecap him if you have to, I don't care. Just make it so he can't let anyone else know we're here until we're gone."

Fang, ever faithful, did exactly what I'd asked. He hauled Leonn through the maze of decorations without a single question.

I turned and ran back for the door.

"Where are you going?" Fang hissed from the edge of the building.

"I need to get my purse. Shit. And Kian and Vaughn. We can't even call them. They're locked in there."

Leonn struggled in Fang's arms, apparently more scared of a kneecapping than he was of outright dying. He clearly didn't like pain. Maybe that came from being a doctor and seeing so many people in so much of it. I stored that tidbit away for future reference.

"Just leave it!" Fang manhandled Leonn a few more steps, turning his attention to him. "Fucking hell, you're scared of a little kneecapping? After what you did to her? You piece of cowardly shit. I should rape you and see how you fucking like it."

Though I knew he was on my side, I couldn't stand there listening to it. I couldn't hear the word rape without wanting to shrivel up and die. I couldn't go back there. To those dark days afterward where I'd lain in my bed in the fetal position and thought about ending it all.

I ran back inside the dark house, swinging the door shut behind me in case anyone else tried coming through this entrance. The locks clicked as they reengaged, which might have been a good thing. At least it would stop Fang from following me back inside. The quicker we all got out of here, the better.

In the living room, I grabbed my purse from the floor and kept going, striding back the way we'd come, the sounds of the party outside getting louder with every step. I reached the glass doors, the party beyond.

Caleb stood on the other side.

His costume a white knight, which was about as ironic as you could possibly get. Even when he was in profile and dressed all in white, I could have sworn I could see the evil in his eye. He talked with a friend, his squinty eyes calculating the entire time.

I couldn't afford to freeze again.

I had my mask back on, but I couldn't walk straight past Caleb.

Something in me knew he'd know, and I had none of the guys here to back me up.

Without them, I didn't trust myself. I was scared I'd revert to the weak pathetic mess, lying on the floor of the living room while men attacked me. While they put their hands on my body. While they broke my spirit.

Caleb shifted in my direction, and I spun on my heel, blindly turning away so he wouldn't spot me. I hurried down the hall, and as the glass doors opened, his evil laugh floated through.

It sent chills down my spine.

I ran.

But his voice followed, casual enough I was sure he hadn't seen me, but that wouldn't last if I just stood there like a stunned mullet. And I couldn't go back the way I'd come, I'd have to walk straight past him while he moved around the kitchen, clinking bottles as he went.

There was nowhere to go. No escape except the locked door that led to the basement.

He wouldn't go down there, surely. He'd get his drinks or food and then he'd return to his guests. I just needed somewhere to hide until he went back outside and then I could creep back up, find the guys, and get the hell out of here.

A second voice joined him in the kitchen, the two of them mumbling something I couldn't quite hear. Was it Hugh? I couldn't be sure. I was too scared to truly listen in case it was, and I was trapped in here with two of my attackers. Their voices seemed too loud, and I was a sitting duck. Fear wrapped its way around my throat, squeezing until I slid the lock to the side and slipped past the door, closing it quietly behind me.

I stood there in the darkness, breathing heavy.

But their voices kept coming. Louder with every second.

I slunk down the stairs, fumbling along the walls for a light switch but then realizing I couldn't just turn a light on. I edged my way around the room, searching the walls and floor for anything I could use to protect myself.

But there was nowhere to hide. It was like the room was completely empty.

Caleb's voice kept coming. Closer with every step. Talking to another man, but terror pounded in my ears, drowning out the exact words. I stared up the stairs at the door, convinced I'd made a terrible mistake.

They were coming down here. At any moment, the door would open, the light would turn on, and I'd be caught.

Behind me, the solid wall changed, and hope reared inside me.

A doorframe. The door. A handle.

It gave way when I put pressure on it, and I stumbled into the room. It was still pitch-black, but for the briefest of moments, I dared to flick on the light.

A simple bathroom, with only a toilet and a sink for handwashing.

I shut the door as quietly as I could and turned the light back off, breathing hard. I pressed my ear to the door, desperate to know where he was, but I couldn't tell. My breaths were too loud. A ringing in my ears piercing.

But he was out there. I knew it.

Stalking me like I was prey.

I was trapped.

Again.

## 32

# KARA

*I* was such a fool. A stupid, stupid girl, just like my father had always told me. I'd thought I'd put that all behind me when I'd left our tiny town in the middle of nowhere Texas. I'd thought I'd escaped his torments and ridicule. I'd thought I'd show him by making it out on my own.

Instead, I'd proved him right.

And found out the real truth about men.

That they were all like him. That movies and TV shows all lied about there being good guys out there. Men who loved and cherished women.

Ha.

How stupid I'd been to hope for any of that.

I'd barely been here a month when I'd met Caleb. When he'd charmed the pants off me, only for me to realize there was no such thing as an honest man.

In the darkness, I rubbed a hand over my swollen belly, the skin stretched so tight it hurt sometimes. But then the little baby inside me kicked, and my heart swelled big enough to take away the ache. Only for me to crash down a moment later when I remembered where I was.

Locked in a windowless room.

Hands and feet tied.

Gag over my mouth so I couldn't scream loud enough to attract any attention.

Not that anyone would hear me anyway.

There was a party going on outside, and at first, I'd thought it my chance to draw attention to myself. To make someone realize I was here.

But though noise filtered through from outside, the house had remained mostly quiet. There'd been no footsteps on the stairs Caleb's friends had dragged me down when I'd been stupid enough to come back here.

I let out a sob of despair. What had I been thinking? I should have just stayed away. Gone on living my life for the baby inside me. But no. I'd gotten greedy. Greedy and stupid. I dropped my head down on bound hands, wrists red raw from the rope around them.

*"Louisa Kara Churchill! Oh my God, where are you? Are you okay? I've been so worried!"*

*I was so grateful to hear her voice I didn't even cringe at the reminder my family still called me by my full name, even though none of my friends had in years because I hated it. "I need help, Mama."*

*There was a pause down the phone line. "What sort of help? Money? I have a few dollars stashed away, but anything more than that, your father will know..."*

*I shook my head miserably. "I'm pregnant."*

*She gasped. "Pregnant? No, that's not possible. By who? You've barely been gone four months."*

*I hung my head in shame. "I know. But please. I need you—"*

*She was interrupted by my father's voice coming down the line. "Is it her? Answer me now, young lady."*

*Despite the fact I was twenty-two, I felt all of five years old when he spoke to me like that. "Yes, Daddy. It's me."*

*"Louisa. You best tell me right now that what I heard your mother say isn't true."*

*His judgment poured through the phone, as strong as if he'd slapped me in the face with it.*

*I stared down at the test clutched in my fingers and the other three on the bathroom vanity. Every single one said I was pregnant. I wouldn't lie. He hated liars. "It's true. I'm so sorry."*

*"Get rid of it."*

*I blinked. "What? Daddy, no."*

*"I said get rid of it and come back home immediately. There'll be no back talk from you."*

*I'd been trained my entire life to obey his commands. My mother did. My sisters. All of us.*

*But there was a baby growing inside me, and I couldn't just get rid of it.*

*No matter how it had been conceived.*

*No matter who its father was.*

*That baby was the only thing I had that was mine.*

*He or she was the only thing no one could take from me.*

*I straightened my spine. "No. You listen to me. I'm keeping this baby. You don't get to tell me what to do anymore."*

*He laughed coldly. "Listen to you. So sure and confident in yourself. Have you even thought it through? What it means to be a parent?"*

*"Of course I have," I fired back.*

"Where are you going to live? Is that baby's father going to support you?"

"I can support myself. I'll find a place."

He scoffed. "The father wants nothing to do with you, does he? That's what you get for opening your legs. How will you work when you have a newborn baby hanging off your tit?"

I blanched in shock. He never spoke like that. But then slowly, anger took its place.

There was never any room for anything but perfection with him. Our skirts had to touch our knees or we'd be forced to change. Our beds had to be made with hospital corners and were inspected daily. We had to get straight A's or we'd be bringing shame on him as a father and as a man. He ruled our house of females with army-like discipline, and the clear disappointment we were all women, and he'd never fathered a son.

I hated him.

Had hated him enough to escape his house in the middle of the night, get on a bus, and travel hours, looking for a better life.

I wouldn't let him drag me down again. "The baby's father is a rich businessman," I declared through gritted teeth. "Very rich. He has a big house in Providence, and he'll pay for his child. And for me." My fingers shook. Or maybe it was my entire body.

"You'll come home now, without that bastard baby in your belly."

He wasn't listening. He never did. Just expected all of us to do as he commanded.

I was done being the girl who listened.

I was someone's mother now. And she would be stronger. Smarter. She'd get everything she needed from the men who owed it to her.

How stupid I'd been to just walk up to Caleb Black and make demands. Now I was probably going to die in this tiny hole of a room, thirsty and starving. And the worst part? I'd be taking my baby with me.

A click from just outside my door had me pausing, staring at the door in a mixture of hope and terror. I hadn't seen anyone since they'd thrown me in here, and right now, even Caleb's evil face would be welcome.

But no one came. The door stayed closed, and a fresh round of sobs overtook me. My brain was playing tricks on me now, making me believe help was coming when there was no one in the world who even knew I was here except for Caleb and his monster friends.

"Hello?"

I whirled around at the quiet, feminine voice. It hadn't come from inside the room, or from outside the door, but it was clear enough that I'd heard her. I glanced around wildly, but there was no light. I screamed as loud as I could against the fabric shoved into my mouth and tied around my head, praying it would be enough to let the woman know I was here.

"Is someone in there?"

I edged close to the wall where her voice sounded loudest. There had to be a grate up near the ceiling. Perhaps an air-conditioning vent? Or a duct of some sort? My hands were bound together, but I banged them against the plasterboard wall weakly, not able to get much momentum going to make a noise but terrified she couldn't hear my muffled screams.

"Oh my God. I...do you need help? I don't think they've come down here yet..." Her voice was barely above a whisper.

I was terrified she was going to go silent. I banged on the wall and made as many noises as I could again.

"Make a noise for yes. Stay silent for no. Okay?"

I made a noise.

"Are you hurt?"

I stayed silent. I wasn't hurt right now, but I probably would be if I didn't get out of here.

"Does Caleb know you're down here?"

I tapped on the wall.

"That son of a bitch! Listen, I don't want you to worry. I mean, fuck, I'm not exactly in the best situation here either, but I've got guys outside who can help... Shit. They had to hand in their phones when we came in, but when they realize I'm missing, they'll get them back. I can call one of them and they'll come down here."

My hope died on its ass.

I had my phone too. But there was a reason they hadn't bothered taking it off me when they'd shoved me in here. There was no reception.

The woman's soft swear seemed to indicate she'd just realized that as well. "Okay, never mind. Plan B. We'll just hang out here for a little bit until Caleb goes back outside to his party guests and then I'll sneak back out and get help."

Panic clawed up my throat at the idea of her leaving, and I banged frantically on the wall again, even though she hadn't asked me a yes or no question.

"It's okay. I won't leave without you. I promise."

A tear fell down my face. I so desperately wanted that to be true.

"I wish you could talk back so you could tell me your

name. Or how long you've been here for. Do you have people who would be worried about you?"

I stayed quiet. My family didn't care. My mother might love me, but she'd never been strong enough to stand up to my father. None of them even knew I'd come storming over here, thinking I was so smart, and ready to show my father what I was made of.

"I'm sorry to hear that."

I was too.

"I can't hear anything from inside the house. I think they've gone back outside. I'm going to go get some help, okay? Just sit tight. I promise. I'll be back."

My heart hammered, and I scrambled to the door, pressing my ear against it, desperate for the woman to be real. For me to not be imagining things, due to a lack of water and food.

Her door clicked open.

Soft footsteps passed my room, and she gave a tiny knock on the door that I echoed back.

In my mind, I could see her in the large basement room on the other side. She must have been in a room like mine, one off the main space. But clearly, she hadn't been locked in like I was. She'd be approaching the stairs, and then she'd just have to make it up them and through the house to get outside to where her friends were…

An evil laughter splintered right through me.

"Ah, look at this. Two of my little sluts, getting all acquainted down here in the dark where they belong."

The woman's scream was ear piercingly loud, but it was quickly cut off.

"Stupid bitch, you think you can come into my house like you fucking own it? You're both as stupid as each other." He slammed his fist against my door. "Hear that, slut?"

I heard. I heard every second of the fight the woman put up. Every grunt and groan and curse Caleb uttered as he fought with her.

She was stronger than I was. Fiercer. Braver.

And with every second that passed, I prayed she'd be the one who came out on top.

Until there were no sounds left.

Except Caleb's evil laughter.

And I was alone again.

## 33

# FANG

*E*verything inside me wanted to kill the man who'd dared to lay a finger on my woman. He was right there, tied up at my feet, staring up at me with piss-stained pants and pathetic, begging eyes.

But he wasn't mine to finish.

I knew what it meant, to take out the person who'd hurt you. There was a closure in it. One that brought peace you couldn't get in any other way.

She needed that.

My little Pix.

I wouldn't take it from her, even if this motherfucker deserved to die a thousand fucking times in a thousand different ways.

I knelt and stared Rebel's rapist in the eye. "Your time will come. And when it does, I'll be standing right behind her, proud as fucking hell. You underestimated her, friend. You think you're scared now? Just wait."

I meant every fucking word.

But if I hung around here any longer, my base desires

that screamed to take out a knife and run it across his throat might get the better of me. I strode around the front of the house and leaned on an overpriced car, while I stared at the front door, waiting for Rebel to reemerge with Kian and Vaughn. She'd closed the door when she'd gone back in, and the fucking thing needed a code to open. One I didn't know.

I pulled out a smoke and lit it up, needing the fucking thing to calm the nerves that mounted with every passing minute.

It was taking too long.

I strode to the gate where we'd entered and eyed the solid silver padlock that hadn't been there earlier. I racked my brain for a single logical reason they would have locked everyone in and came up with nothing.

From the corner of my eye, I spotted the bucket of phones, stashed away, half hidden behind a garden bed. The rising sense of dread intensified. No one on that side of the fence had any way of leaving or even calling out for help. The whole thing screamed red flag.

I should have said something. Should have put a stop to this crazy before it got to this point. But it was too late for regrets now.

I rifled through the bucket, taking out my phone, as well as Kian's and Vaughn's. I picked up my pacing again and called Rebel, but it went straight to voicemail, her chirpy, sassy greeting and directions to leave a message familiar.

Normally it made me smile. I loved every fucking thing about her, from her voice to her body, to the way she made me feel whenever we were in the same room.

I hated how I felt right now, without her at my side.

I stubbed out the half-smoked cigarette. "Fuck this."

I stormed back over to my hog-tied friend and yanked the gag out of his mouth. "Code for the front door and I'll tell her to show you mercy."

He rattled off a simple four-digit code quicker than you could blink.

"Sweet. Thanks. Lied about the mercy by the way. See ya."

I shoved his gag back in, cutting off the pathetic man's howl of despair.

It was easy enough to get back into the house with the code. I stormed through the doorway, not giving a shit anymore about who saw me or tried to stop me. Until I got to Rebel, let them fucking try.

The house was quiet, no sign of my girl or her purse. So why the hell wasn't she answering her damn phone? I knew she hadn't given it up at the gates.

I jerked open glass sliding doors and reentered the party like a man on a mission. I knocked into people as I passed. One guy told me to fuck off but was silenced by the glare I shot him.

I was just itching for a fight. Burning to use up some of this adrenaline and frustration on someone.

From my six-five vantage point, I spotted the bright yellow of Vaughn's Robin cape and Kian's face full of Joker makeup.

I shoved my way over to them, heartbeat picking up with every step.

She'd be with them.

She had to be.

I just couldn't see her 'cause she was really fucking short, and Kian and Vaughn towered over her.

My body didn't believe my brain.

I was running before I even realized it, shoving people out of the way.

I grabbed Vaughn by the shoulder, spinning him around, searching the space between him and Kian for my girl.

"Where's—" Kian and I said in unison, before the music cut out and a chorus of boos drowned us out.

Hugh stood up on a table, clapping and telling the crowd to settle down. "Shut up, all of you. You'll be glad you did when you hear what I have to say."

The look on his face was one not entirely unfamiliar to me.

I'd seen it on men before.

Men who did bad things for bad reasons.

He waved for everyone to settle down. "Now that we're all here, and the gates have been locked, it's time to get the party started!"

Another cheer went up from the men around us.

Hugh was clearly loving every minute, because his grin was ear to ear. "There's drinks in the coolers. Food on the table. And every slut here has been signed away by a man as free use. So take full advantage, boys! Enjoy!"

"What the fuck does that mean?" I asked Kian.

He glanced over at me. "No idea."

But the other men all seemed to know.

A scream came from somewhere behind me, and I spun around to watch two men chase a woman through the yard. A third man caught her around the waist and pushed her onto the ground. A circle immediately formed around them, men leering and cheering at the two grappling on the grass, him yanking her skirt up while trying to get his pants off all at once.

All around us, other circles formed, each one full of men watching while others attacked the small number of women in attendance. Even if they weren't the ones with a woman pinned beneath them, they had their cocks out, stroking themselves excitedly, watching the attacks take place.

Bile churned in my stomach. "What the hell is this?" I asked in horror.

Kian shook his head. "I've no idea, but we need to help them." He lurched in the direction of the nearest woman.

Vaughn grabbed his arm. "Three versus a hundred, Kian," he hissed. "We can't save them all. We need to concentrate on Rebel."

Everything inside me hated that. But the thought Rebel was here somewhere took priority over everything else. As much as I didn't want to admit it, Vaughn was right.

The random guy next to me, who was casually sipping his beer, glanced over at us. "Save them? This is a primal party."

"What is that?" I choked out.

"How sex used to be, back in the day, you know? When men were actually men and there was none of this woke bullshit. See a woman you want? You fucking take her."

"Rape her, you mean?" I could barely hold myself together.

He shrugged. "They like it. They all got signed over when they came in. Don't stress, they can't go crying to the cops. We're all in costume anyway, what are they gonna say? Batman fucked my tight little cunt?" He laughed like it was hilarious.

I couldn't even get a word out.

I'd seen some messed-up shit in my time. I'd seen men do evil things. This was maybe the worst.

Kian stared over at the woman on the ground screaming. "Does she fucking look like she likes it?" He turned around and slammed his palms against Vaughn's chest. "Did you fucking know about this? That this is what you were signing Rebel up for when you brought her here?"

Vaughn shoved him back, his face equally distraught. "Are you insane? Of course I fucking didn't!"

I spun around in circles, desperately searching the yard for Rebel. I checked the face of every woman in every circle, desperately wanting to save them all but knowing I was outnumbered a hundred to one.

A bellowing scream of frustration and fear burst from my lungs when I couldn't find the one woman I would take on a hundred men for. I wouldn't have even given it a second thought.

"She's not here." Vaughn came to the same conclusion I did.

"She has to be!" Kian shouted at him. "She wouldn't just leave." He turned to me. "You were supposed to have her back!"

"I fucking did!" I roared. "She came back for you two!"

"I haven't seen her since we first got here." Kian palmed the back of his neck, eyes wild.

How was that possible? She hadn't been in the house. And she hadn't been out the front. "She never came back out at all?"

He shook his head slowly.

The fear was choking. If one man here had laid a fucking finger on her I was going to burn them all alive. Every single sick fuck here.

"Have you called her?" Vaughn asked, pulling his phone from my hand and checking the screen.

"It goes straight to voicemail." I shoved Kian's phone back at him. "Check your phone."

He looked down but then shook his head tightly. "Nothing."

She wouldn't have just left. I knew it in my gut. She was here. Somewhere. The fact I couldn't get to her was killing me.

Kian paused. "I can find her on SnapChat. She added me last week. If her location is on, it'll show me where she is."

I didn't even know what the hell that was, but I didn't care.

Because something else had just occurred to me. "I don't see Caleb."

Vaughn scanned the party the same way I had. "I don't see him either."

"He's not here," I realized with a start. "If he were, it would have been him up there, making that announcement. Did you see the way Hugh got off on it? You think Caleb wouldn't have wanted that power?"

"Rebel isn't here," Kian announced. "She's...fuck, back at home? How?"

Relief flooded me. "She's home?"

Vaughn turned the screen around and flashed it at me. "If she's with her phone, she is."

I slumped, the relief as soothing as balm on ragged, torn skin.

"Thank fuck for that," Vaughn blew out a breath and ran his thumbs over his phone as the three of us strode to the exit. "I'm calling nine-one-one to get the cops out here."

We got to the locked gate, and I shook my head in disgust, knowing now it was to keep the women in. To keep them from escaping this fucking house of horrors. I slammed one booted foot against the eight-foot fence, taking out all my anger on it, and took the momentary second of joy when it popped the lock straight off the gate.

The three of us strode across the lawn to Vaughn's car. Kian watching his phone the entire time.

"How on earth did she get back home so quick?"

"Uber, maybe?" Vaughn replied, his pace practically a jog in his impatience to get out of there. He looked vaguely green in the light of a streetlamp. "I don't fucking care, I'm just glad she's not still here. You guys have to know that I knew nothing about this. I would never come to something like this if I'd known. This is so fucking messed up." His fingers shook as he ran them through his hair.

You couldn't fake that level of anguish.

He truly hadn't known.

I was still pissed with him though. He'd put her in danger.

But maybe I had too. I'd gone along with all of this.

I'd let her go back into the house without me.

I'd done exactly what she'd told me to do, like a good fucking puppy.

I shouldn't have let her. It was my fault as much as his.

We were halfway across the lawn when Kian suddenly stopped, his gaze pinned on the open garage door.

And the empty space beyond it.

"What if she didn't take an Uber?" Kian asked, his voice as cold and dead as the Halloween decorations around us.

I stared at the empty car space, a new fear rising and swamping me. "We saw him drive in here. His car should be here."

"Call him." My voice was cold. Dead.

Vaughn hit a phone number on his phone, and a moment later, Caleb's laughter came down the line. "Vaughn! Old friend. Are you enjoying the party?"

He didn't even need to say a word. The smugness in his tone told us everything we needed to know.

He had her.

"If you've so much as laid a finger on her, Caleb, I swear to God—" Vaughn clenched his fingers around his phone so hard I was surprised the screen didn't crack.

"You'll what, Vaughn?" Caleb scoffed. "Run off to California again?"

Vaughn said nothing.

Caleb's chuckle was nothing short of menacing. "Relax. We're just having a little private party. You want to talk to her? Cry for them, baby. I bet they like it too."

Rebel's scream came down the line.

I was going to vomit.

"We've called the cops," Vaughn choked out.

The pain in his face was a mirror image of mine, I was sure of it. That scream... I'd never be able to forget it.

Caleb clucked his tongue. "Waste of time. Already paid them off to turn a blind eye tonight."

Vaughn looked to me, then Kian. "We're coming, Roach. Hang on."

"Great!" Caleb crowed. "Just in time for you to watch me fuck her some more then. You know she screams when you take her hard and fast? Oh, of course you do, she lives with you. You probably fuck her tight cunt like that all the time, don't you? Your other friends too? I knew you'd all like my parties. You're my kind of men."

The noise that escaped my mouth as we ran for Vaughn's car was a howl made of outrage and agony. Everything inside me hurt, like someone was squeezing every organ until I was nothing but mush. I couldn't run fast enough. Couldn't breathe. Couldn't fucking help her.

He had her.

And it was all my fault.

Again.

## 34

## REBEL

*Ten minutes earlier*

I blinked my eyes open and quickly shut them again when pain speared through my skull. A moan fell through my lips at the pain spreading from the base of my head all the way through my body. It didn't stop, a constant thumping starting up that pounded its way through every muscle and ligament until even my fingers and toes hurt.

Nausea swelled in my stomach, but when I turned my head to the side to vomit, nothing happened.

A jolt lifted me from whatever I was lying on before sending me crashing back down into it. My head spun in dizzying circles, disorienting me.

The party. Fang and Kian and Vaughn.

A woman locked in a room.

Caleb.

The ringing in my ears died away and was replaced with the roar of an engine.

I forced my eyes open again. This time the horror drowned out the pain.

Caleb was behind the wheel, whistling as he drove.

I twisted frantically, trying to orient myself and realized I was lying across the back seat of his car.

"Good evening, sunshine!" he called out gaily, like we were neighbors greeting each other at the mailbox.

I rolled over onto my stomach with a groan and groped the floor, trying to find something I could use as a weapon.

"Nice of you to wake up. I was worried I was going to have all the fun while you were unconscious."

There was nothing back here. His car was immaculate. I could try smothering him with a floor mat, but I didn't like my chances. The other option was to get the door open and just jump.

I glanced up at the world flashing by outside. Caleb wasn't exactly puttering along at the speed limit. He drove like he was trying out for NASCAR.

I was barely dressed. A Lycra suit wasn't exactly going to be much protection against the road.

But I'd take my chances. Anything was better than being alone in a car with Caleb Black.

I grabbed at the handle.

It moved, but the door didn't fly open the way I expected it to.

Caleb patted his dashboard affectionately when I frantically tried the other side. "Child locks are so handy, aren't they? Good for keeping small children safe. Good for keeping little whores safe too, apparently."

I ignored him, lying back on the seat and kicking at the window instead.

I tried again when it didn't break, but it took all the energy I had.

It produced zero result. How freaking hard could it be to break a car window, for Christ's sakes?

"Don't bother. You've got so many drugs in your system right now your kicks are like the pitter-patter of butterfly wings on the glass. You're only exhausting yourself. We're here now anyway."

He parked the car, and I tried to sit up but found my limbs were really not paying attention to my brain. I was barely half upright when he yanked open the door from outside and dragged me out by my arm.

I peered up at the big house, not drugged enough not to recognize my own home. "How courteous of you to drive me home." My tongue felt twice the size it normally was, and I was sure it wasn't just the ringing in my head that slurred my words.

Motherfucker had seriously drugged me with something.

Either that or I had the concussion from Hell from where he'd smacked me in the head in order to get me out of his house and into his car.

He dragged me from the car parked in the driveway to the big house I'd moved myself into. I fought him every step, but it was like my body was surrounded by molasses. Every step felt like it was happening in slow motion.

"What's the code?" he demanded.

I knew it. Even with drugs in my system and a ringing headache, I still remembered the simple four-digit password. But over my dead body was I going to tell him. This was my damn house. Whatever he was going to do to me, he could do it somewhere else. He wasn't taking away the one place I felt safe. He'd already tainted Psychos. He wasn't having this place too.

"Tell me, bitch."

I muttered out the wrong numbers, stalling, buying time.

Fang would come. He'd bring the others. I just had to stay awake long enough for them to get here. I smiled at the thought of them finding Caleb and drowning him in the pool.

A giggle slipped out.

Caleb stared down at me. "Are you fucking laughing right now?"

I didn't see any point in sparing his feelings. "Yep. Just thinking about how Fang and Vaughn and Kian are going to drown you in the pool. Can you swim? Won't matter. They won't let you live after this."

He stared down at me, then his eyes narrowed. The smile that spread across his face was so chilling it registered even through my drug-addled brain.

His fingers tightened. "Great idea."

He dragged me around the side of the house to the back while I tried to stay on feet that kept slipping out from beneath me. I tried to shout for help, hoping Sasha was home to hear, but he backhanded me again.

Blood seeped from my split lip, tangy on my tongue. My head rang, and I couldn't keep up. My feet stopped cooperating and gave in.

Caleb's phone rang halfway across the yard, and he dumped me unceremoniously on the ground as he fished his cell from the pants of his costume.

From my fetal position, I stared up at him

answering the phone like he was at a business meeting. No care given to the fact he'd just abducted and drugged me.

"Vaughn! Old friend. Are you enjoying the party?"

I tried to lift my head. Vaughn? Why was Vaughn calling Caleb?

Caleb shoved a hand into his pocket. "You'll what, Vaughn? Run off to California again?"

California?

Something that felt a lot like longing and disappointment wrapped its way around me. I didn't want Vaughn going back to California.

Back to his wife.

I wanted him here. With me.

Caleb knelt by my side, running one finger down the side of my face while the other clutched his phone. I tried to cringe away, but he wouldn't let me, his fingers digging into the side of my jaw. A tear slid down my face at him touching me.

"Relax. We're just having a little private party." He leaned in and licked the tear from my cheek. "Cry for them, baby. I bet they like it too."

I sucked up every ounce of energy I had and screamed instead.

Caleb cut me off with another slap to the face. His words went fuzzy, the ringing in my ears taking over again. It took a minute for it to subside.

"...You probably fuck her tight cunt like that all the time, don't you? Your other friends there too? I knew you'd all like my parties. You're my kind of men."

I tried to crawl away, but the drugging slowness made every movement nearly impossible. Caleb's boot connected with my stomach, and I wheezed, blinking up at him.

He'd dropped his phone somewhere, the full extent of his hate now fully focused on me. "You had to find my dirty little secret in the bottom of the basement there, didn't you?"

The girl. "Who is she?"

A dragging noise came from somewhere, but I was too out of it to work out where.

"What do you care? She's as dead as you are."

He jerked me up off the ground and shoved me into an outdoor chair. I couldn't hold myself upright. I slumped to one side, head lolling onto my shoulder while I struggled to keep my eyes open.

He leaned down so we were eye height and ran his thumb over my lips and then forced it into my mouth. "Shame your boyfriends know where we are. I'd quite like to put my dick here and fuck your sweet mouth some. But framing them for your murder is fun too."

He knelt in front of me. I wanted to kick him in the face, but my legs were dead weights, not moving at all.

I had no power to stop him when he spread my knees, strapping each ankle to the legs of the chair.

All I could do was watch through half-mast eyes when he roughly jerked my hands behind my back and tied them there.

He covered his hand with his sleeve and picked up Kian's pocketknife from his work bench.

How many stabs would it take for him to kill me? Only one if he got it in the right place.

That seemed too controlled for Caleb. I braced myself for the frenzy of stabs that seemed more his style.

I was too out of it to move. Too out of it to make any more noise, even though I tried.

But my heart ached. It ached to tell Fang I loved him too.

It ached for Vaughn and the fact he was coming home to witness another murder.

It ached for Kian, whose fingerprints were going to be found on the murder weapon.

Caleb took a handful of my Lycra bodysuit and sliced right down the middle, cutting the fabric right from beneath my neck to my navel, then ripping it the rest of the way until it hung in tatters from my body and I was bared to him again.

Just the way he liked.

Vulnerable.

Weak.

His gaze roamed over me, lingering on the junction of my thighs and my tits. My skin pebbled with goosebumps from the cold. I tried to scream again, but no sound came out. My vocal cords refused to obey.

Caleb pulled out his phone, snapping photos, then grinned at me. "A souvenir for me to get off to later, since I don't have time to fuck you now. Shame. I've missed your tight holes. Dreamed about having you again, and then there you were, slutting it up with my old pal Vaughn and his boys. Such a fucking shame."

He leaned in close. "Maybe I'll share these with Bethany-Melissa too. Maybe now she'll finally understand how big a mistake she made when she left me."

I mumbled something.

He grinned and leaned in. "What was that, little slut?"

I mustered up every ounce of energy I could find,

refusing to go out without at least one final word. "Everyone knows you weren't good enough for her, Caleb. That you couldn't make her come with your tiny dick. That your fiancée went looking for better and found it in a Saint View trailer park. How. Fucking. Embarrassing."

It was his weak spot, and I knew it. The one button I could press to really get beneath his skin.

All Caleb Black had ever cared about was what other people thought of him.

Bliss didn't even know it, but she'd destroyed him when she'd left him. When she'd picked three men from Saint View over Caleb and his fancy house and car. She'd embarrassed him in front of the men he'd spent years trying to impress.

I was only sad she wasn't here to see exactly how bad she'd hurt him.

It was a victory I would tell her gleefully.

Vaughn, Fang, and Kian would be here any minute. They'd kill Caleb and cut me loose, and we'd put this entire thing behind us.

Caleb couldn't touch me.

He'd already taken so much, but now it was my turn.

I knew his dirty little secret, and it wasn't the girl in the basement.

It was that Caleb Black was an insecure boy, desperate for other people's approval.

Caleb's face turned red.

His anger boiled to the surface, echoing out in a screech of frustration. "No!"

But I didn't have to say anything. We both knew the truth.

He could kill me now, but the words were out. I wasn't

the only one who saw it. If I could work it out, then surely his colleagues already had as well.

There was no pretending for him anymore.

No convincing himself he held the respect of anyone.

Somewhere in the distance, sirens wailed.

I smiled. "I win, Caleb," I whispered. "I won, didn't I? They're coming. Vaughn. Fang. Kian. The police. You think stabbing me with that blunt old pocketknife is going to do enough damage I won't survive the minutes until that siren is on top of you? You're all out of time, Caleb. The game is over."

He looked over his shoulder toward the front of the house but then focused back on me.

His eyes darkened. "No, little slut. I always win."

With a grin straight from Hell, he tipped the chair backward, splashing it into the pool.

With me still tied to it.


The end...for now. **Rebel, Fang, Kian, and Vaughn's story continues in book 2, Rebel Obsession.** Get it here.
https://mybook.to/SaintViewRebel2

**Want to read about that public spanking Fang gave Rebel at the Slayers party? And everything that happened after?**
It's in the free bonus scene on my website at www.ellethorpe.com/fangrebelbonus.

**WANT SIGNED PAPERBACKS,
SPECIAL EDITION COVERS, OR
SAINT VIEW MERCH?**

Check out Elle's new website store at
https://www.ellethorpe.com/store

## ALSO BY ELLE THORPE

**Saint View High series (Reverse Harem, Bully Romance. Complete)**

*Devious Little Liars (Saint View High, #1)

*Dangerous Little Secrets (Saint View High, #2)

*Twisted Little Truths (Saint View High, #3)

**Saint View Prison series (Reverse harem, romantic suspense. Complete.)**

*Locked Up Liars (Saint View Prison, #1)

*Solitary Sinners (Saint View Prison, #2)

*Fatal Felons (Saint View Prison, #3)

**Saint View Psychos series (Reverse harem, romantic suspense. Complete.)**

*Start a War (Saint View Psychos, #1)

*Half the Battle (Saint View Psychos, #2)

*It Ends With Violence (Saint View Psychos, #3)

**Saint View Rebels (Reverse harem, romantic suspense)**

*Rebel Revenge (Saint View Rebels, #1)

*Rebel Obsession (Saint View Rebels, #2)

*Rebel Heart (Saint View Rebels, #3)

**Saint View Strip (Male/Female, romantic suspense standalones. Ongoing.)**

*Evil Enemy (Saint View Strip, #1)

*Unholy Sins (Saint View Strip, #2)

*Book 3 (Saint View Strip, #3)

**Dirty Cowboy series (complete)**

*Talk Dirty, Cowboy (Dirty Cowboy, #1)

*Ride Dirty, Cowboy (Dirty Cowboy, #2)

*Sexy Dirty Cowboy (Dirty Cowboy, #3)

*Dirty Cowboy boxset (books 1-3)

*25 Reasons to Hate Christmas and Cowboys (a Dirty Cowboy bonus novella, set before Talk Dirty, Cowboy but can be read as a standalone, holiday romance)

**Buck Cowboys series (Spin off from the Dirty Cowboy series. Ongoing.)**

*Buck Cowboys (Buck Cowboys, #1)

*Buck You! (Buck Cowboys, #2)

*Can't Bucking Wait (Buck Cowboys, #3)

*Mother Bucker (Buck Cowboys, $#4)

**The Only You series (Contemporary romance. Complete)**

*Only the Positive (Only You, #1) - Reese and Low.

*Only the Perfect (Only You, #2) - Jamison.

*Only the Truth - (Only You, bonus novella) - Bree.

*Only the Negatives (Only You, #3) - Gemma.

*Only the Beginning (Only You, #4) - Bianca and Riley.

*Only You boxset

Add your email address here to be the first to know when new books are available!

www.ellethorpe.com/newsletter

Join Elle Thorpe's readers group on Facebook!

www.facebook.com/groups/ellethorpesdramallamas

# ACKNOWLEDGMENTS

First of all, a big thank you to my readers. I've never had a book so highly anticipated, and I really hope Rebel was worth the wait!

Extra big shout out to the Drama Llamas. You guys make my days fun. If you aren't already a member, it's a free reader group on Facebook where I share all sorts of stuff. Come join us, everyone is welcome. www.facebook.com/groups/ellethorpesdramallamas

Thank you to Montana Ash/Darcy Halifax for writing at the club with me every day. I can't wait to work out of our office together!

Thank you to Sara Massery, Jolie Vines, and Zoe Ashwood for the constant support, friendship, and book advice.

**Thank you to my editing team:**

Emmy at Studio ENP and Karen and Barren Acres Editing.

Dana, Louise, Sam, Shellie, Abbey, and Abby for beta reading. Plus my ARC team for the early reviews.

**Thank you to the audio team:**

Denise and Troy at Dark Star Romance for producing this series in multicast audio! Thank you to Troy (again), Michelle, Michael, and Gregory for voicing Kian, Rebel, Vaughn, and Fang.

And of course, thank you to the team who run the store and home front:

To Donna and Ari, for taking on all the jobs I don't have time for. Best PA's ever.

To my mum, for working for us one day a week, and always being willing to have our kids when we go to signings.

To Jira, for running the online store, doing all the accounting, and dealing with all the 'people-ing.' Not to mention, being the best stay at home dad ever.

To Flick and Heidi, for helping pack swag, and to Thomas, who refuses to work for us, but will proudly tell everyone he knows that his mum is an author.

Writing these acknowledgements has made me realize how much my team and my business have grown in the last twelve months. I'm living my dream, and I hope I get to give you all stories for many more years to come.

From the bottom of my heart, thank you.

Elle x

# ABOUT THE AUTHOR

Elle Thorpe lives in a small regional town of NSW, Australia. When she's not writing stories full of kissing, she's wife to Mr Thorpe who unexpectedly turned out to be a great plotting partner, and mummy to three tiny humans. She's also official ball thrower to one slobbery dog named Rollo. Yes, she named a female dog after a dirty hot character on Vikings. Don't judge her. Elle is a complete and utter fangirl at heart, obsessing over The Walking Dead and Outlander to an unhealthy degree. But she wouldn't change a thing.

You can find her on Facebook or Instagram(@el-lethorpebooks or hit the links below!) or at her website www.ellethorpe.com. If you love Elle's work, please consider joining her Facebook fan group, Elle Thorpe's Drama Llamas or joining her newsletter here. www.ellethorpe.com/newsletter

[f] facebook.com/ellethorpebooks

[instagram] instagram.com/ellethorpebooks

[g] goodreads.com/ellethorpe

[p] pinterest.com/ellethorpebooks

Made in United States
Troutdale, OR
02/12/2025

28925558R00241